# MURDER AT
# HENDON AERODROME

*By Christina Koning*

# MURDER AT
# HENDON AERODROME

## CHRISTINA KONING

Allison & Busby Limited
11 Wardour Mews
London W1F 8AN
*allisonandbusby.com*

First published as *Time of Flight* in 2016 under the name A. C. Koning
This edition published by Allison & Busby in 2023.

10 9 8 7 6 5 4 3 2 1

ISBN 978-0-7490-2904-3

Typeset in 11.5 Sabon LT Pro by Typo•glyphix, Burton-on-Trent, DE14 3HE

By choosing this product, you help take care of the world's forests.
Learn more: www.fsc.org.

MIX

Paper | Supporting
responsible forestry

FSC® C171272

Printed and bound by
CPI Group (UK) Ltd, Croydon, CR0 4YY

*In memory of my father Geert Julius Koning (1912–1990), who also knew the Blind Detective rather well.*

*The Albatros came at him out of the sun. His plane was on fire before he knew what had hit him. It was only when he saw it – that little lick of flame just starting to emerge from the engine – that he knew he was done for. His gun had jammed, and it was as he was trying to dodge the blasts of gunfire from his attacker's machine gun that he saw that he was on fire. The flame grew within seconds to a blaze, that would soon, he knew, consume the whole engine before consuming him. His Nieuport was stalled, in any case – if the flames didn't get him, the fall would.*

*The Albatros was level with him now; he looked across at the cockpit where the pilot sat, seeing him, in that instant, as a man much like himself. That rictus grin they all wore when closing in for a kill; he had worn it himself, he knew, on many an occasion. The sheen of sweat on the forehead beneath the leather flying helmet. The fixed stare in the cold blue eyes . . . As he watched, for what seemed a long moment, but which was probably no more that a heartbeat's duration, the man – his enemy – raised a gloved hand, in what seemed like a gesture of farewell. Then the fuselage was enveloped in a wave of fire . . .*

*He woke with a start, his heart pounding, his pyjamas soaked with sweat. For a moment he lay there, waiting for his pulse to slow, his gaze moving slowly around the room, taking in its objects – the heavy brocade curtains on their brass rail; the dressing table with its triple mirror; the box-shaped armchairs; the sleek walnut wardrobe. A room in the furnishing of which no luxury had been spared. He turned his head and saw, on the pillow next to his, a head of platinum blonde hair. It belonged to the woman he had been with the night before; he realised that he had forgotten her name. Some* poule *picked up in one of the bars in the Boulevard Montparnasse, he supposed. He'd have to get rid of her. A glance at the travelling clock on the bedside cabinet told him it was not yet six. Already exhausted at the thought of what the day would bring, he closed his eyes, fragments of his dream still lingering unpleasantly.*

# Chapter One

The world had taken to the air. You couldn't switch on the wireless these days without hearing news of the latest feat by Miss Johnson or Commander Kidson; the newspapers, too, were full of their exploits, and those of the numerous others who'd followed in their wake. Although surely that was the wrong expression, Rowlands thought, being nautical rather than aeronautical? Well, it made not the slightest bit of difference to him, given that he was never likely to set foot in an aeroplane. Not that he cared to: he'd seen enough of the contraptions during his army days. They were more primitive machines then, to be sure – flimsy wooden frames covered with canvas and sealed with dope – but the principle had been the same as with the up-to-date metal-framed models they had nowadays: trusting oneself to the vicissitudes of wind and weather in a thing which resembled nothing so much as a bathtub with wings. At least in these days of peacetime you hadn't to contend with being shot at.

No, it hadn't been his idea of fun then, and it certainly wasn't now even though, as his wife never tired of pointing out, everyone was doing it these days. 'Lot of silly stunts,' he muttered, reaching for the telephone. He knew his ill temper was unreasonable and, in fact, on any other day he'd have taken a different line. But with Miss Lawson getting married in a fortnight and Miss Collins off sick, he was pretty much running the office single-handed. Now there was this Croydon business. Being asked to organise a trip to the aerodrome at short notice for present and former inmates of Regent's Park Lodge, together with a contingent from the Brighton centre, just so that they – the St Dunstaners – could swell the merry throng that would be waiting to welcome home Captain Whatshisname. Well, it was a damned nuisance, that's all.

He picked up the receiver and dialled: CRO 6858. It rang four times before anybody answered. The voice which did so was young, female; a little breathless. 'Hello?'

'Frederick Rowlands speaking,' he said. 'Is that Croydon Aerodrome?' He knew it was; he rarely got numbers wrong. 'Yes,' came the reply, followed by a momentary hesitation. 'But there isn't anyone here at the moment or, at least, only me. They're all out at the airfield at present. Getting it ready, you know, for the day after tomorrow.'

'It was about that I rang,' said Rowlands. 'To confirm arrangements for our visit. The St Dunstan's group,' he prompted when this elicited no response. 'We're invited to the reception.'

'Yes, of course,' said the girl, still sounding a bit doubtful. 'It's just that I don't know anything much . . . I only help out, you know. Stripping down engines,' she added, with a touch of pride.

'Very useful, I'm sure,' said Rowlands. 'Well, Miss . . .'

'Wilkinson. Pauline Wilkinson.'

'Miss Wilkinson, I wonder if you'd mind awfully taking down a message?'

'Not a bit. And do call me Wilkie. Everybody else does.'

'Thank you . . . Wilkie. If you'd just let them know that there'll be thirty-three of us, in two charabancs. That's to say, thirty St Dunstan's men and . . . and three children.'

'Right-ho,' said Miss Wilkinson. 'Hang on. I'll just find a pencil. Thirty-three, did you say?'

'That's right. If you'd pass that along, I'd be most grateful.'

'Will do,' she said cheerily. Then, as he was about to hang up, she added, 'I say – it really is going to be the most ripping fun!'

'Glad to hear it,' he said, smiling at the fervour with which she spoke. Stripping down engines. He'd done a bit of that himself in his soldiering days – not to mention stripping down and cleaning an eighteen-pounder gun. He'd never thought of it as a job for a woman, though. Which all went to show that the world had changed a good deal in the dozen or so years since his army career had been brought to an abrupt end by a burst of shrapnel. 'Well, goodbye.'

'Cheerio,' said the girl, and hung up. Rowlands turned his attention to other tasks. There was still that pension claim to settle; he'd have to see what old Askew thought about it. With the numbers of men they were seeing these days whose sight had only begun to fail since the war's end, the business of allocating funds had become that much more tricky. He felt around on the desk in front of him until he found the letter – written by the applicant's wife (at the former's dictation, he supposed), and read out that morning by his secretary, in a voice thick with rheum. '*Dear sirs,*' it said. '*Hoping this finds you well . . .*' Here, Beryl Collins had been unable to suppress a sneeze. '*I am of a sound constitution myself, with never a day's illness until now . . .*' The letters often started in this vein, with a note of cheerful bravado it soon became hard to sustain. '*A veteran of Mons and Neuve Chapelle, I am forty-two years old, married, with five children . . .*'

'Five! Oh, Lord,' Rowlands had murmured. They'd fought long and hard to get the Children's Allowance extended to include all children of blinded ex-servicemen, and not just the ones born before they entered the service.

Five shillings a week per child wasn't a lot, but it went some way towards covering the cost of food, clothes and shoes – as Rowlands himself had reason to know. '*But with my sight no longer what it was, I find myself unable to do my job . . .*'

'What was his job, exactly, Miss Collins?' he'd asked, having allowed his attention to wander at the crucial moment.

'Factory worker. Making machine tools.' 'Bakig bachib tools' was how it sounded.

'Ah. Might be one for our retraining programme,' he said. In the St Dunstan's workshops in Kentish Town, men with little previous experience were being taught to operate router and borer machines, circular saws and vertical belt sanders – tasks for which they showed considerable aptitude. The scepticism of prospective employers was proving somewhat harder to overcome. 'All right, Miss Collins, I can take it from here.' After which he had sent her home, the poor girl evidently being in no fit state to carry on. Which meant that paperwork which should have been dealt with long before now was still cluttering up his desk. Well, best get on with it. Deftly threading the paper and carbons into the Remington machine, which had been modified only by the addition of tiny circles of fine sandpaper, stuck onto the middle keys – Y, H and N – to enable the typist to check his position, he set the tabs for the address line and paragraph indents, and began to type.

St John's Lodge
Regent's Park

14th May 1931

Dear Mr Askew

*I enclose a letter from Mr Harold Liddell, whose sight, damaged by mustard gas during his war service, has been steadily worsening. It seems to me that he might be just the ticket for the Machinery Department since he already has the necessary skills and would only need a certain amount of retraining . . .*

He finished the letter, signed it, and put it, with Mr Liddell's letter, in an envelope, which he stamped and addressed: 'W. G. Askew Esq', the organisation's Pensions Officer. Lame from childhood, Askew had been passed unfit for the war – a fact which had proved to be of inestimable benefit to the hundreds of men who had returned from it unable to work and in desperate need of some kind of income. It was Askew who wrote letters on their behalf and drafted their appeals to the War Office. Because of him, men who had lost their sight through the gradual effects of mustard gas poisoning rather than in the heat of battle, were now eligible for the basic rate of forty shillings a week, with allowances for wife and children, if any. Men whose blindness had been caused by eye disease, 'aggravated', as the rubric put it, by their war service, could also claim subsistence.

It was advances such as these, Rowlands thought, reaching for the next letter on the pile Miss Collins had sorted into Possibles and Refusals, that made all the difference between a civilised society which looked after those less able to help themselves, and one that was not. This wasn't, he knew, a view shared by everybody. '*I am utterly weary of the lie-down-and-kick-me attitude of the Socialist Government*,' had opined one such malcontent in a letter to *The Times*, which Edith had read out to him only the previous evening; while an eminent Fellow of the Royal Society had been quoted in the same newspaper as being of the opinion that '*it was an hallucination to believe that universal education could ever bring all men to the same level*', and that what he called '*socialistic legislation*' could only result in a '*steady decline in the eugenic fitness of the nation*'. Dorothy would have had something to say about that, he thought, and then pushed the thought away.

He worked until six, alone in the deserted office, with only the ticking of the big clock on the wall for company. In the two years since he'd been running the place, it had come to seem like a home from home. You couldn't say it was as lively as his old office had been, with the phones going all day long and a steady stream of visitors to deal with, but it had its moments, he thought. At least here he was his own boss, working to a schedule that was largely of his own devising. From his days as a sixteen-year-old, working in a factory, up to and including his time at

Saville and Willoughby's when he'd been in charge of the switchboard and a great deal more besides, he'd had to develop ways of doing things that relied on order, method and taking pains. It wasn't always the quickest way, but it got there in the end.

'That's that for today,' he thought, putting the last envelope on the pile ready for posting. He put the cover on the typewriter, and then, as he did every night, straightened the objects on his desk so that they were where he could find them first thing in the morning. Unused stationery he returned to the top right-hand drawer; a file he'd been consulting to the drawer below that. Stamps went back in the tray beside the telephone, with the sections for pencils, pens and paperclips. 'Oh, Mr Rowlands, you're so tidy!' Miss Collins had exclaimed on more than one occasion, as if it were something remarkable in a man. He hadn't thought it worth pointing out that he wasn't just being pernickety: if you couldn't see where you'd put something down, it made sense to return it to the same place each time so that you could find it again.

Blotting paper. He took a sheet from the left-hand drawer and, having discarded the used sheet, tucked the edges of the fresh sheet under the leather corners of the blotter. Paper knife. He weighed it in his hand a moment – there was a pleasing heaviness to it – before returning it to its place. 'You could do yourself an injury with that,' Miss Collins had said, meaning that it was sharp. He couldn't see the use of a knife that wasn't. The only object of no apparent utility on his desk was a pebble, picked up from Brighton beach some years before. When he was thinking about a particular problem or merely abstracted, as he was now, he'd hold it in the palm of his hand, feeling its smooth, round contours, shaped by the sea, over who knew how long? Millennia, perhaps. As he did so, he couldn't help wondering where she was now – the woman who'd been with him that day. Did she ever think of him?

He dropped the pebble back on the desk. He oughtn't to be having such thoughts, he told himself sternly.

Having collected the bundle of letters for posting from the tray, he locked the door behind him, and stepped out into the mild spring air. He drew a deep breath. The best moment of the day, he thought. St John's Lodge was pretty much equidistant from the two Underground stations which served the area; Regent's Park Tube being at the end of the more direct route. A sharp right turn would bring him to the Broadwalk; then another right-angled turn down Broadwalk would lead to the Outer Circle, but it was pleasant, sometimes, not to have to follow such rigid geometries, and he accordingly took a more circuitous path, which led through Queen Mary's Gardens. Beneath his feet, the grass felt soft and springy, and from somewhere close by drifted the scent of flowers. Hyacinths. His mind was flooded, for an instant, by the colour blue. Funny how even after all these years, he still remembered colours.

Something whizzed past his head, just clipping his ear. 'Ouch!' He bent to retrieve the missile. It wasn't, as he'd thought, a paper dart, although it weighed about the same. This was made of balsa wood. A miniature version of the craft he'd seen all those years ago, circling over the battlefields of Mons and Ypres. Flimsy contraptions, which looked as if a puff of wind might carry them away. 'I say – I really am most dreadfully sorry,' said a woman's voice. Rowlands turned towards the sound. Even though he knew perfectly well that a soft voice was no guarantee of a pleasing countenance, he was unable to stop himself picturing the owner of the voice as young and pretty.

He was still holding the balsa wood aeroplane. 'Yours, I think,' he said, with a smile.

'Oh, it's not mine,' she said. 'It's Teddy's. That is, my son's. Teddy, you naughty boy, come and say you're sorry to the nice gentleman.'

'Sorry,' mumbled Teddy, who must have been about five, Rowlands guessed.

'That's quite all right,' he said. 'Even the best pilots sometimes have accidents.' He held the plane out towards the child. 'I expect you'd like this back.'

'Yes,' said Teddy.

'Yes, please,' put in the boy's mother.

'Yes, please.'

Rowlands handed him the plane. At once the child ran off, making the soft buzzing noise small boys made to simulate the drone of an aircraft's engine. 'Well,' said Rowlands pleasantly. 'I suppose I'd better make tracks.' But his new acquaintance seemed in no hurry to relinquish his company.

'We're on our way home, too,' she said, falling into step beside him. 'It's time for his bath. Only I said he might have ten more minutes in the park.'

'It's a fine evening,' he said.

'Yes. He's our only one, you know, so we rather spoil him.' There was no answer to this, and so Rowlands merely smiled. 'I'm Irene Metcalfe, by the way,' she said.

'Frederick Rowlands.'

'So nice to meet you. One doesn't often – meet people, I mean. Or at least, not since we moved to London.'

'Oh?' he said politely.

'Of course, we know people through my husband's work,' she said. 'But . . .' Her voice tailed off. For an instant, he caught a glimpse of her life: a mansion flat, in one of the less fashionable streets near the park. Two servants: a cook (of whom she was probably terrified) and a maid, to do the rough. The child taking up most of her day. Dinner parties, once a month, to entertain 'people from the office'. A dull life for a young woman.

'I'm sure things'll get better,' he said gently.

'I expect you're right.' They'd reached the gravel path that led to the York Gate, and beyond it, the Marylebone Road.

'Well, this is my direction,' he said. On an impulse, he held out his hand. He felt her take it; hers was expensively gloved.

'Perhaps I'll see you again, sometime?' she said.

'Oh, I expect so,' he replied, conscious that he was being evasive. 'I sometimes come here with my own children.'

'That's nice,' she said flatly. 'How many children do you have?'

'Three. All girls.'

'Aren't you lucky? I'd have liked a girl,' she said. 'Well, good night.'

'Good night,' said Rowlands as she walked away.

He was still puzzling over the little encounter as he descended the escalator at Baker Street. Poor girl – how forlorn she'd sounded! Perhaps the marriage . . . He let the thought tail away. The oft-repeated adage that cities could be lonely places flitted across his mind as he stepped off the moving stair and, taking care to keep to the left-hand side, entered the tunnel that would lead him to the southbound platform. Behind and in front of him tramped others – intent, as he was, on getting to where each wanted to go as quickly as possible. It was a largely silent crowd; what he could hear was the sound of hundreds of pairs of marching feet, people in close proximity tending to fall, unconsciously, into step with those around them. The sound echoed and re-echoed from the tiled walls of the tunnel and was overlaid, as he turned the corner, by the plaintive notes of a mouth-organ, playing 'Home, Sweet Home' – its maudlin cadences setting his teeth on edge, even as he reached into his pocket for some change.

*Be it ever so humble, there's no-o place like home . . .*

Reaching his platform at last, he stood well back from the edge, knowing that, in such a crush, it would be all too easy to lose his footing. Still keeping his back to the wall, he shuffled sideways a few feet until he was level with the sliding doors of the first carriage. The train came roaring out of the tunnel, with its hot dragon's breath. There was the usual surge forward, and he got on, squeezing his way between a burly man in tweeds and a woman weighed down with shopping bags. There were no seats left, but in any case he preferred to stand, hanging onto the strap as the train gathered momentum and, with his free hand, unfolding the paper he'd bought. He'd get Edith to read him the salient details later; for now, it was a way of blending in.

At Waterloo, he climbed the steps to the main concourse, listening out for the announcement that would signal the arrival of the Kingston train. There was still ten minutes to go. He started walking, unhurriedly, to the ticket barrier, moving with a deliberation which, he'd found, meant people tended to get out of his way. It was the ones who weren't looking where they were going you had to watch out for. Around him, the crowd seemed a shadow theatre of moving shapes. Like silhouettes projected on a wall by torchlight. There was a game he and Harry had played when they were kids. Making shadow pictures with their fingers – a rabbit, a nibbling mouse, a grinning face. Shifting images that changed, with a flick of one's fingers, into something else. 'Look where you're going, can't you?' said a voice in his ear.

'Sorry!'

'Should think so, too.' Still muttering, the grumbler

moved away, leaving an olfactory trail of peppermint behind him. A swift pint in the station bar, guessed Rowlands, followed by a strong mint to disguise the fact from the wife. And indeed, as he went by, the door of the bar swung open to release a smell of beer and cigarettes. Jovial voices shouted. 'See you tomorrow, old man . . .' A man blundered past him, emitting a gust of beery breath. 'Toodle-oo . . .' And from near the exit, that led to The Cut, came the hoarse shouts of a news vendor: 'Girl's Death on Exmoor Latest!' It had been all over the papers these past few days. An eighteen-year-old servant had gone missing, her body having been discovered some days later in a patch of boggy ground. The Coroner's verdict, Death by Misadventure, had proved an unpopular one with the local populace. Now, it seemed, fresh evidence had called the verdict into question.

Or so it emerged from the discussion two of Rowlands' fellow travellers were having as he took his seat in the carriage second from the front and once more unfolded his paper. 'Stands to reason it's murder,' said the first man. 'I mean, she was half-naked. A young girl doesn't just run out into the night with next to nothing on.'

'Some do,' put in the second man, with a coarse laugh.

'Not decent girls,' insisted the first. 'And they've never found her spectacles, neither.'

'Well, they'll be searching high and low for 'em now,' said a third voice. 'Reckon it was the boyfriend myself.' There came a murmur of agreement. It usually was the boyfriend, in such cases.

Not wanting to be drawn into this conversation, Rowlands feigned absorption in his paper. Although, if it came to that, he thought wryly, he'd had rather more experience of the kind of thing they were discussing than most. A brief and disagreeable memory of the time he'd – quite literally – stumbled across a corpse, passed through his mind. He let it pass. Trying not to think about such things only made it worse, he'd found.

It was a fourteen-minute walk from the station to Grove Crescent; he'd managed it in eleven. Since he'd taken up rowing again, he'd got much fitter, he thought. On this particular evening, there were quite a lot of people about, enjoying a stroll by the river in the mild spring air, and so he couldn't risk striding out the way he might have done first thing in the morning. It was one of the things he disliked most about being blind: the caution it imposed upon one's every movement so that one was forced, at times, to creep along like an old woman instead of going at a smart pace. Even so, it was a pleasant walk, with the river so close at hand. He could smell the weeds and mud churned up by the oars, and hear the shouts of coaches exhorting their respective teams to greater efforts from the towpath. Wouldn't he like to be out there himself on such a fine evening!

He turned into the broad, tree-lined street where he and Edith and the children had moved two years before. The house was thirty years old: square-built and solid; a step up from the shoddy terraced dwelling they'd lived in when they were first married. The money they'd got from the sale of the chicken farm wouldn't have been enough, by itself, to buy a place of this size in such a nice neighbourhood, but it was then that Edith's mother had announced her intention of giving up her own home. 'Because I can't really manage by myself any longer,' she'd said, 'and I do so miss the children.' It was this last reason which was the true one, Rowlands thought. At sixty-five, Helen Edwards could hardly have been called infirm, but her ten years' widowhood had evidently proved a lonely time. Moving in with her daughter and son-in-law had been the solution.

Outside Number 46, Watson was washing his car. It was his pride and joy: a Sunbeam Talbot. 'Evening,' called Rowlands, raising a hand as he reached the gate.

'Evening,' came the reply, accompanied by the sound of a sponge being squeezed out in a bucket of soapy water. Rowlands walked briskly up the path, and let himself into the spacious hall of Number 44.

'I'm home!' he called, into the silence. They must all be in the garden, he thought. But then there came a step on the stair.

'Hello, Daddy.' His eldest daughter, Margaret, descended to greet him.

'All alone?' he said, kissing her. She was growing tall, he thought. Eleven, now. No longer a baby. Not that Meg had ever been babyish in her ways: his serious child.

'I was doing my homework,' she said, in answer to his question. 'Mummy and Granny and the little ones are picking peas.'

24

'Ah.' He suppressed a smile at this description of her sisters; patted her shoulder, slender beneath the broad strap of her navy serge tunic. How proud she'd been, the day they bought the uniform! 'You go back to your studies – what is it this evening?'

'Algebra.'

'Oh! I used to be rather good at algebra. Give me a shout if you find yourself getting stuck.' Not that she'd need any help, he thought; she was getting to be a lot better at maths than he'd been at her age.

'I will.' Then she was gone, slipping back upstairs to her room and her precious books.

When he'd hung up his coat and stowed his briefcase, he went out into the garden where, to judge from the murmur of voices coming from the direction of the vegetable patch, the pea-pickers were still hard at work. After all the rain they'd had this spring, and now this spell of good weather, he was hoping for a record crop. His runner beans had done well the year before, as had his potatoes and cabbages, but he had expectations this year of his vegetable marrows. When they'd moved to Kingston two summers ago, the garden had been a jungle, with the kitchen garden entirely gone to seed, and some fine old roses badly in need of pruning. He'd soon dealt with all of that.

'Daddy!' His youngest daughter was the first to notice his arrival. A moment later, her sturdy four-year-old body threw itself against him, her arms encircling his legs so that he was forced to come to a halt.

'Hello, Joanie.' Disentangling her arms from about his knees, he lifted her up and bestowed a kiss on the top of her head. 'Not in bed, yet?'

'I said they might stay up until you got home,' said his wife from the middle of the pea patch.

'Quite right,' he said. 'It's much too nice an evening to have to go to bed. Evening, Helen.' This was to his mother-in-law. 'And how's my Anne? Good day at school?'

'Yes, Daddy. Daddy, guess what? I'm going to be a pilot when I grow up, like Amy Johnson.'

'Oh-oh,' he said. Ever since he'd brought home the news about their proposed Croydon visit, the girls had talked of little else.

'And just how,' he went on, ruffling his middle daughter's hair, 'are you going to afford flying lessons?' Anne had her answer ready.

'You're going to pay for them, Daddy – until I get my pilot's licence. Then I'll be able to pay you back from the prize money I'll get from flying to Australia.'

'I see. Got it all planned out, haven't you?'

'Yes,' she said simply.

'Well, you won't be allowed flying lessons or any other lessons if you don't finish your homework,' said Edith. 'Go on. You've still got twenty minutes before bed.'

'It's only French verbs,' said Anne carelessly as they began to walk back towards the house. 'I've already done my composition – it's What I Want to Be When I Grow Up.'

'Don't tell me, let me guess,' her father said.

# Chapter Two

'Of course, they're wildly excited,' said Edith as they sat together after dinner, Mrs Edwards having gone up to her room to write some letters, she said, with her customary tact. Since becoming a permanent member of the household, two years before, his mother-in-law behaved, if anything, more like a guest than ever, never failing to ask if she might use the telephone, and making a point of, as she put it, 'leaving you to yourselves' in the evenings. 'Mother, this is your house, too,' Edith had said, exasperated at one such self-effacing display. But Helen Edwards, who could be remarkably firm when she liked, Rowlands had noticed, stuck to her guns. 'Oh, my dear, I don't want you to think me an awful old nuisance,' she'd said. 'I've heard so many stories about people having their relations to stay and ending up detesting them.'

Well, she was right enough about that, thought Rowlands – although, in his experience, the animosity came about from having too many people crowded together in too small a house, like some of the families he'd known growing up in Camberwell. Nine or ten children, parents and grandparents all crammed hugger-mugger into a crumbling back-to-back, with only a tin tub to wash in and the WC in the yard. No wonder people went for their loved ones with the carving knife. You couldn't say they had any such reason to resort to murder here, in leafy Grove Crescent, with electric light, hot and cold running water, and an upstairs bathroom with a bath deep enough to launch a battleship. Four bedrooms so that Margaret could have a room to herself in which to do her homework even if it meant Anne had to share with 'the baby', as she said disdainfully. Then there was a large sitting room, with French windows opening onto the garden, a dining room and a good-sized kitchen and scullery.

It was twice the space they'd had in Gabriel Street, and, for a time, while Dorothy and Viktor had been staying with them, there'd been seven of them in that tiny house. He realised that it was the second time his sister had come to mind that evening. He wondered where she was and what she was doing now. He hoped, wherever she was, that she was happy. It had been three years now. He didn't even know whether she was alive or dead.

'Fred! You haven't been listening, have you?'

'What? I heard every word. You were saying about the girls . . .'

'And Peter. I was talking about Peter.'

His brother-in-law's child. A rather dull little chap, in Rowlands' private opinion. Having a father like Ralph probably hadn't helped. 'What about him?'

Edith gave a triumphant laugh. 'You see! You weren't listening at all. I asked you if you minded Ralph's dropping Peter off on Friday night instead of Saturday morning. Only Diana's got their Bridge party to organise.'

'I don't mind,' he said. Trust Ralph to have to bend arrangements to suit himself.

'It's a pity,' his wife went on, 'that you'd already said you'd go to this Croydon thing, otherwise we could have gone to Ralph and Diana's. You know we were invited.'

Thank heaven for small mercies, Rowlands thought. 'Is there anything in the paper?' he said. Dubious as he was about the aerodrome trip, it made it all worthwhile, just to have an excuse not to go to Richmond. Being condescended to by his brother-in-law, whose position as a bank manager gave him a certain status – in his own eyes, at least – stuck in Rowlands' craw. The trouble was, Edith had rose-tinted spectacles where her brother was concerned.

'What?' she said now, sounding a little affronted at this abrupt change of subject. 'I don't know. I'll just see, shall I?'

It was their custom of an evening for her to read to him. Sometimes, it was a chapter of whatever book they were reading – just now, it was Priestley's *Angel Pavement* – sometimes the newspaper. 'My personal Talking Book,' he called her.

'Please,' he said. She rustled pages.

'There's that awful murder,' she said. 'The poor girl on Exmoor.'

'Yes. I heard about that. Anything else?'

'There's an article about Flying Boats. "*Are they the Future?*" the writer asks.'

He groaned. 'Spare me.'

'Or,' Edith went on mischievously, 'there's a report on the Schneider race. It seems these aeroplanes the French are designing can go up to four hundred miles per hour – imagine that!'

'I'd rather not. Isn't there any real news?'

'Well, there's this – but it's still air-related, I'm afraid. "*Intruders Disturbed at Aerodrome: Police Suspect Sabotage . . .*"'

'That does sound a bit more interesting.'

'I'll read it, shall I?' She cleared her throat. '"*Police last night were hunting for two men, who were seen running away from the scene of a break-in at the de Havilland Flying School near Hatfield. The first is described as being about thirty-five years old, five feet eight inches tall, and wearing dark-coloured clothing and a flat cap; the second as aged about forty, five feet ten inches tall, and wearing a light-coloured mackintosh and a soft hat. Inspector Herbert Rawlins of the Hertfordshire Constabulary stated: 'A hangar was broken into.*

*However, it appears that the perpetrators were disturbed before anything could be taken. The police are keeping an open mind, but have not ruled out the possibility of sabotage.' It is known that de Havillands have invested considerable sums in developing new machines, specifically for competition purposes . . ."* Shall I read on?' she said, swallowing a yawn.

'No, that's all right. Let's have the wireless shall we? There might be a concert worth listening to.'

On any normal Saturday, he'd have taken his usual train, but as he'd the girls and Peter with him, Rowlands resigned himself to catching the slow one. Not that his girls were dawdlers, but their cousin was hardly the speediest when it came to getting himself dressed or eating his breakfast. When he'd realised they were going to have to walk to the station, he'd been unable to conceal his dismay. 'The pater always gets George to run me in the motor,' he'd said – George being the chauffeur.

'Well, it'll be a nice change for you to have some exercise,' replied Rowlands. Still, you couldn't blame the lad. As the only child of doting, well-to-do parents, he was on the way to being spoilt rotten. Knowing the fondness of most small boys for things mechanical, Rowlands had hoped the train journey itself would amuse him. But beyond a passing remark that he was to have a new train set for his birthday, Peter had seemed unimpressed by the experience even though the great engine had let off a satisfyingly loud shriek of its whistle as they'd neared

Waterloo, and a very fierce-sounding guard had passed through the carriage, demanding to see their tickets.

Nor did the office seem to engage his interest much more, although Anne had demonstrated the mechanics of the swivel chair and the adjustable lamp and shown him how to type his name on the typewriter. 'Why don't you take Peter outside and show him the garden?' said Rowlands when these possibilities had been exhausted. 'I've got a bit of work to do.' Again, it was Anne who bore the brunt of this, Margaret having cried off, on the grounds that she had some homework to finish. Threading paper and carbons into the machine before beginning the first of his letters, Rowlands resolved that Anne should have the biggest ice cream money could buy when they reached the aerodrome that afternoon.

By half past twelve, the rest of their party was starting to assemble in front of the Lodge. Rowlands exchanged greetings with a couple of those he knew – Eyre and Barlowe – and drew out the list he'd typed that morning as an aide-memoire. 'Now, Meg,' he said to his elder daughter, 'just read the names out in order, will you? There should be sixteen of them.'

She did so. 'J. E. Barlowe.'

'Present and correct,' said the latter.

'D. J. Calder, R. L. Coxhead, S. M. Eyre.'

'Present!' sang out Eyre. He'd been a pilot during the war, Rowlands recalled, which doubtless accounted for his presence today. 'L. R. Hammond, P. Hewitt.' Another airman, thought Rowlands. 'D. V. Llewellyn-Jones.'

'Here, Miss,' said the Welshman.

'L. L. Neate, C. R. W. Passingham, R. Pope, F. C. Rowlands – that's you, Daddy – G. W. Stratham, J. R. Taylor, S. Twining, and T. S. Turney.'

'That's me,' said a gruff Yorkshire voice. 'This your girl, Rowlands? Grand little lass, isn't she?'

'She's not so bad,' said Rowlands. 'Thank you, Meg. You can hold onto the list, if you will.' Although now he'd committed the names to memory, he'd have no need of a prompt. Just then, the dull roar of an engine in low gear and the crunch of wheels on gravel signalled the arrival of the charabanc. Another would be setting off from Brighton, with the same numbers of passengers, although, thankfully, somebody else would be in charge of that. 'All right,' he said. 'Is everybody here? Or shall I run through the names again? Perhaps people could sing out as they get on board. I wouldn't want to leave any of you behind.'

'Anyone got a light?' said a voice. 'Only I seem to have left my matches behind. Stratham's the name, by the way.'

'Here you are,' said Rowlands, handing him the box of Swan Vestas from his jacket pocket.

'Thanks,' said the other, returning the matches when his gasper was lit. 'I say, would you care for one of these?'

'What are they?'

'Craven A.'

'Thanks, but I prefer my own.' Rowlands lit up. Five minutes more and they ought to get going if they wanted to miss the traffic, he thought.

'I must say,' went on his new friend, 'I'm looking forward to this! Haven't been near an airfield since I crashed my bus at Pop in '17.' So he was a pilot, too, Rowlands thought.

'I had quite a bit to do with you RFC chaps when I was in France,' he said. 'Flanders, too. I was a gunner, you know – eighteen-pounder field guns, not Howitzers – so we rather relied on what your lot could tell us of what the enemy was up to.'

'Well, we tried to make ourselves useful, you know,' said Stratham. Despite the former pilot's becoming show of modesty, Rowlands knew this had been a difficult and dangerous job: flying low over the enemy lines, under raking fire from the Archies, while trying to keep the aeroplane steady enough for the observer to photograph the German gun emplacements.

'Used to watch the dogfights, too,' said Rowlands, pinching out the stub of his cigarette. 'Sometimes there'd be thirty or forty BE2cs, against as many Huns, circling around in the sky. I often wondered how you managed not to crash into each other, but you never did – at least not while I was watching.'

'Oh yes,' said Stratham, sounding almost wistful. 'We had some marvellous times. There's really nothing to beat it. Flying, I mean. Being up there in a cloudless blue sky, looking down on it all, with only your observer for company, and knowing that if you got your kill, there'd be champagne all round in the Mess that night. Really nothing to beat it,' he said.

'I'll take your word for it,' said Rowlands. 'Well, that seems to be all of us accounted for. Perhaps we should get going.'

'I knew him, you know,' said Stratham as he went to get on board. 'Alan Percival, that is,' – this being the man whose exploits they were on their way to celebrate.

'Did you?' said Rowlands since some response seemed necessary.

'Yes,' said the other reflectively 'Back in the old days. Not that he had much time for new bugs like myself – he was already an Ace when I joined 3 Squadron. Always very decent to me, though.' He took a last, deep drag of his cigarette.

'I say, Stratham old man, get a move on, do!' sang out a voice from the back of the bus. Hewitt, Rowlands thought. 'Only I'd rather like to be there before the plane arrives, wouldn't you?'

As the bus drew into the car park in front of the Airport Terminal, there was still half an hour to go before the ceremony was due to begin. If it began on time, thought Rowlands, as his group began to disembark. The Brighton group, he was informed by the steward who met them at the gate, had already arrived. 'Mr Potter's giving them the tour,' he added. 'Your lot might like to join them, seeing as how we've no news from Captain Percival yet.'

'All right,' said Rowlands. 'Where do we go?'

'I'll show you,' replied the steward, whose name, he

said, was Saunders. 'I say, that little chap looks a bit green.' It was Peter he meant, of course, the long journey in the rattling bus having disagreed with him.

'You'll feel better if you're sick,' Anne was assuring him. 'I always feel heaps better after I'm sick.'

Suppressing a groan, Rowlands took charge. 'Come along, Peter, my lad, I need you to show me the way.'

'But Daddy . . .'

'No buts, young lady. Peter's going to be my guide to the airport today, aren't you, old man?'

'Y-es,' said Peter, sounding a bit uncertain.

'Take a deep breath or two if you're feeling queasy. There! Feeling any better?'

Peter said that he was. 'Good show,' said Rowlands. 'Now, if you'll keep Mr Saunders in view, we can all get along quite nicely. I say, I'm looking forward to Captain Percival's arrival in his Gipsy Moth, aren't you? It's quite an achievement, flying all the way from Australia. He's going to break the record, too, I shouldn't wonder.'

'Yes,' said Peter doubtfully. 'But the pater says his machine's not a patch on the new Fairey and Blackburn.'

'Does he?' said Rowlands as the child slipped a small hot hand into his. 'I don't think I know that particular model. Perhaps you'd like to tell me all about it.'

'Daddy . . .'

'In a moment, Anne,' said her father. 'Peter's just telling me about the latest . . . what's it called, again?'

'The S9/30.'

'I could have told you about that,' said Anne.

'Oh, don't think you'll be getting off lightly,' said Rowlands. 'I'll need you to describe the aircraft hangars to me. And all the aeroplanes,' he added.

'All right,' said his middle daughter, somewhat mollified. He felt her take his other hand, and the four of them, with Margaret on her sister's left, fell in behind the St Dunstan's group.

It was a fine, windless day; good flying weather, Rowlands supposed. He drew a deep breath of the mild, faintly petrol-scented air. As they neared the first of the hangars, he could hear what sounded like machinery in operation: the whine of a circular saw, followed by a burst of hammering. 'Our workshops,' said their guide. 'I think this is where we'll find the others. We'll just pop our heads in for a minute.' Which they did, inhaling as they did so the unmistakeable smells associated with such places: the sharp chemical tang of varnish and acetate, mingling with the fresher scents of wood and canvas. The sound of voices, echoing in that vast, cavernous space, indicated that they'd found the Brighton group. 'Well, I'll leave you to it,' said Saunders. 'Hi! George!'– raising his voice to overcome the sound of hammering – 'Here's the rest of the St Dunstan's party.'

'Ah, you made it, then?' said the man Saunders had addressed. 'George Potter's the name. I'm the Airport Manager. I was just explaining to these gentlemen what's going on here.'

'Look, Daddy, they're mending a wing,' cried Anne,

forgetting, in her excitement, that he was unable to follow her injunction.

'Yes, this is the repairs department,' said Potter, who'd overheard her exclamation. 'Running repairs, you know – like the tear in the wing fabric they're fixing now. Anything more serious goes to the machine shop.'

'What kind of plane is it?' piped up one of their party. Stratham, thought Rowlands.

'It's a DH71, otherwise known as a Tiger Moth,' was the reply. 'Lovely little machine. Wingspan's only twenty-two foot six. Built for racing, you see. The one next to it's an Avro Baby. What's the matter with that one, Bert?' he called across to the man who was engaged in overhauling the plane.

'Touch of engine trouble,' said the ground engineer. 'Dirty distributor, it looks like. Nothing a touch of elbow grease can't cure.'

'I remember it well,' laughed Stratham. 'All those mornings in the freezing cold, washing the engine down with paraffin. Not that it made a blind bit of difference,' he added. 'You could get shot down just as easily in a clean plane as in a dirty one.'

'All the craft in this hangar are racers, aren't they, Bert?' said Potter as if he had not heard this remark.

'Next to the Baby we've got a nice little Supermarine. Bright blue, with silver facings. Then there's a Gloster – dark blue, this one, with copper wings and tail. Pretty as a picture, she is. Last one's a Crusader. White, with blue fairings. The Tiger Moth's all in yellow. Like I said, they're pretty things.'

'Go pretty fast too, I shouldn't wonder,' said another voice. Rowlands recognised it as Barlowe's.

'You said it, sir!' was the enthusiastic reply. 'Two hundred miles per hour is the most any of this size of aircraft can reach although it's often closer to one hundred and fifty miles per hour. But you couldn't call any of 'em slow.'

'A bit quicker than we used to manage, eh, Hewie?' quipped Barlowe to one of his fellow pilots – Hewitt, Rowlands guessed. 'Even if we did have the Hun on our tails to lend us speed.'

Leaving the mechanics to their work, the group moved on to the next hangar where they caught up with the Brighton group being given a detailed description of a Blackburn Bluebird. 'It's the metal skin that makes it so aerodynamic,' the guide was explaining. 'If some of you gentlemen would care to put your hands on the fuselage, you'll get an idea of what I mean.' People were accordingly clustering around the big machine –'Mind how you go there! Propeller's just in front of you,' – when Rowlands felt a tug on his sleeve. Peter needed the lavatory, he said.

'All right,' said Rowlands. Telling the girls to stay together, and that he wouldn't be long, he ascertained from Potter where the WC was to be found. 'Come along, then,' he said to Peter.

Skirting the edge of the airfield as advised – 'Wouldn't do to get your heads knocked off by an incoming plane,' said Potter cheerily – they reached the Terminal Building at last. Here, the crowds were thicker than they had been a quarter of an hour before, with people entering by the main doors, only to be told by the official posted there that they'd need to go round by the side entrance if they wanted to get to the stands where the reception was being held. 'Round to the side, ladies and gentlemen,' he was saying, with monotonous frequency. 'That'll be your quickest way. Round to the side.'

'Expecting a good turnout, are you?' said Rowlands to the man as he stood waiting for Peter to emerge from the Gents.

'Something in the region of five thousand,' was the reply. 'He's very popular, is the Captain.'

'I don't doubt it.'

'Broken a couple of records this time, too. Did the Baghdad to Karachi leg in under five days.'

'Very impressive,' said Rowlands, to whom this meant little.

'Yes,' went on the other, 'he's quite a character, is Captain Percival.' He lowered his voice a fraction. 'Bit of a way with the ladies, too, between you and me. Why, only the other day he says to me, "Jock," he says . . .'

'I've a bone to pick with you,' said a voice. A young woman's voice; Rowlands wondered where he'd heard it before. 'I've just seen the list, and my name's not on it. All I can say is, it's beastly unfair.'

'Now then,' said the man who'd referred to himself as Jock, 'I never promised anything.'

'That's just what's so rotten,' she flashed back. 'All these weeks and weeks I've been coming down here and working my socks off – for nothing, mind you! – and you've let me think I was in with a chance.'

'You got the wrong end of the stick then,' was the reply. 'You know as well as I do that girls can't work as ground crew. The men wouldn't like it, for a start.'

'I can't think why. I can service a plane as fast as any man.' Of course, thought Rowlands. That's where I've heard that voice. It was the other day, on the telephone – the young woman who'd enthused about stripping down engines. What was her name again?

'Be reasonable, Wilkie.' That was it: Pauline Wilkinson. *Call me Wilkie. Everybody else does.*

'Reasonable! Ha!' snorted the girl. 'I suppose the men think it's "reasonable" for me to give up my idea of flying altogether? Perhaps they'd like me to stay home and give tennis parties instead?'

'Now, nobody thinks any such thing,' replied the other, in the tone one uses to soothe a fractious child. 'All the lads think very highly of you, you know that.'

'Then why can't I be on the field when Alan . . . when Captain Percival's plane touches down? I've earned the right – you know I have, Jock.' He must have shrugged or made some other gesture of refusal, for she gave an exasperated sigh. 'It's just so unfair,' she said.

'Look, if it means so much to you, I'll have a word with the rest of the men.'

'Don't bother.' She must have turned on her heel, then,

because a moment later she walked slap bang into Rowlands. 'Oh!' she gasped. 'Awfully sorry! I didn't see you there.'

'My fault,' he said politely. 'Miss Wilkinson, isn't it?'

'That's right. I'm afraid I don't know who you are, though.'

'No reason why you should. The name's Rowlands. We spoke on the telephone a few days ago.'

'Oh, that was you, was it?' Her voice was flat and expressionless – a complete contrast to the way she'd sounded on that first occasion. 'I passed on your message, by the way.'

'Thank you.'

'Don't mention it. Look, I'm sorry. I've got to go.'

'Of course,' said Rowlands. He stood aside to let her pass. A moment later, there was the sound of the heavy glass doors swinging shut behind her. The man she'd addressed as Jock blew out his cheeks, expelling a puff of air.

'Women!' he muttered, half to himself. 'Sorry about that, sir. I'm sure she didn't mean to be rude. It's just she takes things to heart, our Wilkie.'

'So I gathered.'

'I'm Jock Stewart, by the way. Chief Ground Engineer.'

'Fred Rowlands.' They shook hands. 'So you're the man responsible for getting the planes down safely.'

'You could say that,' replied Stewart. 'Although you wouldn't hear me say as much in front of one of the pilots. As far as they're concerned, it's all down to their skill and judgement.'

'Well, I won't give you away,' smiled Rowlands. 'I'm just waiting for . . . ah, here he is. My brother-in-law's boy.'

'Hello, young man,' said the Scotsman. A Glaswegian, Rowlands thought. Funny how different it sounded from the Edinburgh accent once you got to know the latter. Chief Inspector Douglas was from Edinburgh, of course, although he'd spent much of his career in the Metropolitan Police. A good man, Douglas. One way and another, he and Rowlands had spent quite a bit of time together. Although it had been two years since they'd last met, shortly before the trial of the murderer both had helped to bring to justice. It had been an ugly case, and one about which Rowlands tried to think as little as possible.

'We ought to be rejoining our group,' he said. 'We're with the St Dunstan's party, as I expect you'd realised.'

'Only noticed it just this minute,' said Stewart politely.

Rowlands smiled. 'I'll take that as a compliment,' he said. 'I don't suppose you could point us in the right direction?'

'With pleasure,' said Jock Stewart. 'Keep going straight towards the big hangar on the far side. It's the middle one of three. You can find your way, can't you, laddie?' This was to Peter. Peter said that he could, and so, with a final wave of the hand, Rowlands set off, with the child tagging along beside him. Rowlands checked his watch. It was a quarter past three. There'd just be time to find their party before they'd need to make tracks for the main event.

'Here we are,' he said as they reached the set of sliding doors that led into the hangar. These were now closed; he slid one of them open. 'Careful!' he said to Peter. 'There's a step.'

But when they entered the great echoing space, with its pungent smells of spilt oil and paraffin, there seemed to be no one there. The hangar, it seemed, was empty of all human presences; its only inhabitants the silent rows of aeroplanes. Rowlands realised this only when moving a few paces away from the door, he'd almost collided with the edge of a wing. 'See anyone?' he said to Peter, who must have shaken his head; unlike Rowlands' daughters, he hadn't been taught to make his responses audible. 'No? They must have moved on elsewhere. Never mind. We'll soon catch them up.'

'And just what the bloody hell do you think you're doing?' said a voice. Rowlands turned towards it.

'I'll thank you to watch your language,' he said evenly. 'There's a child present.'

'Child, my eye!' retorted the irascible stranger. 'You've no business here and you know it. Poking and prying around. What are you – some sort of spy?' Rowlands was left momentarily speechless by this accusation. Even though it was wholly unwarranted on this occasion, it wasn't the first time he'd been called by that unlovely name. Spy. He felt himself flush to the roots of his hair.

'I think you've got the wrong idea.'

'Don't give me that! I saw you. You went right up to it. Had a good look, did you?'

'I don't know what you're talking about.'

Just then came another voice, from towards the back of the hangar. 'What's going on?' said this voice. Rowlands thought it was one he'd heard before.

'You might well ask!' replied the man who'd called Rowlands a spy. 'I caught this man just now, having a dekko at the F7/30. Walked in bold as brass, he did, even though there's a sign saying as plain as day, "No Unauthorised Admittance".'

'I assure you . . .' Rowlands began, but before he could explain, the other man – the one who'd sounded familiar – burst out laughing.

'I say, you are an awful fool, Bill! Can't you see this man's no more a spy than I am? He's with the St Dunstan's crowd, aren't you, sir?' Rowlands nodded. 'You see? Couldn't get a look at your precious plane even if he wanted to . . . No offence,' he added, to Rowlands.

'None taken,' said Rowlands. 'You're the man who was mending the wing when we were being shown around the first hangar.'

'That's me. Bert Higgins's the name. And this is another of the ground crew. Bill Farley. He's got a bit of a temper on him, but he's not as bad as he seems.'

'Sorry,' muttered the man alluded to. 'Only it says "No Admittance".'

'You'll be wanting to join your group,' went on the amiable Higgins. 'My guess is, they'll have started to make their way towards the stands. Want me to take you and the nipper over there?'

'If you'll just give me an idea of the general direction, I think I can manage,' said Rowlands. Having been revealed as an all too unlikely spy, he was nevertheless reluctant to appear entirely helpless.

'Oh, it's no bother,' said Higgins. 'This way. Mind the step. You know,' he went on when Rowlands guessed they were out of earshot, 'I'm sure he didn't mean to be so sharp, poor old Bill. Things haven't been easy for him. Lost a leg in the war, you know, but you'd never guess it, the way he gets about. Bloody good at his job, too. You won't find a better mechanic in the RAF.'

They had by now reached the Terminal building. 'I think I can find my way from here,' said Rowlands, interrupting this panegyric.

'Right-oh,' said the other. 'Well, best be getting back. We've just heard he's been spotted over the Kent coast, the Captain, so it shouldn't be long now. Aren't you excited, young feller?' he said to Peter, the mute witness of the entire exchange.

'Yes,' said the child, but without conviction. He really was a funny little chap, thought Rowlands.

# Chapter Three

Their group, now numbering over thirty, had been allocated a prime position at the front of the tier of seats which had been set up to one side of the airstrip. Here, they found Margaret and Anne. 'Daddy,' said the latter, without preliminaries, 'I sat in the cockpit. The man said I might. When I'm old enough, I'm allowed to take the plane up.'

'You won't be old enough until you're at least seventeen,' observed her sister. 'That's eight years. You'll have forgotten all about it by then.'

'I won't!' There was a dangerous edge to Anne's voice. Rowlands judged it best to change the subject.

'Can anyone see a plane approaching?' he asked. 'I'm

relying on you three to keep a sharp lookout.' Although when Captain Percival's Gipsy Moth appeared from the clouds, there'd be close on five thousand people to give him notice of the fact, he knew. Around him, the air hummed with anticipation. Snatches of excited conversation came from all sides:

'See anything yet?'

'. . . heard he had a spot of engine trouble over Constantinople . . .'

'. . . apparently it has a cruising speed of around ninety miles per hour . . .'

'. . . they say the Mail's paid five thousand pounds for his story . . .'

'See anything?'

'. . . bound to have beaten Hinkler's record, at any rate . . .'

'. . . bit of a playboy. 'Course, they all fall for that type, the women . . .'

'I must say,' said a voice in Rowlands' ear, 'I wish the blighter'd hurry up and get here so that we can all go home.' It was very much what he wished himself. He was about to say as much when the hum of voices around them abruptly ceased. Into the silence, which lasted no more than a split second, Anne's voice sounded clear as a bell, 'There he is, Daddy!' At which the hum began again, and rapidly swelled to a roar.

'I say – jolly good show!'

'He's done it!'

'There he is! Look, there – just above the trees! He's

coming into land.' And indeed there came the sound Rowlands would come to know so well – a low droning, like that of a giant bumblebee – as the Gipsy Moth hove into view, provoking a further outburst of ecstatic cries from those around him, 'Oh, well done! Well done!'

'Look, Teddy, look! Can you see it – the plane? Over there, darling. Look!' The woman who'd shouted seemed almost beside herself with excitement. 'Oh, Teddy darling, look!' she cried again. 'If only I could lift you up so that you could see. But you're much too heavy, darling.'

'Allow me,' said Rowlands, recognising the woman's voice. It was Irene Metcalfe. 'I believe we've met,' he added since she seemed momentarily nonplussed.

'You're the man from Regent's Park!' she exclaimed. 'Look, Teddy, it's Mr . . .'

'Rowlands,' he said. 'Come on, Teddy, let's see if we can't give you a better view.' He picked up the little boy, and swung him up onto his shoulders. 'There! See anything now?'

'Yes,' replied the child. 'I can see Uncle Alan getting out of his aeroplane.'

'So you're a friend of Captain Percival's?' said Rowlands, turning towards the young woman, who now held his arm. 'I hadn't realised.'

'Well, he's really a friend of my husband's,' she said quickly. 'At least, they knew each other during the war.' There was the fraction of a second's hesitation before she added, 'Not that we see much of him, these days.' The object of their interest was now advancing towards them, his progress arrested at intervals by the attentions of the Press. 'Over here, Captain Percival!' 'Just one more picture, Captain Percival!' Adulation flowed from the watching crowd in waves; it was almost palpable, thought Rowlands. He himself, though a sceptic about the whole enterprise from the first, found it hard not to be caught up in it. 'Oh, well done! Jolly well done!' cried the voices, and he, too, echoed the sentiment. To have flown such a distance – twelve thousand miles, much of it overland – and in so short a time, shaving two whole days off the record, well, it was an achievement worth celebrating, if only for the casual daring with which it had been performed.

Just then, Rowlands felt a touch on his arm; a voice said, 'There you are, Mr Rowlands! Jock said I'd find you here.' It was George Potter, who'd been their guide earlier that afternoon. 'And the young ladies, too. Jolly good. Only I thought it would be a nice thing if your eldest were to present the bouquet.'

'Oh! May I, Daddy?' Margaret's voice was breathless with longing. 'Of course you may. Perhaps,' he added to Potter, aware of the acute disappointment Anne must be feeling, 'her sister could go too?'

'The young lady who wants to fly her Moth to Australia? I was just going to suggest it. Come along, Miss . . .' Then they were gone, ducking under the rail to follow the Airport Manager to the podium, Rowlands supposed. He knew that this had been set up at right angles to where they were standing. There were seats for

VIPs – he'd heard two women behind him discussing this earlier. Lord Amulree, the newly appointed Secretary of State for Air, was amongst these dignitaries, as was the elderly Duchess of Bedford – loudly cheered for her pluck in having flown her Fokker FVII to Cape Town and back the previous year.

'Although I think she might have bought a new hat for the occasion,' said Rowlands' neighbour to her friend. 'She does look a frump in that drab old felt cloche . . . Oh, my word! Isn't he handsome?' From which Rowlands surmised that Captain Percival had now come within sight of their section of the stand – a supposition confirmed by the sudden increase in the volume of cheering which came from all around him.

Over and above this rose a woman's voice, 'Go on, Teddy – wave!' It was Irene Metcalfe, of course. Nor could Rowlands dissociate himself from her with ease since the child was still sitting on his shoulders. There was nothing for it but to stand there, grinning inanely, while the wretched woman made a spectacle of herself. For it appeared that the Captain was now level with where they were standing – had perhaps paused, to shake one of the many eager hands which had been thrust towards him, or to pose for yet another photograph. So that when she cried out again, 'Say "well done," to Captain Percival, Teddy!' the aviator had no choice but to respond. There was a moment's pause; then he laughed, a shade uneasily, it seemed to Rowlands.

'I say,' he said, 'I wasn't expecting to see you here, Irene.'

'Oh . . .' She gave a silly little laugh. 'We wouldn't have missed it for the world, would we, Teddy, darling?' The child – well used, it seemed, to having words put into his mouth by his mother – said nothing. It was left to Percival to reply.

'I suppose not,' he said, his voice scarcely warmer than before. 'I see you're wearing your scarf,' said Mrs Metcalfe, with a coyness Rowlands was beginning to see was very much part of her armoury.

'Oh. Yes. Rather,' was the awkward response. 'Jolly nice scarf it is, too.'

'Captain Percival . . .' Potter was growing impatient at this unlooked for delay. 'People are waiting . . .'

'Yes, of course. Must get on,' he muttered, plunging, with what Rowlands guessed was some relief, into the crowd escorting him towards the podium. From here, a few moments later, could be heard the hugely amplified voice of the Secretary of State for Air, welcoming all those who had turned out that afternoon in honour of their distinguished guest – here he had paused to allow a burst of cheering – and to welcome that guest himself (more cheering), to whom he would cede the microphone just as soon as he had finished telling them all how important it was that Britons should become 'air-minded'. This he did for several minutes more as the crowd listened with good-humoured patience, saving its loudest cheers for the moment when these preliminaries gave way to the main event, and Percival himself approached the microphone.

Another outbreak of cheers and whistles meant that it was some minutes before the man himself could be heard to speak. Rowlands felt Mrs Metcalfe clutch his arm. 'How tired he looks!' she murmured. 'He must be utterly exhausted. Why don't they let him speak, instead of going on in that tiresome way?'

The crowd fell silent at last. A series of ear-splitting shrieks and crackles followed as the microphone was adjusted, and then Percival's voice rang out, 'Ladies and gentlemen – fellow aviators and aviatrices – it gives me great pleasure to be here this afternoon. I must say, that when I was battling my way through sandstorms outside Aleppo and near to crashing my machine during violent thunderstorms in the Malay Peninsula, I hardly dared to think that I'd be standing here, on this beautiful afternoon, talking to you now. But then flying is like that – one never quite knows where one is going to come down, nor whether one will make it out alive from one's latest scrape . . .'

There was more in the same vein, from which Rowlands gathered that, whatever his reputation as a ladykiller, Alan Percival was an unassuming sort, who rather tended to make light of his achievements than otherwise. Most of his anecdotes presented him as a sort of amiable incompetent, blundering his way across the world with more luck than judgement. '. . . then there was the time at Rangoon when I overshot the landing strip,' he confided at one point. 'Landed in a ditch with a smashed propeller and a broken wing – not my finest hour!' From his voice, Rowlands guessed him to be in his mid-thirties – old enough to have seen war service. He supposed that once you'd survived that, everything else – even flying halfway across the world in conditions of extreme peril – must seem like a huge joke. '. . . nearly got myself eaten by crocodiles when I came down in a swamp in Tjomal . . .'

The crowd was eating it up, of course. Gales of laughter followed each one of these self-deprecatory stories. But even the most appreciative audiences grow restive after a while and start thinking about matters other than sandstorms and crocodile swamps and whether the altimeter had failed at seven thousand feet. 'I could do with my tea, couldn't you, Florrie?' said the woman behind Rowlands to her friend.

'And so,' Captain Percival was saying, with impeccable timing, 'I'd just like to thank you all for turning out this afternoon, to give me such a splendid welcome . . . I say, that's awfully kind of you!' he added, breaking off these concluding remarks. 'What jolly flowers!' From which Rowlands surmised that Margaret's moment of glory had come.

There came another series of shrieks and howls from the microphone, and George Potter's voice, sounding strangely hollow, said, 'Ladies and gentlemen, tea is now being served in the airport lounge. But first, I'm sure we'd all like to give three rousing cheers for Captain Percival. Hip, hip . . .'

'Hooray!' roared the crowd, now starting to make its way towards the Terminal Building. Rowlands thought it was time he did the same. But first he had to collect the

54

girls. Consigning Teddy Metcalfe once more to his mother's care, he took Peter's hand. 'Let's find Anne and Margaret, shall we? Goodbye, Mrs Metcalfe.'

'Oh,' she replied distractedly. 'Are you going? Goodbye, then. Teddy, say goodbye to nice Mr Rowlands – and "thank you for looking after me".'

'Thank you,' mumbled the little boy.

'That's quite all right,' said Rowlands, feeling guilty for not having offered to escort the child and his mother to the tea lounge. How forlorn she'd sounded at the prospect of being abandoned! But he didn't want to run the risk of losing the girls in the crowd, and so he hardened his heart. 'Come on, Peter,' he said. Together, they plunged into the slowly moving mass. Because of the number of people all heading in the same direction, it took all of five minutes to reach the podium, and then it was only by hoisting Peter – no lightweight – up onto his shoulders so that the child could see over the heads of the crowd, that Rowlands managed to locate his daughters. To his surprise, they weren't alone. As he and Peter drew near, he heard Margaret say, 'We'd like that most awfully. But we'll have to ask Father.'

Then a man's voice – *surely it couldn't be Alan Percival's?* – replied, 'Quite right. I say, is this your papa now? With your little brother.'

'He isn't our brother,' said Anne. 'He's our cousin. Daddy, guess what?'

'I couldn't possibly,' said Rowlands, lowering Peter to the ground.

'Captain Percival's going to take us up in his aeroplane,' replied his daughter breathlessly. Rowlands turned his face towards where he judged the other man to be standing.

'I hope they haven't been pestering you,' he said.

'Not a bit!' laughed Percival. 'As a matter of fact, it was entirely my idea.'

'Oh, do say we can go, Daddy,' begged Anne.

'We'll see,' he said. 'Right now, I think we ought to leave Captain Percival in peace. He's had a long flight, and must be tired.'

'Actually the last bit of the journey was quite short,' said the pilot. 'It was only from Paris, you know. But I can see Potter making faces at me.'

'It's only that people are anxious to meet you,' said the Airport Manager, who had evidently been hovering nearby. 'The Duchess . . .'

'Oh, we mustn't keep her waiting,' said Percival. 'You're one of the St Dunstan's men, I gather?' he said to Rowlands as the whole party began walking towards where the reception was being held.

Rowlands admitted that he was.

'What was your regiment?' the other man pursued.

'Royal Field Artillery.'

'France?'

'And Belgium.'

'I did a bit of flying in Belgium in the last year of the war,' said Percival. 'Sopwiths, mainly.'

'I was out of it by then,' said Rowlands. 'But I know we – the batteries, that is – relied a great deal on what the

56

air crews could tell us of the enemy's position.'

'We did our bit, I suppose,' said the aviator. It was the same casual tone that Stratham had used earlier. Rowlands supposed it must be characteristic of the type, to affect such insouciance. They had by now reached the set of glass doors that led into the lounge. At once a clamour of female voices arose.

'There you are, Captain Percival! We wondered where you'd got to.'

'We're all simply longing to hear some more about your wonderful trip.'

'Tea, Captain Percival? Or would you prefer some of my homemade lemonade? It's really quite good, although I say so myself.'

'Do forgive me,' said the Captain to Rowlands. 'But I really ought to . . .' Then he was gone.

'Twenty minutes,' muttered George Potter. 'Then the car'll be arriving to take him to the Savoy. There's a reception at six. Champagne. The works.'

'A busy week ahead?' asked Rowlands since these remarks seemed directed at him.

'I'll say! There's a banquet tonight with the Lord Mayor; then he's to go to Windsor Castle tomorrow to meet His Royal Highness. The Prince is very interested in flying,' confided Potter. 'Then he's got a full programme of lectures, starting in Brighton and moving onto Oxford and Cambridge – the undergraduates have started a flying club, you know. Then it's Manchester, and Birmingham, and Harrogate.'

It all sounded rather exhausting, thought Rowlands, wondering if Percival would regret his new-found fame. For a man whose idea of fun was spending long hours alone at high altitudes, having to make small talk with eager admirers over tea and buns could not but be somewhat enervating. He wondered if Irene Metcalfe was amongst those now besieging the pilot with questions, 'Oh, do tell us about the time you crash-landed in Karachi.' He couldn't hear her voice, but it didn't mean she wasn't there, silently gazing at the object of her adoration.

For that, he thought, had been what was behind the awkward little encounter he'd witnessed earlier. Poor little Mrs Metcalfe had what was generally known as a crush on the dashing Captain, it would seem. It occurred to Rowlands that one of the hazards, if that was the right word, of being a personable young man who had been thrust into the public eye, was that it made one fatally attractive to the opposite sex.

By the time the bus had dropped them all back at Regent's Park and Rowlands had checked off all its passengers from the list he carried in his head, and they'd said their farewells, and then he and the girls and Peter had caught the Underground from Baker Street to Waterloo, and then the train after that, it was going on for seven. After such a journey, to say nothing of the excitements of the day, the children were tired out; just as well there was no school tomorrow, Rowlands thought. He himself was looking forward to a quiet evening with

Edith once the girls were in bed. Perhaps he'd have a potter round the garden after dinner, to see what was coming up. Tomorrow, after church, he'd plant out those lettuces. Reaching the house at last, he slipped his key into the lock, wondering why the door wasn't on the latch, as usual. 'We're home!' he called, into the silence, ushering the children in. 'Edith?' Perhaps she was putting Joanie to bed.

But then she appeared. 'You're back,' she said flatly. 'Good day?' Her voice sounded strange, Rowlands thought. Perhaps something had happened to upset her.

'Was it a good day, children? he said.

'Rather,' said Margaret. 'It was absolutely ripping.'

'I'm glad,' said her mother, with what seemed a forced cheerfulness. 'Now, go and wash your hands, all of you – yes, you too, Peter. It's time for supper. Granny's made you a lovely shepherd's pie.'

'But, Mummy . . .'

'Tell me about it later, Anne. I need to talk to your father.'

When the children had trooped upstairs to the bathroom, Edith put her hand on Rowlands' arm. 'You'd better prepare yourself for a bit of a shock.'

'What do you mean?'

'You'll see,' she said grimly, opening the door of the sitting room and propelling him ahead of her with a little push. As he entered the room, he heard a faint exclamation from somebody within, then the sound of rapid footsteps coming towards him. 'Who is it?' he said, although he already had half a suspicion.

'It's me, Fred.'

At the sound of that voice, he felt a wild, irrational stab of joy, followed at once by a more complex emotion: anger, mingled with fear. 'What in God's name are you doing here?' he said.

'Oh, Fred . . .' She came closer so that they were standing no more than a couple of feet apart. She took his hands as if trying to draw him towards her. He remained where he was: obdurate, unmoving.

'You shouldn't have come,' he said.

She was crying, now. 'You wouldn't talk like that if you knew what I've been through.' She was still holding his hands; he made an impatient movement as if to free himself from her importunate grasp. His sister, who, because of him, had been banished to the ends of the earth, and whom he had thought never to see again.

'All I know is, you shouldn't be here,' he insisted stubbornly.

'Let her speak, Fred.'

At this unexpected intervention he was silent.

'It's Viktor,' said Dorothy, in a low voice. 'He's dead.' At the unbearable word, she let fall his hands and flung herself forward, against his chest. This time, he brought his arms up to hold her, feeling the sobs shuddering through her, a bleakness in his heart. He had loved Viktor.

'When did it happen?'

'Ten months ago.'

So long, and he had known nothing. 'Couldn't you have written?' he asked, knowing he was being unjust, that communication between them during the three long years of her exile had been too great a risk for either of them to take. She didn't even dignify the question with a reply, but withdrew from his awkward embrace and seemed to make efforts to pull herself together. She blew her nose; drew a deep breath or two.

'I'd like a cigarette,' she said at last. He couldn't stop himself turning towards Edith as if for her sanction. She disapproved of smoking in the house. But she merely said, 'Fred will have some,' as if there were nothing unusual about a guest lighting up in her sitting room. He duly produced his packet of Churchman's, and held the match for her as Dorothy attempted, with trembling fingers, to light it.

'Tell me what happened,' he said when he judged his sister was in control of her feelings once more. But before she could reply, there came a mouse-like tap upon the door, and Helen Edwards put her head in.

'So sorry to interrupt,' she said, with the nervous little laugh she affected at moments of social embarrassment. 'But the children have finished their supper, and . . .' She hesitated.

'What is it, Mother?' asked Edith, with the slightest edge of impatience. The evening's untoward events had evidently taken their toll on her nerves.

'It was only that I wondered if the girls had been told that they're going to have to share a room tonight.'

'Not yet,' replied her daughter crisply. 'I'll tell them in a minute.'

'Peter can come in with me, of course,' said Mrs Edwards, with her customary stoical cheerfulness. She would put up with anything, her tone implied, if it meant others were not so inconvenienced.

'I thought Ralph was picking him up?' said Edith, again without quite managing to conceal her impatience. 'I'd better telephone him, I suppose.' She accordingly disappeared in order to do so, taking her mother with her, much to Rowlands' relief.

He drew his sister over to the sofa, which stood in front of the unlit fire. 'Sit down,' he said.

'I've been sitting down all day,' she replied, but she did as she was told. The smell of her cigarette made him want one; risking his wife's displeasure, he lit up, and drew the sweet smoke deep into his lungs. Both sat silently for a moment. From the hall, Rowlands could hear Edith talking to her brother on the telephone, 'Yes, I know, but I thought we said . . .' He felt a warm affection for her at that moment, and for the life – cosy, ordinary, untroubled – of which she was a part. All he wanted was to preserve that life as far as possible; to protect those he loved from harm. That the woman now sitting beside him – his sister, his nemesis – had always been a disruptive force, he was well aware.

'You'd better begin at the beginning,' he said.

She laughed at that. 'Now there's a thought!' she said. But then she told him what he wanted to know, without further prevarication. When they'd first arrived in Argentina – she and Viktor and the boys – everything had gone well at first, she said. They'd had a house of their own – an old ranch house from the colonial days, it was. She and Viktor had worked hard to restore it to its former glory. 'It was a beautiful house,' she said, with the first note of real warmth Rowlands had heard in her voice. 'With such views! you can't imagine, Fred.'

'No,' he agreed. 'I can't.'

'For the first year, things couldn't have been better. The farm was doing well – he'd five hundred head of cattle, you know, to say nothing of the rest of the estate to run, so there was plenty of work for Viktor. He made sure of that . . .' Rowlands noticed that she avoided mentioning Viktor's relative – *a cousin, wasn't it?* – by name. 'Then he got ambitious,' Dorothy went on, a hardening of her tone suggesting that it wasn't her husband to whom she was referring. 'The farm next to his fell vacant – the owner died, and so he, Dietrich, decided he'd like to buy it. He got it for a knockdown price, of course.' The scorn in her voice was almost palpable. 'He's like that, Dietrich. A true capitalist. Always trying to get something for nothing so that he can make as much profit as possible when it comes to sell.'

'All right,' he said, because her voice had risen. 'Just tell me the bare facts.'

With the property almost twice the size it had been, and with twice the number of cattle, the work had become more than Viktor, as farm manager, could handle on his own. 'Of course he was too mean to pay another full-time manager,' said Dorothy angrily. 'He'd got Viktor on

63

the cheap, as it was.' A succession of assistant managers followed, each more incompetent than the last, Dorothy said. 'Viktor was doing the work of two men, at the very least. Some days he'd been out from dawn to midnight, riding forty or fifty miles a day. He wasn't strong to begin with. But I think it was the worry of it all as much as the work that killed him.' One day she'd come home from taking Billy to school to find Viktor collapsed on the floor. She'd got him to bed, but in the night he'd complained of chest pains. 'He died in the early hours of the morning,' she said, her voice devoid of all expression.

Rowlands reached out a hand towards her, but she pushed it away. 'Let me finish,' she said. 'There's not much more to tell.' Two weeks after the funeral – a simple affair, conducted by the local parish priest, 'although Viktor would have hated all that mumbo jumbo,' said Dorothy – Cousin Dietrich had turned up at the house, wearing his best clothes. 'Stinking of pomade,' she said with disgust. 'He'd brought flowers – can you imagine that?' The proposition he'd wanted to put was simple: she was alone in the world now that poor Viktor was gone; she had the boys to think of, too. He, Dietrich, was happy to provide for them all. 'Can you believe the fat old fool thought I'd jump at the chance?' said Dorothy, with a savage little laugh. 'That I'd be willing to share his bed in exchange for a roof over my head and the chance to see my sons treated as little better than slaves.' She allowed another silence to elapse. 'You see now why I had to get away.'

His silence acknowledged the truth of this. But then he said, 'You know you can't stay here, don't you? It's not safe.'

Again came the bitter little laugh. 'Nowhere's safe, if it comes to that,' she said. 'Why? Are you afraid they'll arrest me in the street?'

He made a gesture of impatience. 'Don't joke about it,' he said. 'You took a risk coming back and you know it.'

'Only because my dear brother decided he'd rather turn me into the police than live with an uneasy conscience,' she said. The words were meant to sting, and they did, all the more because they were not very far from the truth of what had happened. 'Oh, don't look like that!' said Dorothy at last. 'If you must know, I don't hold it against you.'

Rowlands smiled. 'That's good of you,' he said, with the faintest trace of irony.

'No,' she said, apparently oblivious of this, 'I decided long ago that you couldn't help doing what you did . . . any more than I could help . . . what I did,' she added.

'So that makes us quits, does it?' he said, not smiling this time.

'Oh . . .' She gave an exasperated sigh. 'You know what I meant. Don't be so stuffy.'

Rowlands shrugged. 'Whether you've forgiven me or not is rather beside the point,' he said. 'The question remains: what are we going to do with you?' Four years before, Dorothy had committed a crime for which someone else had been about to pay the price. It had been

Rowlands' intervention which had stopped this from happening, and which had necessitated his sister's removal, with her family, to South America. Now she had returned, but her crime remained unpunished. He dreaded lest she should be called to account at last.

'I suppose you want me to go away,' she said sullenly. 'Somewhere as far away as possible, no doubt.'

'I don't want that at all,' he replied gravely. 'I'm just afraid for you.'

'You might have thought of that before you . . .' She broke off. 'Oh, never mind.' *Before you betrayed me* was what she had been going to say, he thought. 'You're right. I can't stay here. So where do you suggest I should go?' Before he could reply, there came a tap at the door; then Edith came in.

'The girls want to say good night,' she said.

'Oh, the precious darlings!' cried Dorothy as they came in. 'Come here, both of you.' She kissed them. 'Such great tall girls you're getting.'

'Say good night to Daddy, and then off to bed,' said their mother.

'Good night, Daddy. Good night, Aunt Dorothy,' said Margaret obediently. Anne echoed these valedictions, then said to her aunt, 'Are you and Billy and Victor going to stay with us?'

'I don't know about that. It all depends,' was the reply.

'On what?' said Anne, never one to be fobbed off easily.

'On lots of things.'

'Well I hope you stay for ever and ever,' said the child.

# Chapter Four

There was in fact nowhere else for Dorothy to go – that much was evident. Her going to Argentina had effectively removed her from the face of the earth as far as the authorities were concerned, at least. It had been as if she were dead, Rowlands thought. Now, she had come back to life. But where was she to live? There was no easy answer to that. Unable to sleep beyond five when the birds started up their shrill monotonous racket, he got up, careful not to disturb Edith, and went downstairs to the kitchen. Here, he made himself a pot of tea, and letting himself out of the back door, took his tin mug into the garden to think things over.

Around him, the air was alive with birdsong and with the fluttering of wings; it seemed to Rowlands that he could feel the air displaced by their movement against his face. Flying was not, after all, so very different from rowing, he thought; it was only the element through which one passed was that of air, not water. God, what he wouldn't give to be out on the river this minute! *Gliding swiftly along in the cool, still morning air, with only the sound of the oars dipping in and out of the water to break the silence, and nothing in one's head but the beautiful rhythm of one's strokes . . .* He became aware that he was not alone. Someone had crossed the lawn, on soundless feet, and now sat down on the bench beside him. He didn't need to hear her speak to know who it was.

'I saw you from the window in the girls' room,' she said.

'Couldn't you sleep, either?'

'No.'

Rowlands blew on his tea to cool it. A blackbird's tuneful whistle pierced the silence. 'In case you were wondering, we won't be here long,' said Dorothy abruptly. 'A few days at most – if that's all right,' she added. Suddenly he was tired of her sarcasms.

'You can stay as long as you like,' he said coldly. 'But you'll have to go somewhere eventually.'

'I know. I thought of Germany. Viktor has cousins there – in Berlin.' It didn't sound like a very practical scheme to Rowlands.

'We'll talk about it,' he said evenly. 'Have you any money?'

'A little. And clothes for the children.' The sum total of her worldly goods, he thought. Dorothy had never cared much for possessions.

'I can help you there – a little,' he said.

'That's kind of you.' Again, the sardonic note. She was silent a moment as if considering her options. 'Of course, there's the money that'll come to Billy when he's of age,' she said. So she hadn't forgotten that.

'It won't be for years yet,' he objected. 'And even then, claiming it might not be as straightforward as all that.'

'What do you mean?'

'I mean that if it could be proved that the money had been acquired by . . . criminal means, Billy might be disqualified from receiving it.'

'That's outrageous.'

'Even so, it's the law,' he said.

She was silent once more. Then, 'I don't know how you could bring yourself to do it,' she said in a low voice.

'Dottie . . .'

'To split on your own flesh and blood.'

'You know it wasn't like that.'

'Wasn't it? You'd have turned me in. And all to save some woman you'd lost your head over.' Now it was Rowlands' turn to be silent. There was no arguing with her when she was in this kind of mood. Besides which, what she said was true – or true as far as it went. In fact, he'd have put his own neck in the noose before letting anything happen to her. He took a last sip of tea. It had gone cold. He threw the tea leaves into the rose bed.

69

'I'm going for my bath,' he said. 'We'll talk about this later.'

'That's right,' she scoffed. 'Run away when things get difficult. That's you all over, Fred.' It was so patently unjust a remark that he didn't bother to reply. As he walked back towards the house, he reflected wryly that his sister had always known exactly how to hurt him.

Several days went by, during which not a great deal happened. Rowlands, at work all day, saw his sister only for those few hours in the evening when, their respective offspring having been put to bed, the three of them – with Mrs Edwards sometimes making a reluctant fourth – sat over cups of tea in the sitting room, feigning interest in some play on the wireless, or making desultory conversation. Dorothy had never been one for smalltalk, nor, it transpired, did she care to play cards. 'What does she do with herself all day?' Rowlands asked Edith as they were getting ready for bed one night.

'Not much,' was the reply. 'Mostly she writes letters – and smokes her cigarettes,' his wife added disapprovingly. 'She takes the boys for walks sometimes. Speaking of which,' she went on, in an undertone since their bedroom and the one where Dorothy and the boys were sleeping was only separated by a thin wall, 'oughtn't Billy to be at school? It's been over a week now.'

'You're right,' he said. 'I'll talk to her tomorrow.' But in the morning, there came another distraction, in the form of a large, square envelope, which arrived with two others very like it, in that morning's post. It was addressed to Mr and Mrs F. C. Rowlands. Edith opened it.

'Oh!' she said when she saw what it contained. 'It seems he's been as good as his word, your Captain Percival.'

'Well, read it, then.'

She cleared her throat. '"*Lord Amulree, Air Chief Marshall Sir John Salmond, and The Trustees of the Royal Air Force request the pleasure of your company at the Twelfth Annual Display on Saturday 27th June 1931 from three – six p.m. at Hendon Aerodrome . . .*"'

'Mummy, may I open mine?' interrupted Anne excitedly. Because one of the envelopes was addressed to her, it appeared; the other to Margaret.

'When you've finished your breakfast. You'll get marmalade all over it, Anne, if you will insist on holding it.'

'I must say,' said Rowlands. 'That was very decent of him. I never thought . . .'

'Yes,' said his wife. 'And there's something written on the back, too.' She read aloud, '"*Hope you and your dear little girls can still join me for a spin.*" What does that mean, I wonder?'

'It means,' laughed Rowlands, 'that Anne will get her wish of flying a plane at last. Or at least, flying in a plane,' he added. 'And Margaret and I will be forced to go along too.'

'I don't mind,' said Margaret quickly.

'What's all the excitement?' Dorothy had just come in. This was early for her; usually she and the boys didn't come down until Rowlands had gone to work. He explained about the Air Show.

'How nice,' she said with only the faintest shade of irony. Yawning, she took the seat just vacated by her brother. 'A pity you can't take Billy. He loves all that sort of thing.'

'I'll see what I can do,' said Rowlands, already heading out the door. Perhaps, if nothing else, including his sister's elder boy in the proposed family outing might go some way towards healing the rift between himself and Dorothy.

Work continued to be very busy. Fortunately, Miss Collins was over her cold and back in the office, and the new Temporary, Miss Peachey, had started on Monday. Even so, Rowlands was kept busy dealing with what seemed an ever-increasing number of pension claims, housing problems and urgent requests for employment to be found, as well as his regular task of supervising the buying and distribution of materials for the organisation's homeworkers. These were men too disabled to fit into the ordinary working world, but who could make a living making furniture, leather goods, baskets and other household items, to be sold in the St Dunstan's shop in Great Portland Street. It worked out cheaper all round for St Dunstan's to buy the materials wholesale – these included wood, leather, willow and cane, string and twine, as well as the tools needed for working them – and to act as middleman too, in selling the goods. The proceeds, all but a small percentage to cover transport costs, went to the craftsmen. It was a good system, offering a measure of independence and self-respect to men otherwise unemployable. But it all took a good deal of organisation.

That day, Rowlands had been to visit the firm in Whitechapel which supplied them with yarn, and other kinds of haberdashery, for the making of useful items such as pot holders, dusters, penwipers and needle cases. There'd been complaints from some of the men about the poor quality of the stuff; he'd agreed to take it up with the firm's proprietor. Returning from this somewhat disagreeable excursion – the owner of the wholesaler's, a Mr Beasley, had said he was sorry, but there was nothing he could do; prices were going up, quality was going down; it was the same everywhere you looked – Rowlands took a short cut across the park. After a couple of hours spent wrangling over costs and percentages, he felt like a breath of air.

It was a beautiful afternoon. A light breeze blew the scent of almond blossom from the trees on either side of the path into his face. He drew a deep breath, glad to be out of the stink of London traffic, albeit temporarily. 'Mr Rowlands!' A woman's voice. 'It is Mr Rowlands, isn't it?' The voice belonged to Irene Metcalfe. She sounded a little breathless, as if she had been running. 'I saw you from across the way. I was just crossing the street, on my way back from the shops, and I said to myself, I know that man! You hold yourself very upright, you know. Once a soldier, I suppose . . .'

'Hello, Mrs Metcalfe.'

'Irene, please!' she said. 'I say, you wouldn't fancy a cup of tea, would you? I only live just over there.'

'It's awfully nice of you,' he replied. 'But I really ought to be getting back.'

'Oh, do say you'll come! It'd be such fun to chat.' Her voice, though seemingly cheerful, had a plaintive undertone he was powerless to resist.

'Well . . . perhaps just for a few minutes,' he said. The flat was on the fifth floor of one of the newly built mansion blocks in Gloucester Place: entering through heavy, plate-glass doors into a spacious foyer, he had an impression of sleek, modern comfort. The Metcalfes' flat reinforced this impression.

'We've just had it decorated,' Mrs Metcalfe said as they walked in. 'Eau-de-Nil and silver. Rather restful, I call it. But Neville can't stand it. "Insipid" was the world he used.' She laughed. 'So like a man.'

'It sounds very nice,' said Rowlands tactfully. He was starting to regret the moment of weakness which had brought him here. She really was rather a silly little thing.

'I expect you'd like some tea?' said his hostess brightly. 'So nice to have a guest, for once.' It occurred to him to wonder why this should be an infrequent occurrence. Didn't she have any women friends? But his reflections were cut short by the arrival of the maid, summoned no doubt by a touch of the electric bell. 'Tea, Mabel,' said her mistress, with some asperity. 'And bring some of those wafer biscuits, will you?'

'Yes'm.'

'Do sit down, won't you?' said Irene Metcalfe to her reluctant guest. There was an air of artificiality to her way of speaking which reminded Rowlands of a little girl, playing at tea parties. Just so would four-year-old Joan address her favourite doll. 'There's an armchair just behind you,' she went on. 'Oh, do look out!' Because in locating the chair – a low, square item upholstered in some kind of slippery fabric – he had inadvertently tripped over the glass and chrome side table beside it. He managed, just, to keep his balance. 'I'm sorry,' she said. 'I forgot.'

'Doesn't matter a bit.' But he felt a painful blush run over him. He hated looking a fool. 'No Teddy today?' he said, to cover his embarrassment.

'He's at his piano lesson, poor little scrap,' she said. 'He will be wild to have missed you!' She laughed, and Rowlands had the odd sensation that something had been left unsaid. He smiled.

'Did he enjoy himself at Croydon on Saturday?' he asked.

'What? Oh yes!' The maid appeared at that moment with the tray. 'Put it down there,' said her mistress, 'and tell Cook I'll want some more hot water.' The girl disappeared into the outer recesses of the flat. Mrs Metcalfe poured the tea. 'He adored every minute,' she said, placing a full cup on the low table beside Rowlands' chair. 'There's sugar in the silver basin. So thrilling,' she went on. 'Seeing him come into land. Like a god descending from the heavens.' It was not, of course, her son to whom she was referring.

'Yes,' said Rowlands, a little uneasy at this fanciful turn of phrase. He wondered what on earth she'd come out with next.

She must have realised that she'd gone too far, for she said quickly, 'I wouldn't want you to think that Captain Percival and I are anything but good friends.'

'Of course not.' The tea was the perfumed kind he rather disliked. *Earl Grey, was it?* He sipped it gingerly. 'We meet very occasionally, that's all. At social events,' she added, as if he couldn't have worked this out for himself.

'Oh?' said Rowlands politely.

'Yes. Neville's at the Air Ministry, you see, and so if it's anything to do with aviation, he's sure to be invited,' she said, with a little simpering laugh. 'And of course with Alan being so famous . . .' But Rowlands' acute hearing had detected the sound of a key turning in a lock.

'I wonder if this can be your husband now?' he said.

In sharp contrast to his wife's air of vague helplessness, Neville Metcalfe gave the impression of not suffering fools gladly. If one of the fools was the woman to whom he was married, that was a pity, his manner seemed to say, but hardly his fault. Now he stood, having thrown down his coat and briefcase upon a chair, surveying the room and its occupants with what seemed a sardonic bemusement. 'Have I forgotten something?' he said, addressing his wife, who had got up at his entrance and was presently fluttering around him.

'I don't think so,' she replied, walking into his trap.

'Only I wasn't aware we were having visitors this afternoon,' he finished smartly.

'Oh!' She gave a little gasp. 'That's right, you haven't met, have you? Neville, this is Frederick Rowlands.'

Rowlands, who had got to his feet at the other's appearance, now extended his hand. 'How do you do?' he said. The hand which took his, after an interval not quite long enough to be offensive, was cold and dry, and belonged to a man of slightly below average height. A wiry build, Rowlands guessed, feeling the strength in the other's grip – again, a deliberate show that he wasn't to be trifled with.

'Delighted,' he said, his tone implying that he was anything but. 'And where did you and Mr Rowlands meet?'

Irene Metcalfe gave another little gasp of laughter. 'I . . . We met in the park the other day.' She seemed incapable of dissembling – at least, where her husband was concerned. A rabbit transfixed by a stoat, Rowlands thought. 'That is, I . . .'

'Mrs Metcalfe was kind enough to offer me a cup of tea,' said Rowlands, hating himself for what he was about to say, but seeing no alternative to it. 'I'm one of the St Dunstan's crowd, you know.'

'Ah.' Metcalfe must have taken a closer look to verify this, for he said in an altered tone, nicely balancing concern and condescension, 'Of course. We often see the men out and about in the park, don't we, Reenie?' The use of his wife's pet name signified that he was prepared to overlook her indiscretion – inviting a man she'd picked up in the park into their home – or at least, that he was prepared to let things lie for the present. 'Sit down, sit down,' he said to Rowlands, in a tone of great affability. Still disgusted with himself for having played what he privately thought of as the cripple card, and angry with Irene Metcalfe for having forced him to do so, Rowlands shook his head.

'I really ought to be going,' he said. 'I have to get back to the office,' he couldn't resist adding, to dispel the impression he'd just created that he was some kind of charity case.

'Oh, but you mustn't leave on my account!' said Metcalfe, his voice now coming from the far side of the room: a large room, Rowlands judged, and no doubt furnished in the best modern style, with a well-stocked cocktail cabinet in blonde wood an essential feature. Sure enough, there came the clinking of ice into a glass. 'I'm going to have a proper drink,' went on his new acquaintance. 'Care to join me?'

'Thanks, but it's a bit early for me.'

'Suit yourself,' said the other carelessly. 'After the day I've had,' he added, subsiding with a grateful sigh into an armchair, 'I need a stiff whisky and soda. Well, if you must go you must.' Because Rowlands had turned and was moving towards the door. 'Drop in again sometime, why don't you?' Rowlands nodded. He'd no intention of setting foot in this blessed flat again if he could help it.

'Thank you for the tea, Mrs Metcalfe,' he said. 'Say hello to Teddy for me, won't you?'

'Yes.' She gave another of her nervous little laughs. 'I'll see you out,' she said, although there wasn't the slightest need for this, the entrance hall being only a narrow strip between the sitting room and the front door. 'Did you have a hat?' she asked, in a clear, bright voice, perhaps designed to carry.

'No, I never wear one,' Rowlands replied. He was still a bit irritated with her for putting him through the charade of the past few minutes. She probably didn't even realise that he had saved her skin. But then she did something which caused him to reverse his opinion. As he went out onto the broad landing which led to the lifts and stairs, she followed him, laying a hand on his sleeve to detain him.

'I'd be grateful,' she said in a low voice, 'if you wouldn't say anything to my husband about my having been at Croydon that day, with Teddy. Only I forgot to mention it at the time, and it'd look rather odd if it came out now, don't you think?'

The week leading up to the day of the Air Show had been wet and stormy, leading to fears – frequently expressed on the part of Rowlands' middle daughter – that the whole thing might be called off. But the Saturday in question dawned clear and windless; by midday, as they were getting ready, it was starting to feel quite warm.

'Hats, I think,' said Edith, provoking a chorus of protests from her daughters. It wasn't the hats they disliked so much as the elastic which held them on, and which had an unpleasant tendency to cut into the soft flesh under the chin. Their mother was adamant, however. 'It's going to be hot. I don't want you getting a touch of the sun.'

'Daddy doesn't wear a hat,' said a still mutinous Anne.

'Daddy's a grown-up. And don't chew the elastic – you'll make it all soggy.'

'Does that mean I won't have to do as I'm told when I'm a grown-up?' Anne never did know when to leave off in these contests with her mother.

'That's enough,' said Edith, but Rowlands, overhearing this exchange, couldn't refrain from laughing. 'Not having to do what you're told is one of the few consolations of being a grown-up,' he said to the child.

'I do wish you wouldn't encourage her,' grumbled his wife. 'She's quite bumptious enough. What time did you say the car would be here?' she said, not for the first time that morning.

'Half past one. We've plenty of time.'

'Do you think my figured georgette will be smart enough? Only the silk two-piece is a little warm for this weather.'

'What? Oh yes, rather.'

'I must say, it's awfully good of Ralph to let us have the car,' she said, also not for the first time.

'Yes, isn't it?' Because for once, Edith's brother had turned up trumps. Since his son was once more to be of the party, he saw no reason, he said, why they shouldn't have the use of the motor; its driver, too. Rowlands suspected that it was the fact that the invitation had come from Alan Percival himself which had prompted this unprecedented display of magnanimity. That, and the fact that the Rowlandses were to be entertained in the VIP tent afterwards. Ralph never missed a chance to 'get in with the right sort', as he'd have put it. But Rowlands kept these thoughts to himself. And it was decent of Ralph to lend them the Vauxhall given that the alternative would have been for them to travel in by train and out again by bus – not the most appealing prospect, with four children in tow.

His mother-in-law had offered to look after Joan. 'Such fun we're going to have, aren't we, my poppet?' Mrs Edwards was perfectly happy to stay at home, she said, with her customary air of martyred cheerfulness. 'Oh, I've heaps of things to be getting on with. And Joan can help me, can't you, Joanie?'

Dorothy, too, was to remain behind, with little Victor. Quite apart from the fact that she hadn't been invited, there was the feeling Rowlands was unable to shake off that by appearing in public she might be risking a more serious exposure. Which was absurd, of course, because who – apart from himself and the two or three others most intimately connected with the case – knew that his sister was a wanted woman? But it would be tempting fate to risk it, he thought. It was yet another manifestation of what Rowlands had come to think of as 'the problem of Dottie', a problem which had loomed large this past week or so. The fact was, there was nothing for her to do, except sit around the house all day, smoking her eternal cigarettes and getting under Edith's feet. She couldn't go anywhere, except for walks along the river. 'I'll be fine,' she said, irritably now when he asked her if she would be all right; adding, 'I can't think of anything more boring than standing around watching a lot of grown men showing off.' Which appeared to have settled the matter.

But Rowlands had reckoned without the quixotic side of his sister's nature – something which had got her into trouble more times than he cared to think of in the past. The car had arrived, and Edith was settling the children in the back of it before getting in after them; Rowlands was to sit in front with George, the driver – an arrangement that suited him down to the ground. George was a good sort; a veteran of Vimy Ridge. They'd have a smoke, and a chat about the old days. But into this tranquil prospect there entered a note of dissension. Suddenly, Billy, his sister's elder boy, piped up, 'I'm not going.'

'Why, whatever's the matter?' said Edith.

'I'm not going,' he repeated stubbornly. He'd got back out of the car by this time.

'What's wrong, Billy?' enquired his mother, seemingly not at all put out but this show of independence.

'I'm not going if you're not going,' he replied, with the doggedness that already seemed a feature of his character. Instead of telling him not to be so silly, as Edith would have done, had Anne shown a similar inclination to be difficult, Dorothy merely said, 'That's kind of you, old chap. But you know I have to stay with Vicky. He's too little to be left on his own.'

'Look, we really should be going . . .' Edith began. But just then there came another intervention.

'If that's all that's stopping you, then you needn't worry about it any longer,' said Helen Edwards, who had emerged from the house at that moment. 'Dear little Victor and Joan are having such a lovely time together. Playing tea parties, you know. I thought we'd make some fairy cakes. You go and enjoy yourself, my dear,' she said to Dorothy. 'I've brought up two children of my own. I think I can manage these for an afternoon.'

For a long moment, the four of them – himself, Edith, Dorothy and the recalcitrant Billy – stood frozen to the spot while Mrs Edwards, oblivious of the havoc she had caused, awaited a reply. Then several of them spoke at once. 'I don't think . . .' Rowlands began, while Edith said again, 'We really ought to go.' Both these utterances were cut short by what Dorothy said, however.

'Thank you, Helen. I'd love to go. If you're sure you really don't mind?'

'Not a bit,' replied Mrs Edwards happily. 'No, you needn't say goodbye to Victor. Much better not to give him a reason to fret. If he asks, I'll tell him Mummy's gone out for a little while.'

'But . . .' Edith started to say. Rowlands put a hand on

her arm. 'Are you quite sure about this?' he said to his sister, in as neutral a tone as he could manage. He didn't have to see her, to picture the little toss she gave her head.

'Quite sure.'

'Oh, let the poor girl have some fun!' cried Mrs Edwards. Then there was nothing for it but to get into the car where the rest of the children were waiting with diminishing degrees of patience.

'I hope you know what you're doing,' Rowlands said under his breath to Dorothy. To which she said nothing. Nor did any of them speak until they were a good way along the road to Hendon – each of the adults wrapped up in his or her private thoughts; the children perhaps picking up that something was amiss from the silence. It was Edith who, typically enough, broke the impasse, with what sounded like a challenge.

'Well,' she said. 'This is going to be an interesting afternoon.'

And, after all, thought Rowlands, as the car joined the slowly moving stream of vehicles heading towards the aerodrome, there was no earthly reason why his sister shouldn't have come with them. One could be as invisible in a crowd as in a quiet suburban street – arguably more so. It can't have been much fun for Dorothy, these past few weeks, hanging around the house all day, he thought. No wonder she'd jumped at the chance of a change of scene. It was just the way she'd done it that had raised his hackles. But then, you could never have called her tactful.

# Chapter Five

By the time they reached the section of the viewing stands to which their invitations admitted them, a large crowd had assembled – Edith put the numbers at around ten thousand. Quite a number of these had come in cars, and now perched themselves on bonnets and roofs, in the hope of getting a better view, she supposed. Others were crowded into a fenced off area at the edge of the airfield, with little or nothing in the way of seating, and no shelter from the baking sun. They themselves suffered no such discomfort: the VIP section was not only provided with tiers of cushioned seats, but had its own tea tent, serving refreshments of all kinds. They'd also been issued with souvenir programmes, on one of which Rowlands traced the embossed letters that read, *Royal Air Force: Twelfth Annual Display* and then, in smaller letters underneath, *27th June 1931.* 'So what death-defying stunts are we going to be treated to first?' he said.

But before Edith could reply, there came a booming from the loudspeaker above their heads, and a voice said, 'Ladies and gentlemen, it gives me great pleasure to welcome you to Hendon on this glorious afternoon . . .' Rowlands supposed this must be Lord Amulree, who had been appointed Air Minister following the untimely death of his predecessor Lord Thomson in the R101 airship crash the previous year. After some further preliminary remarks, the speaker announced the first item on the programme. This was an aerobatic display, featuring six aeroplanes – all Gipsy Moths – under the command of Flight Lieutenant B. E. Embry. Rowlands knew he would have to rely on others' accounts to get more than a vague impression of this; fortunately, his daughter Anne was on hand. 'They're taking off now, Daddy . . . the first plane first . . .'

'Well, obviously,' muttered Margaret.

'And then the second one. Third. Fourth . . . Oops! That one's a bit slower than the others. Fifth. Sixth. All of them are in the air now, Daddy. They're going up all together as if they were aiming for the same spot. I hope they don't crash.'

'They won't crash, you silly.' Margaret again.

'. . . and all trailing smoke. It's ever so pretty.'

'It isn't smoke,' said Margaret. 'It's called a vapour trail.'

'Now they've reached the top,' went on her sister, ignoring this. 'And ... Oh! They're turning over and coming back down again.'

'Looping the loop,' said Margaret.

'No, it isn't a loop – more of an arch,' Anne corrected her. 'Oh Daddy, it's so pretty. I wish you could see it.'

'But I can see it,' he said. 'Exactly as you've described it. What colour are the Moths?'

'Red.'

'Against a blue sky. How lovely! I suppose they're climbing back up again?'

'Yes! How did you know?'

'A good guess,' smiled her father. 'You see, you needn't tell me everything. Some of it I can work out for myself.'

This aerobatic ballet was followed by a display of parachute descents from a Jupiter-engined Vimy. This flew slowly from one side of the field to the other, dropping its fragile cargo as it went. As each man fell, there was an instant, signalled for Rowlands by a momentary hush on the part of the watching crowd, when it seemed as if the trick might, after all, fail, and the afternoon's enjoyment turn to horror. But then the parachute would blossom, and a collective sigh of relief would pass around the field. This happened twelve times – each exhalation of breath, as a parachute opened, indicating that a human life had once more been, against the odds, preserved.

Parachutes had been invented long before the war, of

course, but it had not been thought expedient by the British High Command to issue them to the pilots of the Royal Flying Corps (as the RAF had been called then), although the Germans had had them from 1915. It was thought they might encourage cowardice or the unnecessary jettisoning of an expensive machine. And so thousands of men had died who might otherwise have been saved. It was one of the worst deaths, Rowlands thought, amongst the many terrible ways there had been to die. To burn to death in a cloud of flaming gas. No wonder most fliers took a loaded pistol with them, for use in the eventuality of being shot down.

He was roused from these dark thoughts by a touch on the arm. 'Fancy a cup of tea?' said Edith. 'There's a break before the next event.' With Edith on one arm, Dorothy on the other, and the children bringing up the rear, he accordingly made his way through the crowd that, doubtless with the same thought in mind, was moving towards the marquee. Once inside, however, it seemed their hopes of finding refreshment were to be disappointed. So crowded was it that there seemed little chance of their reaching the front of the queue within the allotted twenty minutes. But then Rowlands heard his name called.

'I say! Over here!' cried a familiar voice. It was Alan Percival. 'Thought I'd spotted you,' he said, now joining them. 'What a crush!'

'Captain Percival, do let me introduce my wife,' said Rowlands when the two had shaken hands. 'How do you do?' said Edith.

'Delighted to meet you, Mrs Rowlands,' was the reply. 'My daughters you already know.'

'Rather! Hello, girls. You've brought your cousin, I see.'

'Two cousins,' said Anne. 'This is Billy and this is Peter.'

'Hello, Billy and Peter.'

'And this is my sister,' said Rowlands, because not to introduce the only other member of their party would have seemed odd, to say the least. 'I hope it's all right?' he said, conscious that she hadn't been included in the invitation. But if Percival heard him, he gave no sign of it. In fact he said nothing at all.

'Hello,' said Dorothy, in the offhand tone she habitually adopted with strangers.

'I say, h-how do you do?' Percival managed at last. 'It's awfully good of you to come.'

It struck Rowlands, not for the first time, that his sister seemed to have this effect on men. Reducing even the most confident to babbling schoolboys. She'd always been good-looking, of course. But it was the combination of this and her air of complete indifference to her admirers that seemed to have such a devastating effect. 'But you haven't had tea,' the Flying Ace was saying. 'You must have some tea. We're just over here,' he went on, ushering them all towards a roped off section of the tent. Here, tables and chairs had been set up for those taking part in the day's events, and their guests.

At one of the tables, some people were already sitting. 'Let me introduce you,' said Percival. Before he could do so, Anne said in a thrilled whisper, 'Mummy, that's Olave Malory. Next to Amy Johnson, she's the best woman pilot in England.' There was general laughter at this.

'There you are, Olave darling,' said a man's voice. 'You'll have to be content with being second best.'

'I didn't mean . . .' said Anne, sounding mortified. But then Percival said, 'Olave, I'd like you to meet a friend of mine. Miss Anne Rowlands. She's going to be the next best woman pilot in England. So you'd better look to your laurels.'

'I will,' said Miss Malory. 'How do you do, Anne?'

'And this is Cecil Harmsworth,' said Percival. 'Cecil's not a bad pilot, either. He'll never be as good as I am, though, will you, old boy?'

'That's a matter of opinion,' said Harmsworth with a laugh that sounded more like a sneer, Rowlands thought. He had the impression that there wasn't much love lost between the two men.

'Sit down – all of you,' their host was saying. 'There'll be some tea in a moment. Cakes, too. And strawberries. If you like strawberries . . .' It evidently wasn't the children he meant, although they were the ones who took up his offer with most enthusiasm. Since there wasn't room for them all at the table, another was brought, and within a few moments everyone was seated, Dorothy having been offered a chair next to Alan Percival and adjacent to Rowlands' own at the second table so that he couldn't help being a party to the conversation between them. 'So tell me . . .' This was Percival. 'Are you enjoying the show so far?'

'Oh . . . Yes. Billy's enjoying it, aren't you, Billy?' Dorothy replied. 'This is my son,' she added, to Percival. He took a moment to digest the information.

'Then you're married?'

'Yes,' she said. 'Or I was. I'm a widow.' To Rowlands, listening to this exchange, it seemed that the young man brightened.

'Ah,' he said. 'The war, I suppose?'

'No.' What she said next was lost in the rattle of cups and saucers being brought by the waitress, and tea being poured and handed round. Rowlands, in any case, was determined not to listen to any more. It was none of his business whom his sister chose to talk to, nor what she chose to say, although he hoped, for her own sake, that she wouldn't give too much away. Others were not so restrained, however.

'What are you two whispering about?' called Olave Malory, from the far side of the table. It struck Rowlands that she was rather more interested in Percival's conversation with Dorothy than her languid tone suggested.

'Oh, nothing,' was the reply. 'I was just telling Mrs Lehmann here what a feckless life we fliers lead. Never knowing where we'll lay our heads on any given day.'

'Yes, it must have been awfully muddling for you these past few weeks,' said Cecil Harmsworth sarcastically. 'Not knowing which country you've woken up in.' Or with whom you've woken up, his tone seemed to imply. But Percival seemed impervious to this banter.

'One gets used to it,' he said. 'And I'd rather have the flier's life, for all its instability, than have to get my living any other way. Well, can you imagine me behind a desk?'

'I see what you mean,' said Miss Malory, and again, it seemed to Rowlands that her careless manner concealed a more serious intention. 'You'd be simply awful at anything that required you to turn up on time. I've lost count of the number of times you've stood me up for dinner,' she added with a laugh that – to Rowlands, at least – sounded less than convincing. 'Fortunately, I'm a forgiving woman.' Which was a not too subtle way, Rowlands thought, of letting the rest of them know that she and Percival were involved, if that was the word.

Now he came to think of it, hadn't Edith read something out from the paper, a day or two before? 'This'll interest you, Fred. "*Newly returned to England after his record-breaking flight from Australia, Captain Percival enjoys a joke with glamorous aviatrix Miss Olave Malory, winner of the Ladies' Challenge Cup at the Reading Aero Club last month . . .*" There's a photograph. He's rather good-looking, I must say. And she's handsome enough, if you like tall, willowy brunettes, although I always find those kind of looks rather hard.' He hadn't paid much attention at the time. Now, the truth of the matter was brought home to him. No wonder Miss Malory had seemed so interested in what the Flying Ace was saying to Dorothy, and no wonder she'd felt the need to stake a claim. What was it Jock Stewart had said about

Percival? 'Bit of a way with the ladies.'

As if to underline the point, there came another interruption. 'Well!' cried a voice he knew. 'This is a nice surprise! Isn't it a nice surprise, darling?' It was Irene Metcalfe. With, Rowlands supposed, her husband – an assumption that proved correct a moment later. 'Hello, Percival,' said Neville Metcalfe stiffly. There was the slightest pause before Percival replied, 'Metcalfe. And Mrs Metcalfe, too. Well, this is jolly!'

'Just thought we'd drop by to wish you luck,' said Metcalfe. 'You're on later, I gather?'

'Yes.' Was it Rowlands' imagination, or was there a note of ironic amusement in Percival's voice? 'I'll be doing a few stunts.' Another pause, longer than the first, ensued, before Percival said, 'But do join us.'

'That's good of you, old man, but we don't want to intrude, do we, Reenie? As a matter of fact, we're with the Minister's party.' The self-satisfaction in the man's voice was all too evident. 'His speech went down rather well, I thought . . .'

'So it should have done,' put in his wife, as if on cue. 'Since you wrote most of it.'

'Let's not exaggerate, my dear! Although I did make one or two suggestions . . .'

'Now, who don't you know? said Percival, ignoring this blatant bit of self-promotion. 'Miss Malory you've met, I'm sure, and Harmsworth. But I don't think you know Mr and Mrs Rowlands . . .'

'Oh, but we do,' sang out Irene Metcalfe, to Rowlands's

discomfiture. 'Mr Rowlands, at least. We're old friends, aren't we?'

'Well . . .' Having got to his feet at her arrival, Rowlands now felt himself caught in an awkward crouch, halfway between standing and sitting – a posture entirely expressive of the embarrassment he was feeling. The wretched woman had a knack of wrong-footing him. Nor did her husband's brusque acknowledgement of their acquaintance make things much better.

'Hello, Rowlands. Didn't see you there. This your wife?'

'Yes.' Seething inwardly at the man's patronising tone, Rowlands performed the introductions.

'This is Mr Rowlands' sister, Mrs Lehmann,' said Percival, who seemed to be making a point of his own where Metcalfe was concerned. Once again, Rowlands was conscious of the momentary silence to which Dorothy reduced any man confronted with her dark good looks and air of aloofness. She was, he rather imagined, the very opposite type to the one offered by the winsome Irene Metcalfe. 'She's rather grown into her looks,' Edith had said, referring to her sister-in-law, some days before. 'Some women do as they reach thirty. And she's always known how to dress.' Which came from his sister's having worked as a seamstress all those years, Rowlands supposed – she had the knack of making clothes that looked as if they'd been professionally tailored.

'You know, it's a funny thing,' said Percival. 'I was only saying to Mrs Lehmann a moment ago how much

94

I'd have hated doing a desk job, and here you are, to tell us how wrong I was.'

'Oh! I don't know about that,' said Metcalfe stiffly. 'My job's not what you'd call exciting. But then we can't all be daredevils.'

'Just as well, or you'd be out of a job, Percival, old man,' drawled Cecil Harmsworth. 'Speaking of which, isn't it time you went and got ready for your turn?'

'Thanks for the reminder! Mustn't let my public down, must I?' laughed Percival. 'Good to see you, Rowlands. Mrs Rowlands. I hope,' he said, addressing Dorothy, 'that you'll drop by the airfield sometime, Mrs Lehmann? Perhaps when I take Rowlands and the girls up for their spin? Good. That's settled, then.'

Beyond a vague remark that it was 'awfully nice' of Captain Percival to have invited them to join his party, Edith made no reference, as they walked back towards the stands, to what had taken place in the previous half-hour, although Rowlands guessed she was burning to know how it was he knew the Metcalfes. But it seemed the presence of her sister-in-law deterred her from too pointed a line of questioning. No doubt she'd save that for the privacy of their bedroom, Rowlands thought wryly. He himself was troubled by quite another train of thought. The fact that Dorothy had attracted the attention of Alan Percival was the cause of this alarm. A month ago, his sister had been invisible – a kind of ghost, even to her closest family members. Now she risked making herself all too conspicuous. I'll talk to her, he thought, knowing that it would make little difference. Dorothy had always gone her own way; nothing he had ever said in the past had caused her to alter her behaviour in the slightest.

Even so, she must be made to see sense, Rowlands argued with himself, as they took their seats for the second half of the programme. Because if his sister's presence in the country were to become known to the authorities, then she stood a good chance of finding herself on trial for murder. These sombre thoughts were curtailed by the announcement, issuing from the loudspeakers above their heads, that the mock battle was about to start. This was between two squadrons of Wapitis, and would involve the dropping of smoke bombs, the announcer said. The ladies should feel no alarm, however; these would just be for show, and would present no danger to the crowd.

'I wish they were real bombs,' muttered Billy, who was sitting on Rowlands' left.

'I think you'll find they'll be quite realistic enough,' said his uncle, thinking, not for the first time, what an odd little chap Billy had turned out to be. Not an outgoing sort, like his mother, but so quiet that one often forgot he was there. Although, he reminded himself, that was as much to do with the fact that he – Rowlands – was blind, and therefore impervious to others' looks and gestures, as it was to do with the child's predilection for silence.

The 'battle' duly began, with a satisfying amount of noise and smoke, if the children's excited comments – and his own ringing ears – were to be believed, but

Rowlands wasn't sufficiently caught up in it to follow much of what was going on. He'd seen quite enough of what real bombs could do during the war to find such a display very entertaining now. He concentrated instead on what he could see, with the little amount of vision that was left to him: one-eighth of the sight remained in his right eye, which meant he could tell light from dark, and make out shapes of things.

Just now, with the sun pouring down from a cloudless sky, it was if his field of vision were washed with golden light. He bathed in the sensation – not so very different from that experienced when looking at the sun through half-closed eyelashes. As he did so, he breathed in the smell of sun-bleached grass, asphalt and corrugated iron, which was the smell of the place, overlaid with the more pungent odours of oil and cordite, from the smoke drifting back over the field of battle. 'Captain Percival's on next, Daddy' said Anne, clutching his arm. 'I think that's his plane over there. The yellow one.'

'All right. Keep an eye on it, and let me know what happens,' he said. Even though it wouldn't mean much to him, he'd take an interest in this one item on the programme if only out of gratitude to Percival for the kindness he'd shown. Although thinking about that, brought back Rowlands' anxieties about Dorothy. Had Percival really been paying court to her, or had he merely been displaying the charm he turned on every woman? Whatever the truth of the matter, one thing was certain – it couldn't go any further. Dorothy had made herself quite visible enough, these past few hours, without becoming more involved with one of the most famous men in the country – a man now being hailed, as he took his seat in the yellow Moth and prepared for take-off, as 'the world-renowned Flying Ace, just back from his record-breaking trip to Australia, and now about to dazzle us with his aerobatic expertise.' Well, he could 'dazzle' them all he liked, thought Rowlands grimly; he'd better not get any ideas about 'dazzling' Dorothy.

To loud cheers from the watching crowd, the plane took off, and made a circuit of the field before starting to ascend. It climbed higher and higher until (Anne said) it almost seemed to reach the sun. Then, to delighted gasps from the crowd, it looped-the-loop – the first of a breathtaking series of such manoeuvres. From his daughter's commentary, Rowlands got most of what was happening; the rest he could supplement from his store of memories. That aerial battle he'd watched over Ballieul, in the summer of '17, for instance.

Four German Albatross, emerging from the sun, like bright silver insects against the blue of the sky. Three British Nieuports wheeling round to face them. Then the battle itself – seeming, at that distance, to be no more than the harmless skirmishing of toys. Only when one of the beautiful machines caught fire – it was an Albatros, he recalled – did the game's deadlier purpose become apparent. Watching it fall, like Icarus, in flames, Rowlands had found that he was praying. 'Dear God . . .' Unlike some of his compatriots, who'd whooped and cheered themselves hoarse to see another Hun burn, he could take no pleasure in the sight.

'Daddy, he's turned the plane right over,' said Anne. 'Now he's flying upside-down. I hope he won't crash,' she added in a small voice.

'Of course he won't, silly.' This was her older sister. 'He only makes it look as if he might. See? He's right side up again. I don't suppose it's a bit dangerous.'

'Well, I certainly wouldn't like to try it,' said her father drily. But just then there came a murmur from the watching crowd.

'Look, Daddy! There's another plane!' cried Anne in the same moment. 'It's a red Avro... a Tutor, I think... It's flying straight at Captain Percival's plane. Oh, Daddy, I'm afraid they're going to crash.' Others must have been thinking the same, for there was a collective gasp from the crowd.

'That was a near thing,' said Edith a moment later when it appeared that the danger was past. 'I suppose it wasn't really as risky as it looked.'

'Just another stupid stunt,' was Dorothy's comment. But even she sounded faintly rattled. Only when Percival, to a roar of appreciation from the crowd, brought his Moth safely in to land at last, did the tension in the atmosphere slacken. Rowlands, for one, had had enough of it for one afternoon.

'Now, who's for an ice before the Grand Finale?' he asked. 'Anne, you can come with me, to help carry the ices.'

'And to stop you getting lost,' she said.

'And to stop me getting lost,' Rowlands agreed.

In the decade and a half that he'd had to navigate his way through the world without his sight, he'd developed strategies for doing so. Using his other senses more thoroughly than most people did was one of them; training his memory another. Thus, he could deduce, just by paying attention, quite a bit about any new acquaintance: his age, height and general state of health, from the rapidity or otherwise of his footsteps, the level at which his hand emerged when he shook hands, as well as the vigour, or otherwise, of the handshake. Voice and its many variations of volume, tone and timbre, offered further clues.

But it could be exhausting, all of this, requiring as it did a good deal of concentration. Not for him the lazy assumptions of the eye; his was a cryptographer's mind, constantly engaged with the minutiae the sighted overlooked. In a crowd, it was especially taxing, deciphering the mass of information disparate bodies in motion emitted. Then, it wasn't just a matter of coolly judging, but of making rapid assessments of those nearest to one. Fail to do so, and you'd come a cropper. This woman, for instance, talking loudly to her friend, 'I do think he's handsome, don't you?' She wasn't looking where she was going, of course. 'Oops! Ever so sorry.' Or this group of men emerging from the beer tent: '. . . the Siskin'll beat your Avro hands down in a fair fight . . .'

The sheer volume of noise was confusing. Children crying. Dogs barking. Engines revving. And the smells! The sickly-sweet tang of toffee apples and lemonade, mingling with that of petroleum, hot metal and trodden down grass. It was all rather overwhelming. Rowlands was glad, if only for quickness' sake, that he had his daughter to guide him through the melee. Now she seized hold of his hand. 'Come on, Daddy!' she cried. 'Or they'll be sold out.'

'Coming,' said Rowlands.

But then above the general murmur of the crowd came a voice he knew; a voice raised in anger, 'You bloody fool! I ought to knock your teeth down your throat!'

'Oh, dry up, old man. It was only a bit of fun.' Rowlands knew that voice, too.

'Fun!' Alan Percival sounded almost choked with fury. 'You could have killed us both, pulling a stunt like that.'

'There was never the least danger of that,' drawled Cecil Harmsworth, with what seemed a calculated insolence. 'I'm far too experienced a flier.'

'You're a colossal idiot, that's all I know. I've had just about enough of you and your antics.'

'What's that supposed to mean?'

'You know damn well what it means. One of these days, my lad, you're going to get your fingers burnt.'

'Am I?' There was a sneering tone in Cecil Harmsworth's voice.

'Oh, do stop fooling around!' snapped the other. 'It's a dangerous game you're playing, young Harmsworth, and you know it.'

'That's as may be. At least I'm not behaving like an insufferable cad,' said the other, silkily.

'What did you say?'

'Daddy!' Anne's patience was wearing thin.

'You heard me. Now, if you don't mind,' said Harmsworth, 'I need to get out of this infernally hot flying suit.'

'You're not going anywhere until you explain exactly what it was you meant.'

'Isn't it obvious, old man? Only a cad would have behaved as you did to Miss Malory just now. Flaunting your latest conquest.'

'Take that back,' said Percival, between gritted teeth, 'or by God I'll . . .'

'You'll what?'

Rowlands decided he'd heard enough. But before he could take himself out of earshot, there came the unmistakeable sound of a slap, followed by a muffled curse from Harmsworth. 'You may live to regret that, old man,' he said, and his tone was murderous.

They'd just reached the front of the queue, and he'd given his order to the man in the kiosk (an Italian, of course) when someone came rushing up to them. 'I say – it's Mr Rowlands, isn't it?' Now here was another voice he knew. It took him a moment to place it, unusually for him. Mostly he got it straightaway. Training one's memory to remember voices being essential if one were not to be left behind in the complex game of Who Am I? in which they were all engaged.

'And you're Miss Wilkinson,' he said, getting there at last.

'Oh, call me Wilkie – do! What a ripping day!'

'Isn't it?' he said. He realised what it was now: this ebullient young woman was the one he'd spoken to on the phone – as different as could be from the sullen creature he'd met two days later at Croydon Aerodrome. Yet they were one and the same person. Rather a volatile type, our Miss Wilkie, he thought. 'So are you enjoying the display?'

'Rather! It's been simply marvellous,' she said. 'I thought Captain Percival put on a ripping show, didn't you?'

'Well . . .' He wondered if she'd realised how limited his appreciation of this had been. But if she knew she'd made a faux pas, she gave no sign of it, rattling on happily about ailerons and wind speed until he wondered how he'd ever get away.

'Is this your little girl?' she asked. Rowlands suppressed a smile. She was scarcely more than a child herself, he thought. Surely no more than sixteen or seventeen. But he replied gravely, 'Yes – this is my daughter. Anne, say hello to Miss . . . to Wilkie.'

'Hello,' said Anne.

'Wilkie helps out at the aerodrome – looking after the planes,' he said.

'Do you really?' Anne sounded suitably impressed.

'That-a will be one and fourpence,' said the ice cream man. Rowlands handed over the money, and gave two of the cones to Anne to carry. A thought struck him as he took the remaining two.

'Would you care for an ice, Wilkie?'

'Gosh. That's awfully kind.'

'One more, please,' he said to the man. He handed the cone to her. 'Well,' he said, with a smile. 'It was nice to see you again.' Assuming, as he spoke, that she'd be wanting to join her friends wherever these might be. But she seemed in no hurry to leave them, tagging along beside Rowlands and his daughter as they threaded their way back through the crowd. Before they reached the VIP stand, she and Anne had become fast friends, chatting enthusiastically of Furies and Flycatchers, and other things aeronautical. By the time Rowlands had handed over the (by now rapidly liquifying) ices, Wilkie seemed quite a fixture, pointing out the details of this machine or that for the edification of the other children, and discoursing knowledgeably on the merits of the new Armstrong Whitworth XVI Fleet fighter as opposed to the Hawker Hoopoe or the Jupiter-powered Gloster SS19 multi-gun fighter.

'But the best of the lot is the Vickers bomber,' she was saying, to a rapt audience consisting of Anne, her sister and the two boys. 'It's a scaled-up version of the B19/27 bomber, of course.'

'Where did you find this prodigy?' murmured Edith in Rowlands' ear. He grimaced slightly, but made no other reply.

'I'm going for a smoke,' he said. At which Dorothy said she'd join him. The two of them made their way towards a part of the field where the crowd had thinned out a little. Here, in the shade cast by the beer tent, they lit up.

'Rather talkative, isn't she, your Miss Wilkie?' his sister said after a moment. 'Doesn't she have any friends of her own?'

'Apparently not.'

'I suppose it's rather an awkward age,' said Dorothy, with which he concurred. Then they said nothing for a while, but smoked their gaspers in what might have seemed a peaceful companionship, had the peace not been shattered, at intervals, by the roar of aircraft taking off, and the murmur of the crowd. 'You needn't worry, you know,' his sister went on, exhaling a lungful of smoke. 'Nothing's going to come of it. It's just the way men of his class behave.' He didn't have to ask who it was she meant.

'I hope you're right,' he said. 'I don't think he's at all the right man for you.'

'When I want your opinion, Fred, I'll ask for it,' she said tartly.

'I'm sorry. I only meant . . .'

'As it happens, I agree with you. He isn't the kind of man who could ever interest me in the least. I don't care for those playboy types. I mean, what has he ever done with his life except amuse himself and fly about in some expensive machine?' He fought a war, thought Rowlands, but judged it best to say nothing. 'Besides which,' his sister went on, in a softer tone, 'you must know I could never care for another man after Viktor.'

# Chapter Six

The complexities of his sister's love life necessarily took second place, in the two weeks that followed, to more pressing matters. With the financial crisis worsening and unemployment at unprecedented levels, Rowlands found himself increasingly busy at the office. Set against the fact that three and three-quarters of a million were out of work, most of them able-bodied men with families to support, the needs of a mere few thousand blind men seemed insignificant. And yet – as Rowlands never tired of pointing out, in letter after letter, written on their behalf – these men had families too, for whom they were often the sole breadwinners. Hadn't they lost their sight in the service of their country? But time and again, the answer came back: '*We regret to say this position has been offered to a more able candidate . . .*' – that is, when an answer came back at all. 'Look, I'm sorry,' said the manager of a button factory Rowlands had telephoned on behalf of one man. 'We had a hundred and fifty applicants for that job. I don't have the staff to answer every letter.'

Sometimes Rowlands wondered what they'd fought the Germans for if this was all there was to be at the end of it. Hardship, and struggle, and being made to feel you were no good for anything. It wasn't much of a reward for four years of fighting. He knew he himself was in a privileged position, working for St Dunstan's, whose continued existence was guaranteed by charitable donation. Although one couldn't take anything for granted these days. In 1915, when the organisation had been set up by Sir Arthur Pearson, the aim had been to get blind men off the streets and into decent jobs; now those jobs were drying up, and there were more beggars on the streets than ever.

Preoccupied with these heavy thoughts, he was engaged, one particular evening, on his weekly chore of mowing the lawn and then rolling it flat with the garden roller. He'd reached the second stage of this task, whose Sisyphean aspect rather suited his present mood, when he heard Edith call from the open French windows. 'Telephone, Fred.' He'd been so sunk in thought that he hadn't heard it ring. Propping the handle of the heavy iron roller against the trunk of the cherry tree so that he could find it again without difficulty, he followed his wife back into the house, taking care to wipe his feet; she wouldn't be very pleased if he dropped grass cuttings all over the carpet. In the hall, the receiver lay on its side; he picked it up.

'Frederick Rowlands speaking.'

'Ah, hello, Rowlands. Alan Percival here.'

'What can I do for you, Captain Percival?'

'The thing is . . .' said Percival with a certain air of diffidence. 'I was wondering if you . . . and your sister . . . might be free on Saturday. To go for that spin I promised you. The girls too, of course,' he added.

'Thank you,' said Rowlands. 'That's kind of you, but . . .'

'Good. I'll pick you up at nine. If it stays fine like this, we should have a good three or four hours flying.' He hung up. Inwardly cursing himself for not having made some excuse, Rowlands stood for a moment, still holding the heavy receiver. Perhaps, he thought, grasping at straws, Saturday would turn out to be wet, and the arrangement would have to be cancelled.

The airfield where Percival kept his Moth belonged to a private club in Surrey; it took little more than half an hour to drive there in his Lagonda. For Rowlands, sitting beside the driver, the experience was an agreeable one: whisking along at speeds of fifty miles an hour or more, on what appeared to be empty roads, with the wind in one's face and the smell of petrol mingling pleasantly with that of the new-mown hay from the fields on either side. It was probably less enjoyable for Dorothy, he thought guiltily, squashed as she was in the back of the car with the three children. He'd given her the choice, but she'd said, 'I'll sit with Billy and the girls. You men have things to talk about.' Although, as it happened, they'd hardly exchanged a word.

'You know, you don't have to come if you'd rather not,' Rowlands had said to his sister the night before. 'I can make some excuse – say you're not well.' She'd laughed at that.

'You mean you'd lie for me? That's a turn-up for the books!' she'd said. 'But no, as it happens, I rather want to go. And Billy will want me to be there,' she'd added, as if this clinched the matter.

The airfield had been built on what had once been farmland. The barn in which Percival's plane was garaged was to be demolished in due course to make way for a proper hangar, he said. 'But of course we make do for the present,' he added, with a laugh. 'Even though the door's half off its hinges and the roof leaks like a sieve.' If they were to come back in six months' time, they wouldn't recognise the place, he went on, as their little party – Rowlands and Percival on either side of Dorothy, with the children running ahead – crossed the windswept stretch of grass. Instead of fields, there'd be a smooth tarmac runway he said; ramshackle farm buildings would be replaced by gleaming new hangars, and a club house.

'Oh, it'll be the last word in modernity, you see! You'll be able to have cocktails in the lounge, and then hop on a plane to Paris to do your shopping.'

Rowlands supposed that this remark was meant for Dorothy, although she made no response – or none of which he was aware. It occurred to him that it would be perfectly possible for his sister and her admirer to conduct the most outrageous flirtation under his nose, without his being any the wiser. Clandestine looks conveying more than mere words. But he dismissed the thought as unworthy. Hadn't Dorothy already made it clear she'd no time for the dashing flier?

A few minutes' walk brought them to the barn. Its doors stood open, Rowlands guessed, from the by now familiar smell of engine oil and dope that came from within. Nor were they the only people there, he gathered, as a murmur of voices came towards them. 'Did you remember to test the airscrew bolts?' said one.

'Of course,' was the reply. 'You know I always do.' He recognised both voices, but before he could put a name to the first, Percival said, 'Ah, there's Bill now. My chief mechanic, you know. I'll introduce you. Bill, this is Mr Rowlands and his sister, Mrs Lehmann. I'm taking them up in the Moth.'

Rowlands held out his hand. 'I believe we've already met,' he said, to Bill Farley. 'At Croydon, a few weeks ago.'

'So we have,' said Farley, somewhat gracelessly. After a moment, he remembered his manners enough to shake Rowlands' hand. 'And this, if I'm not mistaken, is our

110

good friend Wilkie,' Rowlands went on. 'Say hello to Miss Wilkinson, girls.'

'Well, I'm blowed!' said the young woman in question. 'I wasn't expecting to see you here, Mr Rowlands. And the dear little kiddies, too,' she added, ignoring Dorothy.

'If it comes to that,' said Rowlands with a smile, 'I wasn't expecting to see you again so soon either.'

'Oh, I always help out at Fairoaks on a Saturday, don't I, Alan? Captain Percival, I mean. That is, if they don't want me at Croydon. Soon as I know there's going to be some flying done, I just hop on my motorbike and . . .'

'Yes, we couldn't manage without our Wilkie,' agreed Percival heartily, cutting across this enthusiastic outburst. 'She's the one who keeps everything ticking over – eh, Bill?' To which Farley merely grunted an affirmation. He was scarcely more civil to Percival when the latter enquired, 'I take it we're all set?'

'As much as we'll ever be,' was the reply. 'Oi, Bert!' This was to his teammate, Bert Higgins, Rowlands supposed. 'You can bring her out now. The Captain's ready to fly.'

'I'll take the lady up first,' said Percival, addressing the engineer. 'Then the nippers, I think. Might have to make it two flights, as there's three of 'em. Mr Rowlands'll go last . . . if that's all right with you, Rowlands?' he added.

'Quite all right,' said Rowlands, who'd have ducked out altogether, given half the chance. A roaring drowned out his words as Higgins started up the engine in readiness for wheeling the machine out from under cover.

'Stand back, everyone!' shouted Percival, his voice barely audible above the din. At the same time, Rowlands felt a powerful gust from the propellers. He needed no second bidding to step back, out of the path of the great mechanical bird. 'We're in luck,' Percival shouted in his ear. 'Perfect flying conditions. Not too much cloud and very little wind. It'll be like a millpond up there.' Rowlands nodded his comprehension but made no other reply. Millpond or not, he'd rather be safely on the ground.

With a throaty rumble, the Moth taxied away across the field, the noise of its engines diminishing the further away it got. 'Ready, Mrs Lehmann?' said Percival.

'I think so,' she said; then, to her son, 'Wish me luck, old chap.' A brief pause ensued, during which she and Percival made their way to the waiting aeroplane. A moment later, those remaining behind heard the engines start up again. 'Chocks away!' shouted someone – Farley, Rowlands guessed, although it was hard to distinguish voices over the roar of the engines and the loud whirring of the propeller. The sound swelled until it reached a crescendo and then – just as suddenly – it diminished again.

'They're in the air!' cried Anne excitedly. 'Oh, Daddy, I can't wait until it's my turn.'

To Rowlands, waiting on the ground, it seemed as if they were gone a long time, although it could not have been more than twenty minutes from the moment when the plane left the ground and disappeared into the clouds (he had the children to thank for this piece of information) and its re-appearance, 'Look, Daddy – there's the plane!

Just above that cloud. How tiny it looks! Like a funny sort of insect.' It struck him that, had Percival wanted to have Dorothy to himself, he could not have chosen a better way of doing so. Alone together, in such close proximity, and with nothing but the empty sky around them, how could they fail to become more intimate? He told himself sternly that it was not his business, uncomfortably aware that, like it or not, his sister's peculiar circumstances made it very much his business.

At last they were down again, and if anything had passed between them during their sojourn above the clouds, it was not apparent to Rowlands. 'I must say, it's rather wonderful,' was all Dorothy would say. 'To look down from such a height. The world seems quite perfect, you know – like a child's toy farm, with painted fields, and woods made out of painted cotton wool, and little houses. Oh Billy, you will enjoy it!' she cried, catching the child in an embrace from which – to judge from his abashed protests – he tried to wriggle free. They'd been quite a distance, she said. 'As far as Richmond and . . . I don't know where else. Dorking, I think. We flew over Box Hill. The Thames looked like a great silver ribbon, winding its way through green fields. You can't imagine anything more beautiful,' she said, with a fervour Rowlands had hitherto only heard her employ when talking of some cause close to her heart.

The children's jaunts took up far less time: the few minutes it took to make a circuit of the airfield and come back down again. They were all suitably thrilled by the experience, however – Anne vowing that she was going to save up her pocket money 'for years and years' in order to pay for flying lessons. Then it was Rowlands' turn. 'You know, this is rather a waste of your time,' he said to Percival as the latter handed him the leather flying helmet he was to wear, and guided him towards the plane. 'Given that I won't be able to see anything.'

'Flying isn't only about what you can see,' was the reply. 'You may find there's more to it than you imagine. Gently does it! That's right. Put your near foot on the edge of the wing, and swing your other leg up over the fuselage. You'll find the seat quite comfortable.' Which indeed it proved to be. Even so, thought Rowlands, he was glad to have been the last of their party to go up; having to picture the girls in the precarious position in which he now found himself, exposed to the elements in this flimsy shell of wood and canvas, would have added considerably to the anxiety he'd felt during the few minutes his children had been airborne. 'All set?' shouted Percival, above the noise of the engine – a low rumble Rowlands seemed to feel in his viscera. He shouted a reply, but it was lost in the tremendous roar of the engine's starting up.

The plane began to taxi. Away over the bumpy ground it went. The wind came in a rush from behind as they plunged on, gathering speed. It seemed to Rowlands that it would never end – this rattling, roaring, headlong momentum, which reminded him of nothing so much as the time, soon after he'd been posted to the Front, when he'd been ordered to drive a ten-ton lorry over muddy ground near Amiens. Faster and faster they went, the wind rushing past with a whistling sound. Rattle and roar. The machine seemed as if it might shake itself to pieces. Then – suddenly – Rowlands felt the whole thing lift. An extraordinary sensation. His heart seemed to fly into his throat. His stomach . . . but where his stomach had got to, he hadn't the least idea. He wondered for a moment if he might be sick.

But then, as quickly as it had come, the sensation of nausea went away, to be replaced by something altogether more pleasurable. A lightness. A fluidity. Like the feeling one had on water, taking the skiff out, when the blades of one's oars cut through that element with the swiftness of a hot knife through butter, and one found oneself released, for those few moments, into absolute freedom. Freedom from time, from death, from the gross limitations of the body. A soaring, swooping sensation. They were airborne, evidently. He let out the breath he'd been holding, aware that now, after all the commotion of taking off, it had grown magically quiet. 'You see?' came the voice of the pilot, drifting back towards him, 'There's more to it than people think.'

'Oh yes,' said Rowlands. 'I see that, now.'

And indeed for those few minutes that they were airborne, it seemed to him as if there could be nothing better than just this feeling of being, quite literally, above it all. With only Percival's comments to offer a clue as to where they were – '. . . just passing over Chobham

Common. Some quite pretty country around here . . .' – Rowlands could surrender himself to the pure sensation of flying. How utterly peaceful it was! Even the slight queasiness he'd felt at the beginning had vanished. There was nothing between him and the air itself, he thought, but the flimsy shell of the flying machine in which he sat, cocooned. Overhead was the sun, shining down in all its glory. He could feel its steady warmth upon his face. And oh, how bright it was!

'It seems lighter up here,' he said. Meaning not just the illusion of weightlessness which came with being airborne, but the brilliance of the light itself.

'What? Oh, it's certainly that,' came the reply. 'I thought we'd nip round over Chertsey, take a quick look at the river, then head back via Woking.' It made little difference to Rowlands whether they went via the moon, just as long as he could go on enjoying this extraordinary sensation of being . . . bathed in light, was the nearest he could get to it.

'Whatever you say,' he said.

'There's a piece in the paper about Captain Percival,' said Edith. 'Mother found it earlier, didn't you, Mother?' It was later that evening. The children, exhausted but happy, had been put to bed, and the adults were sitting out in the garden, enjoying the last hour of daylight. It struck Rowlands how much of a difference it made, the light – even to one like himself. Those few minutes he'd spent above the clouds, in the full glare of the sun, had been like nothing else he'd ever experienced. For that brief moment, he'd remembered what the sun could be. Now, in the twilit garden, he thought of the golden radiance with which everything had been permeated as he and Percival had ascended higher and higher. Called back to earth, he made a sound vaguely expressive of interest. 'Yes, he does seem to have made quite a splash recently,' his wife went on. 'We were only saying, weren't we, Mother? Ah, here it is.'

She cleared her throat. '"*Captain Percival, the celebrated Flying Ace, whose record-breaking flight from England to Australia in his Gipsy Moth made headlines across the world last month . . .*"' She broke off. 'Are you going in, Dorothy? I thought you of all people would be interested.'

'What made you think that?' was the cool reply. 'As it happens, I'm going to check on Victor.'

'Suit yourself.' There had never been much love lost between Edith and her sister-in-law. 'Now, where was I? "*Captain Percival . . . celebrated Flying Ace . . .*" etcetera . . . "*is a man who has the luck that so often attends the adventurous. He was shot down over France during a dogfight with an enemy aircraft during the war, and escaped without a scratch, as he himself puts it; he has survived the perils of motor racing at Brooklands. He alone escaped alive when an airliner, returning from Berlin, crashed near Caterham in 1929, killing the pilot and other passengers; six months later, a motorboat, in which he was doing fifty knots in the Solent, hit a rock* and sank under him. '*I was lucky again that time,*' he laughs. '*The luck of the devil, you might say.*' *Admirers of Captain Percival's daring stunts in his Moth will be wishing him all the luck in the world when he competes in the King's Cup Race next Saturday . . .*" I suppose you'll be going?' said his wife, with only the faintest trace of irony.

'Not I.'

'Only I thought, after this afternoon's escapade, that you'd become quite an enthusiast for flying,' Edith said innocently. Rowlands laughed.

'I won't deny that I found it a lot more enjoyable than expected. But I think I've had enough of aeroplanes for a while.'

'Well, that's a relief,' said his wife. 'Shall we go in, Mother? It's starting to feel a bit chilly.'

Something had woken him. The sound of a car door being slammed in the street outside; of a car driving away. Perhaps he'd been dreaming, he thought. Well, he was wide awake now – whatever it had been that had disturbed him. Insomnia was a condition with which he was all too familiar, there being no clear demarcation for him between night and day. He checked his watch: it was just gone one. He lay there for a moment, listening. But the house was quiet. The only sound was his wife's soft breathing and the drumming of the rain on the window. If this kept up, he'd have to put off creosoting the fence, which he'd been planning to do for a fortnight. It could wait another week, he supposed, now resigned to sleeplessness. On an impulse, he eased himself out of bed, taking care not to wake Edith, and reached for his dressing gown. He'd just make absolutely sure.

But when he put his head into the girls' room, there was only the sound of Anne, grinding her teeth in her sleep, and of Margaret's even breathing. He paused for a moment outside his sister's door, but thought better of opening it. She wouldn't thank him for waking the baby.

In the morning, the rain had stopped, but it was still heavily overcast. 'You'd hardly think it was July,' said Edith.

'I suppose not. Is there another cup of tea in the pot?' he asked.

'Mm.' She took his cup from him and filled it. 'All right, girls. You can get down. Billy, will you see if Mummy's awake?' She waited until the child had gone out. 'Only it's past nine o'clock. You'd have thought . . .' Just then Billy came in, accompanied by his little brother.

'Mummy's gone,' he said flatly. 'And Vicky wants his breakfast.' When questioned as to where his mother had gone, he said he didn't know. He'd been asleep, he said. 'But this was on her pillow,' he added. A letter; Edith read it aloud. '"*Out all day. Back late.*" Well!' Conscious of the children's presence, she restrained herself from further comment.

'And you're sure she didn't say where she was going?' Rowlands persisted, knowing that Dorothy – unadvisedly, in his opinion – often made a confidant of the boy. But if he knew anything, he wasn't saying.

119

'I was asleep,' he repeated stubbornly.

'Of course you were. It doesn't matter,' said Rowlands. 'I think I've pretty good idea where your mother might be.'

The bus dropped him off outside Hendon Aerodrome. It wasn't a regular stop, but the driver – who'd been in the trenches at Chateau Wood in '16, it transpired – had made a point of taking him right to the gates. 'We old soldiers should stick together, that's what I say,' he said. 'Going to watch the King's Cup Race, are you?' Rowlands admitted he was. 'That's nice,' said the driver. 'Hope it clears up for you, that's all. No, I don't want your money, thanks,' he'd added when Rowlands had proffered his fare. 'Seems to me you've already paid more than enough.' From which uncompromising position Rowlands was unable to shake him.

At the ticket office just inside the gates, they seemed no less uninterested in taking his money. 'Oh, your party's already here,' said the young woman behind the counter. 'You are with the St Dunstan's group, aren't you? I couldn't help noticing your badge.' A flaming torch, in silver; he always wore it pinned to his lapel.

'Ah. Yes. The St Dunstan's group,' he echoed, playing for time. Now he came to think about it, there had been some talk at the Lodge a few days before about getting up a party to go to Hendon Stratham and Hewitt and a few of the others who'd come to the Croydon show had been the ones behind the plan – all former RFC men, Rowlands recalled.

'They're in the Club House,' his obliging young friend was saying. 'I'll get someone to take you there, shall I? Only I can't leave the desk.'

'No, of course not. As a matter of fact, it was Captain Percival I was after.'

'If he's here, he'll be at the hangars. But I'm not sure he's arrived yet.'

'I can wait,' said Rowlands. Having reassured the girl that he could make his own way there, he set out along the perimeter road that led from the main gate to the far side of the airfield where the hangars were to be found, and which was, she said, his quickest route if he wanted to avoid all the people. These had started to arrive in numbers even though the race wasn't due to start for another three hours. But already the rattle of charabancs and other motor vehicles could be heard. The feeling of urgency, expectancy and mild hilarity, which a large crowd bent on amusement brings with it, was in the air. As Rowlands threaded his way through the press of bodies, snatches of conversation came his way:

'. . . fewer entries this year, but still an interesting field . . .'

'. . . twelve Gipsy Moths, five Puss Moths, five Avians, five Bluebirds, four Spartans, four Widgeons . . .'

'. . . hope the weather holds . . .'

'. . . two Martlets, a Comper Swift, a Civilian Coupe, an Arrow Active, and a Warren-strutted Curtiss-Reid Rambler.'

Leaving behind this excited babble of voices,

Rowlands walked briskly in the direction he'd been shown, his thoughts preoccupied with a subject quite unconnected with flying: his sister's propensity for landing herself in trouble. Of course, he thought grimly as – the path being otherwise deserted – he quickened his pace, it might be that he'd got it wrong, and that she wasn't with Percival at all. But he didn't think so. 'Ten minutes' walk', hadn't that girl said? 'Past the Nissen huts, then sharp left, through the shrubbery. You can't miss it.' He found the path, and was making his way in what he guessed was the right direction, guided by the low rumble of aircraft engines being started up, and the *whup-whup* sound of propellers.

It was then that he heard the scream. It came from the direction of the hangars. It was a woman's voice, sounding raw with terror. He couldn't make out the words at first, but then came another choking cry, 'Help! Somebody help me! Oh God! Help! Murder!'

Careless of his own safety, Rowlands broke into a run. At that moment, someone coming the other way ran past him, too quickly for him to get a sense of who it might be. 'Hi, there!' he shouted; then, when this had no effect, 'Stop!' He was about to go in pursuit of the malefactor – for surely, someone who failed to stop when challenged must be up to no good – when someone else ran full tilt into him. Trim little body in a silk dress. Rather a lot of perfume. A woman, evidently.

'Oh!' It was Irene Metcalfe, he realised; it had been her voice he had heard. The brief, but forceful contact seemed to knock the breath out of her. 'My God,' was all she could say. 'Oh, my God . . .' She began to cry, in great gasps, her whole body shuddering with the effort.

'What's happened?' he said, trying to shake sense into her. Then, when the anguished sobbing seemed to go on and on, 'It's all right, Mrs Metcalfe. You're safe now. If you'd just tell me what's happened.' But she seemed incapable of saying anything coherent, merely sobbing over and over, 'My God. My God . . .'

'Look, if you'll just calm down a moment . . .'

His gentle injunction must have had some effect, for her sobs now dwindled into a soft whimpering, like that of a child just woken from a bad dream. 'It's all so horrible,' she said. 'I walked in and he . . . he was just lying there.'

'Who was lying where?' he asked, trying to make sense of this. But before she could reply, there came another voice.

'What the bloody hell's going on?' Someone came running up. 'Is this man bothering you, Miss?' said a voice fiercely. Then, 'Oh, it's you.' The speaker was Bert Higgins. 'Sorry, Mr Rowlands, sir, I thought . . .'

'Mrs Metcalfe has had a shock,' said Rowlands. 'I don't suppose there's anywhere she could sit down?'

'There'll be a chair in the office at the back of Hangar Three. If you'll just come this way . . . No, it's all right, Ginger.' This was to one of the ground crew, Rowlands guessed. 'The lady's feeling a bit poorly.' But when, with Rowlands supporting her, the mechanic tried to usher the weeping woman back in the direction from which she had come, she flatly refused to budge.

'I'm not going in there again,' she said, the shrill note of hysteria in her voice. 'It's too horrible. I won't go in there. I won't!'

'All right, all right,' said Higgins, in a placatory tone. 'No one's going to make you go in there if you don't want to. It's only the hangar where the Captain keeps his machine,' he said in an undertone to Rowlands. 'God knows what's upset her so. P'raps it was a mouse. Some women do take against 'em.'

'I hardly think . . .' Rowlands began.

'Or maybe Bill gave her a piece of his mind. He doesn't take kindly to members of the public poking their noses in when he's trying to work.'

'Yes,' said Rowlands. 'I know. Let's take a look, shall we?'

'Right you are. Ginger, look after the lady, will you?'

Another few paces brought them to the door of the hangar. 'I don't understand it,' muttered Higgins. 'Bill's supposed to have opened all this up, in readiness for when the Captain gets here. He will be mad if he finds we've let ourselves get behind.'

'When are you expecting him – Captain Percival, I mean?' said Rowlands, for whom this was of some significance.

'Any time now,' was the reply. 'The race doesn't start till two, but he likes at least an hour to run through his checks. Take care. There's a step.'

124

'Thanks.' He went in first. The first thing that struck him was the utter silence.

'Bill!' called Higgins; then, under his breath, 'Now, where's the bugger got to?' He must have moved past Rowlands then and gone a few steps further into the hangar, for his voice sounded more distant, echoing hollowly in that vast, empty space. 'Slipped off for a crafty fag, I shouldn't wonder . . . Bill!' Then came a stifled exclamation. 'Christ!'

'What is it?' said Rowlands, taking a step towards the place from which the cry had come.

'It's Bill,' came the reply. 'Dead as a doornail, poor bugger. Looks like somebody bashed his brains in for him. No, I shouldn't come any closer,' said Higgins, in a queer, half-strangled voice. 'There's rather a lot of blood.'

# Chapter Seven

The police had been telephoned by the efficient young woman in the ticket office and Rowlands was settling himself down to wait in the Club House. To his worries about his sister's whereabouts had been added another concern – just how exactly he was going to get her away from here before the forces of law and order arrived – that is if she turned up at the aerodrome at all; he had only his hunch to go on. And yet, looking back over the events of yesterday, certain things seemed significant. The fact that Dorothy hadn't said goodbye to Percival when he'd dropped them off at Grove Crescent was one thing; at the time, Rowlands had put it down to her cussed off-handedness where men were concerned. Now he wondered if it hadn't been because she knew she'd be seeing Percival later. Then there was that note: *Out all day. Back late.* The cool effrontery of it was typical of his sister.

He was roused from these reflections by the sound of sobbing, Irene Metcalfe evidently having given way to another attack of nerves. Although this could doubtless be put down to delayed shock, it was also noticeable that Mrs Metcalfe's mood had worsened considerably since she'd been told that she'd have to give a statement to the police. 'It's so horrible,' she was saying, between sobs, 'to think that it might have been Alan . . . Captain Percival . . . lying there . . .'

'What makes you say that?' said Rowlands.

'Well, it stands to reason, doesn't it? The . . . the body was next to Captain's Percival's plane. That dreadful man must have thought it was him.' Tears overwhelmed her. 'Oh it's too awful,' she wept. 'I don't know what Neville's going to say.'

But he was struck by something she'd said. 'Which man are you talking about exactly?' he said. 'Did you actually see anyone when you went into the hangar?'

'It was only for a m-moment,' she stammered. 'And it was awfully dark.'

'Yes, but you did see someone?' he persisted.

'I . . . I can't say for certain.' Again came a fresh storm of tears. 'Oh, I want to go home!' she cried. 'Why can't I go home?' She was working herself up. Rowlands, whose wife had never been prone to such emotional outbursts, was uncertain how best to deal with them.

'Perhaps,' he began, 'a cup of tea might be the thing.'

'Anything I can do?' said a familiar voice. Rowlands turned towards it with some relief.

'Miss Wilkinson . . . Wilkie. What a piece of luck to find you here!'

'Oh, I never miss one of the big races,' said the girl.

'Of course not. I don't suppose,' said Rowlands, 'that you could get this lady a cup of tea?'

'Nothing easier,' said the obliging Wilkie. 'I say, Mr Rowlands, you do get about! Have you brought the kiddies with you?'

'No, it's just me today.'

'They will be fed up, not to see the race!'

'They will, won't they? Wilkie, if I could just leave you to look after Mrs Metcalfe for a minute, there's something I ought to . . .' Because Rowlands' sharper hearing had caught the sound of a Lagonda drawing up outside. A moment later, Alan Percival burst into the room.

'What on earth's going on?' he demanded. 'I've just been down to the hangar, expecting that everything'd be ready for me, only to find it all locked up, and as silent as the grave.' The simile was all too apposite, thought Rowlands.

'I'm afraid something rather dreadful's happened,' he said. 'Bill Farley's been murdered.'

'What!' There was a moment's stunned silence before the pilot found his voice again. 'I don't believe it. Are you absolutely sure about this?'

'I'm afraid so,' said Rowlands.

'Oh, he's dead all right,' chipped in Bert Higgins. 'Mr Rowlands and I found him, didn't we, Mr Rowlands?'

'Well, as a matter of fact,' said Rowlands, 'it was Mrs Metcalfe who found him.' At this, Irene Metcalfe, who had quietened down somewhat as a result of Wilkie's ministrations, burst into tears again.

'Oh, Alan, it was awful,' she sobbed. 'Seeing him like that . . . all covered in blood. And the worst thing was, I thought it was you, at first.'

'Now, now,' murmured Percival unhappily. 'No need to upset yourself, Irene. Wilkie, what do you know about this?' he added to the hovering girl.

'Me? I've only just got here,' was the reply. 'I haven't been near the hangars.'

'Well, I must say, it's all a bit of a bloody mess, if you'll excuse my French,' said Percival. 'I suppose the police have been called?' But an answer to his question was rendered superfluous by the sound of a big Wolseley pulling up, followed by the slamming of car doors. A moment later, three men walked in – the first of these introducing himself as Inspector Hawkins of the Metropolitan Police.

'And this is Sergeant Gerrard,' he added. He didn't trouble to introduce the uniformed man. 'Now then. Which of you is Mr Frederick Rowlands?' Rowlands identified himself. 'So you're the gentleman who found the body?' said the Inspector.

'Yes. That is, I was one of the first on the scene,'

amended Rowlands guardedly. 'This lady was the one who alerted me to what had happened. Then Mr Higgins and I went into the hangar and . . .'

'We'll be coming to that shortly,' said Hawkins. 'I'll need your name first, madam, if you don't mind.'

'I didn't have anything to do with it,' said Irene Metcalfe shrilly. 'He'll tell you that.' She clutched Rowlands' arm. 'He knows what happened.'

'We'll be taking Mr Rowlands' statement in good time,' said the policeman. 'Now. Perhaps you'd like to sit down again over there and tell Constable Timms all about it?' His subordinate duly complied with these instructions, drawing the nervous woman towards the row of chairs on the far side of the room, from whence he could be heard putting his questions, his emollient tone in marked contrast to the senior officer's more abrasive manner.

'I take it,' said this official, evidently addressing Percival, 'that you haven't anything further to add to what this gentleman has told us, sir?'

'Nothing at all,' was the reply. 'I've only just got here, as a matter of fact.' But his remarks were cut short at that moment by the door's opening, and someone coming in whose step was all too familiar to Rowlands.

'Can anyone tell me what's going on?' said Dorothy Lehmann. 'There appear to be policemen everywhere.'

'I thought I told you to wait in the car,' said Percival.

'You did,' she said. 'But I got tired of waiting. Oh! Hello, Fred. I wasn't expecting to see you so soon.'

'I don't suppose you were.' No one who didn't know him well would have been able to tell from Rowlands' voice that he was angry.

'And who might you be, Miss?' said Inspector Hawkins. Before she could reply, Rowlands said, 'She's my sister.'

'Ah. Miss Rowlands, is it?'

'That's right,' said Rowlands before Dorothy could reply.

'I say—' Percival began, but Rowlands cut across him.

'Captain Percival has very kindly offered to show us around the aerodrome, hasn't he, dear?'

'Well . . . yes.' She sounded faintly amused.

'All right,' said Hawkins. 'We'll take all your statements in a minute. First things first. Which of you is Albert Higgins?' Higgins, who had been hanging back since the appearance of these representatives of the Force, now spoke up.

'That's me.' The Inspector's voice shifted from the deferential tone he had used in addressing *the gentry* to a brusquer register.

'You were the one that found the body – after this lady here?'

'I was,' said Higgins. 'Horrible, seeing him like that, poor bugg . . .'

'That'll do. You can tell it to my sergeant. You're the one who's got the keys to the place, I take it?'

'Yes. Thought as I'd better lock up in case anyone . . .'

'No doubt. Well, you'd better give 'em to me,' said the Inspector. 'Time we took a closer look at the scene. Come

131

on, Sergeant. You can stay with Mrs Metcalfe,' he added to Constable Timms. 'And you'd better come along, too.' This was to Higgins, Rowlands surmised. 'It isn't often that I get three principal witnesses under my eye at one time.' The three of them were on their way out when Percival intervened.

'I say, Inspector, I'd like to join you, if I may. Farley was one of my employees, you know. A good man, if inclined to be a bit surly at times. But a very competent mechanic. We worked pretty closely together.'

'I don't see any reason why you shouldn't come along,' said Hawkins drily. 'Am I right in assuming that you're *the* Captain Percival?' Reassured on this point, he said, 'My wife's a great admirer of yours' – the implication being that he himself wasn't. They went in two cars – Higgins in the police car with the Inspector and his assistant, Dorothy and Rowlands in Percival's Lagonda. At the last minute the girl, Pauline Wilkinson, asked if she could come with them. Rowlands thought this a bad idea, and said so. Wilkie insisted.

'We were good chums, old Bill and I,' she said, in a choked voice. 'He taught me everything I know about engines.'

'I don't suppose the police will want a kid hanging about the place,' said Alan Percival.

'I'm not a kid.' There was a steeliness to the young woman's voice Rowlands hadn't noticed until now. 'I'm seventeen.'

Percival sighed. 'Have it your own way. No, you can

132

hop in the back, next to Mr Rowlands,' he added when the girl went to climb in beside Dorothy. 'There isn't room for you in the front.' He let out the clutch and, having waited for the Wolseley to lead the way, began driving slowly back along the perimeter road that led to the hangars. 'You never said that you'd reverted to your maiden name,' he went on, now addressing Rowlands' sister.

'I haven't,' replied Dorothy.

'Then why . . . Oh I see!' Percival's next remark was obviously meant for Rowlands. 'You were trying to keep her out of it. But it won't work, you know. The police'll find out her real name as soon as they start asking around. In any case,' he went on, sounding increasingly puzzled, 'what does it matter what she calls herself? Anyone would think you'd got a criminal record, darling,' he added jokingly to Dorothy.

'Oh, I killed a man once,' she replied, her tone as flippant as his.

'I'm sure he deserved it,' laughed Percival.

'He did.'

All too conscious of the presence of Wilkie, no doubt drinking all this in, Rowlands gave a warning cough. Would his sister never learn sense? Fortunately for his peace of mind, they had now arrived at their destination. Car doors were being slammed as those inside the police vehicle got out. 'Here we are,' said Percival. 'I can't say I'm looking forward to this one bit.' He got out of the car, followed, a moment later, by the faithful Wilkie. It was obvious that the girl had a serious crush on the fellow, Rowlands thought. But at that moment he had other things on his mind, apart from Percival's fatal tendency to ensnare every nubile female within sight.

'What the hell do you think you're playing at?' he said to his sister in an undertone. 'Do you want to put your head in a noose? Because I can assure you, you're going the right way about it!'

'Dear old Fred. Always looking on the bright side,' she said, but there was anger underneath the facetiousness.

'You can joke about it all you like, Dottie, but . . .' The nearside door opened and Percival put his head in.

'Are you coming, or not?' he said to Rowlands. 'Dorothy . . . or should I say *Miss Rowlands* . . . I think you should stay in the car. This isn't something a woman should see.'

'Oh, I'm hardened to such things, aren't I, Fred?' she replied, with the mixture of mischievousness and defiance Rowlands had come to dread. One never knew quite where it would end, with Dorothy. But in the end, it was the Inspector who put his foot down.

'I shan't want you, Miss, begging your pardon,' he said as the three of them, with Wilkie tagging along behind, walked over to where he was standing. 'Nor you, young lady. It's Mr Rowlands' account of things I need. Now then, sir, can you show me where you were when you heard Mrs Metcalfe scream?'

Rowlands thought for a moment. 'Let's see. I'd just turned off the road, and was heading down the path towards the hangars . . .'

'Can you take me to it?'

'I believe so.'

'All right,' said Inspector Hawkins. The two men, with Rowlands leading the way, walked slowly back along the path that led through the shrubbery towards the perimeter road. When they were fifty paces from the hangars, Rowlands stopped.

'It was about here.'

'Don't take this the wrong way,' said the policeman. 'But how can you be sure?'

'It's quite simple, really,' said Rowlands. 'In my situation, one gets quite good at estimating distances. And there's a bend in the path, just here, where the paving stones are broken. It nearly tripped me up, the first time I came this way. That's how I know. Also, from this spot it's possible to hear the sound of the aircraft engines being tuned. Nearer the road, you can't hear it quite so well.'

'All right, all right, I get the picture,' said Inspector Hawkins. 'So you were about here. You heard a scream. Then Mrs Metcalfe ran up.'

'No, that was later. Someone else ran past me, a moment or so before Mrs Metcalfe appeared. It must have been at about a quarter past eleven because . . .'

'Don't tell me you'd just heard a clock strike?' said the other drily.

'I won't,' replied Rowlands. 'As a matter of fact, I'd just checked my watch a few minutes before. It was twelve minutes past then, so . . .'

135

'I can see you're going to prove a useful witness, sir,' said the police inspector. 'That'll help us establish the time of death. Now then, this man you heard running past you . . . can you tell me anything else about him? Height? Build? Age?'

'I'm afraid not,' said Rowlands. 'In that respect, I'm not much use as a witness. It would have been a different story if I'd actually collided with the man, but I didn't. What I can tell you is that you'll probably find a bit of the shrubbery's broken just about here. When I shouted at the fellow to stop, he went crashing through there.' He gestured towards the laurel hedge that grew alongside the path. The Inspector went to investigate.

'I believe you're right,' he said. 'Some of the twigs have been snapped, here and there. The ground's quite soft and muddy after last night's rain, so we may have some footprints, too . . . Hello! What's this?' He must have bent to pick something up, for he emitted a small grunt of effort. 'A button. Navy blue. Still with a few threads attached. It looks as if it might have been torn off whatever our man was wearing.'

At that moment the sergeant came up. 'The MO's arrived, sir,' he said. 'Said as I was to ask you if you wanted him to carry on, like – or if you wanted to view the body first.' Hawkins sighed.

'I suppose I'd better take a look,' he said. 'I'd like you to come with me, Mr Rowlands, if you will. You' – this to the sergeant – 'can take charge of this.' Rowlands guessed it was the button he meant, for he added,

'Carefully, mind! Yes, your handkerchief will do. We're unlikely to find any useful fingerprints on it, but you never know.'

'There you are, Inspector!' said a voice Rowlands took to be the Medical Officer as the three of them walked up. 'I'd like to get on with this, if it's all the same to you. Got a poisoning case in West Drayton to see to when I'm done here.'

'All right, Dr Coles. I won't detain you much longer,' said Hawkins. 'I'll just have a look at the scene. Higgins, I'd like you to come along as well. You, too, Captain Percival, if you don't mind.'

'Not at all,' said Percival.

The six men entered the hangar where a uniformed copper stood guard. Rowlands was again struck by the profound silence; the extraordinary feeling of absence one encountered in the presence of death. It was a feeling he'd had before, on more occasions than he cared to remember. There was the smell of death, too, as they drew nearer. 'Hmph,' grunted the Inspector as they reached the spot where the body lay. 'Someone has made a mess of him, haven't they? What do you make of it, Doctor?'

The Medical Officer took his time considering the matter. 'From the way he's fallen – on his back – I'd guess he was hit from in front . . . perhaps even while he was lying on the ground. Quite a heavy blow, to do that much damage to the skull.'

'Indeed,' said the Chief Inspector. 'Don't suppose we'll find the weapon lying about in here, but you might as well take a look around,' he added, to his subordinate.

'My God,' said Percival, in a hollow tone. 'Poor old Farley.' He drew a shuddering breath. 'To think that only a few hours ago, he was alive and kicking.'

'Yes, we'll need to know when you last saw Mr Farley, and where,' said Hawkins. 'Sergeant Gerrard'll take all your statements in a moment.' He was silent for a few seconds, apparently lost in contemplation of the scene and its various elements, at which Rowlands could only guess. The vaulted hangar, whose darkness was broken only by the light streaming in through the door. The great winged machine, with the dead man lying beside it. 'I suppose the overalls he's wearing must be pretty much the standard variety?' mused the Inspector as if an idea had just occurred to him. 'Navy drill.' Rowlands wondered if this detail was meant for him, but then Higgins said, 'That's right. We all wear them – although some of the RAF lads prefer khaki.'

'Mm,' said the Inspector. He must have stooped for a closer look at the victim, for he gave a grunt of surprise. 'You didn't mention he had a tin leg,' he said, addressing Percival.

'It didn't occur to me to do so,' was the mild reply. 'He got it after a wound went bad during the war – isn't that right, Bert?' Higgins agreed that this was so. 'Why? Is it important?'

'It might have made a difference when it came to defending himself,' said the Inspector. 'Well, I don't

138

suppose there's much else we can do here,' he went on. 'Fine-looking aeroplane, this.' He slapped his hand down on the fuselage of the Gipsy Moth. 'Is it the one you flew all the way from Australia, sir?'

'Yes, it is. On which subject,' said Percival, 'I don't suppose you can tell me how much longer all this is going to take? Only I'll need access to the plane if it's to be ready in time for this afternoon's race. It'll need to be serviced, which should of course have been done by now,' he added irritably. 'But it can't be helped. Just as long as I can run some routine checks.'

'Out of the question, sir, I'm afraid,' said Hawkins cheerfully. 'This is a crime scene. The aeroplane'll have to be thoroughly examined for fingerprints.'

'But that's terrible!' cried the pilot. 'I'm supposed to be taking that plane up in a couple of hours.'

'What's *terrible*, if you don't mind my saying, sir, is that a man has lost his life,' replied the Inspector severely. 'I'd say everything else was merely unfortunate.'

Outside Hangar Number 3, a crowd had now collected. In the few minutes during which Rowlands and the others had been engaged in their grim task of inspecting the corpse, the news of what had happened had spread around the airfield. Now the excited babble of voices – some of them with a distinctly foreign sound – rose to a crescendo as the five of them emerged, with the pilot being the focus of the attention. 'Say, Percival!' cried a man Rowlands guessed from his accent to be an American.

'Is it true what this guy says – that a man's been killed?'

'Quite true, Mr Harrington, I'm afraid,' said Percival grimly. 'Worse than that, he appears to have been murdered.'

'*Mein Gott*!' exclaimed another voice. A German, evidently. 'Will the race go ahead?'

'Your guess is as good as mine, Count von Lowenstein,' was the reply. 'One thing's certain, though – I won't be flying my plane. The police have taken charge of it.'

'But . . . they can't do that!' cried Wilkie, sounding more distraught than Rowlands had ever heard her. 'You've been training for this race for weeks.'

'It's purely a temporary measure, I assure you, ladies and gentlemen,' said Inspector Hawkins, with the patience borne of many years of dealing with the public. 'Now, if you don't mind, I'll need you to clear the area. This is a murder enquiry, not a day at the races.' Muttering rebelliously in its various accents – as well as those he'd already identified, Rowlands thought he detected an Italian and a Frenchman – the crowd began to disperse. But just then there came another intervention, this time in unmistakably native tones.

'Will someone tell me what the hell is going on?'

'Hello, Harmsworth,' replied Percival. 'I wondered when you'd turn up.'

'Yes, just got here, actually. Olave gave me a lift in her pretty little motor, didn't you, Olave?'

'Yes,' said that lady, with a certain constraint in her manner.

'I heard there'd been a murder,' Harmsworth went on.

'You heard right, old boy.' Was there a jeering note in Percival's voice? 'It's one of my ground crew who's been killed, as a matter of fact.'

'Well, I think it's bloody outrageous,' snapped the other. 'They've locked up all the hangars. I can't get access to my machine.'

'No more can I,' said Percival, who seemed to Rowlands to be taking a certain malicious pleasure in his rival's discomfiture.

'As I've said,' repeated the Inspector with some asperity, 'this is only a temporary measure.'

'But what does that mean exactly?' someone asked – it was Olave Malory. 'Are you going to let us have the aeroplanes back before the race?' she went on, addressing the Inspector in an imperious tone. 'You can't keep them locked up indefinitely. We're expecting ten thousand people to turn up this afternoon. Are we to send them all home?'

Inspector Hawkins sighed. 'I don't see why you shouldn't have your race, miss,' he said. 'Just as soon as my men have finished searching the area.'

'Searching for what?' said someone else.

'The murder weapon, I guess,' came the reply – the American, Harrington. But Inspector Hawkins refused to be drawn on this, or any of the other wilder speculations which were flying around.

'If you'll just move along, ladies and gentlemen,' he said. 'We can get on all the quicker.'

* * *

The police had set up their HQ in the Club House; in order to reach it, the three of them – Percival, Rowlands and Dorothy – were obliged to push their way through an excited crowd of people which had assembled near the entrance to the aerodrome. Among these voices, clamouring to know if the event would still be held, was one which was familiar to Rowlands. It was Stratham's. 'Look here,' he heard the former pilot say, presumably addressing the young woman to whom Rowlands had spoken earlier. 'Can you tell me what's going on? I'm with the St Dunstan's group, you know.'

'I've no news at present, sir,' said the girl, sounding harassed, as indeed she might, thought Rowlands. 'If you'll just be patient.'

'That's all very well,' said the blind man. 'But we've been here since half past ten, and . . .'

'Perhaps I can help?' said Rowlands, tapping the other on the shoulder. 'I heard you chaps were somewhere about.'

'Rowlands! Am I glad to see you!' Like most of their generation of war-blinded, Stratham didn't think twice about using such expressions; it was only the sighted who ever thought it odd. 'I've been trying to explain to this young lady here that I've a group of half a dozen men who've been kicking their heels since this morning, in the hope that there'd be some flying to watch this afternoon, only to find that the whole thing might be called off. I say,' he added in a lower voice, 'there isn't any truth in this fantastic story about a murder, is there?'

142

'I'm afraid there is,' said Rowlands. 'A man's been killed. The police are looking into it now.'

'Good Lord!' said Stratham. 'That's a facer, and no mistake. Well, chaps,' he went on, addressing the group of St Dunstaners. 'It looks as if the race may be called off, after all.' There was a general murmur of discontent at this; then Rowlands said, 'Look, why don't we all go and wait in the Club House until we know what's what?'

'Good idea,' said Stratham. 'I must say,' he went on as they began to walk towards the building. 'I never knew you were such an enthusiast for flying, Rowlands, otherwise I'd have asked you to join our party.'

'Oh, I'm afraid I'm here under false pretences,' replied Rowlands, with a lightness he did not feel. 'Who else is with you? I thought I heard Hewitt's voice.'

'The very same,' said Hewitt. 'You know Eyre, of course? And Barlowe, and Ronnie Pope.'

'All the RFC boys, in fact,' said Rowlands as they entered the Club House.

'Except Aitchison here,' said Stratham. 'He was in the PBI, weren't you, Jim?'

'That's right,' replied the man thus addressed. 'Always wanted to be a flier, but they wouldn't take me, worse luck.'

'But lucky for the Air Force,' quipped someone else. Barlowe, Rowlands thought. It occurred to him that he ought to find Dorothy.

He was on the point of making his excuses when he heard himself loudly hailed, 'Hi! Rowlands! I say – over here, man!' It was Neville Metcalfe, his tone, as ever, peremptory; his manner supercilious. 'Perhaps you can explain what's going on?' he said as Rowlands turned to answer his summons. 'Irene tells me a man's been murdered, and that the police require some kind of statement of her movements. I must say,' he went on, sounding increasingly indignant, 'I can't see what on earth she can have to say about it. She only stopped by the aerodrome for a minute – to return a scarf that Percival . . . Oh, there you are, old boy,' he said as the latter joined them. 'I was just saying to Rowlands here that I take a pretty dim view of all this.'

'Yes, it is rather beastly,' said Percival, calmly lighting a cigarette. 'Oh, I'm sorry, Rowlands. Would you like one?' he said, not extending the offer to Metcalfe, Rowlands couldn't help noticing. He shook his head.

'Thanks. I've got my own.'

'Well, I call it disgraceful,' Metcalfe persisted, apparently oblivious to this slight. 'Dragging a woman into an affair like this.' A woman to whom you happen to be married, thought Rowlands, guessing that the civil servant's indignation was as much on his own account as it was on his wife's. Just now, he had other things on his mind.

'I don't suppose you've seen my sister anywhere about?' he asked Percival, hating to have to ask such a question of the man, and annoyed with Dorothy for putting him in such a spot.

'She's around somewhere,' was the cool reply. 'I think

she went to powder her nose . . . Oh, there she is!'

He must have waved at her, for she came over. 'Looking for me?' she said, slipping her arm through Rowlands'.

'I was, as it happens. Stratham, I don't believe you've met my sister? Dorothy, this is a friend of mine from the Lodge.'

'Delighted,' said Dorothy.

'I think you and Captain Percival already know one another, don't you?' said Rowlands to his fellow St Dunstaner. Stratham gave an awkward laugh.

'Well, it was an awfully long time ago,' he said. 'You were already a bit of a legend in the Squadron.' Now it was Percival's turn to sound embarrassed.

'I was a reckless young fool,' he said. 'We all were, if it comes to that . . . Stratham. Of course, I remember you now! Skinny young chap, with a shock of ginger hair.'

'Yes, I've lost most of it now,' said the other ruefully.

'Oh, we've all changed a bit since those days,' said Percival.

'Well, you sound just the same,' Stratham remarked. 'And from what I can gather, you're still getting up to the same daredevil stuff.'

'Oh, I wouldn't call myself a daredevil,' said the aviator. 'Most of what I do is pretty routine, you know.' There was general laughter at this piece of self-deprecation. Then Metcalfe said, 'Far be it from me to interrupt these touching reminiscences, but I'd like to know how soon we'll be allowed to leave. My wife's had a very unpleasant shock.'

The woman in question now piped up, 'It's all too horrible,' she said in a faint voice. 'I do wish you'd take me away, Neville.'

'There, there, my dear . . .' her spouse began, but then broke off, evidently becoming aware of the presence of the police. 'I suppose you must be the man in charge of all this,' he said, addressing Inspector Hawkins.

'I believe I am,' was the pleasant reply. 'And who might you be, sir?'

'Metcalfe's the name. I'm with the Air Ministry.'

'Are you, sir?' said the policeman, his tone nicely balanced between deference and sarcasm. 'I'll be sure to keep it in mind. I take it you're this lady's husband?'

'I am. And I must say, I consider it quite indefensible that she should have been subjected to questioning. Her nerves are far from strong, and—'

'You've taken the lady's address?' said Hawkins to his sergeant, cutting across this protest.

'Yes, sir.'

'Good. Then I needn't keep you,' said the Inspector to Metcalfe.

'You mean we're free to go?'

'Certainly. Now then, Sergeant, let's have the first of 'em in,' said the Inspector, paying no more attention to the Permanent Secretary and his wife. 'Who've we got? A French gentleman, by the sound of him. Lieutenant Bourgault,' he added, making a valiant attempt at pronouncing the name. 'Yes, sir. Gentleman says as he saw a suspicious character running away from Hangar

146

Three at around the time we're looking at.'

'Did he indeed?' said the Inspector. 'Then you'd better lead me to him.'

'That must have been the same man that I saw,' cried Irene Metcalfe excitedly. 'He ran right past me, you know.' She gave a little, shuddering laugh. 'Quite terrifying.'

'Don't be ridiculous, my dear,' said her husband sharply. 'You weren't anywhere near the place. You couldn't possibly have seen anything.'

'But Neville . . .'

'You're letting your nerves get the better of you, again,' said Metcalfe. 'Come along. I've got a car waiting. I said I'd have it back at the Ministry by one.'

It crossed Rowlands' mind as the couple – still arguing in an undertone – made their way towards the exit, that it had taken Metcalfe surprisingly little time to reach the aerodrome if he had come from Central London. Even in a fast car (and a Ministry car would surely be that), it couldn't have taken him less than three-quarters of an hour. They'd spent around twenty minutes down at the hangar, during which time Irene Metcalfe must have telephoned her husband. Five minutes to make the call left barely half an hour to make a journey which should take an hour, at the best of times. It couldn't be done, thought Rowlands – unless of course the man had been in the vicinity already. 'I remember Metcalfe,' said Stratham, breaking into these reflections. He must have been standing there all the time, thought Rowlands. 'He was in the Squadron, too – at the same time as I was, although

147

we were never what you'd call friends. Funny running into him again. Not that he remembered me. Seemed awfully het up, I thought. Stands to reason, I suppose. This murder business. Enough to put anybody's nose out of joint.'

'Yes,' said Percival. The uncomfortable silence which followed was broken by someone shouting from across the room.

'I say, Percival, old man! Got a minute?' It was Cecil Harmsworth.

'Oh, Lord – what does *he* want, I wonder?' muttered the airman; then, to Harmsworth, 'Be right with you . . .' At which he excused himself, and was gone. A moment later, he could be heard addressing his fellow pilot, his tone far from amused, 'All right, what's this all about?' Harmsworth's reply was lost in the general murmur of talk surrounding them, but something about the little exchange seemed to strike Stratham, for he murmured, 'I know that voice. He was in the RFC at the same time as the rest of us. What was the blighter's name? Hapgood, or Hollingsworth, or some such . . . Harmsworth. That's it! He joined the Squadron right after I did, in the spring of '15.'

'I imagine there must be quite a few of you about,' said Rowlands drily.

'Yes,' was the reply. 'Although it's rather odd to find him still hanging around Percival. After what happened, I mean. I shouldn't have thought they'd have much to say to one another.'

148

'Oh?' said Rowlands, more out of politeness than because he wanted to hear what was doubtless no more than a piece of Service gossip.

'Yes,' the other went on. 'It caused rather a stink at the time. Well, I mean, it's a bit like when a man gets accused of cheating at cards, only rather worse,' he said. 'There's no proof, either way, but it creates a bad impression, do you see?'

'Well . . .' said Rowlands, not sure that he did. But before Stratham could go on to explain, there came a cheerful shout from across the room.

# Chapter Eight

'I say, Stratham!' It was Hewitt, with another of the St Dunstan's men. 'Are you going to stand there gassing all day, or are we going to get some beers in?'

'Do excuse my friend, won't you?' said Stratham, with an embarrassed laugh. 'The excitement seems to have gone to his head. It was awfully nice to meet you, Miss Rowlands.' Then he was off, to join his chums at the bar.

'Nice chap,' said Dorothy to her brother.

'Yes, isn't he? Look,' he went on since he'd got her to himself for a minute. 'There's a bus back to Kingston in half an hour. I think we ought to be on it.' Even as he said it, he knew he hadn't much hope of persuading her. But surely, he thought, even someone as perverse as his sister could see how dangerous it was – for her to be caught up in a murder investigation when barely three years before she'd been implicated in another such case? She refused to see reason, of course.

'We can't leave now. What about the race?'

'But . . .' he began to object. Because surely even she wouldn't insist on staying if Percival wasn't going to take part? Just then Percival himself returned.

'I've just had some rather good news,' he said. 'Harmsworth's going to let me use his spare machine.'

'That *is* good news,' said Dorothy.

'Decent of him, isn't it? Especially when . . .' Percival let the sentence tail away, but it was clear what it was he meant. Especially when he and Harmsworth had been rivals for so long and had been at one another's throats not half an hour before. Yes, it was certainly decent of Harmsworth. 'Of course, I'm familiar with this particular machine,' Percival was explaining. 'Or it'd be out of the question to take her up, with so little time to prepare.'

'Yes, I see that,' said Dorothy. 'Rather like getting behind the wheel of a car one hasn't driven before.'

'Exactly like that.'

'I didn't know you could drive,' said Rowlands, making a determined effort to interrupt this tête-à- tête.

'Oh yes,' she replied coolly. 'I learnt when I was in Argentina. You had to, there.'

Resigning himself to the inevitable, Rowlands determined to stick as close to his sister and her companion

151

as possible, at least while there was still the chance that they might be taken for a couple by the other members of their party, or indeed by the Press, whose members were now in evidence. A group now stood around the Club House bar, awaiting developments in the murder story. 'If I don't file soon,' Rowlands heard one of them say, to sympathetic murmurs from his colleagues, 'it won't make the early editions.'

Yes, it wouldn't do to leave Dorothy at the mercy of such types, he thought. Because although playing gooseberry wasn't much to his taste, if it meant that his sister might escape an appearance in the gossip columns of the *News of the World* as 'Captain Percival's attractive, dark-haired companion', then he was willing to put up with it. Not that she was a bit grateful for this brotherly solicitude. 'You needn't hover quite so obviously, Fred,' she muttered as Percival excused himself once more – to go and see about the plane, as he put it – leaving them momentarily alone together.

'Was I hovering? I'm sorry,' said Rowlands innocently. 'I'm afraid I can't much help it. Not being able to see when I'm in the way, you know.'

Dorothy's answer to this was a disbelieving snort. 'I suppose,' she said after a moment, 'we might as well go and find ourselves something to drink. All this standing around is making me thirsty.'

'A cup of tea would be nice,' he agreed.

'I wasn't thinking of tea.'

'You've certainly changed your tastes,' he remarked as

they stood waiting for the barman to fetch their orders: a whisky and soda for Dorothy and half a bitter for Rowlands. Another snort. But then she said, 'As a matter of fact, I got the habit in Argentina. We liked a whisky every now and then, Viktor and I.' At this mention of her late husband, Dorothy's voice softened. 'As for my having "changed",' she went on. 'I don't think I *have* changed much. I've always known how to enjoy myself.' Which was true enough, thought Rowlands, recalling one particular episode in the past when his sister's love of pleasure had overwhelmed her judgement. Not that he was in any position to talk, he reminded himself. Their drinks arrived.

'Well, here's luck,' he said, raising his glass.

'Here's luck,' she echoed, touching her glass to his.

'I say – are we having a toast?' said a voice from behind Rowlands. It was Olave Malory. 'I think we should have a toast, don't you?' She thrust herself between the siblings so that she was standing close to Rowlands, so close that he could smell the gin on her breath. '*I'll* give you a toast. A toast to all the fliers – and one in particular. May he rot in hell,' she added, under her breath. It seemed to Rowlands that the room had fallen silent. So that his sister's words, although pronounced without undue emphasis, would have been audible to anyone standing near, the journalists at the bar amongst them.

'I don't think I'll drink to that, if it's all the same to you.'

The other woman laughed. It wasn't a pleasant laugh. 'I don't suppose you will,' she said. She took a swig of the

153

drink she was holding. 'It won't last, you know,' she added, still addressing Dorothy. 'So I wouldn't get your hopes up.'

'I don't know what you're talking about.'

Again came the laugh. This time it ended in a coughing fit. 'Oh, that's *too* killing,' gasped the aviatrix when she could speak. 'You'll be telling me next that you didn't spend the night with him.'

'That's enough,' said Rowlands.

'And who the bloody hell are you?' demanded Miss Malory. Then, placing him, 'Oh yes. You're the blind brother.' The thought seemed to amuse her. 'What the eye doesn't see, eh?'

'Why don't you put a sock in it?' said Dorothy fiercely.

'Heavens!' was the mocking response. 'I knew he sometimes went for the common sort, but *really* . . .'

Before she could expand upon this, there came another intervention, 'What on earth is going on?' said Alan Percival. 'Olave, I could hear your voice from outside the Club House.'

'Hello, my sweet,' was the reply. 'I've just been explaining to your latest popsy here that you're not to be relied upon.'

'You're making a spectacle of yourself,' said Percival coldly. 'And I don't think I'm going to stay here to listen to any more of your nonsense. Are you coming, Dorothy? We should be in time for some lunch before it all starts.'

'That's right,' said Olave Malory. 'Run away. Just as you always do. I'll tell you one thing, though – you'll

154

never get that plane of Cecil's up to scratch. They're temperamental machines, Avians.'

'Oh, I think I can handle it,' replied Percival. 'Rowlands, do join us for a bite,' he added, offhandedly. 'Can't promise that it'll be anything special, mind – but it'll keep the wolf from the door.'

'Thanks.' Ten minutes before, Rowlands would have been glad of any excuse to get out of the place, even at the behest of the man who'd so thoughtlessly compromised his sister's reputation. Not that it mattered a damn to him whom she slept with. She was a grown woman, wasn't she? It was the unwelcome publicity he'd hoped to avoid. Now, of course, the damage was done; couldn't have been much worse, in fact – a supposition confirmed as the three of them made their way towards the exit. Suddenly, one of the group of pressmen who'd been standing at the bar detached himself from his fellows.

'A word, if I may, Captain Percival,' he said. 'The name's Smythe – of *The Express*. I wonder if you'd like to say something to our readers about your hopes for the race?'

'I never comment on a race beforehand,' said Percival curtly.

'Yes, I suppose it could be seen as tempting fate,' laughed the journalist. 'What about this murder, though? You must have something to say about that. Seeing as how it happened right next to your plane.'

'I've nothing to say about that or anything else.'

'Like that, is it?' said the irrepressible Smythe. 'Well, you can't blame a man for trying! Perhaps a quick snap of yourself and the lady? Maybe she'd like to say a word or two? Our readers always like to get the woman's angle.'

'If you don't get that camera out of my face,' said the pilot, in a dangerously quiet voice, 'I'll make sure you never cover the King's Cup Race again. Or any other race, for that matter. Now let us pass, will you? I've a plane to fly. Jackals,' he muttered as they made their escape at last. 'They simply won't leave one alone.' He said it with real anger, but it occurred to Rowlands that even Percival could hardly have failed to see the connection between this journalistic intrusiveness and the fame he himself had courted.

Something of the sort must have occurred to Dorothy, for she said wryly, 'Tedious for you.'

'You might think it's awfully funny,' said Percival bitterly, 'but I can assure you it's not. Why, for two pins I'd . . .' But he was never to say what it was he would have done, because at that moment there came another interruption.

'Captain Percival, sir . . .' It was Bert Higgins, sounding as if he had been hurrying to catch up with them. 'Just to say as she's all ready for you, sir. The Avian, that is. Engine sounds as sweet as a nut. Although she's still not a patch on the Moth, if you want my opinion, but she'll do.'

'Good show,' said Percival. 'Who's down at the hangar now?'

'Just Ginger and one of the other lads, sir. But I've locked the place up. Thought it best, sir.'

'Quite right. Don't want any more funny business, do we? Chaps getting themselves killed and so forth.'

'No, sir.'

'Because I must say,' said Percival, as if to himself, 'I'm fed up to the back teeth with it all.'

Lunch, in spite of Percival's disclaimer, was very good: Beef Wellington with roast potatoes and carrots, washed down with a glass or two of a decent Bordeaux. Since the Club House restaurant was not large enough to accommodate the competitors – Rowlands judged there to be around fifty of these – trestle tables, covered with starched cloths, had been set up in a marquee. Here, they found a space between a group eagerly discussing the merits of the new Italian machine, and another comparing speeds achieved in the recent trials at Southampton Water. 'Hello, Percival!' called a voice Rowlands guessed from the accent to be that of the Count von Lowenstein. 'I hope you will not be too disappointed this afternoon.'

'Why should I be?'

'Why, when you fail to keep your title of winner of the race,' replied von Lowenstein, with evident satisfaction at this sally. 'Because you will have lost to me, you know.'

'I don't think so,' said Percival, with a laugh. 'You forget that I'm flying Harmsworth's Avian.'

'I do not forget. It is a good machine,' said the German,

with no less affability. 'But not, I think, as good as my Fokker.'

'That remains to be seen,' said the champion. 'And now, if you don't mind, old boy, I'd like to finish my lunch.'

'I'm surprised you can eat,' said Dorothy. 'Don't you have any nerves at all?'

'None. Which is why I'm so good at what I do,' said Percival. 'The last time I felt sick before flying was during the war, and that was only because I didn't like being shot at. Compared to that experience, this is a piece of cake. Oh Lord!' he said suddenly. 'There's that wretched child again. I do wish she'd stop following me around.'

'Who?' Dorothy made no attempt to conceal her interest. 'Oh, you mean your Miss Wilkie.'

'She isn't *my* Miss Wilkie,' said Percival. 'Kid's got a bit of a crush on me, that's all. Now she's looking this way. Don't catch her eye, will you?'

'I'm afraid she's already seen us.'

'Damn and blast' said Percival in an undertone; then, with forced heartiness as the girl appeared, 'Oh, hello, Wilkie. Come for a spot of grub? I'm afraid you've left it a bit late.'

'I say – look out!' said Dorothy. In the same moment, came an anguished cry from Wilkie – 'Oh no!'– and then the sound of a glass breaking.

'That was clumsy,' said Percival after the silence which followed. 'Awful waste of good wine. You've ruined that pretty frock of yours, too.'

'Never mind.' This was Dorothy. 'I'm sure it'll come

out.' The tone she used in speaking to the girl was unusually gentle. 'Come on. Let's go and find some water, shall we?'

'I can manage by myself, thanks,' said Wilkie coldly. It was obvious that she had taken a dislike to Dorothy. Without another word, she dashed off.

'I think you were a bit hard on her,' said Dorothy.

'Do you?' Percival's tone was one of bored indifference. 'Perhaps I was. But you've no idea how maddening it can be, having some star-struck kid making sheep's eyes at you all day long. I mean, it's hardly my fault if . . .' He let the sentence tail away. 'Good Lord! Is that the time? I'd better be pushing along. I say, wish me luck, old thing.'

There followed the sound of a kiss.

'Good luck,' said Dorothy.

'Not that I'll need it, of course. Be seeing you, Rowlands, old man.'

'Yes,' said Rowlands. The two men shook hands. 'And best of luck.'

'Thanks.' Percival went to join the throng of pilots streaming out of the marquee towards where the aeroplanes were waiting.

'Well,' said Rowlands when his sister showed no sign of moving. 'I suppose we ought to be making our way, too. Since you're determined to see this race.'

'Mm,' she said absently. 'You know, it's the strangest thing . . .' But whatever it was she'd been going to say, she never got the chance to say it, for at that moment there came the announcement that the race was about to

159

start. They found the seats Percival had reserved for them with minutes to spare as the loudspeaker was blaring out the names of the contestants, of which there were forty-one, all told. Most of the names meant little to Rowlands, but a few caught his attention as belonging to those he'd heard in the vicinity of Hangar Three, after the murder.

'First to make his appearance at the starting line, ladies and gentlemen is Lieutenant Bourgault, in his Nieuport-Delage. The dashing Frenchman has three wins to his credit – the last being at the Paris Air Show, two years ago . . . and now here's Signor Mazzini in his Macchi . . . a very fine-looking machine . . . Another face familiar to flying enthusiasts is Mr Hank Harrington, in his Bluebird . . . I understand Mr Harrington is planning another cross-Atlantic flight before too long, after the one he was forced to abandon on account of bad weather . . . Count von Lowenstein is now climbing into his Fokker VII . . . the Count has high hopes for this race, I gather. He has twice broken the speed record for planes in his class at the Berlin Air Show . . .'

Any one of them could have murdered Bill Farley, thought Rowlands, and yet what motive did any of them have? Until that was established, there could be no hope of catching the killer.

'Just taxiing up to the starting line is Miss Olave Malory, in her apple-green Puss Moth, with flying suit to match. If there were a prize for the most elegant turnout, I'm sure the charming Miss Malory would win hands down!' A cheer went up. 'And here's the champion now,' went on the announcer, perhaps superfluously. 'A very popular contestant is Captain Percival, now flying Mr Harmsworth's Avian instead of his usual Gipsy Moth.'

'I don't like the look of those clouds,' said Dorothy in Rowlands' ear. 'Surely they won't let them take off in this?'

He shrugged. 'I'm sure they know what they're doing.'

'I hope you're right.'

Why was she so nervous, all of a sudden? he wondered. It wasn't like Dottie at all. But just then the announcer's voice, which had been going on all the while, grew louder. '. . . and this is the moment, ladies and gentlemen – the moment we've all been waiting for.' All around, the excited murmur rose to a crescendo before subsiding into anticipatory silence. There came the crack of the starting pistol. 'They're off!' Forty-one engines roared into life, and forty-one sets of propellers began to revolve. Even though he couldn't see what was happening, Rowlands couldn't help but feel a surge of excitement as the great winged machines began to move along the runway, gathering speed. He remembered the extraordinary feeling of freedom he'd felt that day with Percival as they took to the air. It was true what they said about flying, he thought. There was nothing like it.

The announcer was almost beside himself now. 'There goes Mrs Fenishaw, in her cherry-coloured Avro Baby, taking an early lead . . . with Captain Harmsworth on her tail, in his silver Widgeon . . . then Signor Mazzini . . . the Count . . . Mr Harrington . . . Flight Lieutenant Phillips . . . Mr Carr . . . Miss Snow . . . Flying Officer

Martindale ... and Captain Percival. Now they're all airborne, except for Miss Malory. Looks as if she might be having a spot of engine trouble ... Yes, the mechanics are running over to see what's what. So it's forty planes, not forty-one, who'll be on their way to Southampton. What a splendid sight, ladies and gentlemen!'

For Rowlands, this spectacle was translated into sound: forty engines, droning in unison, like a swarm of angry bees – a sound that grew gradually fainter as the aeroplanes disappeared into the distance. 'They're flying straight into the storm,' murmured Dorothy. 'It's pitch black over there.'

'Now you'll see them start to climb to fifteen hundred feet,' continued the voice from the loudspeaker. 'Weather's looking a bit uncertain, but I'm assured it will clear up later ... At the moment, visibility's rather poor, but you can just make out the leaders as they start to make the turn towards the south-west ... The Fokker's in the lead ... No, it's being overtake by the Avian ...'

'That's Alan's plane,' said Dorothy.

'Yes, it looks as Captain Percival has established a clear lead,' said the announcer, confirming this. 'Will he be able to maintain it over the distance, I wonder, and make this the hat-trick? Only time will tell, and there are certainly quite a few challengers to his title competing today ... Oh, I say! That's nicely done! He's beginning his turn ... banking quite steeply towards the left ... In a moment you'll see him start to correct his course so that he doesn't ...'

There came a gasp from the watching crowd.

'My God!' The announcer's voice was a shocked whisper. 'What's happening? The plane's flipped over . . . He seems to have completely lost control . . . The plane's spiralling down and . . . Oh, my God! This is too awful . . .'

The voice broke off abruptly. What followed was the terrible sound of an explosion.

The moments immediately following the crash had the quality of a nightmare. Pushing their way through the press of bodies milling around the stands seemed to take forever. Nor were they the only ones who wanted to get out. 'I say – will you let us get by?' said a man behind Rowlands, in agitated tones. 'My wife's feeling rather faint.' Other voices, no less vehement, came from all directions:

'. . . ought never to have let him fly. It wasn't his plane, you know . . .'

'. . . awful for the kiddies to see something like that . . .'

'. . . too late to call it off. Still, you'd think, under the circumstances . . .'

Over the hubbub came the announcer's voice, hoarse with desperation, 'Ladies and gentlemen – please! Remain in your seats – do! There's really no cause for alarm.'

Rowlands' head rang with the noise. He felt stupefied; unable to take in what had happened. It didn't seem possible, he thought. One minute Percival had been talking to them, the next . . . He shook his head in disbelief.

Ridiculous. The waste . . . He felt Dorothy clutch his arm as if she were afraid she might fall if she did not. 'Are you all right?' he asked her gently. She made no reply; nor did he really expect one. 'Let's go and see if there's anything we can do,' he said, knowing that it was unlikely they or anyone else would be able to do anything for Alan Percival now. Just then, there came the sound of a clanging bell, and a moment later, an ambulance passed them, going at full tilt towards the site of the crash, Rowlands guessed. 'Perhaps, after all . . .' he started to say, but his sister cut across him. 'You didn't see what happened. I did,' she said. 'No one could have walked away from that.'

In the Club House, people were standing around, talking in shocked tones. 'Does anyone know what happened?' said someone as Rowlands and Dorothy came in.

'God knows,' was the reply. 'Engine failure, one supposes.' Then someone else came up to them: it was Olave Malory.

'Is it true what they're saying?' she demanded. 'I mean that it's Alan's plane . . .'

'Yes.' He didn't attempt to soften the blow, and her reaction, in any case, seemed more angry than shocked.

'I told him he should never have taken up Cecil's offer!' she cried. 'He hadn't had nearly enough flying time in that machine. Now he's killed himself, the bloody fool.'

'We don't know that he's dead,' objected Rowlands.

'Oh, he's dead all right.' Her laugh had the shrill note of hysteria. 'Or if he isn't, I hope he soon will be. You

164

obviously haven't seen what happens to the pilot when a plane crashes.'

'I have,' said Rowlands. 'But there's still a chance he'll have survived.'

'Yes, worse luck.' Suddenly she burst into tears. 'Oh, the bloody fool, the bloody fool,' she wept.

'Look . . .' Rowlands began awkwardly. But it was Dorothy who took charge.

'Come on,' she said. 'You need a drink.'

'I've had enough, wouldn't you say?' But she allowed the other woman to order her a brandy.

'You'd better have one, too,' said Rowlands to his sister.

'I'm all right.' But her hand, when he touched it, was cold as ice. 'Do you think he could have lived through that?' she said.

'I don't know.' He found a couple of chairs and made both women sit down. 'People survive all sorts of things. We'll have to wait until the ambulance comes back.' Around him, the conversational murmur rose in volume as people argued over what exactly had happened. He thought he recognised the voice of Smythe, the journalist.

'Yes, they're holding the front page until we get all the facts,' he was saying. What was it Percival had said? Jackals. Well, he'd been right about that. In death, as in life, it seemed, the Ace was headline news.

A few minutes passed during which nobody said very much at all. Like the pressman and his colleagues, they were all waiting for the facts of the disaster. Then came the clanging of the ambulance's bell as the vehicle sped towards the gate. This precipitated a rush to the door, on the part of the Press crew. 'Looks like he's still alive, after all,' said Smythe, who seemed to have appointed himself their leader.

'We need to get someone to the hospital,' said another of their number. 'Joe, you stay here, in case there's a statement from the aerodrome about what caused it.'

Just then, the door opened and someone came in.

'Any news?' demanded Smythe.

'He's alive – just,' was the reply. It was Bert Higgins who'd spoken. 'We managed to pull him out, but . . .' His voice tailed off, and he seemed to be struggling to find the words. 'P-plane's a complete wreck,' he managed at last. 'What I don't understand is . . .'

'Did he say anything?' someone else interjected. It was Wilkie, Rowlands realised. She must have been there all along, poor kid.

'He couldn't hardly speak, poor blighter.' Higgins sounded close to tears. 'All he said was something about the ailerons jamming. It didn't make no sense. We checked the thing from top to bottom, not half an hour before he took off. Give me a beer,' he said to the barman. The latter seemed reluctant to comply with this request.

'Now then, Bert. You know we're not supposed to serve ground crew in here.'

'Oh for the love of God!' cried Olave Malory. 'Give him a bloody beer. You can put it on my account,' she added.

'That's awfully good of you, Miss,' said Higgins. 'Only this business with the Captain's upset me something terrible.' It took a bit of persuasion on the aviatrix's part to get him to join their party. 'It doesn't seem quite right, miss, thanks all the same. You being with your friends, like.'

'Oh yes, we're all the best of friends here,' she said sarcastically. 'Sit down, for heaven's sake, man. Do you think any of that matters now?'

Rowlands went over to speak to Pauline Wilkinson, who was sitting by herself on the far side of the bar. 'Can I get you anything?' he asked. 'A cup of tea, perhaps?'

'No, thanks.' Her voice was a dull monotone.

'Only you've had a shock,' he persisted gently. 'A cup of tea or . . . or a lemonade might do you good.'

'I said I didn't want anything!' snapped the girl.

'All right.' He was just turning away when she said, with a tremor in her voice that suggested she was close to breaking down, 'Do you think he'd have suffered?' He knew it was Percival she meant.

'I don't know,' he said. 'We can only hope that he didn't know too much about it.' It occurred to him that she ought not to be by herself. 'Why don't you join us?' he said. 'You know Miss Malory, don't you – and Bert, of course? And I think you've met my sister.'

'Thanks, but I'm quite all right here,' said the girl, in the same flat voice as before. He realised that in her present state – almost, it seemed to him, as if she hadn't quite taken in what had happened – she wasn't to be persuaded.

167

'Well, the offer's there,' he said. 'Sometimes it helps to have company.'

Not that the rest of his party seemed to be deriving much comfort from one another's presence if their morose silence was anything to go by. 'What I don't understand,' Bert Higgins said after some minutes had elapsed, 'is how it happened. I checked the machine myself. There was nothing the matter with it. I suppose they'll say it was my fault,' he added gloomily, taking a pull of his beer.

'If he'd only listened to me,' said Olave Malory, the effects of the brandy and whatever else she'd been drinking before that now apparent in her slurred speech. 'I told him that plane was no good.'

'That's utter rot and you know it,' said a voice from the door. The aviatrix gave a gasp.

'Cecil! What on earth . . . I thought you'd be on your way to Southampton by now.'

'I turned back. After I'd seen the Avian go down . . . Well, I didn't think it was right to carry on, that's all.'

'Decent of you,' muttered Miss Malory into her glass.

'You can sneer all you like, Olave, but I felt it was the right thing to do,' said Harmsworth. 'Give me a whisky,' he added in an undertone to the barman. 'Percival was a friend of mine.'

'I know, I know.'

'We went through the war together, damn it! As for the plane being no good, as you put it, I can assure you it had passed all the latest safely checks.'

'That's the truth,' put in Higgins. 'I'll swear to it.'

'You may be having to swear to something else, my lad,' said a voice from the door where a commotion of heavy boots announced the arrival of Inspector Hawkins and his cohorts. 'I'd like you to come with me, if you will – and look sharp about it.' But Higgins, since it was evidently he who had been addressed, wasn't prepared to fall in with this request without demur.

'Why? What have I done?' he said. 'If it's about Captain Percival's plane, I can tell you right now that there was nothing the matter with it.'

I don't know anything about a plane,' said Hawkins. 'Although I'm sorry to hear about the Captain's accident. This is about something else. Your friend Farley's murder, to be exact. Perhaps, in all the excitement, it'd slipped your mind?' he added sarcastically.

''Course not,' mumbled Higgins.

'Good. Then perhaps you'll come with me?'

'But I don't see why. I've told you all I know,' protested the mechanic. Rowlands got to his feet.

'Inspector, I don't know what this is all about,' he said. 'But I'm sure I can vouch for Mr Higgins' movements around the time of the murder.'

'Can you?' said the policeman. 'Then perhaps you can explain this. All right, Sergeant,' he added to one of his subordinates, who now stepped forward. He must have produced some item of evidence – was it the murder weapon, Rowlands wondered, because there was a murmur of surprise from those standing nearby. Someone

– one of the Pressmen, he guessed – let out a low whistle.

'What is it?' he asked Dorothy, exasperated that he, out of all of them there, was the only one not to be 'in the picture'.

Before she could reply, the question was answered for him. 'Those are my overalls,' said Higgins in a wondering tone. 'Indeed,' said the Inspector grimly. 'They were found in your locker just now. With – you'll note a button missing,' he added, perhaps for Rowlands' benefit.

'But . . . how did they come to be covered in blood? You don't think . . .' Higgins must have made a bolt for the door, for there came the sound of a scuffle, and a barked instruction from the Inspector, 'Hold him, lads!'

'I didn't do it,' panted Higgins, thus restrained. 'You'll not pin it on me!'

'Pipe down,' said the Inspector severely. 'Well, you've asked for it, my lad. Since you refused to come quietly, I'm afraid we'll have to do the business here. Albert Higgins, I am arresting you on suspicion of the murder of William Farley. I should warn you that anything you say . . .'

'I tell you, I didn't do it!'

'That's enough. Take him away,' said Hawkins to his sergeant. 'I'll thank you to keep this unfortunate incident to yourselves for the time being, ladies and gentlemen,' he went on, addressing the rest of the occupants of the Club House, who now stood in a silent huddle. 'You' – this was to the journalists still remaining at the bar – 'can say there's been an arrest, that's all. There'll be further details given out at the press conference.'

# Chapter Nine

The stunned silence after the police had left lasted for what seemed to Rowlands a long time. It was as if, coming on top of the horror of the crash, the fact that the killer had been caught was too much to take in. He himself found it hard to believe. Surely it didn't add up? 'If the overalls are his,' he mused aloud, 'then he must have been wearing them when he rushed past me, through the shrubbery. But I don't see that he'd have had time to change out of them – the bloodstained ones, I mean – and into the clean pair he must have been wearing when he spoke to Mrs Metcalfe.'

'Well he obviously must have had time, or the police wouldn't have decided to arrest him,' said Olave Malory.

'To think,' she went on, with a shudder, 'that I actually invited him to join us. It isn't every day that one can say one's had a murderer as a drinking companion. But I suppose this isn't like any other day,' she added bleakly.

'Do we have to talk about it?' said Dorothy. 'It's all too horrible.'

Another silence followed. We're all waiting, thought Rowlands, although no one seemed very sure what exactly they were waiting for. 'Perhaps we should go,' he said to Dorothy, but she rebuffed the suggestion angrily.

'We can't leave now. There might be some news from the hospital.'

'Yes. But it might not be for hours yet.'

Suddenly she broke down. 'Oh, Fred,' she wept. 'I can't bear it.'

He put his arm around her. 'Chin up, old thing,' he said. Why was it that one always said such meaningless things at these times? 'It'll be all right, you'll see.'

'It's just that it's brought it all back. What happened with Viktor . . .'

'I know.' He took the clean handkerchief from his breast pocket, and gave it to her.

'Thanks.' She blew her nose.

'Come on,' he said. 'There's no sense in hanging around here. We can telephone the hospital when we get home.'

But as it turned out, there was no need. Because as they got to their feet, the door opened and someone hurried in. 'Give me a large whisky,' said this person to

172

the barman. It was Smythe, the journalist. He gulped the drink down. 'That's better,' he said. 'Give us another, will you? The paper'll pay.'

'You've come from the hospital, haven't you?' demanded Dorothy. 'Is there any news? How is he? Has he come round?'

Smythe gave a sour little laugh. 'Oh, it's you,' he said. 'The mysterious Dark Lady. I don't suppose you'll give me a story now? Thought not. News? Yes, I'm sorry to say there is some news – but not the kind you were hoping for, I'd guess. Alan Percival died twenty minutes ago. God rest his soul,' he added sanctimoniously. 'And I,' he added to no one in particular, 'am going to get stinko. You see if I don't.' But no one was paying any further attention to the journalist. Because it was then that there came a cry from the far side of the room, followed by the thud of a body falling to the floor.

'It's that girl,' said Dorothy. 'She's fainted, poor kid. You stay here,' she added to Rowlands. 'I'll see to her.'

'How is she?' said Rowlands in a low voice to his wife. It was the evening of the same day; they'd had dinner, and the two of them were sitting over their coffee in front of the unlit fire in the sitting room – it being too cool to sit outside – at the end of what had been an unseasonably stormy day.

'She was almost asleep when I looked in,' replied Edith. 'I've given her a couple of aspirin, with a mug of Ovaltine to wash it down. It's supposed to be good for the nerves,' said she, who never suffered from them.

173

'And what about . . . ?' He jerked his chin upwards, to indicate another member of their household.

'She's reading to the boys,' said Edith. 'But I think . . .'

'Shh . . .' he said, hearing the creak of a footfall on the stairs. But it was only Edith's mother. 'All quiet on the home front,' she said cheerily. 'The girls are asleep, and when I peeped into dear Dorothy's room just now, she was curled up on Victor's bed, with the little boys on either side of her. All three of them dead to the world.'

'Glad to hear it,' said Rowlands. 'After the day she's had . . .'

'Yes, it must have been dreadful for you both,' said Helen Edwards, sitting herself down in her usual chair across from where the two of them were sitting. 'Now, where did I put my embroidery? Ah, there it is! All I need is my glasses. Quite dreadful. Given that you were such good friends with Captain Percival.'

'Hardly that,' said Rowlands. 'But it was certainly a shock.'

'How the dear children will take it, I dread to imagine,' went on his mother-in-law. 'Anne especially. She's a sensitive child, you know, and she quite hero-worshipped that poor young man.'

'I'll tell her tomorrow,' said Edith. It had been tacitly agreed not to say anything about the accident to the girls before it was unavoidable. With one distraught child on their hands – because what else was Pauline Wilkinson if not that? – to have coped with the distress of the others would have been too much for them both, Rowlands thought.

'You know,' said Mrs Edwards as if she half-guessed this, 'I'd have been happy to have the poor young thing in with me tonight. Ridiculous to have that large room all to myself.'

'That's kind of you, Mother, but I'm sure we'll manage,' said Edith firmly. After a brief discussion between her and Rowlands, it had been decided to put up the camp bed in their bedroom where, as Edith (a former VAD) had put it, she could keep an eye on the patient. Rowlands would rough it that night on the sofa, which was not, he'd remarked humorously, the worst bed he'd ever slept in. In the morning, always supposing Miss Wilkinson had got over her attack of nerves, he'd see about returning her to her family.

Establishing where this was to be found and of whom it consisted hadn't been easy. There was an aunt, she said – that is, when Rowlands was able to get her to say anything. After she'd come round from her faint, the girl had fallen into what seemed like a catatonic fit, speaking only when spoken to, and then in monosyllables. The aunt had a house in Maida Vale where Wilkie had a room, it eventually transpired. Since the girl made no mention of her parents, Rowlands supposed that they were out of the picture. Perhaps they were dead; he hadn't liked to press her on the point.

All he'd succeeded in getting from her was the aunt's telephone number. 'Because she'll be worried about you, won't she?' he'd said. To which she made no reply –

175

unless it was a shrug. He'd telephoned as soon as they got home, because when all was said and done, she *was* only seventeen. The telephone had rung for what seemed to him a long time before someone – a woman; elderly from the sound of her – had answered. 'May I speak to Miss Wilkinson?' he'd said.

'Who?' He repeated what he'd just said.

'There's no one of that name here.' He tried again. 'I mean Pauline Wilkinson's aunt. This is Kilburn three-nine-four?'

'It is. You mean Miss Denham, I expect.'

'Yes, that's right. Could you put me through to her, please?'

'She's resting.'

'Well then, perhaps I could leave a message?' Which he accordingly did, to the effect that Pauline would be spending the night with friends, and would be back the following day. He left his number and address, adding for good measure that he was Secretary to St Dunstan's in Regent's Park, in case Miss Denham should want to check his bona fides. So far she hadn't seen fit to, which made Rowlands wonder a bit about the kind of woman she was.

'Would you like the wireless on?' his wife was saying.

'I don't think so, thanks, if it's all the same to you.' It'd be all over the news, he thought – the plane crash, and probably the murder, too; although the death of the celebrated Flying Ace would doubtless trump that of the ground engineer. What a day it had been! He hoped Dorothy was all right. She'd hardly said a word on the drive home. It had been Olave Malory who'd brought them back to Kingston in her Aston Martin. 'I absolutely insist,' she'd said when it had emerged that he and Dorothy, with their young charge in tow, had intended getting the bus. 'It's practically on my way.' She lived in Richmond. 'And after you were so decent to me.' He hadn't been particularly decent. But he let it pass, knowing that, for her, it had meant something that they'd been together when they heard the news of Percival's death.

'I wish I could have persuaded Miss Malory to stay to supper,' said Edith. Sometimes his wife's ability to read his mind stuck him as uncanny. 'Of course, it was only cold meat and salad, but . . .'

'She said she had to get back.'

'I know. Poor thing, it must have been terrible for her,' said Edith. 'Given that they were practically engaged, if one believes what the papers say.' Never a good idea, thought Rowlands. He made a noncommittal sound. For obvious reasons, he'd been unable to put Edith in the picture with regard to Dorothy's relationship with Percival. Not that he was entirely sure what that was himself. As matters stood, it might be best to let sleeping dogs lie. The telephone rang in the hall.

'That'll be the aunt,' he said. He got up to answer it. 'Miss Denham?' he said. 'This is Frederick Rowlands. I expect you've rung about your niece.'

'What's that?' said a voice he recognised. 'I don't have a niece. You must be thinking of someone else.'

'Hello, Mrs Metcalfe,' he said. 'Yes, I was expecting another call. What can I do for you?'

'I heard what happened,' she said. 'I was listening to it on the wireless . . . the race, I mean . . . when they said . . .' She broke off, then went on after a moment. 'They said it was his plane that had crashed. That he'd been badly injured and . . .' Again she seemed unable to get the words out.

'It must have been a dreadful shock,' said Rowlands gently.

Irene Metcalfe drew a shuddering breath. 'Just now, I heard it on the news. That he was . . .'

'Yes,' he said. 'I'm sorry.'

'Then it's true?'

'I'm afraid so.'

She was crying, now.

'Mrs Metcalfe. Please . . .' Where the blazes was her husband, he thought irritably. Surely he ought to be the one to comfort her, instead of a virtual stranger, like himself. But then it occurred to him that Neville Metcalfe was hardly the ideal person to console his wife over the death of a man with whom she gave every sign of having been in love. As if conjured by his thought, he heard a voice at the other end of the line call, 'Reenie?' and then a gasp from Irene Metcalfe.

'That's my husband! Won't be a minute, darling,' she said loudly. 'I have to talk to you,' she said to Rowlands in a lower tone. 'It's about what happened.'

'You mean about Captain Percival's death?'

178

'No. Before that. The murder. The fact is, I've remembered something.'

'If it's about the murder, don't you think you ought to telephone the police?' he said. But she insisted stubbornly, 'It's you I want to talk to. I know you'll be able to help me.'

'Irene!' came the peremptory summons once again.

'I have to go,' whispered Mrs Metcalfe. 'Promise me you'll come and see me. Tomorrow.'

'It's Sunday tomorrow,' he reminded her. 'I won't be at the office until Monday morning.'

'Well, make it Monday then,' she said. 'Teatime would be best. I'll be on my own then.'

'All right,' he said. 'Monday at teatime it is. But I still don't see how I can possibly . . .' She'd rung off. Cursing his luck, which had made him a magnet, it seemed, for unpredictable females, he stood for a moment, the receiver heavy in his hand, and the feeling that something, somewhere, wasn't right.

He was on the point of pouring himself a second cup of tea when he heard someone come downstairs. It wasn't Edith: he knew her step, and in any case, she was getting Joan dressed. He heard a door being opened across the hall, and a moment after, the door of the breakfast room was flung open and Pauline Wilkinson came in. 'I say!' she cried. 'What a jolly house! It's got ever so many rooms. I looked into the other one first – the sitting room, I mean – but then plumped for this one. Second time

179

lucky!' she laughed. 'I say – is it all right if I help myself to toast? I'm ravenous.'

'Go ahead,' said Rowlands, a little taken aback by this metamorphosis. The stricken waif of yesterday had vanished, replaced by this bouncing tomboy. She really was the most volatile young woman he'd ever met, he thought. 'There's a cup of tea in the pot,' he said.

'Thanks, but I don't care for tea,' she said. 'A glass of milk'd be just the thing, though.' She helped herself, and took an appreciative gulp. 'That's better. Nothing like milk to set one up for the day. But where are the kiddies?' she demanded suddenly. 'I was sure they'd be up and about by now.'

'It's the school holidays,' Rowlands pointed out. He assumed that this loud cheerfulness must be no more than a front, to cover up her real feelings. If so, she was making a good job of it. 'They'll be down in a minute, I expect.'

'Jolly good. I wouldn't want to leave without saying hello to young Anne,' said Wilkie, buttering herself a slice of toast. 'Scrumptious marmalade, this. Is it homemade?'

The door opened, and Edith came in with Joan. A moment later, Margaret and Anne followed, with their grandmother bringing up the rear. 'Oh, hello, Mrs R,' sang out Wilkie. 'I was just saying what awfully good marmalade this is.'

'Yes,' said Edith. 'I heard you. Anne, sit down, please.'

'I don't want any breakfast,' said the child.

180

'Then you can just sit at table until the rest of us have had ours,' replied her mother. 'And don't bite your nails.'

'I say, Anne, I'll bet you anything you can't eat your toast as fast as I can eat mine,' said Wilkie. 'Go on, take a piece. Want me to butter it for you?'

'No, thank you,' said Anne.

'Yes, I know it's beastly that Captain Percival's dead, but we've all got to carry on, haven't we?' said the young woman. 'Margaret's eating her toast – look!'

'Margaret didn't care about Captain Percival as much as I did,' said Anne.

In the end, their young guest was with them another night. 'Oh, Auntie won't mind,' she said when it was suggested that Miss Denham might want her at home. 'She knows I'm with friends. I often spend weekends away,' she added airily. And really, Edith pointed out, she was no trouble at all. She'd come with them to church, and positively insisted on helping with the washing-up after lunch. In the afternoon, she and the three older children had taken a picnic on the river.

'Wilkie's ever so good at climbing trees,' said Anne when the four of them returned from this excursion. 'She's got a knife with five blades, and a corkscrew, and a thing for taking stones out of horses' hooves. And she showed us how to make a fire so that we could boil the kettle.' Anne, though still in mourning for Captain Percival, was evidently in the process of transferring her affections to someone else.

On Monday morning, Rowlands offered to escort

Miss Wilkinson back to the airport so that she could collect her motor bicycle, but she wouldn't hear of it. 'I'm quite capable of getting the bus by myself,' she said. Because of course, he reminded himself, as he walked back from the bus stop, appearances notwithstanding, she wasn't a child, but a grown woman. Appearances. How one stuck with the old ways of thinking! After all the years he'd had to make do without sight, he still persisted in trying to form a mental picture of what people looked like. Some of this was automatic: one could estimate a person's height, and build, and a good deal about their general state of health and vigour, from simply shaking hands; the height at which someone's voice emerged was another useful clue.

He'd have put Wilkie's height at five foot nine, or thereabouts, which was tall for a woman. Edith was five foot four. As to build, and general vigour – well she was a healthy modern girl, that much was obvious – not one of your sensitive, bookish types. Short hair, he guessed – red or light brown in colour – and blue, or perhaps hazel, eyes. Whimsically he added a snub nose and freckles. Yes, it was funny, the pictures one built up in one's mind. It was rather like the images of people one saw in dreams: one recognised them without ever looking directly at them; their features remained shadowy although one knew who they were beyond the shadow of a doubt. And in his dreams, like the blind poet Milton, he'd always been able to see – a trick of memory, he supposed.

He was whistling – a habit contracted in his St Dunstan's

days – as he lifted the latch of the garden gate and walked up the path to the front door of Number 44. Most of the men he'd got to know at the Lodge in Regent's Park, during the early days of his blindness, whistled, hummed or sang as they walked along, by way of alerting others to their presence. All in all, they'd been quite a musical bunch. He was still smiling at the memory as he went to put his key in the lock. Before he could do so, the door opened suddenly. 'Now that sounds like a happy man,' said a voice he knew.

At once the smile froze on his face. 'Chief Inspector Douglas,' he said, at which the other laughed delightedly.

'Aye, it's me, right enough. Now what gave me away, I wonder? You'll be telling me it was the accent, but I've always said it was the other man who had the accent, d'ye see?' Chuckling at his own joke, he stepped back to let Rowlands come in.

'What brings you here, Chief Inspector?' Rowlands made an effort to keep his voice level. They've caught up with her at last, he thought. A cold horror filled him. 'I take it this isn't a social call?'

'No, indeed,' said Douglas. All laughter had now gone from his voice. 'It's about a very serious matter indeed.'

'I see.' He must play for time, he thought. 'Well, I'm not sure how I can help you.' All he could think about was that Dorothy was upstairs, perhaps still asleep. Did this man, whom he'd once thought of as his friend, mean to drag her from her bed, in front of her children, in order to arrest her? If so, he'd better think again. Blind as he was, Rowlands knew he was still capable of putting up a fight. Unconsciously, he squared his shoulders. Had Douglas come alone, he wondered, or were there a couple of police constables waiting outside in the car? 'You'd be surprised,' Douglas was saying. 'You see . . .'

'No need to stand about in the hall, Chief Inspector,' said Edith from the doorway of the sitting room. 'Do please make use of this room. It'll be more comfortable.'

'That's kind of you, Mrs Rowlands,' said Douglas meekly. 'After you, Rowlands.'

'I'll make some tea,' said Edith. As she brushed past him, on her way to the kitchen, Rowlands felt a sharp pinch on his arm. A warning of sorts. But this left him none the wiser.

'You seem distracted, Mr Rowlands, if I might say so,' said the Scotsman. 'Is there anything particular on your mind?'

It took an effort of will for Rowlands not to gape at him. Was this some kind of cruel joke? 'No. That is . . . You might have telephoned to say you were coming,' he managed to reply. 'I . . . I have to leave for work in the next few minutes.'

'Oh, this won't take long,' said the other. 'It's just that you're in a position to help me, y'see.'

'I don't see how.'

'Let me explain. It's come to my attention that you were one of the last to see Captain Percival alive.'

So this was about Percival! Rowlands tried to keep the relief from his voice. 'That's true,' he said. 'But I still don't see . . .'

184

'You were there when the accident took place, I gather?'

'Yes.'

'Perhaps it might make things clearer if I tell you that it wasn't an accident. It appears the plane was tampered with.'

'What!'

'Och, yes, there's no doubt about it at all. I'm no expert on these matters, so you'll have to bear with me, but apparently a piece of wire was introduced into the mechanism of the aeroplane in such a way that it caused the ailerons – is that the right term? – to jam. So that when the pilot – Captain Percival, that is – tried to perform some crucial manoeuvre, the whole thing seized up, as it were, and went into a spin.'

'He said something about the ailerons,' said Rowlands. 'Alan Percival, I mean. It was after they pulled him out of the wreckage.' He frowned. 'But wasn't the plane completely smashed up?'

'It was,' said Douglas. 'Burnt to a cinder, too. Yes, there wasn't very much left of it at all. Although if you knew what to look for, the fact that it had been tampered with was obvious, I'm told. They found the wire, you see. Wrapped around the chain that controlled the movements of these ailerons we've mentioned. A cotter pin had been put in the wrong way round, too. That by itself could have been accidental, but with the wire there . . . well, it was a clear case of sabotage.' He allowed a pause to elapse. 'I can see you're wondering what alerted them –

the investigators – in the first place. It's this: they found that another plane had been fixed in the exact same way. Cotter pin the wrong way round, wire wrapped around the chain so that the cogs would seize up and the ailerons – such a useful word! – would jam as a result.'

'Whose plane was it?' asked Rowlands, although he'd guessed what the answer would be.

'Captain Percival's. Not the one he eventually flew, but . . .'

'The Gipsy Moth.'

'Got it in one,' said the Chief Inspector. 'So you see it wasn't an accident.'

'No,' said Rowlands. He was silent a moment. 'I don't believe Bert Higgins could have done such a thing,' he said at last.

'He had the know-how,' the other replied.

'Yes, but what was his motive?'

Douglas laughed. 'I knew I could count on you not to be taken in by appearances, Mr Rowlands,' he said. 'As it happens, there doesn't seem to be any clear motive as yet as to why Higgins should have sabotaged that plane. But he had the opportunity, and so, given that he killed Farley . . .'

'Has he confessed to that?'

Another chuckle. 'I'm glad to see you're still as hard to convince as ever,' said the Chief Inspector. 'No, as it happens, he denies all knowledge of Farley's murder. Although you'll admit it looks pretty black for him, with those overalls covered in Farley's blood being found in the man's locker.'

'I suppose they could have been put there by someone else,' said Rowlands.

'That's just what Higgins says,' was the reply. 'Och, he swears blind he had nothing to do with it. But Hawkins – you met Inspector Hawkins, did you not? – has hopes of breaking him down before too long.'

'I gather you think the two deaths are connected?'

'I find it awful hard to believe they're not,' was the reply. 'I mean to say, what are the chances? Two murders taking place almost on the same spot, within a matter of hours. It has to be more than a coincidence, wouldn't you say?'

'Well . . .' began Rowlands. But just then Edith put her head around the door. 'Fred, I wonder if you could give me a hand with the tea tray?'

'Right you are.' She'd never asked for help with carrying anything in all the years they'd been married.

'I must say, you might have asked the Chief Inspector to sit down!' said Edith. 'He'll think us very inhospitable.'

'Och, not at all,' said Douglas politely.

'Do smoke if you'd like to, Chief Inspector,' she added brightly as she drew her husband after her into the hall, and closed the door behind them. When she spoke again, it was in a low voice, meant for Rowlands' ears alone. 'She's taken the children down to the river. I told her not to come back until one of us goes to fetch her.' He didn't need to be told who 'she' was. 'It was a bit of luck that I spotted the police car from the window,' his wife went on. 'I bundled them out of the back door as he' – it was the Chief Inspector she meant – 'was knocking at the front.' It struck Rowlands that his wife was rather enjoying all this. 'Here you are.' She took his hands and placed them on either side of the tea tray. 'It's heavy, mind. I thought he might like a slice of cake, to sweeten him up.'

'Where would I be without you?'

'I wonder that myself sometimes,' she said.

In the sitting room, they found Douglas contentedly smoking his pipe. 'I took the liberty of opening a window,' he said as Rowlands set down the loaded tea tray on the low table in front of the fireplace. 'My late wife never could abide the smell of smoke in the house.'

'No more can this one,' smiled Rowlands as Edith began to pour out. 'I get chased out into the garden if I want a cigarette.'

'I don't mind the smell of pipe smoke quite so much,' said his wife untruthfully. 'It's more ... aromatic, somehow. Won't you have a slice of cake, Chief Inspector? I made it myself this morning.'

'In which case, I certainly won't say no,' was the reply. After which Edith left them to it. The relief Rowlands had felt on learning that his sister was out of the house was tempered by a suspicion that the Chief Inspector wasn't being quite straight with him.

'If you've reason to believe Higgins is the killer,' he said, when both men were seated with their cups of tea, 'then why have you come to see me?'

# Chapter Ten

It was a bold challenge, and Douglas seemed to recognise it as such, for he gave a bark of laughter. 'Why indeed? Apart from the pleasure of seeing you again, and of partaking of your wife's excellent cake.' He took a bite of the same, and swallowed it before going on. 'No, the fact is, as soon as I saw your name on the list of witnesses Hawkins had drawn up, I said to myself, this is too good an opportunity to miss. Why, I said, can it really be the same Frederick Rowlands who's proved himself so useful to me in the past? I determined to find out, you see. Because there was your name, written down in black and white, with another name, written below it. "Miss Rowlands" it was. No initial.'

Rowlands found he was unable to say a word.

'And I thought to myself,' the Chief Inspector went on, 'That has to be a mistake. Because I don't know of a Miss Rowlands in your household – unless it's one of your delightful daughters, o' course.'

Still Rowlands said nothing.

'And then I thought, Why, it's probably just that some young fool of a constable has written down Miss instead of Mrs. Because I suppose it must have been you and your wife who were Captain Percival's guests at the Air Show on Saturday?'

'That's right,' said Rowlands.

'Glad we cleared that little matter up,' said Douglas. 'And now to your question: why have I come to see you? The answer's simple: I think you're the man to help me. You were at the scene – and I know from past experience what a good man you are for noticing things.'

'When you put it like that,' said Rowlands wryly, 'I see that I must be indispensable. I'll tell you all I know, of course, even though I've already told it to Inspector Hawkins.'

'Yes, I saw your statement. As precise as I'd have expected of you with regard to times and places. If all our witnesses were as admirably lucid in their recollection of events, our clear up rate would be a lot better than it is,' said the Chief Inspector. 'But it's not the time leading up to the discovery of Farley's body that I'm interested in – that's been well documented already. Len Hawkins may not have much imagination, but he's a thoroughly efficient copper. No, the period that interests me, Mr Rowlands, is the four-hour gap between the time the body was discovered and the time – just after three p.m., I believe – when Captain Percival lost control of his plane. You were at the aerodrome all that time, weren't you?' Rowlands nodded. 'What I want to know is if you saw . . . I mean if you heard . . . anything untoward, which might cast some light on what happened.'

'I'll do my best.' It occurred to him to tell Douglas about the phone call from Irene Metcalfe. But then Rowlands remembered how reluctant she'd been to bring the police into it. He supposed she was all too aware of how dim a view her husband would take of any such involvement. Perhaps, after all, he ought to keep it to himself until he knew what it was she had to tell him. Stupid to get the wind up over what might turn out to be nothing.

'I gather that the plane Captain Percival was flying when he crashed – an Avro 616 Avian racing model – had been lent to him by a Mr Harmsworth,' said the Chief Inspector.

'That's right.'

'Mr Harmsworth was also taking part in the race, I believe?'

'Yes.'

'Would you say he and Captain Percival were on good terms?' asked Douglas. Rowlands hesitated.

'I couldn't say,' he replied guardedly.

'Oh, come now, Mr Rowlands!' said the other impatiently. 'Surely you can do better than that? You were in the Club House, were you not, when Mr Harmsworth made his generous offer – remarkably generous, when one considers the circumstances.'

'I was,' said Rowlands, refusing to be drawn by the last remark, 'but I didn't actually hear what was said.'

'Would it surprise you to know that hard words were exchanged between Mr Harmsworth and Captain Percival, with the latter saying in front of witnesses, and I quote, "If this is another of your half-cocked stunts, I'll wring your bloody neck for you."?'

'No,' admitted Rowlands, recalling the quarrel he'd overheard that day at the RAF show. 'It wouldn't.'

'I thought not,' said Douglas drily. 'And do you have any idea to what Captain Percival was referring when he made this remark?'

'I've no idea,' said Rowlands. 'But I think it's pretty clear that they were rivals.'

'Indeed! And in more ways than one,' replied the Chief Inspector. 'I take it you've met Miss Olave Malory?'

'I have.' Rowlands was beginning to see where all this was leading, and he didn't like it one bit. 'Were you aware,' said Douglas, 'that she and Captain Percival were once engaged to be married?'

'I didn't realise it was an official engagement,' said Rowlands. 'Although I know there was some speculation about it in the papers. But I tend not to pay too much attention to that sort of thing.' It certainly explained Olave Malory's bitterness towards the dead airman, and indeed her antagonism towards Dorothy, he thought.

'Very wise,' said the Chief Inspector. 'It's usually no more than a tissue of lies. But in this instance, it seems as if there was some substance to the rumour. In any case, the engagement was broken off a few weeks ago. It appears the late Captain Percival had rather a wandering eye where the ladies were concerned, and Miss Malory took exception to it. Speaking of which,' the policeman added, 'I'm told he was with a woman on Saturday.'

Rowlands' heart gave a thump. 'Oh?' he said. Foolish to think they'd have got away with it so easily. In the hall, the telephone began to ring. He supposed Edith would answer it.

'Yes,' Douglas was saying. 'A dark-haired young woman. Very attractive she was, too, according to my informant. I don't suppose,' he added slyly, 'you happened to notice her yourself?'

Rowlands forced a smile. 'I'm hardly the man to ask, Chief Inspector.'

'I don't agree. It seems to me that, in your own way, you've as much an "eye" for a pretty woman as the next man. So you weren't aware of Captain Percival's lady friend?'

'I'm afraid not.'

'Strange, that,' said Douglas. 'Because she was seen coming out of the Club House with Percival at exactly the same time as you were.' By that journalist fellow, no doubt, thought Rowlands. 'I wonder if your wife would remember?'

'Remember what?' said Edith, putting her head round the door at this moment. 'Fred, it's the office,' she went on. 'Do you want a word, or shall I say you're on your way?'

'Say that by all means,' said Rowlands. He forced himself to sound casual. 'Edith, the Chief Inspector was wondering whether you'd noticed an attractive dark-haired woman with Captain Percival. When you were with me at the Club House on Saturday,' he added deliberately, keeping his face impassive. His wife seemed momentarily lost for words.

'I . . .'

'Of course, it might have been Miss Malory,' put in Rowlands quickly. 'Isn't she a brunette?'

'No, I've spoken to Miss Malory,' said Douglas. 'She says she doesn't recall seeing any woman apart from Mrs Rowlands here. Although she too seems to have been under the impression that you were Mr Rowlands' sister,' he said to Edith. 'Odd, that. But then she was rather vague about the entire period.'

'I think Miss Malory was suffering from shock,' said Rowlands.

'I don't doubt it. She'd had a good deal to drink, too, according to Inspector Hawkins,' said the Chief Inspector with evident disapproval. 'Told him she couldn't remember much about Saturday at all. So do you remember seeing a dark-haired lady, Mrs Rowlands?' he persisted.

'No,' replied Edith after a moment. 'I can't say I do.'

'Thank you,' said the policeman. 'That's all I wanted to know. Yes, it's a complicated case, this,' he went on when Edith had gone to pass on Rowlands' message to the office. 'First there's this business with Farley having his brains knocked out by person or persons unknown, and then there's the matter of a plane, piloted by one of the top airmen in the country, being found to have been sabotaged. It's a conundrum, you'll admit.'

'Yes,' said Rowlands. 'It's certainly very puzzling.'

'What interests me,' went on the Chief Inspector, in a speculative tone, 'is where the Metcalfe couple fit into all this. I mean, the harder you look at it, the less their account of things adds up. He says he arrived at the aerodrome at approximately ten minutes to twelve. His wife had telephoned him sometime after eleven – he says he didn't notice the time, but we know it can't have been before eleven-fifteen at the earliest – and he got his man to drive him to Hendon straight away. All I can say is he must have been going at quite a pace to get from the Air Ministry in Holborn to Hendon Aerodrome in under an hour.'

'You don't think he had anything to do with Farley's murder, do you?'

'I don't know what to think. All I know is, he's lying about the time he arrived at the aerodrome. But we'll let that lie, for the present. What I'd like to to know is what she was doing there in the first place, our Mrs Metcalfe. Pretty little woman, if you like the helpless type.' It sounded as if the Chief Inspector didn't. 'She says she was returning a scarf to Captain Percival.'

'Yes, I heard her say that.'

'White silk, with his initials stitched in gold. Sounds a bit gaudy to me. Apparently, he thought it brought him luck. Although it can't have done him much good last Saturday,' remarked Douglas with a certain gloomy satisfaction. 'Anyway. It begs the question as to how the scarf got into Mrs M's possession, in the first place.'

'I expect he left it at her flat. They were friends, I believe,' said Rowlands.

'You know that for a fact, do you?' said the policeman slyly.

'Mrs Metcalfe told me as much,' said Rowlands, feeling more and more uncomfortable at this line of questioning.

'Before or after she was screaming her head off?'

'Before. I mean,' said Rowlands with some reluctance, 'it was on a previous occasion.'

'Oh ho,' said Douglas. 'So you know the lady, do you? You might have mentioned this before, Mr Rowlands.'

'There wasn't much to mention. I'd met her, very briefly, a couple of times – well, three times, actually – before I ran into her at Hendon. Or she ran into me,' amended Rowlands drily. 'It hardly seemed important.'

'Perhaps not,' said the Chief Inspector. 'Although you do seem to have quite a way with the ladies, if you don't mind my saying.'

'I do mind, as a matter of fact,' said Rowlands. 'It's hardly my fault if people latch onto me.'

'All right, keep your hair on! Just trying to establish the facts,' said Douglas. What really interests me is what your Mrs Metcalfe was doing down at the hangars, between ten-thirty a.m. – when she says she arrived at the aerodrome, by taxi, apparently – and ten minutes past eleven, when she stumbled across Farley's body.'

'Looking for Percival, in order to return the scarf, I imagine,' said Rowlands.

'Yes, but why not wait for him at the Club House once she knew he was yet to arrive?' said Douglas. 'There was no need to visit the hangars at all.'

'I suppose not.' Although as he spoke, a very clear picture arose in Rowlands' mind of the incorrigibly romantic Irene Metcalfe lying in wait for Percival in the one place she knew he'd be bound to turn up: the Gipsy Moth's hangar. With the excuse of the scarf to return (and how had she got hold of it, he wondered; he wouldn't put it past her to have purloined it), she could be pretty sure of finding him alone.

'Unless she had some other reason for seeking him out, apart from returning the scarf,' said the Chief Inspector, uncannily echoing Rowlands' thoughts.

'She couldn't have sabotaged that plane,' said Rowlands. 'Nor killed Farley, if it comes to that.'

'I never suggested she could. What interests me is why she lied.'

Rowlands was silent a moment. 'Go on,' he said at last.

'She says she put her head in at the front of the hangar, to see if Percival was there, and that the murderer ran past her before she knew what had happened. It was only then, when she went further into the hangar, that she found Farley's body, lying beside the Gipsy Moth.'

'Isn't that what happened?' said Rowlands.

'Not quite,' was the reply. 'You went into the hangar, didn't you, with Hawkins and the rest?'

'Yes.' Rowlands suppressed a shudder at the memory: the smell of dust and oil that had greeted them, and the sharper tang of blood that overlaid it.

'You'll remember that the front of each of the hangars is closed off with a kind of metal shutter so that the aeroplanes can be moved in and out? There's a door to one side of this, to allow the service crews to enter. The door was unlocked when you were there, I take it?'

'Yes. Higgins unlocked it.'

'Indeed. But during the time our Mrs Metcalfe says she was at the hangar the door was locked. So she couldn't have "put her head in", the way she says she did. I'd like to know why she was lying. Although I've got a pretty good idea,' said Douglas. When Rowlands said nothing, the Chief Inspector went on, 'What you may not have realised is that there was another way into the building – through the office at the back of the hangar. There's a door – usually kept locked – and a window, usually left on the latch, or so I'm told. The opening's quite large enough for a slim young woman to climb inside if she were so inclined.'

'I see,' said Rowlands. 'So you think Mrs Metcalfe must have broken into the office – or at least found a way in – some time before the murder?'

'I'm certain of it.'

'Do you think she saw more of . . . of what happened than she's let on?'

'It seems likely.' The Chief Inspector sighed. 'The trouble is, Mr Rowlands, no amount of taking her over her story and asking her to reconsider can make her admit it, although Inspector Hawkins has tried, you can be sure! But she just clams up, and says she doesn't remember. That husband of hers doesn't help. He's already threatened to complain to the Chief Constable if we don't stop persecuting her, as he puts it.' A silence followed. 'I don't suppose,' began Douglas. 'Seeing as you're so friendly with the lady . . .'

'I barely know her,' said Rowlands. But the thought of the arrangement he'd made with Irene Metcalfe later that day troubled his conscience as he spoke.

'Yes, yes, so you've said,' replied the policeman with an edge of impatience. 'But if you could see your way to maybe having a wee chat. She might talk to you, that's all.'

'I'll see what I can do,' said Rowlands.

'Good man. Well, I'd better let you carry on' said Douglas, suddenly brisk. 'I'd offer you a lift to town, only I've a few more enquiries to make at the aerodrome. It seems that the late William Farley may have been involved in some rather shady goings-on. Selling his employers out to a rival concern being one.'

'Oh!' said Rowlands, pausing in the act of opening the door for the Chief Inspector. 'That's why he reacted the way he did the first time I met him.' Briefly, he described his encounter with Farley at Croydon Airport, the day of Percival's return from Australia a month before. 'I couldn't understand why he got so hot under the collar. He kept accusing me of being some kind of spy.'

'It's he who was the spy,' said Douglas grimly as they walked towards where his car awaited. 'One theory we're working on is that somebody who knew about his activities might have been putting the squeeze on him.'

'Higgins, you mean?' said Rowlands as the Chief Inspector's driver, who must have been waiting patiently all this time, got out of the vehicle and hastened to open the door for his superior. 'I can't see him as a blackmailer, somehow.'

'Perhaps not,' was the reply. 'Which leaves us with the question: who else wanted Farley dead? Good to see you again, Mr Rowlands.' The two men shook hands. 'I'll be in touch,' said Douglas. 'All right, Hobbs,' – this to the driver – 'you can take me to Hendon. Quick as you like, man. We've no time to waste.'

As the half-empty train rattled through Hampton Wick, Teddington, and Strawberry Hill, on its way to the metropolis, Rowlands reflected on what the Chief Inspector had said concerning the Metcalfes. There was certainly something about both their stories which didn't add up. And while Irene Metcalfe's evasiveness about the whole affair might have an obvious explanation – her wish to conceal from her husband the fact that she'd been intending to meet another man that day at Hendon

Aerodrome – Neville Metcalfe's behaviour also seemed more than a little suspicious. How was it that he'd managed to arrive at Hendon so soon after Farley's body had been discovered – unless he'd actually been in the vicinity all along? Had he perhaps been following his wife, having got wind of her intention? It certainly couldn't be ruled out.

One thing was certain: whether Metcalfe had been lying about the time he'd got to the aerodrome or not, he could have had no motive for murdering Farley. It was Percival, surely, against whom he'd have had a grudge? Still trying to make sense of this, Rowlands arrived at the office to find things in a state of mild chaos. Miss Peachey, the Temporary, had failed to show up – 'boy trouble', said Rowlands' secretary, Miss Collins, darkly – and the telephone had been ringing 'off the hook' (Miss Collins again) because a delivery of cane and raffia, essential for the manufacture of those household items whose sale provided the only source of income for a score of housebound men, had failed to arrive. On top of these minor emergencies was the usual pile of letters to be answered; the most urgent, concerning money, he dealt with first.

What with one thing and another, it was gone four o'clock by the time he remembered his appointment with Irene Metcalfe. It was rather a nuisance, he thought, because he'd all this work to catch up with, and Miss Collins had already said with a martyred air that she had hoped to be able to go by half past, as she'd got her

eye on a nice pair of beach pyjamas in the Debenham &
Freebody sale. He supposed he could always come back
to the office for an hour or so after he'd heard what the
woman had to say. 'That's all right, Miss Collins,' he
said to the secretary. 'You can go now. Thanks for
holding the fort,' he added as she got up to leave. The
last thing he wanted was for her to take umbrage, and
hand in her notice.

'Don't mention it,' was the gratified reply. 'And thanks
ever so for letting me go early. I wouldn't have asked,
only they're down to twenty-nine and six. Green-and-
white spotted washing silk. *Ever* so pretty.'

Rowlands made a vague sound expressive of polite
interest, although privately he thought the idea of wearing
pyjamas on the beach rather an odd one. He supposed
Edith would know all about it; he was always the last to
cotton on to such fashions. Which was hardly surprising,
he thought, as, locking the office door behind him and
pocketing the key, he set off across Regent's Park towards
Gloucester Place. The last women's fashion he'd been
able to appreciate fully had been the one for skirts and
coats of a military cut, worn with sailor blouses. He
remembered his sister sporting just such an outfit, the last
time he'd been home on leave, in the spring of '17.

A quarter of an hour later, he climbed the shallow
flight of steps leading to the entrance of the mansion
block where the Metcalfes lived. He promised himself
that he wouldn't stay more than a few minutes. Surely
whatever she had to tell him wouldn't take too long in

the telling? He suspected that the real reason she'd asked him to call was in order to be able to unburden herself of her feelings, in the wake of Percival's death. Well, let her do it, poor woman, if it made her feel better. With regard to the official reason for his visit, he felt rather less sanguine. Damn Douglas, with his 'wee chat' – the homeliness of the phrase didn't disguise what it really was: the interrogation of a suspect. He thought of what the Chief Inspector had told him concerning the discrepancies in Mrs Metcalfe's story. How was he to approach the subject, he wondered. It'd be no good confronting her with what she'd said, and asking her to explain herself, the way the police seemed to have done. She'd only take fright.

No one challenged him as he pushed open the heavy glass doors and crossed the echoing foyer. If there were a porter on duty, he was keeping very quiet about it, Rowlands thought. Eschewing the lift, he took the stairs – always his preference where possible. It was one way of getting some exercise; that was something you didn't get enough of, being blind. With walking, you could never go fast enough, hamstrung as you were by the fear of tripping over some unseen obstacle, or of crashing into somebody. Rowing was better, but you needed a sighted companion for that. It was weeks since he'd last got out on the river. Perhaps this Saturday if it turned out fine and Edith wasn't too busy.

Arriving, with a heart that beat gratifyingly fast, outside the door of the Metcalfes' fifth-floor flat, he took a moment to get his breath back. Must be getting old, he thought; either that, or it was the cigarettes. Straightening his tie, and smoothing his hair into place (just because he couldn't see, it didn't mean he had to look a sight), he rang the bell, then checked his watch. Half past four. He supposed it still counted as tea time? A few moments passed. He strained his ears for the sound of footsteps from within. Nothing. After half a minute or so, he tried again. If she were in her bedroom, she might not have heard him. Although you'd have thought the maid . . . Then he remembered that she'd said she'd be alone. Another thirty seconds passed. It had been this afternoon she'd said, hadn't it? Perhaps, when he hadn't appeared at four, she'd given him up and gone out? Feeling increasingly foolish, he rang once more, hearing the shrill sound echo within. Still no reply. He tried knocking. 'Mrs Metcalfe?' he called. 'It's me. Frederick Rowlands.' Drat the woman. Would she never come? Mingled with the irritation he was feeling was a stirring of unease.

He descended the stairs at a faster pace than he'd climbed them. Reaching the porter's desk, he put his finger on the bell and kept it there until the man appeared. 'Yes?' said this individual, making no effort to hurry himself. 'What can I do for you? Sir,' he added as an afterthought.

'Did you happen to see Mrs Metcalfe go out?' asked Rowlands, with an edge of impatience. 'Only I've been trying to raise her, and there's no reply.'

'Flat Five, would that be? No, I haven't seen her.'

'Are you sure?' demanded Rowlands.

'Quite sure. The only ones I've seen come down in the past hour, apart from yourself, sir, is the Colonel, from Flat Three – he always takes his dog for a walk around this time – and the delivery boy.'

'Oh?' said Rowlands. 'And when was this?'

'I couldn't say, offhand. About three-quarters of an hour before you yourself turned up, I reckon. I'll need to check my ledger.'

'If you would,' said Rowlands. With evident reluctance, the porter did so. 'Yes, here we are. Three forty-three: arrived. Three fifty-five: left the building. Rather a long time, just to deliver a bunch of flowers, but you know what these chaps are!' The porter chuckled. 'Prob'ly stopped on his way down to have a quick smoke.'

'I'd like you to let me have the key to the Metcalfes' flat,' said Rowlands, cutting across this humorous speculation.

'Oh, I don't know as I can do that, sir,' was the reply. 'Whatever would Mr Metcalfe say?' Rowlands insisted, however, and the two of them ascended in the lift to the fifth floor, the porter grumbling all the while that it was more than his job was worth, and that if Mr Metcalfe got to hear of it, he – the porter – would be looking for another position sooner than you could say 'knife'. Outside the door of Number 5, he fumbled so long with his bunch of keys that Rowlands was tempted to snatch them from his hand. At last the door was open, and Rowlands, with the other man muttering in his wake, went inside.

# Chapter Eleven

'Hello? Mrs Metcalfe?' he called, into the profound silence. Because it was obvious from the moment he set foot in the place that there was no one there. The big sitting room, with its box-shaped sofas and chairs, and glass and chrome occasional tables – one of which had nearly tripped him up, the day he'd been there for tea – now echoed hollowly to the sound of his footsteps.

'Why, look,' he heard the porter say. 'Here are the blessed flowers, dropped on the floor. Seems an awful waste. Somebody ought to put 'em in water.'

But Rowlands was no longer listening. 'Hello?' he called again. 'Anybody home?' He pushed open the door of what he took to be a bedroom – hers, he guessed, from the smell of face powder and perfume. A second door yielded more masculine odours of leather and Bay Rum. Still nothing. And yet the porter had sworn he hadn't seen her go out. He tried another door. This must be the child's room, he thought. A smell of cough drops, and clothes airing on a fender. Next to this was a bathroom, to judge by the echo, as well as the faintly medicinal smell.

'If you're quite finished, sir . . .' said the porter from the room beyond. But Rowlands hadn't finished. Not yet. There was still a door left unopened. He opened it, and at once knew his worst fears had been justified. Because the smell that rushed out at him was the smell of death. Of blood – copious amounts of it. He took a cautious step inside the room, and felt his foot bump against something that was on the floor. At once he drew back and, careful not to disturb things any more than he had to, knelt down and reached out a hand to where he guessed she must be lying. 'Mrs Metcalfe? Irene?' he said softly, knowing that she was, in all probability, beyond hearing now.

Her head was the first thing he found – its crisp marcelled waves of hair had kept their shape, even in this extremity. He made himself feel down across the face to the throat, in case a pulse still beat there. But there was nothing; nor could he feel even the faintest breath. 'My God,' he murmured, pity and horror rising up in him at once. 'Who could have done this?' He moved his hand down the limp body until he found the place, just above the heart, where the fabric of the dress, now soaked with blood, had been pierced. Was there a flicker of movement? He couldn't be sure. Using his clean folded handkerchief as a rudimentary pad, he placed both hands over the wound and bore down as hard as he could.

''Ere!' said a voice from behind him. 'What's going on?' The porter. He'd forgotten all about him.

'Stay back,' he said sharply. But his warning must have been ignored, for a moment later, there came an exclamation.

'Oh, my Gawd.'

'You'd better ring for an ambulance,' said Rowlands. 'Well, go on, then, man! Don't just stand there.' He knew his anger was as much at himself for having arrived too late, as at the porter's dilatoriness.

'All right, all right,' said the other. Rowlands heard him go through to the hall where the telephone was, he guessed. A moment later, he could be heard asking for the Operator.

'You'd better call the police, while you're about it,' called Rowlands after him. Because as the minutes passed with no sign of life from Irene Metcalfe, he realised that his attempts at first aid were futile. It was a corpse, and not a living woman, that lay there – a suspicion now confirmed by the porter who, having finished his call to the emergency services, now returned.

'You're wasting your time if you think there's any chance of bringing her back,' he observed. 'Dead as a doornail, I'd say she is.'

'Did you ask for an ambulance?' said Rowlands, ignoring this.

'I did. For all the good it'll do,' said the man. 'My Gawd,' he went on, in tones of fascinated horror. 'To think of her lying here, all the time we was talking, and I never knew.' It was a thought which had also occurred to Rowlands. If he'd only got here sooner! He left the pad where it was, over the wound – although the fact that it had remained dry should have told him all he needed to know – and took off his jacket. With a confused sense of its being the right thing to do, he spread it over the poor crumpled body. A dull anger rose in him at the senselessness of it all.

He got to his feet, conscious that the knees of his trousers were wet from where he had been kneeling, blood having formed a spreading pool across the kitchen's tiled floor. Whoever had killed Irene Metcalfe had made a thorough job of it, Rowlands thought. He guessed she had been stabbed several times, and was glad that he was unable to confirm this.

'I'm sure I don't know what I'm going to say when they ask me how the man got in,' the porter, Grundley, was saying as the two of them went back through the flat towards the open front door. But Rowlands had heard something which made him grow cold all over: the sound of voices, coming up the stairwell.

'We'll see what your mama has to say about that, Master Edward.' It was the maid, Rowlands thought. Then came the child's voice, 'Mummy said I could have

209

another half an hour in the park. She *said*!'

'I keep telling you – you've had your half-hour, and more. Now it's time for your bath, and . . . Oh!' she exclaimed, as Rowlands, who had run full tilt down the stairs, now came face to face with the pair of them.

'Hello, Teddy,' he said, trying to keep his voice light. 'Remember me?' To which the child of course said nothing. 'Been flying that plane of yours again?' said Rowlands; then, when the boy tried to wriggle past him up the stairs, he put a hand on his shoulder. 'Shouldn't go up there, if I were you, old chap. Nor you.' This to the girl. 'Mabel, isn't it? Fact is, there's been a bit of an accident. So we're all going to go back downstairs again, and have a cup of tea – you can make tea in that cubbyhole of yours, can't you?' he added to Grundley, who came stumping down the stairs at this moment. The latter grunted an affirmative. 'Good. Then let's all go down together.'

'But I don't want to go downstairs, protested Teddy.

'Now then, Master Edward . . .'

'I want to see Mummy,' said the boy stubbornly.

'Tell you what,' said Rowlands, his heart heavy within him. 'You can have my watch to look at, if you like. It's a rather special one.' He unstrapped the watch from his wrist and put it into the child's small warm hand. 'See those dots around the face of it? They help me to tell the time even though I can't see.' They had by now reached the porter's lodge. It struck Rowlands that, with the police and ambulance due to arrive at any minute, Teddy and his nurse had to be got out of the way. While the child was momentarily distracted, playing with the watch, he drew the maid aside. 'Here,' he said, pressing two half-crowns into her hand. 'I want you to take Teddy to the nearest tea shop, and buy him – and yourself – a decent spread. Don't come back for at least an hour. Do you think you can manage that?'

'Yes, sir,' she said doubtfully. 'It's just if the Mistress was to ask where I was, like . . .'

'Don't you worry about that,' he said. 'An hour, do you understand?' That should give the police time to get here, and do what they had to do, he thought. Mabel duly collected her charge, and – to Rowlands' immense relief – ushered him out of the building. It was only just in time, for a few minutes later, there came the sound of a clanging bell growing nearer and nearer, followed by that of a vehicle pulling up outside. Two men came briskly up the steps and into the foyer.

'Who was it reported an incident?' one said. 'Woman found stabbed . . .'

'I did,' said Grundley, emerging from his cubbyhole. 'The fact is, he must've been ever so sharp to have got past me, the way he did.'

'Fifth floor,' said Rowlands, interrupting this self-serving explanation. 'I'd take the lift, if I were you. You'd better give them the keys, Mr Grundley.'

'And who might you be, sir?' said the second of the

two ambulance men. 'I've only got one name written down here.'

'The name's Rowlands. I was the one who found her.'

A swift examination by one of the ambulance men confirmed that Irene Metcalfe been dead for at least an hour. It was now twenty to six, which suggested that the man the porter had seen going up in the lift half an hour before Rowlands himself had arrived was the one responsible. If I'd only got here a bit sooner, I might have stopped him, he thought. It was not a comfortable thought. Still less enjoyable was the grilling he'd received from the police inspector who'd taken charge of the case: a dour individual by the name of Lorrimer, he evidently took a dim view of Rowlands' story that he'd been keeping an appointment with the dead woman.

'So you say she'd asked you to visit her – this Mrs Metcalfe?'

'Yes, that's right.'

'Friend of yours, was she?'

'Not exactly. I'd say she was an acquaintance.'

'Indeed.' The Inspector managed to convey a good deal of scepticism in that single word. 'And what reason did this "acquaintance" of yours give, for inviting you to her home? Rather a strange thing to do, wasn't it, since according to you, you hardly knew one another?'

Rowlands hesitated. He wondered what the response would be if he said that Irene Metcalfe had wanted to give him some information about a murder. 'She was going to ask my advice about something.'

'Was she now! It sounds as if she regarded you as rather more than a casual "acquaintance",' said Lorrimer, with some satisfaction. 'Was this the first time you'd been to the flat?' Rowlands admitted that it was not. 'Ah, now we're getting somewhere,' said the policeman.

'I think you've got the wrong idea,' said Rowlands. 'On the one previous occasion I was in the flat, Mrs Metcalfe's husband was also present.' Although only for the last five minutes, he amended silently. 'Mrs Metcalfe had kindly offered me a cup of tea,' he went on, despising himself for what he was about to say. 'I'm with the St Dunstan's home for blind men, you see, and so I imagine she was just being charitable.'

'Hmm,' said Lorrimer. 'Yes, I spotted that you were blind right away. You've got a way of looking off to the side instead of straight at a man when you're talking to him that rather gives it away. Still, blind or not, it doesn't alter the situation. Just why were you going to see Irene Metcalfe?'

'I'm afraid I can't tell you that.'

'Oh! And why not? If it was all as innocent as you say, then why the secrecy?'

'Look,' said Rowlands. 'You're barking up the wrong tree, Inspector. Mr Grundley – the porter – will tell you that I arrived after Mrs Metcalfe was killed. He was with me when I discovered the body. As the police surgeon has confirmed, she'd been dead for at least half an hour. Quite apart from anything else, I didn't have time to kill her.'

'That's as may be,' was the gruff reply. 'You must admit, though, Mr Rowlands, that it does look awfully suspicious – your being in the flat so near the time the woman was murdered.' Rowlands shrugged.

'I can't help that,' he said. 'But I really think you should be concentrating your efforts on tracing the delivery boy. The one who brought the flowers. He's a much more likely suspect, if only because the times fit. You see . . .'

'Thank you,' said Inspector Lorrimer with asperity. 'We're already looking into that aspect of the case. Now, about this telephone call you had with Mrs Metcalfe . . .' But Rowlands had remembered something.

'I'm sorry, Inspector,' he said, getting up from the chair where he had been sitting – one of the fashionably box-shaped items in Irene Metcalfe's sitting room. 'I can't talk to you just now . . .' Because Mabel and the boy would be back at any minute, he thought. Even though the body had now been removed – the police surgeon having finished his examination – still it was unthinkable that the child should come back here.

Rowlands was across the room before anyone thought to stop him. It was only when he went to open the front door that the constable stationed there intervened. 'Just a minute, sir!' A heavy hand descended on Rowlands' shoulder.

'Let go of me, there's a good fellow,' said Rowlands. 'This is important, don't you see?' Because his sharper hearing had caught the sound of the lift rising up the shaft, and coming to a stop on the landing outside.

'And what,' said Inspector Lorrimer, 'can be so important, I wonder?' Then to the junior officer, 'That's all right, Horrocks. You can leave hold of him now.'

Before Rowlands could answer, there came the sound of a key in the lock. The door opened. 'Oh Lord,' muttered the Inspector, seeing who it was that stood there. 'You might have warned me.'

'I was just about to,' said Rowlands. 'Hello, Mabel,' he went on, addressing the girl. 'Did you have a good tea?'

'Lovely, sir, thank you,' was the reply. 'I did try and keep him out as long as possible, like you said, but . . . Here!' she cried, evidently catching sight of the uniformed man standing behind Rowlands. 'What's going on? You didn't say the police was here.'

'I take it you're the maid?' intervened Lorrimer, in the brusque tones he evidently thought fit for one of her class. 'Perhaps you'd like to tell me where you were this afternoon?'

'I . . .' she began, then stopped, apparently dumbfounded by the question. 'I was taking Master Edward to the park, like I always do.'

'Quite so,' replied the Inspector. 'And what time was this?'

'I . . .' she began again; but before she could get out the rest of it, there came another interruption. It was the child, this time.

'Where's Mummy?' he said. And then, when no answer seemed forthcoming, 'I want to see Mummy.'

\* \* \*

215

After he had finished speaking, Edith was silent a moment. 'Poor little mite,' she said, her voice not quite steady. 'Of all the rotten things to have happened.'

'Yes,' said her husband. 'To tell the truth, none of us knew how to answer him. One thing was certain, though – he couldn't be allowed back into that flat. Not with his mother's blood all over the kitchen floor.'

'Fred, please . . .'

'I'm sorry. It's been a hellish day.'

'So what happened then?' said Edith. They were speaking in the hushed tones customarily reserved for talk of a bereavement, which this was, thought Rowlands, if not one they themselves had suffered. But with children in the house, to say nothing of an elderly lady of a sensitive disposition, such horrors could only be discussed in whispers.

'Fortunately, at that moment, the father turned up.'

'Was that the man we met at the Air Show?'

'Yes. Neville Metcalfe. Works at the Air Ministry. They'd sent a car to fetch him.'

'That was decent of them.'

'Mm,' said Rowlands. Although it occurred to him that there might be another reason why the police were so solicitous towards the bereaved man. If he were a suspect, then it made sense to lay hands on him as soon as possible. But he kept this thought to himself. 'Let's drop this now, shall we?' he merely said. Because he had heard his sister's step upon the stairs. A moment later she came in. 'Children asleep?' asked Rowlands.

'The little ones are,' she replied. 'Tired out after their long walk. Margaret's reading. I said she might finish her chapter. Billy's playing with his crystal set. It's hard for them to get to sleep, these light evenings.'

'Yes. Look here, old girl . . .' Rowlands hesitated before going on with what he had to say. It would be all too easy to upset her. But she took the words out of his mouth.

'I'm going to have to leave,' she said. 'Oh, you needn't look so surprised, Fred! I'm quite capable of working things out for myself. After what happened today, I'd be a fool to stay here any longer,' She laughed. 'Although I'm sure you both think I've made a fool of myself already.'

'Dottie . . .'

'No, let me finish, Fred. I'm sorry if I've made things awkward for you . . .' That was putting it mildly, Rowlands thought. 'But I'd not the least idea when I came here with the boys, of how things would turn out. With . . . with Alan Percival, I mean.' She was silent a moment. 'No, I couldn't have predicted that,' she said softly.

'Look, I'll leave you both to it.'

'No, don't go, Edith. I want you to hear this,' said her sister-in-law. 'I've been selfish, I know, staying here as long as I have. But the boys seemed to settle down so well and . . .'

'You don't have to leave,' said Edith.

'Thank you. That counts for a lot. But Fred's been right all along when he said I shouldn't have come. What happened today, with that policeman turning up, only goes to show how right he was.' Dorothy gave a tremulous little laugh. 'In fact, if it weren't for your quick thinking, Edith, I'd be sitting in a police cell this minute.'

'There's no evidence against you,' said Rowlands, surprising himself; then, as she started to object, 'The only case Douglas has is based on hearsay. Mine,' he added, in case she'd missed the point. 'There were no witnesses to our conversation. And nothing's going to make me repeat a word of what I said, you can be sure of that.'

'Oh, Fred . . .' A moment later, she flung her arms around his neck.

'Which doesn't mean that I don't agree with you,' he went on, giving her an awkward little pat on the back. 'With the Chief Inspector and his chums likely to pop up at any minute, it isn't safe for you to remain here . . . at least, not for the present.'

'I'll write again to Viktor's cousins in Berlin,' said Dorothy. But Rowlands shook his head.

'Oh, I don't think you need go as far as Berlin,' he said.

A brief paragraph on the Home News page gave the bare details of Irene Metcalfe's murder. At his request, Edith read it to Rowlands as he was having his breakfast next morning. They were the only two up at that hour, the rest of the house being still asleep. But after yesterday, Rowlands thought he should get in early; unsurprisingly, he'd not made it back to the office the previous night, after all. '"*Civil Servant's Wife Found Murdered*"' began Edith, then stopped. 'Are you going to eat that toast, Fred, or just break it into little pieces?'

'What? Oh.' He put a piece of toast in his mouth and chewed it absent-mindedly. 'Go on,' he said.

'All right. "*Police were called to a flat in Gloucester Place yesterday afternoon after the porter, Mr Ernest Grundley, alerted them to the presence of the body of Mrs Irene Evadne Metcalfe, aged twenty-nine who was found stabbed to death at around four-thirty p.m. . . .*" No mention of you,' said Edith.

'No,' he said. 'I'm glad of that.' He had in fact bumped into a man he guessed must have been a reporter as he was leaving Gloucester Mansions just before six. The man had asked him, in a confidential tone, if he knew which was the 'murder flat'. He'd said he had no idea. Percival was right when he'd said men like that were jackals.

'"*Blonde, attractive Mrs Metcalfe, whose husband, Mr Neville Metcalfe, is Permanent Secretary to the Minister for Air, is thought to have surprised a burglar . . .*"'

'One bearing gifts,' said Rowlands.

'What? Oh, you mean the flowers? Yes, I wonder why they haven't mentioned that.'

'Trying to put the murderer off his guard, perhaps. If he *was* the murderer,' said Rowlands. 'Sorry, I interrupted you.'

'There's not much more,' she said. 'Just a comment from the porter. I must say, he does seem to have pushed himself forward! "*'Mrs Metcalfe was a charming lady,'* *said Mr Grundley, sixty-three, who has worked at* *Gloucester Mansions ever since the luxury flats were put* *up last year. 'Always ready to pass the time of day with a* *smile and a pleasant remark. I can't think what kind of* *man could have done this terrible thing.'*" That's all,' said Edith. 'Will you be late home tonight?' Because having finished his toast, and gulped down his second cup of tea, Rowlands was now on his way out the door.

'I shouldn't think so.' He dropped a kiss on her cheek. 'I'll telephone if anything comes up.'

But in fact the day proved uneventful, which was the way Rowlands liked it. Having been through the war, he'd come to appreciate the value of a quiet life; for him, the everyday could never be taken for granted. And so he signed letters, and answered telephone calls, and with Miss Collins' assistance, went through invoices, and filed receipts. At four o'clock, because there was nothing much for her to do, he sent her home. 'I'll just finish off here,' he said as she collected the letters for posting. 'See you in the morning.'

'Yes, Mr Rowlands.' High heels clicked across the linoleum. The door closed behind her, and he was alone. In truth, there wasn't anything he had to do, or nothing that couldn't wait. He just wanted some time to himself, to think things out in peace. The events of the past three months – from that day at Croydon Airport when he'd first met Alan Percival, to those hideous few minutes in Irene Metcalfe's kitchen – were surely part of a pattern, if only he could work out what it was. Farley's death. The accident which had claimed Percival's life, and which had turned out not to be an accident after all. The murder of Irene Metcalfe. All were links in a bloodstained chain. And yet . . . Even if one supposes that Higgins killed Farley, for some as yet unknown reason, as well as tampering with Percival's plane, he can hardly be held responsible for killing Mrs Metcalfe, Rowlands argued with himself.

Barely conscious of what he was doing, he picked up the pebble from the desk in front of him and weighed it in his hand. Something about the circumstances of Irene Metcalfe's death troubled him. But when he tried to put his finger on what it was, it slipped away.

'I very much hope,' said the Chief Inspector when Rowlands had finished saying what he had to say, 'that there's nothing else you're holding back from me, as regards this case.'

'No,' said Rowlands. 'That's all.'

'I'm glad to hear it. Withholding information can have serious consequences, as I'm sure you realise.' They were in Douglas's office at New Scotland Yard. Big Ben had just struck six, its resonant chimes seeming to fill the room where they sat, so close were they to the famous edifice. Rowlands wondered idly how anyone in the building managed to do any work with that sonorous racket going on at measured intervals throughout the day. He supposed one got used to it.

221

'Yes,' he said, picking up on the implications of Douglas's remark. 'If I'd spoken out earlier, Mrs Metcalfe might still be alive.'

'Perhaps.' Douglas had his back to Rowlands, and so his words sounded muffled. Shouts from passers-by in the street below – or perhaps from lightermen on the river beyond – drifted up through the open window where he stood. 'And then again, perhaps not. Because even if you'd prevented him from carrying out his intentions in the first instance, he'd have tried again. They always do, in these cases.' Having finished stuffing his pipe with the pungent tobacco he favoured, he struck a match, and applied it to the instrument. A powerful whiff of Navy Cut soon arose. 'Aye,' he went on, sitting himself back down in his accustomed chair, 'this is a very nasty little crime, planned in cold blood, I'd say. I take it you've met the husband, Neville Metcalfe?'

'Yes. But you surely don't think . . .'

'Why not?' said the Chief Inspector. 'The man's been lying himself black and blue. For a start, he wasn't at the aerodrome last Saturday at the time he said he was. And he's the one who ordered those flowers.'

'Flowers?' echoed Rowlands. 'Aye. Two dozen red roses, from Eloise Fleurs of Mayfair. Ordered and paid for in person by one N. Metcalfe, Esq.'

'But I still don't see . . .' began Rowlands. 'No more did I, at first,' said the Chief Inspector. 'Oh, he's been very clever, there's not doubt about that. Bribing the delivery boy. Although as it turns out, that was his first mistake.'

'Then . . . you've found the delivery boy?' asked Rowlands, still not following. Familiar as he was with Douglas's telegrammatic utterances, they were sometimes hard to decipher.

'Aye. Name of Davy Hughes. Age: sixteen. Picked him up on his way to Cardiff. Five pounds in his pocket.' The Chief Inspector puffed away at his pipe for a moment. 'At first we thought he was our man. But a number of things made that seem unlikely. For a start, there was no blood on his clothes. "Oh," you'll be saying, "he might have changed his clothes", as indeed he might. But, as it happened, he didn't. Wearing the same short jacket and trousers, with the monogram EF – for Eloise Fleurs – on the breast pocket, as he had on when he left the shop. They give 'em a uniform, ye ken, these smart Mayfair florists.'

'I see.'

'There was also the fact that nothing had been stolen – from the Metcalfes' flat, I mean – which rules out a simple case of breaking and entering . . . or, in this instance, a forced entry, with the flowers as his excuse. No, he didn't seem a very likely candidate for our murderer,' said Douglas. 'Even if he did have a new five-pound note in his possession.'

'So you think Metcalfe is our man?' said Rowlands. 'But wasn't he at his office when the murder was committed?'

'I was coming to that,' replied the Chief Inspector. 'He was certainly at the Ministry during the crucial period –

call it half past three to a quarter past four – with witnesses to prove it.'

'Then how . . . ?' began Rowlands.

'All in good time,' said Doulgas, who was clearly enjoying himself. 'First of all there's the maid's evidence to consider.'

'Young Mabel, you mean?'

'The same. Says she overheard the Master and Mistress having a violent altercation, that morning. She'd just let herself into the flat – she lives out, as does the cook – when she heard them going at it, hammer and tongs. They must not have realised she was there, says our Miss Mabel, because she'd never heard them quarrel like that before.' The Chief Inspector shuffled some papers on his desk. 'Here we are. I knew I'd got a note of it somewhere. According to the girl, her mistress was in tears. "*You've got it all wrong*," she kept saying. "*It wasn't like that . . .*" And then he – Metcalfe – shouted, "*If you think I'll believe that, you must take me for a fool. You've gone too far this time, Reenie. I tell you, I won't put up with it!*"'

A moment later, Mabel says, Metcalfe comes rushing out with a face like thunder, grabs his hat and coat and slams out of the flat, leaving Mrs Metcalfe sobbing her heart out in the bedroom. The girl says she didn't know quite what to do, so she just put on her cap and apron and carried on with the dusting, as per usual. Presently, Mrs Metcalfe calls from the bedroom that she's got a headache, and won't be getting up. She often suffered from these sick headaches, says Mabel, and so this was nothing unusual. At half past nine, the cook, Mrs Chandler, arrives, and prepares breakfast for Mrs Metcalfe and the boy.'

'I was wondering about the boy.'

'He's in good hands,' said Douglas shortly before returning to his notes. 'At lunchtime, Madam was well enough to get up – she'd had her breakfast in bed, it seems – and Cook served her some lunch upon a tray. Then, after lunch, she (Madam, not Cook) told Mabel to take the child to the park, and that was the last our girl saw of her.'

'What about the cook?'

'She left at half past two after doing the washing-up. Her husband's on nights, so she had his tea to prepare,' said Douglas. 'That left the field clear for Metcalfe's little plan to work . . . Oh, there was one other thing I should have mentioned,' he added slyly. 'Metcalfe's telephone call.'

'Oh?'

'You might well say "Oh,"' said the Chief Inspector. 'The girl, Mabel Smith, took the call at around ten past twelve. Apparently, Metcalfe asked to speak to his wife, and she – the maid – told him that her mistress was indisposed, and couldn't come to the telephone.'

'Isn't there an extension in the bedroom?' asked Rowlands.

'There is, as it happens. But she usually liked the servant to answer. You know these society women. Too weak to pick up the receiver,' said Douglas scornfully. 'Anyway. He said he'd leave a message – and this is where it gets interesting.' The policeman's Edinburgh accent grew more pronounced, the more excited he got. '"*Be sure and tell your mistress,*" he says. "*That's she's to stay in this afternoon. There's a surprise on its way to her,*" he says. What d'you think of that?' cried Douglas triumphantly. '"A surprise!" I should say it was certainly that.'

'Don't you think he meant the flowers?' said Rowlands. 'I imagine they were a sort of peace offering after the quarrel he'd had with her that morning . . . I mean, even if he was planning to kill her, he'd hardly want to announce the fact.'

'Yes, man – but don't you see?' cried the other. 'He made sure she'd be at home, just at the time he wanted her there.'

'I thought you'd established that he had an alibi for the period in question,' said Rowlands.

'Oh, he did,' was the reply. 'That's the clever thing about it. He was nowhere near Gloucester Mansions when his wife was murdered. That doesn't mean he didn't know all about it.'

Rowlands was beginning to see daylight. 'Are you suggesting that he hired someone else to kill her?'

'Exactly so.' There was a note of self-congratulation in the Chief Inspector's voice. 'Young Hughes has been telling us all about it. Says that when he arrived at Gloucester Place there was someone waiting for him there, outside the flats. Tall youth wearing overalls and a cloth cap. Had a scarf across the lower part of his face. The lad – Hughes – thought he must have been disguising his voice, because he spoke in a kind of hoarse croak, as if he'd got laryngitis, Hughes said. Told him he could make himself some easy money if he handed over the flowers, and made himself scarce. Didn't take much persuading once he saw that nice crisp fiver,' added Douglas sourly. 'So you see,' he went on. 'That's how it was done. Ingenious. But not quite ingenious enough.'

'What makes you think Metcalfe's the one behind it?' said Rowlands. 'I mean, is there anything to tie him to the murder itself? Apart from that phone call.'

'No, but we're working on him,' said the policeman. 'As a matter of fact, I'm on my way down there now. I'll see you out.'

# Chapter Twelve

The interrogation rooms were on the ground floor, just above the cells; a convenient arrangement for all concerned, said Douglas. 'O' course, we don't hold 'em here for very long. *Habeas corpus*, ye ken. In Metcalfe's case, it'll be for no more than a night. Perhaps two, if he proves difficult. But I've high hopes we'll get a result before that.' A result being a confession, Rowlands surmised. He wondered what had made the police so very sure of Metcalfe's guilt.

'I suppose you've found someone who saw him at the aerodrome on Saturday, at an earlier time than the time he said he'd got there,' he said as the lift, groaning like a damned soul, came to a halt. Douglas gave a short bark of laughter.

'You do like to work things out for yourself, don't you, Mr Rowlands?' he said. The lift doors clashed open. 'Yes, we have found somebody, as it happens. Chappie by the name of Stanley Perkins. "Ginger" to his friends.'

'Oh yes.' Rowlands remembered Ginger. 'One of the ground crew, isn't he?

'He is. Worked with Farley and Higgins, so you can be sure we gave him a grilling. Turns out he saw Metcalfe acting in a suspicious manner outside the hangar where Farley's body was found, at around a quarter to eleven that day. Says he though it odd, because the man in question "looked like a gent" and seemed to have no good reason to be there. Thought he must be one of Percival's friends, come to look him up before the race, and so thought no more about it.'

'Well, he was,' said Rowlands as they turned down along the corridor – empty at this time of evening – which led to the interrogation rooms. 'A friend of Percival's, I mean.'

'Aye,' said the Chief Inspector grimly. 'If you can call it friendship, to fake up a man's death, and then kill the woman you believe has betrayed you with that "friend" . . . But whsst! I've said more than enough. If you follow the corridor to the end, the exit's on your left.'

'Thank you,' said Rowlands. 'Well, goodnight, Chief Inspector.'

'Goodnight,' said the other, a little distractedly. Because at that moment, the door of the interrogation room opened, and someone came out. 'Ah, Hawkins. Just the man I want to see. Has he said anything yet?'

'Not yet. His lawyer's with him.'

'Who's he got?'

'Caulfield.'

'No expense spared, I see,' said Douglas drily. 'Len, you know Mr Rowlands, I believe?'

'You're the gentleman that was at the aerodrome last Saturday. With a young lady – a sister, wasn't it?' Rowlands felt his face flame. He opened his mouth to reply, but before he could do so, the Chief Inspector answered for him.

'I think you'll find that was Mr Rowlands' wife. One of your lads must have got the details wrong. All right, Len,' he went on briskly before the other could respond to this. 'You can give me an hour. We won't be able to hold him for much longer without charging him, in any case – not with Mr Julius Caulfield sitting at his side.'

'We've had to let him go.' Douglas's tone was one of weary disgust. 'Even though, in my opinion, he's hiding something. But with that expensive brief sitting there, and nothing more than circumstantial evidence, we couldn't hold him.'

'Frustrating for you,' murmured Rowlands. They were in the public bar of the Red Lion in Parliament Street, around the corner from Scotland Yard; it was the evening of the next day. Sometimes Rowlands wondered if his role in the Chief Inspector's life wasn't rather that of a Father Confessor. Someone to whom one's weaknesses and occasional slips from grace could be confided, without fear of the consequences. He sipped his pint of Fuller's, and kept the thought to himself.

'We've got a witness who saw him going into a telephone box in High Holborn at five minutes to twelve on the day of his wife's murder,' the policeman was saying. 'Now who was he telephoning to, I wonder? He says it was to his broker, about some shares he wanted to sell. Then why not telephone from the office?'

'Perhaps he didn't want to be overheard.'

'I'm sure he didn't.' The Chief Inspector gave a gusty sigh as he set down his glass. They were seated at a table in the recess at the far end of the pub's massive carved oak bar – an arrangement which gave them a modicum of privacy, screening them, as it did, from the room at large. The place was full, which was just as the Chief Inspector liked it. Far less likelihood of being overheard, he said, with a crush of people all shouting at the tops of their voices. 'I just don't know where I'm going with this case at all,' he said morosely.

'If he's telling the truth, I suppose that lets him out,' said Rowlands.

'I don't see that it does, necessarily,' replied the policeman. 'He might just have used the call to his broker as an excuse, to cover the fact that he was making another call.'

'Couldn't that be traced?' said Rowlands.

'Almost impossible, I'm afraid,' said the other. 'These public telephone boxes are a godsend to criminals. But we'll catch him, never fear,' he added grimly.

'Then you think he *is* guilty?' said Rowlands.

'I gather from your tone of voice that you don't?'

'I find it hard to believe that a man so devoted to his wife that he couldn't bear her infatuation with another man would have been capable of killing her, that's all.'

'Indeed?' The Chief Inspector's voice was heavy with irony. 'Then just who do you think killed him?'

'I couldn't say. But I can't see Metcalfe as the murderer, somehow.'

Douglas emitted a dry chuckle. 'You're a hard man to please, Mr Rowlands. Another pint?'

'Thank you,' said Rowlands, then as the other man began to get to his feet, 'Surely you're not suggesting that Metcalfe killed Farley?'

'As it happens, I'm not. Farley's murder may turn out to be unconnected to either of the other two. I believe I mentioned that he was mixed up in this de Havilland affair?'

'Passing on secrets to a rival firm, you mean? You did, indeed,' said Rowlands. 'We haven't yet managed to get Higgins to confess that he was involved in it, too,' said Douglas. 'But I have every confidence that we'll get the evidence we need before long.'

'Which suggests you still think that Higgins killed Farley,' said Rowlands. 'Presumably to silence him.

That is,' he added, in a sceptical tone, 'if we suppose Farley was blackmailing Higgins, and not the other way around.'

Douglas guffawed. 'I do so enjoy our little discussions,' he said. They keep me on my toes, as it were.' He absented himself for a few moments, returning with a couple of brimming pints. 'Here we are,' he said; then, continuing from where they'd left off, 'Yes, it had occurred to me that since it was Farley who was selling the secrets, it ought to have been Higgins who got it in the neck, always supposing he'd been tapping Farley for money. But I happen to think there might have been another side to the story. Supposing Higgins was in on it, too – and we do know that more than one of 'em was involved – Farley might have been getting greedy, and threatened to expose Higgins' part in it so that he – Higgins, that is – was obliged to put him out of the way.'

'It's possible,' said Rowlands, not quite managing to disguise his scepticism. 'I don't suppose,' he said, 'that I could have a few minutes' conversation with Higgins?'

'Any special reason?'

'Not really. That is . . . I wondered if he'd said anything about exactly how the plane was sabotaged. Given that he's something of an expert on such matters. Aeroplanes, I mean.'

'It's all in the notes,' grunted the other man, taking a sip of his pint. 'Lovely, that. Better than the first. I suppose

I could let you have a gander at 'em, if you like. Unofficially, o' course.'

'I don't think that would be much good to me,' said Rowlands, with a smile.

'True enough. Is this one of your famous hunches?' said the Chief Inspector, to cover up his blunder. 'Because if it is, you'd better let me in on it PDQ.'

'I'd just like to get a clearer idea of what happened,' said Rowlands. 'Talking to people seems the best way since, as you've pointed out, I'm not in a position to read the case notes. Even if those were to be made available to me,' he added quickly, to avert an outburst from Douglas. It came anyway.

'You do realise,' said the policeman in a furious undertone, 'that if it got out that I'd allowed a material witness – that's you, Mr Rowlands, in case you didn't know – to interview another witness, it could jeopardise the whole case?'

'I can see that it might,' said Rowlands meekly.

'It's completely against the rules.' The Chief Inspector sighed. 'Sometimes I think I need my head examining,' he muttered. 'All right, all right. I'll have a word with the prison governor. He owes me a favour. You can have ten minutes with the suspect – no more. On one condition, mind. If you do get anything of interest out of Higgins, I want to be the first to know. None of your haring off on your own private little investigations, as you've done in the past.' This was an allusion to an earlier case, in which Rowlands had been involved. In following his own line, as he had, he'd almost succeeded in getting himself killed.

'Don't worry,' he said. 'I've lost my taste for grappling with murderers.'

As it happened, he had enough on his plate, dealing with his sister's now all too urgent flight from London. Because the more Rowlands thought about it, the more it seemed to him that Douglas knew, or guessed, where Dorothy was hiding. That piece of obfuscation he'd come out with, concerning the identity of the 'dark-haired young woman' who'd been with Rowlands the day of the fatal crash at Hendon Aerodrome, had been the Chief Inspector's idea of a warning. He'd even repeated the falsehood in front of his junior officer. No, thought Rowlands, he'd be a fool to ignore such warnings from such a quarter. Despite what he'd said to Dorothy, he wasn't at all sure that he couldn't be made to testify against her.

The letter had accordingly been typed, and an answer received – as Rowlands had hoped – the following day. '*Dear Old Fellow,*' it began. '*Cecily and I would be delighted to have Mrs Lehmann and her boys to stay. I knew her before she was "Mrs Lehmann" in fact. She came to St Dunstan's several times, as I recall – for concerts and the like. I remember thinking what a jolly kid she was . . .*' A few further remarks followed, concerning the weather in Cornwall – hot, but inclined to be stormy – and the national financial crisis: '. . . *rather worrying, just at present, don't you think? It sounds as if the grand panjandrums at Westminster are decidedly rattled – with even the PM cutting short his holiday to come back and tackle the crisis. Is this what we fought the war for, I wonder?'* Then came a postscript: *'Ciss has just put her head around the door to say that, as we've no guests booked at the hotel until the middle of next month, she sees no reason why Edith and the girls shouldn't come too . . . that is, if you don't mind being abandoned by your womenfolk for a week or two, old man . . .'*

He didn't mind a bit. An acceptance was sent, and a couple of days of frantic washing and ironing commenced before the suitcases were packed with all the clothes and equipment – sandshoes, bathing dresses, sun hats – essential for a seaside holiday. Then all that remained was to make the sandwiches (for the train journey would be a long one) and for a taxi to be called to take the lot of them to Kingston Station, on the first stage of the six-hour journey by Great Western Railway from London to Penzance. Edith's mother, who was to stay with friends in Poole, was to go some of the way with them, and Rowlands was to see the whole party off at Paddington Station.

Quite apart from the satisfaction of knowing that his wife and family would soon be enjoying themselves in a place they knew and loved, was the relief he felt at the thought that Dorothy would be out of harm's way. The ever-present dread that she might be taken up by the police, which had haunted him all those weeks, was lifted. He could breathe at last, he thought. 'Are you sure you're going to be all right?' said Edith.

'Of course I'll be all right.' He drew her to him and kissed her. 'Telephone when you arrive, won't you?'

'Of course.' Still she hesitated on the platform. 'There's that egg and ham pie in the larder for your supper,' she said.

'I know.' He squeezed her hand. 'Better get a move on, old girl,' he said as the guard went past, ostentatiously slamming doors.

'All right,' said Edith. 'Look after yourself, won't you? Don't go getting yourself into any scrapes.' A judiciously edited summary of the previous day's conversation with the Chief Inspector had clearly given his wife food for thought.

'I'll try not to. Now off you go – unless you want the children to end up in Cornwall all by themselves.'

'I'm going.' He held her hand until she was safely on board. Then he turned to Dorothy.

'Be good, old thing,' he said. They exchanged a brief hug. 'And give my best to Jack.'

'I will.' Then she, too, got on – not a moment too soon, for the guard now blew his whistle, and a cacophony of slamming doors and shouted farewells ensued as the six minutes past ten to Penzance began its stately departure. Its great wheels began to grind, slowly at first, then inexorably gathering speed, and clouds of smoke belched from its stack, leaving a taste of soot. A window was flung up. 'Goodbye, Daddy!' cried a voice – Anne's

237

– from the moving train. He waved his hand, hoping she'd see even though, chances were, he'd be invisible to her, lost in a swirling cloud. It was wrong to have favourites, he knew, but he'd always had a soft spot for his middle daughter.

It was the Dog Days. The weather, which had been dull and rainy, suddenly took a turn for the better. London sweltered in the heat. In the parks, the grass had a scorched look, and the leaves were turning brown on all the plane trees. At Dickens & Jones, there was a run on panama hats and white flannel trousers, while bathing dresses had long sold out at Harrods. As the Prime Minister and his Cabinet, suitably clad in frock coats and wing collars, thrashed out a solution to the current National Emergency, Kent beat Surrey at the Oval, in temperatures the BBC commentator described as 'hotter than Calcutta'. At Goodwood, the opening race was won by Lord Abergavenny's Knight of the Vale, beating Pretty Boy by a length, and in the Court of Criminal Appeal, the Lord Chief Justice – perhaps affected by the stifling atmosphere of the courtroom – reduced a sentence of five years' penal servitude, passed on Frank Jones at the Wiltshire sessions for breaking into the booking office of a railway station and stealing a Swiss roll and two pork pies, to eighteen months' imprisonment with hard labour.

After his week's incarceration, Bert Higgins seemed crushed and defeated – a far cry from the cheerful individual Rowlands had met three months before at Croydon Airport. He seemed pathetically grateful to see his visitor, exclaiming at intervals, 'I must say, this is very good of you, Mr Rowlands, sir,' and seeming on occasion to be on the verge of breaking down. 'They're going to hang me, sir, as sure as eggs is eggs,' he said at one point, reaching to clutch at Rowlands' hand across the table. 'But I didn't do it. What reason would I of had? Bill was a mate of mine. Not but that he couldn't be a surly bugger when he wanted to be – begging your pardon, sir – but bash 'is brains out for 'im? Nah. What would of been the good of that?'

So it went on, for almost the whole of the time allocated to the visit, with Higgins' hoarse sing-song interrupted from time to time by bouts of coughing – brought on by the rough tobacco in the hand-rolled cigarettes he favoured, Rowlands supposed. His gift of two packs of Capstan had been received with fervent gratitude – 'I must say, this is very good of you, Mr Rowlands, sir' – and a solemn declaration to 'save 'em for later' that Rowlands suspected was a polite way of saying he preferred to smoke his own. To what Rowlands already knew of the two hours leading up to the discovery of Farley's body Higgins could add little, however.

He'd arrived at the aerodrome at nine on the Saturday morning, he said. He'd gone straight to the hangar. Farley was already there – at work on the Gipsy Moth – and the two of them had carried on working for the next hour and forty-five minutes. Around ten o'clock, they'd been joined by Ginger Perkins, who'd pottered around doing odd jobs – 'sweeping up and suchlike,' said Higgins – before Farley noticed they'd run out of dope, and sent the lad to the workshop to fetch some. At a quarter to eleven, Higgins and Farley had gone to the tea hut for tea and a smoke since they weren't allowed to light up in the hangars. It drove the Captain wild to have people smoking too near the machines, said the chief mechanic, what with all the drums of fuel that were standing about.

They'd got to the hut, which was where they kept the kettle and a gas ring, said Higgins, and brewed up. Then, after about ten minutes, Farley noticed his knife was missing – he'd been going to cut up a bit of sausage he'd brought along for his dinner. He thought he might have dropped it in the hangar, he said, and so he went back for it. That was the last time Higgins had seen him alive. 'The next I knew, sir, was some woman – begging your pardon, sir, I mean that Mrs Metcalfe – screeching her head off. I ran out of the hut, and round the side of Hangar Three, and found you, sir, with the lady.'

'And did you see anyone else?' asked Rowlands. 'Apart from Mrs Metcalfe and myself?'

'Well, no, Mr Rowlands, sir, I can't say as I did. Only young Ginger, but if you knew 'im, sir, you'd know 'ee wouldn't hurt a fly.'

When the subject of Percival's death was touched on, the ground engineer waxed even more loudly indignant than he had at the suggestion that he might have murdered Bill Farley, 'They're trying to say I fixed that machine so's it'd crash,' he said. 'The idea!' The anger in his voice was mixed with scorn. 'That I'd queer the engine so's it'd stall in mid-air . . . or whatever it was the bugger did. Well, it beggars belief, that's all. Not but that I couldn't of done it,' he added, pausing to relight the stub of roll-up he'd been smoking all the while, 'but I wouldn't of done it like that, sir. Even if I had done it – which I ain't.'

'How would you have done it?' asked Rowlands, struck by the fact that Higgins didn't appear to know how it was the plane had actually been sabotaged. Unless of course he was being extraordinarily cunning, but Rowlands didn't think he had it in him. This feeling was strengthened when Higgins replied, 'Why, bless you, sir, I wouldn't of gone monkeying around with the engine at all, not when an Ace like Captain Percival, Gawd rest 'im, was flying the machine. With his experience flying crates in the war – some of 'em pretty much held together with string and glue, sir, you may be sure – he'd 'ave been able to get 'er down, no trouble at all, even with the engine stalled. See, when you come down to it,' went on the chief mechanic warming to his theme, 'an aeroplane's no more than a fancy sort of glider. Captain Percival would 'ave been well able to bring 'er out of a spin like that, sir, and land 'er as easy as winking . . .'

'Why didn't he then?' interrupted Rowlands. 'If, as you say, he was perfectly capable of landing the plane in the event of engine failure.'

'Couldn't say, sir,' replied Higgins. 'What I will say is that unless there'd been a mechanical failure of some kind, there's nothing the Captain couldn't of got himself out of – being the pilot he was. I'd stake my neck on it,' he added, apparently oblivious to the fact that he already had. 'No, in my opinion, the only thing that'd have done for the Captain would be if someone had used the wrong kind of petrol in the Avian. That would of clogged the filters, see, and made the engine seize up.'

'According to you, he'd still have been able to get out of it,' said Rowlands.

'Not if he was overcome with fumes, like,' was the reply. 'Then he'd have been a goner, all right. Oh, I've seen some nasty crashes caused by a filter's being clogged,' he said. 'Fumes go the wrong way, you see, and the pilot gets overcome. Horrible way to go,' he added. Aside from this account of the various ways that the plane might have been 'fixed', Higgins was unable to cast any more light on the day of the fatal crash. Yes, he'd spoken to the Captain just before he'd gone to have his lunch – 'You yourself can bear me out, sir' – and no, he hadn't spoken to him before he'd taken the plane up. 'Not beyond a wave to say everything was A-OK – which as far as I knew, it was, sir.'

Asked to account for the bloodstained overalls which had been found in his locker, Higgins pronounced himself mystified. 'They're my overalls, all right. Got my initials – AWH – on the pocket, right enough. The missus did 'em after a couple of pairs went missing. We have to buy our own, you see. As to how they got to be in the state they're in, I couldn't say, Mr Rowlands, sir. Reckon somebody must have it in for me,' said the chief mechanic, in a voice that trembled slightly.

There was not much more to be got out of Higgins in the few minutes that remained, and Rowlands took his leave of the prisoner, feeling that he was no further forward. For while he felt in his bones that Higgins was telling the truth, there was still that crucial period to account for – between five minutes to eleven, when Farley had left the tea hut, and thirteen minutes past – when Higgins had rushed out of the building (or so he claimed) after hearing Irene Metcalfe's screams. That was eighteen minutes unaccounted for, during which he'd have had ample time to follow Farley to Hangar Three, kill him, and return to the tea hut, having first concealed his bloodied overalls in his locker, to be disposed of later.

Seated on the jolting tram that was taking him from the stop near Pentonville Prison along the Euston Road to Regent's Park, Rowlands frowned and shook his head. Something wasn't right. Even if Higgins had managed to carry out the murder without being seen – and hadn't Metcalfe been spotted by Ginger Perkins outside the hangar at about that time? – he'd still have had no way of knowing for certain that the body would be found before he returned to the hangar himself. He was taking an awful risk, thought Rowlands. Always supposing he did it, which he was inclined to doubt, what were the chances that he'd have been the first person to find the body?

He – Higgins – could have had no notion that Irene Metcalfe would be the first to raise the alarm. Unless he'd known she was there, in the office, all along, in which case, why hadn't he killed her, too? Back and forth in Rowlands' mind went the arguments for and against Higgins' innocence as the crowded tram lurched and rattled along, forcing him to hold tight to the back of the seat in front in order to avoid bumping into his neighbour – an elderly lady with a large shopping basket, the edge of which connected uncomfortably, from time to time, with Rowlands' ribs. 'It doesn't make sense,' he muttered to himself at one point, forgetting he wasn't alone. 'No, that's right,' said his neighbour, evidently thinking he was referring to something else. 'A shocking waste, I call it.'

'Great Portland Street!' shouted the conductor, obviating the need for Rowlands to reply. He got to his feet. There was a stop further down, along the Marylebone Road, but he wanted a chance to think things out. Besides, the walk across the park would do him good. Even though it was not yet ten, it was already hot; it would be stifling by midday. Having been pointed in the right direction by the said conductor – who'd lost a brother at Passchendaele, he said – Rowlands skirted Park Square Gardens and went in through the gate that led onto the Broadwalk. Here, with the crunching of gravel underfoot to warn him of the advent of other passers-by, he could walk in relative safety, released from the ever-present need to be vigilant that dogged his steps elsewhere. Yes, there were those eighteen minutes, and there was the fact of the bloodstained overalls. Both pointed to Higgins' guilt. And yet somehow Rowlands couldn't see the man as a murderer. Farley, now . . . But Farley was dead.

Then there was the question of who it was that had fixed Percival's plane and caused the fatal crash. Farley had certainly had the opportunity since he'd been alone in the hangar for at least some of the time after he'd left the tea hut. Had Higgins gone in search of him, and found him tampering with the Moth? Had a struggle ensued, in which Farley had come off worst? Then why the hell didn't he say so? said Rowlands to himself. He'd have been able to make a case that it was self-defence. Of course, there was the inconvenient fact that the other plane had also been sabotaged, and certainly not by Farley unless he'd done it the night before. Which meant it could only have been Higgins – or another, as yet unknown. 'Damn and blast this case!' muttered Rowlands, striking out across the grass towards the Inner Circle. 'It just gets more and more confusing.'

# Chapter Thirteen

The heady scent of late summer roses greeted him as he reached Queen Mary's Gardens – a favourite spot in the early days of his courtship of Edith, and still a place in which he found a kind of refuge. As he strolled past fragrant beds of Ena Harkness and Madame Hardy, and ducked under trellises heavy with the scented blooms of Blanche Moreau, it struck him with painful force that it was here, or not far from here, that he'd first met Irene Metcalfe and her boy. He wondered what had become of the child, with his mother dead, and his father now under suspicion of having killed her. Could Metcalfe really have arranged his wife's murder? He was something of a cold fish, it was true, but was he capable of such extreme cold-bloodedness? During Rowlands' time in the army, he'd seen death in many forms – most of them ugly. But this, the savage slaughter of a defenceless young mother, in her own home, seemed to him one of the worst.

With some reluctance, he turned his thoughts to the events of that day, now over a week ago, when he'd found himself once more the first on the scene of a murder. Again, the timing was very tight, he thought. Whoever had killed Mrs Metcalfe had had the luck of the devil. There'd been that bare half-hour between the florist's boy, Davy Hughes, arriving at Gloucester Mansions with the flowers sometime after half past three, and his own arrival at the Metcalfes' flat. The only witnesses had been the lad himself, and Grundley, the porter. As the Chief Inspector saw it, it had been Metcalfe's telephone call to the killer which had set the whole thing in motion.

Yet again, it seemed so risky, he thought, with so much depending on the perpetrator's knowing in advance about the movements of other people. Knowing that the maid would be out with the child – the cook, too, for that matter. Knowing that the florist's boy could be bought. 'How could he have known it would work out the way he wanted it?' muttered Rowlands as he let himself into the office.

'Did you say something, Mr Rowlands?' It was Miss Collins, already tapping away at her typewriter. He really must get out of the habit of talking to himself, Rowlands thought.

'Oh, good morning, Miss Collins. No, it was nothing,' he replied. 'Have those invoices come in yet?' He'd put the whole thing out of his mind, he told himself. Maybe if he stopped thinking about it so hard, an answer to the conundrum of who killed Irene Metcalfe would come to him.

And yet as he dictated letters and answered telephone calls, Rowlands couldn't prevent himself from worrying away at the loose threads of what one might have called, for want of a better name, 'The Aeroplane Murders'. Because if he was certain of one thing, it was that the three killings had to be linked . . . and what linked them was their connection with flying. Leaning back in the sturdy wooden swivel chair, he thought about each in turn. Farley's murder had come first, it was true, but had he perhaps been killed because he'd been about to prevent the murderer from carrying out his real purpose, which was the killing of Alan Percival? He felt he was finally on to something, here. What if it had been Metcalfe who'd been tampering with the plane when Farley unexpectedly returned? Metcalfe had certainly been seen outside the hangar at around the time of the murder. That, at least, made a kind of sense, thought Rowlands.

Far from being premeditated, Farley's murder had been the act of a man driven by panic and fearful of discovery. A man, moreover, with enough aviation experience to know how to sabotage a plane. Again, Metcalfe fitted the bill, thought Rowlands unhappily. But then there was the question of those overalls. Had it been mere coincidence that they'd been hidden in Higgins' locker? He turned his attention to the faked accident. It was this that didn't hang together with the rest. Even supposing that Metcalfe had sabotaged the first plane, how could he have known that it was Harmsworth's machine that Percival would end up flying? He'd left the aerodrome by then, so he'd have had no opportunity for carrying out the sabotage. Unless . . . The possibility that Metcalfe had paid someone else – Higgins, perhaps – to tamper with the aircraft crossed Rowlands' mind. It would fit with the way he'd, allegedly, carried out his wife's murder.

'I just don't like it,' said Rowlands aloud. Fortunately, the office was empty, apart from himself, Miss Collins having gone out for her lunch. As with the killing of Mrs Metcalfe, there were too many things which could have gone wrong, or which depended on other things happening. In the drowsy, late summer heat of the silent office, he considered once more the question of who had wanted Alan Percival dead. Of the two main candidates for this dubious distinction, neither entirely matched up with the facts as they were known to him. Higgins had had the opportunity, to be sure, but where was the motive? This was a man whose principle virtue was loyalty; hardworking, unimaginative and, one assumed, fundamentally decent. Could he really have connived at selling his employer's secrets to a rival firm, then killed his co-conspirator in a brawl over money? It seemed unlikely to Rowlands.

Metcalfe – who had, at least, a motive for doing away with the rival who'd stolen his wife's affections – seemed to have had less of an opportunity to enact his revenge. Perhaps, thought Rowlands. I need to start looking at this in a different way. All at once, he felt in need of a breath of air. Miss Collins wouldn't be back for a good half-hour; he'd take a turn around the grounds, to clear his head. It was one of the joys of the place, he thought – the fact that you could almost believe yourself in the heart of the country, surrounded by fields and woods, while being in fact smack in the middle of London. Only the distant sound of traffic on the Marylebone Road gave the lie to this impression.

Crossing the wide lawn shaded with spreading cedars that lay behind the Lodge, he encountered a group of St Dunstan's men, who were clearly of the same mind. 'Fine day,' he said; then, when further pleasantries had been exchanged, 'Is Stratham about, do you know?'

The man thus addressed, a cheerful Lancastrian, by the name of Featherstone, replied, 'I haven't see him.' Then, to another of their party, 'What about you, Jock?' The latter, who wasn't from north of the border, but a Canadian, by the name of McCallum, said that he hadn't run across Stratham that day, either.

'Never mind,' said Rowlands. 'It's not terribly important. If any of you do see him around, tell him to look in at the office, will you?'

Back in the office, he got on with what needed to be done – all of it routine stuff, thank heaven – while all the time his thoughts were elsewhere. It was just possible, wasn't it? He considered the timing of the thing. Yes. If the man he had in mind had arrived at the aerodrome half an hour earlier than the time he'd said, then it was certainly possible he could have fixed the Moth and murdered Farley. As for the murder of Alan Percival – who else had had a better opportunity to sabotage the plane in which the airman had suffered his fatal crash, but the man to whom the plane belonged? Of course, Rowlands had to admit, he wasn't the only one to whom the idea had occurred: hadn't the Chief Inspector raised the fact of Cecil Harmsworth's rivalry with Percival right at the start?

With regard to the earlier act of sabotage – well, if it could be proved that he'd lied about the time he'd got to Hendon that would go some way towards confirming his guilt. As for the killing of Irene Metcalfe . . . 'I'm just off, now, Mr Rowlands,' said Miss Collins, breaking into these sanguinary thoughts.

'Yes, that's all right,' he replied. 'Thank you, Miss Collins. I'll see you in the morning.'

After she'd left, he sat for a few moments without stirring. With Edith and the children away – and thank the Lord that Dorothy had gone with them – there was no need to hurry back. Nor did the heat of the day encourage energetic movement. Instead, since he was now alone, he allowed himself the luxury of removing his jacket. Something had occurred to him just now before Miss Collins had spoken. Ah, yes . . . Let's suppose Metcalfe didn't do it, he thought. Then who else had a motive to kill her? A small sound, as of somebody fumbling with a door handle, brought him back to the here and now. 'Who's there?' he said. 'Is that you, Miss Collins?' Although it wasn't her step. The door opened.

'Rowlands?' said a voice.

'Hello, Stratham. Yes, do come in. There's a chair to the left of my desk, about two paces from the door.'

'Thanks,' said the other, seating himself upon it. 'You wanted to see me?' he said.

'Yes.' Rowlands hesitated a moment, not sure how best to put the question he wanted to ask. He decided that a forthright approach was best. 'It's about Harmsworth. When we met at Hendon last Saturday, you said something about there having been a bit of bad blood between him and Percival. It was as a result of something that happened during the war, I think you said.'

'That's right,' said Stratham. Now it was his turn to pause. 'May I ask why you want to know?'

'Just interested,' said Rowlands, aware that his interest might seem merely prurient, in the aftermath of Percival's death. 'It stuck in my mind, I suppose.'

'Only after what's happened – with Percival going west . . . Well, I wouldn't want to stir things up again.'

'No, of course not. I can promise you that it won't go any further,' said Rowlands, making a mental reservation that it depended on what the story was. Stratham seemed satisfied with this, however.

'I suppose it can't do any harm for you to know,' he said. 'It was running into them both again after so many years that brought it all back. Almost as if . . . I don't know . . . the years had melted away, and we were all a bunch of scrubby schoolboys, and back in uniform again. I don't know if that makes any sense to you?'

'Perfect sense,' replied Rowlands.

What followed was a not uncommon tale of a young, inexperienced man trying to impress a more seasoned peer, the latter having been Alan Percival. 'You have to understand that to us he was like a god,' Stratham said, sounding in that moment like the youngster he had been in those days of war and adventure. 'He was only twenty-two – I was eighteen myself, at the time – but he'd already notched up twenty kills in three months. He was absolutely fearless.'

He broke off, as if trying to marshal his thoughts. 'This was the spring of 1915. Harmsworth had just joined the Squadron. I remember that, because it wasn't long after I'd arrived at the base myself. We were all pretty green, except for Percival. As I said, we were all a little in awe of him. But it was Harmsworth who really worshipped him. It was all: "Need a light, old man?" every time Percival got out his cigarettes, and "Tell us about the time you downed that Hun crate over Abbeville," about some exploit or another. We all got a bit sick of it in the end. But that was Harmsworth for you. Always out to please. You know the type, I expect.' Rowlands did. 'Well, as I said, this kind of thing went on for a while, with Harmsworth ingratiating himself more and more.'

'How did Percival take it?'

'I don't think he liked it much. But then, one never really knew what Percival was thinking. It was as if his mind was . . . I don't know . . . elsewhere. He wouldn't have let a thing like that bother him. And then of course, he and Harmsworth had known one another from before.'

'Had they?'

'Oh yes. Harmsworth was his fag at school, I believe. Their people knew each other. So even if he'd wanted to give him the brush-off, it would have been awkward for him.'

'I see.' From outside, came the sound of laughter and voices upraised in friendly argument. Some of the men taking a turn around the grounds before supper, thought Rowlands 'Go on with what you were saying,' he said since Stratham had once more fallen silent.

'Oh! Yes, of course. Well, it was one day a few weeks after Harmsworth arrived. He'd been sticking to Percival like glue all this time, as I was saying. We were all of us sitting in the Mess, playing cards, when a message came in that a German reconnaissance machine had been spotted over the trenches at Arras . . . I say,' said Stratham. 'Do you mind if I smoke?'

'Not a bit. Here, have one of mine.'

'Thanks.' A few moments passed while both men lit up. Then Stratham went on, 'Where was I? Oh, yes . . . Percival was first to his machine, of course.

Harmsworth followed hard on his heels. He wasn't going to miss the chance of sharing in the glory. His own score up to this point, you understand, hadn't been anything to write home about. Six or eight kills in as many weeks. Of course, he was only a novice . . .'

Stratham paused a moment, as if the very act of narrating had brought it all back to him: that day, and its particular sensations. *The smell of aviation fuel mingling with that of sun-bleached grass of the airfield. The roar of aeroplanes taking off growing gradually fainter as they disappeared above the treetops. The ethereal blue of the sky.* 'I was still at the airfield when they came back, two hours later,' he went on. 'There was something wrong with my machine, as I recall – the altimeter kept getting stuck – and so I saw them come in. Percival first, swooping down in that lazy way he had, as if he was leaving it to the very last second to bring the nose up and land the thing safely; Harmsworth bringing his kite down a few minutes later like a small boy scrambling after a bigger one. Keen to impress, you know.'

He laughed. 'Funny,' he said. 'The things you remember. But it was what happened next that struck me as odd. Because as Percival was walking back across the field towards the huts – not looking especially pleased with himself, but then he never did, you know – Harmsworth got out of his plane and came running up behind him. He said something to Percival which made him stop dead and stare at him as if he'd gone insane – Harmsworth, that is. I actually heard him shout: "You must be off your head!"

and then turn and walk away, with Harmsworth tagging along at his heels, like some eager little dog. "We got him all right," I heard Harmsworth say. "Surely you saw him go down? He was hit all right. I'll swear to it." To which Percival said not a word, but just kept on walking as if he wanted to shake the other man off, like a burr that had got stuck to his coat.

'Later that night, in the Mess,' Stratham went on, 'there was champagne all round, on account of Percival's latest kill, which of course he shared with Harmsworth since they'd gone on the mission together. Percival's score was now up to thirty, so he wasn't about to contest it, but I remember he looked pretty sick at the time, as if his heart wasn't in it. And I couldn't help noticing – we all did – that he spoke not a word to Harmsworth the whole evening.'

'Are you saying that Harmsworth lied about the German plane going down?' asked Rowlands. 'That's exactly what I'm saying,' was the reply. 'The thing is, Percival was hardly going to call him out about it when his own reputation was at stake, to say nothing of the fact that the chap had been his fag and all that. One doesn't accuse a friend of cheating. But it made for some bad feeling in the Squadron, I can tell you, with some people saying that Percival was just a fake . . . Not me,' he added. 'I knew it wasn't his idea to add that plane to his tally.'

'Maybe they really did shoot the plane down?' said Rowlands. 'What proof was there, either way?'

'None,' said Stratham. 'Although a couple of the chaps who flew over the area next day said there wasn't any sign of debris. Not that there always was if the fire was bad enough, you know.'

'No,' said Rowlands. 'I can see that. But even so . . .'

'Even so, people got the feeling that there'd been a bit of dirty work. Fliers are strange creatures,' said Stratham. 'Hero-worship a man one day – the next, his name's mud . . . But as I said, it was all a long time ago. And Percival's dead. It doesn't matter now.'

The story Stratham had told him didn't of itself offer a satisfactory motive for murder, in Rowlands' view. It was an uncorroborated tale about a rather shabby piece of behaviour, which had occurred a long time ago. More than that, one of the men it most concerned was dead. There was no one now to know, or care, whether it was true or false. Except Stratham, of course, and he himself had said it was best to let sleeping dogs lie. That the story should have surfaced at all after fifteen years, was fortuitous – the result of a chance meeting between men who hadn't seen each other in more than a decade. Rowlands thought again about the quarrel he'd overheard, that day at the RAF show, and of the very real venom there'd been in the voices of the two airmen. Had one of them been driven to murder the other over something which had happened in the past? Or was it simple rivalry over a woman that lay at the heart of it?

It struck Rowlands all of a sudden as he locked up the office and set out across the park on the first stage of his homeward journey, that it might have been a combination of both. If Percival, knowing his rival's attraction towards the beautiful aviatrix, had threatened to expose Harmsworth's disreputable act, then what had been merely an old story, of no interest to anyone, might have become more significant. A reason to kill, in fact . . . 'It's certainly a thought,' he murmured to himself, striding out across the grass.

He'd reached the Outer Circle and was strolling along past Cumberland Terrace; a vague recollection of its handsome white stucco mansions flitted across his mind. It was odd how, even after almost a decade and a half of blindness, his memory still supplied such images so that his world, far from being the unrelieved darkness of popular imagination, was made up of glimpses and halftones: a chiaroscuro of remembered sights and shadowy impressions. Just now, for instance, the evening sun, striking the dazzling white surface of the tall buildings, cast its reflected glow full on his face. He'd always been grateful for the small amount of sight he had left, even if, in the early days, it had made it harder to adapt to the realities of being blind.

The rude blare of a klaxon interrupted these thoughts, making Rowlands jump half out of his skin. 'Sorry!' he mouthed, although as far as he could tell, he hadn't been about to step out in front of the motorcar – a powerful one, from the sound of the engine – which was even now pulling up alongside him. He was even more startled to hear himself hailed by the driver.

'Hello! It's Mr Rowlands, isn't it?'

'Miss Malory.' His heart was still pounding from the shock. Ridiculous. He forced a smile, remembering the circumstances under which they had last met. 'I . . . I didn't expect to run into you in this part of the world,' he stammered, feeling more and more foolish.

'No?' she said carelessly. 'I suppose it isn't my usual neck of the woods. I had some things to do in the neighbourhood, as a matter of fact.'

'Ah.' It really was no concern of his what she was doing here, he thought. 'Well don't just stand there gaping! Hop in,' she said. 'I take it you are on your way back to Kingston?'

'Yes. That is . . .'

'I'm going that way too, as it happens,' said Olave Malory. 'Come on! There's a police constable coming this way, with a very fishy look in his eye.'

'Right-ho,' said Rowlands, thinking, as he climbed into the passenger seat of the Aston Martin, that he'd never get a better opportunity to check up on the movements of Cecil Harmsworth, not to mention those of Miss Malory herself.

'Here,' said his companion, handing him the leather helmet and goggles. 'You should probably put these on. I like to put my foot down, and it throws up quite bit of dust.' He did as he was told, uncomfortably reminded of the last time he'd worn such headgear – the day of his joyride in Percival's Gipsy Moth. As if she'd been privy to the thought, Miss Malory said, 'I was just picking up some things from Alan's flat. Books I'd lent him. Letters. The usual rubbish,' she added, with an attempt at lightheartedness. 'One doesn't like to think of strangers pawing through it.'

'No, of course not.' So that was why she was here! Rowlands couldn't remember if Percival had ever mentioned he'd had a flat in Cumberland Terrace. He supposed Dorothy must have known, although she'd kept it dark. The powerful car moved off, and presently joined the stream of early evening traffic heading westward along the Marylebone Road. In the confined space in which they sat – really not so different from the cockpit of an aircraft, he thought – Rowlands could not but be aware of his companion's physical presence. Once or twice, as she was changing gear, her hand inadvertently brushed his knee, and an agreeable scent – *Chypre, was it*? – wafted towards him from the silk scarf she wore. They'd gone some way along the busy thoroughfare before the aviatrix broke the silence, or what passed for silence in an open-topped car.

'He mattered to me,' she said, her voice just audible over the throaty purr of the engine. 'Although you might not think it.'

'It's really not any of my business . . .' he started to reply, but she forestalled him.

'I was appallingly rude to you when we last met,' she said. 'To your sister, too,' she added, somewhat grudgingly.

'We were all rather upset,' replied Rowlands, choosing to overlook the fact that the offensive remarks in question had been made *before* the fatal accident which was the cause of the upset. 'People often say things they don't mean.'

'Oh, but I *did* mean them,' said Olave Malory calmly. 'I've got a beastly temper.' As if to illustrate this remark, she gave a blast on the klaxon, evidently irritated by the slow progress of the traffic up ahead. 'Do get a move on!' she shouted. 'Why people can't learn to give way, instead of hogging the middle of the road, I've no idea.' Only when the traffic jam at the mouth of Paddington Station had been left behind, and she was able to 'put her foot down' at last, did she expand on her earlier statement. 'We were going to be married, you know.'

Just in time, Rowlands restrained himself from replying that he did know. 'I'm sorry,' he said.

'Oh, I was the one who ended it,' said Olave Malory, her bright tone belying the seriousness of her words. 'To tell you the truth, I got rather fed up with playing second fiddle to Alan's other women.' This time, Rowlands said nothing. Nor did his companion seem to require a response. It was as if she were talking to herself as much as to him, Rowlands thought, raising her voice over the roar of the car's engine, and the buffeting of the wind in their faces. 'We quarrelled about it endlessly, of course. The worst of it was, Alan's being such public figure meant that every time he had a fling, it ended up in the papers.'

Rowlands recalled Percival's bitterness on the subject of the Press. No wonder he'd been so angry if a consequence of his notoriety had been the breaking of his engagement. 'Anyway, just before it . . . happened, I'd decided I'd had enough,' Olave Malory said. 'I told him it was either the popsies or me – he couldn't have both.' She laughed, a little wildly, Rowlands thought. 'Do you know what he said?' she cried. '"I can't help it. It's just the way I am." Can you believe that? Looking at me with such a hurt look in his eyes. Like a small boy who's been told he can't have any more sweets.'

# Chapter Fourteen

They'd reached Chiswick Bridge before she spoke again, sounding vaguely apologetic. 'I say, I hope you don't mind, but I was thinking of calling in at the Air Park.' By which she meant Hendon, Rowlands surmised, knowing that this was the name under which the aerodrome had been known when it was first set up three years before as a private flying club. 'It's practically on our way.'

'Of course,' he murmured.

'I've something to collect,' Olave Malory said, again sounding a little abashed. 'It shouldn't take long.' They made good time once out of the built-up areas. 'Dreadful, this suburban sprawl, isn't it?' remarked Miss Malory as they roared through Perivale and Greenford and were soon turning in along the drive that would take them to the gates of the aerodrome. Instead of driving up to the Club House, however, she took the turning to the right onto the perimeter road that led to the hangars, along which Rowlands himself had walked, that fateful Saturday. They had gone no more than a few hundred yards before they came to a stop.

It seemed to Rowlands, judging by the distant sounds of engines revving, that they must be in the vicinity of Hangar Three – an impression confirmed a moment later when Miss Malory said, 'Just popping into the big shed. He . . . he left his spare flying jacket, you know.' She was already getting out of the car, with a swish of long legs in linen trousers. 'If you'll just wait here, I won't be long,' she called, her voice now coming to him from a few feet away.

She'd be taking the short cut, he supposed, giving her a few moments' head start. He'd of course not the slightest intention of staying put. She'd left the keys in the car, he discovered, deciding to pocket them just in case. He couldn't imagine that anyone familiar with Miss Malory's distinctive vehicle, or with that lady's temper, would be so foolhardy as to risk taking the Aston Martin for a joyride, but you never knew with airmen. He got out in turn, and was soon striding along the path the aviatrix had taken, and along which he himself, not six weeks before, had almost run slap bang into the man who'd just murdered Bill Farley.

Around him, a smell of rotting leaves told him that, notwithstanding the dry spell they'd had, the ground here, covered as it was by dense clumps of evergreens, remained damp. He wondered if the police had ever made anything of that footprint – a size ten, wasn't it? That suggested a bloke of reasonable height. Reaching the hangars, he paused for a moment to get his bearings. In spite of the impression he might have given to the Inspector that day, it wasn't always a straightforward matter when you were blind. Sounds were one way of orienting yourself, but sounds, when they came from several directions at once, could be confusing. Just now, there was the engine noise he'd heard earlier – a lorry, he thought, not a motorcar, judging by the low frequency. There was also somebody shouting instructions, 'Bit more to your left, mate . . .' He'd rather not have to explain his presence there to anyone else, least of all one of the ground crew. He was, he supposed, technically trespassing.

But he knew he wouldn't get another chance like this – to put to the test his own particular theory about Farley's murder. And so, finding himself within another few paces up against the corrugated-iron wall of the first of the hangars, he took care to go in the opposite direction from the one from which the ground engineer's voice was coming. Having checked the time on his watch, he made his way cautiously along the iron wall until he reached the passageway between Hangars 2 and 3, along which he guessed Farley's killer had run, on his way to what he supposed was safety. Only there had been somebody in his path . . . I must have given him quite a turn, thought Rowlands wryly.

Of course, the man had been damned lucky in that the 'somebody' in question was blind. He couldn't have known that, thought Rowlands. So why didn't he kill me, too? The question was not one to which he could supply an answer. The obvious one – that the murderer had simply panicked, and run away – was unsatisfactory, somehow. Turning down the narrow alley, Rowlands felt his way along it until he came out on the wide expanse of concrete in front of the hangars. Just now, there seemed to be no one else about, apart from the man he had heard earlier, who was still shouting instructions to the lorry driver. Both were some way off, he judged, trusting to luck that neither would look round at that moment. He edged his way along the front of the second hangar. As he reached the open doorway, the sound of voices brought him up short, 'I've told you a hundred times, my lad, you've got to check the oil before you do anything else.'

'But Gaffer, I thought . . .' began a second, younger-sounding voice. A trainee, Rowlands guessed, wondering what had become of young Ginger.

'But me no buts,' replied the older man sternly. 'You'll do it all again, or I'll want to know why. Flight Lieutenant Harmsworth won't be very pleased if he gets here and finds his machine in that state, I can tell you.' So Harmsworth was expected, was he? Well, it was a fine evening. He couldn't imagine there'd be a cloud in the sky. Holding his breath, Rowlands slipped past as noiselessly as he could, and reached the safety of Hangar Three. Cautiously, he stepped inside the great echoing box. The smell of the place was as he recalled it: a mixture of engine oil, paraffin and dust, overlaid with that of hot metal, from the sun beating down on the roof all day, Rowlands supposed.

He took another pace or two into the building, mindful that, at any moment, he might blunder into something. Under conditions such as these, he'd adopt a tactic he'd learnt during his rehabilitation at St Dunstan's, all those years ago. It was to hold his right arm out in front of him, with the fist lightly clenched, like a boxer squaring up to an opponent. It wasn't a foolproof way of avoiding collisions, but it meant he had a better chance of meeting any obstacle in advance of the rest of his body. Sure enough, he'd hardly gone another two paces before he encountered a curved metallic surface which turned out to be the edge of a wing. I wonder if it's the Gipsy Moth, he thought. If so, it must have been just about here that the murder had taken place, watched, from a little way off, by a horrified Irene Metcalfe.

'You must be mad!' said a voice he knew, breaking into these dark speculations. He recognised the voice as Cecil Harmsworth's.

'I tell you, the police suspect something,' said the person he was addressing. Olave Malory, of course. Rowlands had guessed all along that the story about the flying jacket was just a blind. 'You know,' she went on, 'I really think you ought to tell them that we didn't arrive together that day.'

'What – and put my head in a noose?' Harmsworth sounded close to hysteria. 'Thank you *very* much!'

'You know I didn't mean . . .' she began. Then she broke off. 'Keep your voice down, will you? I think there's somebody there.' Because, in edging closer, Rowlands had inadvertently stumbled over one of the aeroplane's protruding wheels, only saving himself from an ignominious tumble by clutching onto the wing. Cursing himself for his clumsiness, he decided that his only option was to come clean.

'It's only me,' he called, into the cavernous silence which had descended since the aviatrix's muttered warning. 'Frederick Rowlands.'

'Oh!' A moment later, she was beside him. 'Mr Rowlands.' She sounded annoyed. 'I thought you were going to wait in the car.'

'I was.' He gave an apologetic shrug. 'I felt like stretching my legs, that's all.' It was a feeble excuse, he knew, but it was the best he could come up with. They were joined at that moment by Harmsworth.

'I didn't expect to see you here, Rowlands,' he said. 'You do realise,' he went on, in the blustering tone Rowlands recognised as one the other man resorted to when he was rattled, 'that this is a pretty dangerous spot for someone like yourself? I mean,' he added with an unpleasant little laugh, 'you wouldn't want to get your head knocked off by an incoming plane, now would you?'

Rowlands smiled, as if the words had been no more than a joke. 'No,' he said, 'I wouldn't want that at all.

But I've taken care not to go anywhere near the landing area. As a matter of fact,' he went on, thinking that he might as well be hung for a sheep as a lamb, 'I was looking for the tea hut.'

'The tea hut?' Harmsworth seemed momentarily disconcerted by this admission. 'Why the blazes would you want to go there? It's hardly worth the trouble, old boy. Just a ramshackle old potting-shed of a place where the ground crew can brew up that fearful muck they drink, and smoke their filthy roll-ups. Unless it was a cup of tea you're after?' he added spitefully.

'No, I can do without the tea,' replied Rowlands. 'What I was interested in was finding out how long it would take to get from the tea hut to the path leading to the perimeter road.'

'Why, that's easy,' said Olave Malory. 'One could do it in six or seven minutes, I'd say.'

'Three minutes at a run,' murmured Rowlands. 'Yes, that would certainly fit.'

'Fit with what, exactly?' asked the aviatrix. 'You're being very mysterious, Mr Rowlands.'

'Yes,' put in Harmsworth. 'Anyone would think you were some kind of detective.' He emitted another burst of laughter, to point up the patent absurdity of this.

'I'm just interested,' replied Rowlands calmly. 'Only Bert Higgins says he was in the tea hut when he heard Mrs Metcalfe scream, and so I wanted to check that it was possible for him to have reached the shrubbery when he did, which was about a minute after I got there, you know.'

'But why does it matter what he said?' demanded Olave Malory impatiently. 'He killed poor old Bill, didn't he? He must have been in the hangar when he heard the scream. Probably thought he'd better make himself scarce.'

'Yes, but the fact remains that he wouldn't have had time to change out of his overalls,' said Rowlands. 'They'd have been covered in blood, you see.'

'Yes, I *do* see,' snapped Harmsworth. 'Which is rather more than *you* do, old boy!'

'Cecil, *really* . . .'

'No, let me speak, Olave. It's time this fellow was taken down a peg or two. You've been poking your nose into a lot of things which aren't your business,' he went on, addressing Rowlands. 'It's high time you realised that you're not wanted around here.' There was real venom in the words. It occurred to Rowlands that, if it hadn't been for Olave Malory's presence, Harmsworth's anger would have taken a more physical form. To his relief – and, he suspected, Miss Malory's too – there came an interruption. 'Why, if it isn't Mr Rowlands!'

He turned towards the new arrival with a smile. 'Hello, Wilkie.'

'We do seem to keep bumping into one another, don't we?' laughed the girl. 'You must spend almost as much time at Hendon as I do – and I'm here practically every day, aren't, I, Cecil? I mean,' she corrected herself. 'Flight Lieutenant Harmsworth.'

'Yes,' agreed that gentleman. 'You're pretty hard to avoid. Did you find that spanner, by the way?'

''Fraid not,' was the reply. 'Hangar Two said they hadn't seen it, and Hangar One said they'd done an inventory of their tools only the other day, and it came to just the right number, so they—'

'I get the picture. Well, I suppose that's that,' said Harmsworth. 'Damn nuisance, of course. Tools are expensive,' he added, perhaps for Rowlands' benefit. 'But they do go missing, from time to time, worst luck.'

'Yes,' said Rowlands. A thought occurred to him, but he kept it to himself, resolving to ask the Chief Inspector at the earliest opportunity whether they'd yet turned up the murder weapon. A blunt instrument. *What was a spanner, if not that*? 'Anne was asking after you the other day,' he said to Wilkie. 'She enjoyed your picnic on the river.'

'Did she?' The girl didn't sound as if this meant very much to her. Perhaps she was embarrassed at being reminded of more childish pursuits in front of her employer, Rowlands thought, a supposition which was confirmed when she said abruptly, 'I'll get on with cleaning those plugs, shall I, Flight Lieutenant Harmsworth?'

'Yes, carry on,' said the pilot, in an offhand tone. But then, as the girl started to walk away, he said, 'On second thoughts, you can take Mr Rowlands here over to the tea hut. Since you're so keen to see it, Rowlands.'

'There's really no need.'

'No, I insist. You don't mind, do you, Wilkie?' The girl said she did not. If this was a strategy for getting Rowlands out of the way so that he – Harmsworth – could continue

271

his conversation with Miss Malory in private, it didn't succeed, for the latter seemed suddenly to tire of her fellow aviator's company.

'Well, I'm off,' she said. 'I'll wait for you in the car, Mr Rowlands.'

'All right. I won't be long,' he said; then, remembering something. 'You'd better have these.' He handed her the car keys.

'I had, hadn't I?' she said. 'What a very cautious chap you are!' But she sounded amused rather than annoyed by his presumption.

The tea hut, when they reached it, was nothing to write home about. As Harmsworth had said, it was just a bolthole for the men, and a pretty basic one at that. No more than ten or twelve feet square, it was furnished with a deal table, covered with an oilcloth, and four chairs. A smell of oily rags, cigarette butts and milk just on the turn prevailed. 'What's so interesting about the old hut, anyway?' said the girl, making him jump. He hadn't realised that she'd followed him in until she spoke.

'Nothing much.' He shrugged. 'I only thought it might help me get a better idea of what happened that day – the day of Captain Percival's accident – if I could take a dekko at where it all happened. Farley's murder and . . . all the rest,' he finished awkwardly.

He made a move towards the door of the hut, but she was standing in his way. 'And has it?' she said, sounding genuinely interested. Rowlands smiled.

'Not really. Now, if you wouldn't mind, I'd like to go

back to the car. It's Miss Malory's Aston Martin – I expect you know the one. It's parked on the perimeter road, behind the shrubbery. If you'll just point me in the right direction.'

'I'll walk back with you,' said the girl. 'Cecil . . . Flight Lieutenant Harmsworth . . . won't need me for another few minutes.'

'That's kind of you,' said Rowlands, although really he'd have preferred to make his own way back. But he gave in with good grace. 'What's going to happen to the plane?' he asked as the two of them began to walk back across the concrete apron in front of the hangars. The airfield itself, like all others of its size, was grass; a fact which had surprised Rowlands when he had been told of it. Even Croydon hadn't yet been concreted over. 'The Gipsy Moth, I mean,' he added when she didn't reply at once.

'I know. I was just wondering about that myself,' she said. 'They'll sell it, I expect. No one'll want to take it up again, not after what happened.' She sounded so morose, that Rowlands wished he hadn't mentioned the subject. The poor kid was obviously still terribly cut up about the whole affair, as well she might be, he thought.

'You know, you really must come and see us one day,' he said as they reached the path that led towards the shrubbery. 'Perhaps when the girls return.'

'I didn't realise they were away.'

'Yes. They're in Cornwall for a couple of weeks.'

'How ripping,' she said in a flat little voice. 'Do give Anne my love, won't you?'

'I will,' he said. Then she was gone.

He found Olave Malory leaning on the bonnet of her car, smoking a cigarette. 'Did you find what you were looking for?' she said.

'I'm not sure.' Rowlands hesitated. 'I'm afraid I overheard what you and Mr Harmsworth were saying just now,' he said.

'I rather thought you might have.' She didn't seem too put out by his admission, however. 'Cecil's in love with me, the silly fool,' she said. 'It makes things rather awkward.'

'I can see that it might.'

'I was just about to have things out with him when you arrived,' she said.

'I'm sorry,' said Rowlands.

'You needn't be. It wasn't the right time and place. And Cecil was in one of his stubborn moods,' she said. She gave a short, bitter little laugh. 'As for that ridiculous girl . . . What a bore she is! It used to drive me wild, the way she used to hang around Alan. Now it looks as if it's Cecil's turn to be hero-worshipped.'

'It's her age,' said Rowlands. 'She'll grow out of it, I expect.'

'I jolly well wish she'd hurry up and do so,' said the aviatrix fiercely. 'I've had about as much of young Pauline as I can stand.'

Seated once more in the Aston Martin, Rowlands barely had time to put on the helmet and goggles before the car took off; soon they were racing along the Bath Road towards Kingston at a speed which made him almost glad he was oblivious to oncoming traffic. 'Do you always drive this fast?' he yelled, above the roar of the engine. Olave Malory laughed.

'It's the only way to drive,' she cried. 'Next best thing to flying, I always say.' Well, you should know, he thought.

'How long have you known Flight Lieutenant Harmsworth?' he shouted, although really, conversation under these conditions was next to impossible. It didn't seem to bother her, though.

'A couple of years,' she shouted back. 'Alan introduced us, as a matter of fact.'

'What?'

'I said Alan introduced us.'

'Oh.' He nodded his head violently, to show he understood. His hopes of getting much more out of Miss Malory seemed doomed to failure. Then she said, 'I say, do you fancy a drink?'

'Very much,' he said.

'Good! There's a pub on the river. The White Swan – do you know it?'

'I can't say I do.'

'What?'

'I said . . . Yes, that'd be grand.'

Ten minutes later, they were comfortably seated in the big bay window of the quaint old pub, with their drinks – beer for him, a Gin and It for her – on the table in front of them. 'Pity you can't see the view,' she said. 'It's rather a pretty one, with the river and all that. A lovely evening, too.'

'Yes,' he said. 'I can tell.' The feel of the air on his skin was enough, and the faint sound of voices drifting in through the pub's open door from people strolling along the riverbank.

'You know, you interest me, Mr Rowlands,' said his companion suddenly.

'Do I?' He sipped his drink. *Nice pint*. 'I can't imagine why.'

'I hope you won't be offended if I say that I've not met many people like you.' She meant people of his class, he supposed.

'I'm not offended in the least,' he said. 'If it comes to that, I haven't met all that many like you.'

She laughed. 'Touché! But what I meant was, you're rather an unusual sort. Alan liked you,' she said. 'And he was generally a good judge of character. Of men, at least,' she added. Rowlands wondered where all this was leading. Knowing that people will come out with what's on their minds if one gives them the chance to do so, he stayed silent. It was as well, because what she said next left him temporarily speechless. 'I saw Celia West the other day. I gather you two know each other rather well.'

He felt the blood rush to his face. 'I wouldn't go that far.'

'Wouldn't you?' She seemed to be enjoying his discomfiture. 'She says you saved her life.'

'That's putting it a bit strongly. I . . . I was in possession of some information which proved useful to her when she was in tight spot, that's all.'

276

'You see, you *are* an unusual sort. Most men would be cock-a-hoop at the thought that Celia regarded them as her saviour. But I can see you're different.'

'I've got used to being different,' he said wryly. His pulse seemed to have returned to its normal rate. 'May I ask you something?'

'Ask away.'

'How did my name come to be mentioned? As far as I know, it wasn't in any of the press reports of Captain Percival's death.'

Olave Malory was silent a moment. 'It wasn't in connection with what happened to Alan,' she said at last. 'Or at least, not the accident.' Again, she paused, as if trying to think how best to put what it was she had to say. 'I . . . I happened to mention your sister's name,' she said. 'I was telling Celia about the awful row I'd had with Alan on the day he died and . . .'

'You told her he'd been with another woman,' Rowlands finished for her. This was worse than he'd feared.

'Yes,' she said. 'It was funny, because as soon as I said he'd been seeing a Mrs Lehmann, Celia said, "That woman haunts me. If it's the same one." Then we compared notes, and it emerged about her brother – you, I mean – being blind. It was then that Celia said that queer thing about your having saved her life.'

So she knew that Dorothy was back in England, thought Rowlands. If, as he suspected, Chief Inspector Douglas was also aware of this fact, then the situation was fast becoming untenable. The sooner his sister went away again – preferably as far away as possible – the better for everyone. Thank God she was out of London! The place was becoming increasingly hot for her, it seemed. Something else struck him. 'Is Lady Celia back in London, then? I thought she was in New York.' The last he'd heard of her – the woman with whom he'd once been so besotted – she'd been about to marry an American financier.

'Yes, she's been back for several months.'

'Wasn't she engaged to be married? I thought . . .'

'Oh, *that* ended ages ago. After poor Hamilton lost his shirt in the crash, you know.' Of course, that was the man's name, Rowlands thought. Eliot Hamilton III. He'd seemed a pleasant enough chap, on the one occasion Rowlands had met him. So he'd been one of the unfortunates caught out when the market collapsed in '29, had he? The shock waves of that particular financial disaster were still being felt across the world. 'Of course Celia hasn't a bean,' his informant was saying. 'That husband of hers left her with nothing but a pittance when he had the bad taste to be murdered. Awful case. I don't suppose you remember it, but . . .' He remembered it all too well. He got to his feet.

'Care for another?' he said.

'What? Oh, thanks. That'd be lovely.'

As he stood at the bar, waiting to be served, he could hear the cheerful shouts of those in passing pleasure boats. There must be a place nearby where you could hire a skiff, he thought distractedly. So Celia West was back in London. The knowledge seemed to bring her closer, out of the realm of the might-have-been into the here-and-now. 'That'll be two-and-ninepence,' said the barmaid. He paid her, then made his way back to where his companion was sitting, taking care not to spill a drop. She took the glass from him.

'I'd better watch out,' she said. 'Or I'll be getting squiffy. Chin-chin!'

'Cheers,' said Rowlands. 'So,' he went on, deciding that he'd had enough of beating about the bush, 'if Harmsworth didn't arrive at the aerodrome when you did, when *did* he arrive?'

Olave Malory was silent a moment. 'I'm not entirely sure,' she said. 'All I know is he was at the hangars when I got there.'

'Was he indeed? Do the police know of this?'

'Not so far.' She sounded distinctly uncomfortable. 'But they've been asking some very awkward questions. That Scottish one – the Chief Inspector – can be horribly persistent.'

'I know,' said Rowlands drily. 'So Harmsworth was definitely there when you arrived?'

'Yes. That is . . . I think so. But he'd only just got there,' she said. 'We'd two hours to go before the race and so . . .' She broke off. 'You can't seriously think' she went on, 'that Cecil had anything to do with that man's death?'

'That's not for me to decide,' he said. 'What I am

interested in is why he should have lied to the police. Saying he'd arrived with you when he was there already.'

'I . . . I'm sure I haven't the faintest idea,' she said. She took another swig of her drink. 'Just why are you so interested, anyway? Cecil says . . .' She broke off. 'Oh, never mind.'

Rowlands smiled. 'I don't imagine Mr Harmsworth's idea of me is a particularly complimentary one,' he said.

'No.' She hesitated. From outside, came the carefree sounds of people messing about in boats. 'But after what Celia said about you, and now all these questions . . . Well, I can't help wondering if you're not some kind of detective.'

'Oh, I wouldn't say that exactly,' he said. 'I just want to get to the truth, that's all.' He wondered how far to take her into his confidence. Even though she'd implied she didn't care for Cecil Harmsworth, there might be more to that than met the eye, he thought. 'The fact is, there are too many different versions of what went on that day,' he said at last. 'None of them quite add up.'

'But surely . . .' He could tell from her voice that she was frowning. 'The police have already made an arrest. That man Higgins.' She gave a little, shuddering laugh. 'I wish now I hadn't stood him a drink,' she said. Sometimes it was better to say nothing, Rowlands thought. Often as not, people arrived at a conclusion without any further prompting. 'I mean,' Olave Malory went on, 'what reason could Cecil have had for killing the man? He didn't even know him . . . or only to nod to, the way one does with most of the chaps around the Air Park. Why,' she laughed, 'if he was going to kill anyone, I'd say he had far more reason to kill Alan Percival. They were always at one another's throats about something or other.'

'Yes,' said Rowlands. It occurred to him that she didn't know that Percival's death hadn't been an accident. The police had been keeping that dark, on purpose. 'Why did you think he lent him the plane? Flight Lieutenant Harmsworth, I mean.'

Miss Malory took another swig of her drink, and set down the glass rather too decisively. 'You know, I haven't the least idea,' she replied. 'Unless he was trying to make up for having been such a swine earlier on.' Rowlands recalled the acrimonious little exchange he'd overheard between the two airmen in the Club House bar.

'That must be it, of course,' he said.

But the subject, once raised, appeared to fascinate her. 'You're not suggesting Cecil did something to that machine to make it crash?'

'I'm not suggesting anything.'

'Alan would never have been such a fool as to accept if he'd suspected anything of the kind,' she said. But she didn't sound convinced. 'I can't believe it of Cecil,' she went on. 'He can be an awful ass, it's true, but . . . murder?' She lowered her voice on the final word, although as far as Rowlands could tell, they were the only ones in the bar. 'No, I just don't believe it,' she said.

# Chapter Fifteen

'So you think it's Harmsworth, do you?' said Douglas. They were in the Chief Inspector's office at the Yard; the clock on Big Ben had just struck six o'clock.

'I don't know,' said Rowlands. 'It's a possibility, that's all.'

'Possibility!' echoed the policeman in a disgusted tone. 'This case has too many "possibilities", if you want my opinion. The trouble is, that's all they amount to. It's possible that Higgins killed Farley. It's possible that whoever killed Mrs Metcalfe was put up to it by her husband. Now you're telling me it's *possible* that Harmsworth fixed that aeroplane. But where's your proof?' he demanded. The heat was making the Chief Inspector bad-tempered. Now he pushed back his chair with a horrible scraping sound, and strode to the window, which was already open a crack. He flung up the sash. 'It's too hot, that's the fact of it,' he grumbled. 'A man can't think in this.' And indeed, the air outside the window was as warm and sluggish as the air inside; nor did any freshness come from the river, but only a smell from the mudbanks, now exposed at low tide, and a low rumble of motor vehicles, crossing Westminster Bridge.

Rowlands, whose shirt was sticking uncomfortably to his back beneath his jacket, murmured his concurrence with this view. 'I don't suppose,' he said, 'That there've been any further sightings of the chap we're looking for? The one who delivered the flowers, I mean.'

'I know who you mean,' said Douglas. His tone was tetchy. '"Further sightings", apart from those we had in the first instance from the lad and the old man? No, there've been no further sightings, as you put it. If you ask me, he's disappeared into thin air. We've not found hide nor hair of him, although you may be sure we've searched every corner of W1 and a great many more parts of the metropolis besides. It's my belief he's lying low,' said the Chief Inspector, sucking the stem of his unlit pipe – a habit when he was thinking, Rowlands knew. 'Going about his business like any other citizen. Trouble is, he probably looks like any other citizen, too. You'd think from what you read in the papers that a man needed two heads to carry out a murder,' he added gnomically. 'Yet they're usually the most unexceptional of men.'

'Do we have a description?' said Rowlands. He knew that physical appearance was something he tended, perforce, to overlook. The Chief Inspector laughed. It was not a cheerful laugh.

'We do,' he said. 'For what it's worth.' He rummaged about amongst the papers that lay on his desk. 'This is the lad's. Young Hughes, that is. "*He was tall. Taller than me.*" The boy's only five foot three, so that doesn't help us much. "*Dressed in blue overalls*" – or they might have been black, he can't be sure. "*He had a cloth cap on. Pulled down over his face. A scarf round the lower part of his face . . .*" Doesn't help us much,' said Douglas gloomily.

'What about his voice?' said Rowlands.

'Ah, we made sure to ask him about that! But again, he'd nothing much to say. It was a "*gruff voice*" he thought, "*as if the bloke had a frog in his throat . . .*" Disguising it, o' course,' said Douglas. 'Then there's old Grundley's description. Between you and me, I don't think he got much of a look at our man. Taking a nap in his cubbyhole at the time, I shouldn't wonder. This is what he says.'

Douglas cleared his throat and read, in a pompous manner Rowlands recognised as that of the Gloucester Mansions porter. '"*I only caught but a glimpse of the perpetrator as he was running upstairs. It seemed to me he was wearing some kind of dark-coloured clothing. He didn't speak, but merely waved the bouquet of roses he was carrying, as if to indicate his purpose in being there. I assumed he must be deaf and dumb . . ."* And not the only one!' snorted the Chief Inspector contemptuously. 'Ask me no questions and I'll tell you no lies is old Grundley's motto, I'd say. So you see,' he concluded, 'we've nothing much to go on.'

'Dark blue overalls,' said Rowlands.

'Oh, as to that,' said the other, 'I'd say half the working men in London must be wearing something o' the sort. But I know what you're driving at,' he went on, still chewing at his pipestem. 'You mean they could be the same overalls that our man was wearing when he killed Farley.'

'Well, not exactly the same,' said Rowlands. 'But it is a coincidence, you'll have to admit.'

'A coincidence, aye. This case is full o' those. What with "possibilities" and "coincidences", I don't know whether I'm coming or going,' said the Chief Inspector wearily. 'The fact is,' he went on, 'the more I think about it, the more I find myself coming to the conclusion that we've not one murderer but two on our hands . . . Ridiculous as that may sound,' he added with a sour little laugh. 'Because the fact of it is . . .'

'That even if Higgins did kill Farley, and fixed that plane, he couldn't have killed Mrs Metcalfe, for the simple reason . . .'

'That he was in prison at the time. Agreed,' said Douglas. 'No, my theory is that Higgins was put up to it

285

– the murder and the sabotage – by someone else. Metcalfe seems the most likely. Given that he'd used precisely the same method to do away with his wife. Recruiting someone else to do the deed, I mean.'

'Yes,' said Rowlands doubtfully.

'Except the blessed theory only works if one can prove that there's a link between Higgins and Metcalfe, which so far we've failed to do,' said the other. 'Metcalfe denies ever clapping eyes on the man until that day at the aerodrome. Higgins says much the same. If we could only find that wretched delivery boy,' he groaned. 'But the blighter's vanished off the face of the earth.' The Chief Inspector was silent for so long that Rowlands wondered if he'd dropped off. 'As for this notion of yours about Mr Harmsworth,' he said at last. 'I don't fancy it myself. Yes, yes, I know you're going to say he had a reason to kill Percival, although it seems a pretty flimsy one. Whether a German plane was shot down or not . . . But even if one allows that as a possible motive, what's his motive for killing poor little Mrs Metcalfe? It won't wash, I tell you.'

With which Rowlands had to be content. He was, in any case, not convinced that Harmsworth had anything to do with it himself. The man had lied, undoubtedly, but that was rather in his nature, it appeared. 'Well, I'm off,' he said, getting to his feet. 'Unless you need me for anything else, Chief Inspector?'

'What? Och, no, you get away home,' said the other.

'I've a few things I need to finish off here. If only it weren't so infernally hot. A man can't breathe in this weather, let alone think,' he said.

Rowlands left the building by the side entrance, and after a murmured 'Good night' to the police constable on duty, turned into Parliament Street, and from thence past the Houses of Parliament and the statue of Boadicea, to Westminster Bridge. The home-going crowds had thinned out by this time, and so it was easier to walk than it would have been an hour before; even so, he kept close to the parapet on his left, conscious that it was the only barrier between himself and a fifteen-foot drop to the swiftly flowing river passing beneath it. Reaching the middle of the bridge, he drew a deep breath. If there was one thing he loved about London it was this: the sense one had of its being defined by the river.

He supposed all great cities had this in common – recalling pleasant hours spent wandering along by the Seine during a twenty-four hour leave in Paris, during the war. But to a Londoner born and bred, as he was, the Thames was the only one worth mentioning. *Earth has not anything to show more fair* . . . Old Wordsworth had it right, although even he might have found it hard to recognise the view he'd described so memorably a hundred and thirty years before. The fields had long since disappeared; nor could you have called the air 'smokeless'. A tram rattled past at that moment, while a motorcar, braking to avoid colliding with this or some other obstacle, left a powerful stench of burnt rubber in its wake. No, it certainly wasn't the 'bright and glittering' city of the poet's vision, Rowlands thought; that had all changed with the advent of the combustion engine.

Having descended the steps that led down to the Embankment, he began walking in the direction of Waterloo, passing the massive edifice of County Hall. The image he had of this, as of all the buildings which had been completed since the war, was necessarily vague. He remembered when they'd started laying the foundations, though. The excavations had gone on for many months. People joked that the esteemed members of the London County Council would have to hold their meetings from the bottom of a pit. From the river to his left came the hooting of a siren. A steamer hauling coal from Greenwich Docks, he guessed. It was still a working river. As a boy, he'd liked nothing better than to watch the ships pass under Tower Bridge, into the Pool of London. If the river was the reason for the city's existence, the ships and their cargoes – machine tools, tin trays, cotton goods and other essentials manufactured for export to the far reaches of the Empire – were the reason for its prosperity.

As he strolled, enjoying the relative cool afforded by the shade of the dusty plane trees along the Embankment, he thought about what Douglas had said about Irene Metcalfe's murderer: 'The blighter's vanished off the face of the earth.' Rowlands supposed it must be easy enough, in a city the size of this one. He stood and rested his elbows for a minute or two on the stone balustrade overlooking the river, breathing in the pungent-smelling, not quite fresh city air. Somewhere out there, he thought, in that tightly woven maze of brick and stone, was a man to all intents and purposes like himself, but with this one distinction – that he had murdered two people in cold blood and, as cold-bloodedly, brought about the death of a third.

It seemed an impossible task, that he could ever be tracked down. And yet it would happen, Rowlands thought. At this very moment, there were men out there under orders to do nothing else. For a minute he felt almost sorry for the fugitive. But then he thought of the dead woman, lying still and silent in a pool of blood, and of the child who would now be motherless. 'We'll find you,' he murmured under his breath, addressing the as yet unknown perpetrator. 'You can be sure of that. Better to give up now.' A train coming out of Charing Cross rattled overhead as he passed under Hungerford Bridge, and a woman put her hand on his arm.

'Lookin' for company, dearie?' He shook her off, not unkindly, and made his way at a brisker pace to the station.

Seated on the slowing-moving train, he allowed his thoughts to drift to what had been hovering at the back of his mind all day – and all the previous night, too – ever since the Malory girl had mentioned it. Celia West. Specifically, her presence in London, and the fact that she was still 'Celia West'. Because she hadn't married that

American, after all. Even though in a part of his mind he was sorry that she'd failed yet again to find happiness, in another, ignoble part, he couldn't help feeling glad. Which was ridiculous, he thought, since it could make no difference to him, either way. And yet he couldn't stop thinking about her. What was it Olave Malory had said? 'She said you'd saved her life.' Well, it was true enough, he supposed. Although in doing so, he'd – unforgivably, it seemed to him now – exposed his sister to the fate from which he'd rescued Lady Celia.

Forty minutes later, he let himself into the quiet house – how empty it seemed, with the girls away! The only sound was the ticking of the mantelpiece clock, and the softer sound of a tap dripping. He'd been meaning to fix a new washer to the kitchen tap for the past fortnight; he'd get onto it tonight, he thought. There were some letters on the mat – circulars and a bill or two, he ascertained; he'd take those into the office first thing on Monday. Miss Collins could write the cheques and he'd sign them, a system that had worked up to now. Reading his post was the only thing he couldn't manage in Edith's absence; even the newspaper – extracts from which she read to him most nights – wasn't essential, with the wireless to hand.

He switched it on, and then went to change out of his working clothes; the newsreader's voice followed him up the stairs and into the bathroom, its clipped tones intermittently obscured by the sound of splashing water. 'Mr Baldwin and Mr Neville Chamberlain arrived at

Number Ten, Downing Street, for consultation with the Prime Minister and Chancellor of the Exchequer on the worsening economic crisis . . .' Rowlands hung up his jacket and stripped off his sweaty shirt with a sigh of relief. Now for his gardening togs. He could put in a good couple of hours tonight, he thought. Get the whole lot tidied up, ready for Edith's return with the girls next week. Whistling softly, he descended the stairs and went into the kitchen to fix himself a bite to eat.

'A man who was said to have begun a criminal career after receiving a head wound during the war was yesterday sentenced to six months' imprisonment with hard labour at Southwark Crown Court after pleading guilty to obtaining two pounds by false pretences . . .' Poor devil, thought Rowlands. It seemed a harsh sentence, even if it wasn't a first offence. He filled the kettle and placed in on the hob. *Now where were the matches? Ah. Where he'd left them, of course.* He lit the gas. 'Detective Constable Hart said that the defendant went to France in 1916 and was awarded the MC and mentioned in Dispatches. He was wounded in the head, and after his return to France was wounded four more times. He was four and a half years in mental hospitals after the war.'

It was the kind of story with which Rowlands had become all too familiar in recent years, doing the job he did. Men who'd been damaged by the war – and not only in the physical sense – and who'd become incapable of adapting to civilian life. In this case, the chap was obviously mad, poor blighter. Hospital would have been the place for him, not prison. Something that Viktor had once said on the subject came back to him – what was it, now? He could almost hear the gentle voice, its German accent barely eradicated by all the years he'd lived in England, 'In my view, those who commit crimes – *ja*, Friedrich, even murder! – should not be imprisoned at all, but should be sent to hospital until they are well in their minds.' At the thought of his late brother-in-law, Rowlands felt his throat constrict. He was a decent sort, Viktor. If there had ever been any animosity between them on account of the war, it hadn't lasted long. He'd been a good husband to Dottie, too. Well, there was no sense in regretting what was past.

'At the inquest on the body of Mrs Mabel Cracknell, of Kettering Street, Streatham, it was shown that her death was due to a dose of cyanide of potassium . . .' Rowlands switched off the wireless. He'd had enough of murder, for one day. He cut himself a hunk of bread from the end of the loaf and a slab of cheddar to go with it. That'd do for his supper, he decided. Edith would have scolded him if she'd known, but Edith wasn't here. Much as he loved his wife, she had notions about the 'proper' way of doing things which sometimes struck him as excessive. In his opinion, a meal of bread and cheese was as good, if not superior, to one of three courses eaten off bone china. But he'd never get Edith to agree. Having finished his scratch repast, he put cup and plate in the sink for washing-up later. Now for the garden.

But at that moment, the telephone rang, its shrill,

peremptory jangle resounding through the silent house, like a summons from another, more uncertain world. Had Edith said she'd telephone this evening? He didn't think so. Unable to suppress the vague feeling of apprehension which an unscheduled call always provoked, he went out into the hall, and lifted the heavy receiver from its cradle. 'Hello? Kingston five-four-nine,' he said. There was a brief pause, then a voice he knew said, 'Is that you, Mr Rowlands?'

'Hello, Miss Malory. Yes, it's Frederick Rowlands speaking. What can I do for you?'

'Oh, good! I hoped you'd be in,' she said, ignoring his question. 'Only it seems a shame to waste such an evening, and I was sure you'd want to come when you knew who else was coming.'

'I'm afraid I don't understand,' said Rowlands, a little stiffly. There was a peal of laughter from the other end of the line. 'Of course, I should have said. I'm having a party,' was the reply. 'Now do say you'll come! I'll send the car for you.' Then, as he was starting to protest that he didn't want to put her to the trouble, 'Not another word! It's no trouble at all. Whatever are cars for if not for the convenience of one's friends?'

Olave Malory's house was an eighteenth-century cottage tucked away at the end of a lane leading down to the river. This much Rowlands discovered from his hostess, who greeted him at the door. 'Come in – don't worry, you're not the first. Take care. There's a step. And do

293

mind your head! The ceiling's a bit low just here.' She laughed, and it struck him that, under her studiedly casual manner, she was quite nervous. 'It's an awful little hovel, I'm afraid, but it does for weekends.'

'I'm sure it's very . . .' But his polite protest was cut short.

'I must speak to you,' she said, in a low voice. 'There's something . . .'

'I say, Olave old thing! We've run out of Vermouth,' yelled someone from the room beyond.

'Be right there, Dickie,' she called. She took Rowlands' arm and drew him after her into what he guessed must be the sitting room. 'I won't be a moment,' she murmured, leaving Rowlands stranded. To judge from the noise, the room was already full of people. Snatches of shouted conversation came from all sides.

'. . . thought it was frightfully funny. The scene with the butler . . . I nearly died laughing.'

'. . . ever tell you about that little escapade in Cairo in '29? Priceless . . .'

A man standing close to Rowlands said, 'Yes, I thought I might get in some shooting. Fly the old crate up to Inverness, and then pop in on Hamish and Judy.'

'Sounds like a swell idea.' This voice was familiar, thought Rowlands. American. Now, where had he heard it before?

'Why don't you come, too, old boy?' said the first man. 'Bags of room in that draughty old castle of theirs. I can give you a lift in the Avro, if you like.'

'Thanks. But I'll be at Calshot all month. These time trials for the new S6B are turning out to be a real pain in the neck.'

'Let me introduce you to some people,' said Miss Malory, returning from dealing with the Vermouth crisis. 'I don't think you know Hank Harrington, do you? Hank, this is Frederick Rowlands.' The two men shook hands.

'As a matter of fact, I believe we have met,' said Rowlands.

'That so?' said Harrington affably. 'I can't say I recall the occasion, but then I meet a lot of people in my line of work.' Rowlands remembered in that instant when it was that he had first encountered the American, and cursed himself for a fool. This wasn't the time or place to bring up the subject of the aerodrome murders.

'I'm sure you must,' he said quickly, to cover up his faux pas.

'Say, you don't have a drink,' said the pilot.

'I was getting to that,' said their hostess. 'Dry Martini all right?'

'Thanks.' Rowlands would have preferred a beer.

'Bobby, be a dear and fetch Mr Rowlands one of your specials, would you?' She turned her attention once more to her guest. 'And this is Peter Coulson – "Stinker" to his friends. Although he always smells perfectly sweet to me. Stinker's what we in the trade call an enthusiast.'

'She means I collect planes,' said the other cheerfully. 'Last time I looked I had eight of the things. Can't seem to stop, you know. Latest's a cherry-red Avro Baby. Pretty little machine.' From which Rowlands gathered that the young man must be immensely rich.

'Pamela is Stinker's better half, if that's the word,' went on their hostess as a tall girl with a nervous giggle, shook Rowlands' hand.

'Awfully nice to meet you,' she said. 'Do you fly, too?'

Rowlands smiled and shook his head. 'I think that might be a bit risky for everyone else,' he said. Olave Malory must have signalled something to the same effect at that moment, for the girl sounded abashed.

'Awfully sorry! I didn't realise . . .'

'Don't give it a second thought.' His drink arrived, and he took a grateful swig, wondering why he'd let himself be persuaded to come.

'And this is Clarissa Foy. She doesn't fly, either.'

'Heavens, no! I'm terrified of heights,' said the lady thus introduced. 'There seems to me something decidedly unnatural about careering around at three thousand feet. Can't imagine how you do it, Olave.'

'No more dangerous than getting on a horse,' said Miss Malory briskly.

'Oh, horses are different,' replied Clarissa Foy. 'Four hooves on the ground. *Much* safer. Give me a horse any day.' She hooted with laughter, and it occurred to Rowlands that she was rather tight. Judging by the strength of these cocktails, he soon would be, too, if he didn't watch out. Miss Malory introduced him to some more people. A Mr Davenport, who worked for the Foreign Office.

'I fly in my spare time, you know. Haven't crashed yet, ha, ha!' A Miss Holyoke, who painted.

'Rosalind's frightfully talented,' said Miss Malory. 'She did some beautiful screens for the big show at the Mayor Gallery last spring.' Miss Holyoke gave a self-deprecatory murmur. 'Oh, but you did, you know! I bought one myself,' said her hostess. 'It shows the *Spirit of Speed* – without a stitch on, you know, except for her winged helmet,' she explained for Rowlands' benefit. He replied that it sounded most attractive. 'Oh, it is. It was Alan's engagement present to me, as a matter of fact. We were going to get Rosalind to paint us a mural on the same theme in the London flat . . .'

She broke off. 'I say!' The brittle gaiety of her manner struck Rowlands as artificial. 'I don't suppose you'd care for a breath of air? It's so beastly hot in here.'

It was a lovely night. The air still held a little of the day's heat, but without the oppressiveness which had prevailed earlier. A warm breeze blew from the west, bringing with it the smell of the river, which Rowlands judged to be close at hand, and sweeter scents of flowers. 'Lovely roses,' he remarked.

'What?' Her surprise sounded in her voice. 'Oh . . . Yes, they do smell rather delicious, don't they? Such a pretty old rose. *Souvenir du Docteur Jamain*. They've simply *smothered* the summerhouse.' Because they were now close to that edifice, from whose open doors and windows came sounds of music and laughter, 'You utter beast, Simon! if you don't hand me that soda siphon this minute, I'll . . .'

'Children, children!'

'I've been thinking,' said Olave Malory, under cover of this merriment, 'about what we were talking of the other day.'

'What happened at the aerodrome, you mean?'

'Yes. The fact is . . .'

'Simon, you rotter!'

'Children, please!' screamed the voice from the summerhouse. 'Oh, someone put a record on the gramophone,' said someone else. 'If we can't be civil to each other, we might as well dance . . .' A moment later, the strains of 'I Can't Give You Anything But Love' floated out upon the night air, and the sound of drunken laughter gave way to that of shuffling feet as a contingent of guests took up the music's invitation.

'It's about Cecil,' said Miss Malory, in a low voice. She hesitated as if uncertain how to go on. 'He was there, wasn't he?' Rowlands prompted. 'That morning . . .'

'Yes. But it's not what you think . . .' Again she broke off. 'He'd kill me if I told you,' she said. Rowlands had the sense to say nothing. 'I'm afraid he's involved in something rather unsavoury,' she went on, speaking rapidly now that she'd made the decision to unburden herself. 'He flies to Paris every week, you see, and so it's easy for him to pick up the stuff.'

Rowlands was beginning to understand. 'By "stuff" I suppose you mean drugs?'

'Yes. Cocaine. Everybody takes it nowadays.' Her

laugh sounded forced. 'It's become quite the thing at parties.' Including this one, thought Rowlands.

'So what you're saying,' he persisted, 'is that he was at the aerodrome that morning in order to unload a consignment of drugs he'd been smuggling?'

'I wouldn't be able to swear to it, of course, but . . . Oh!' She broke off. A moment later, he knew why.

'There you are,' said a voice. It was Cecil Harmsworth. During the brief, awkward silence which followed, Rowlands wondered how much of their conversation he'd overheard. 'I couldn't find you in the house,' he went on, ignoring Rowlands. 'And so I thought I'd have a look out here. But I see you've got company,' he added rudely.

'Yes. You know Mr Rowlands, Cecil.'

'Evening, Harmsworth.' Rowlands kept his tone light. But his mind was already whirring. If the man wanted to cover up the fact that he'd been smuggling cocaine, then he might have had a reason to kill anyone who threatened to expose him. Alan Percival, for instance. But then something happened to drive this, and all other thoughts, out of his head.

'So this is where you're all hiding!' He knew the voice, of course. The delicious scent she was wearing was familiar to him, too. 'What an absolutely blissful night,' she said. 'Clever of you to choose it, Olave darling. Why, Mr Rowlands! How perfectly lovely to find you here.'

He held out his hand, and felt her take it. 'Good evening, Lady Celia,' he said.

# Chapter Sixteen

'Well,' said Celia West as, a few minutes later, they strolled across the lawn that sloped down to the river. 'I knew you had a wide circle of acquaintance, Mr Rowlands – how *is* the dear Chief Inspector these days? – but I'd never have thought to find you in with the flying crowd.' Rowlands laughed.

'No more would I,' he said.

'I take it it's something to do with this murder?' She sounded as calmly detached as if she'd been remarking on the likelihood of the evening's remaining fine. 'Olave's told me all about it,' she went on when he did not reply at once, their hostess having gone inside, taking Cecil

Harmsworth with her, to supervise the supper arrangements. 'She said you suspected Cecil of having sabotaged Alan Percival's plane.'

'I hate to contradict a lady, but I never said any such thing.'

'Oh, I know he can be an absolute rotter,' she went on, paying no attention to Rowlands' protest, 'but I don't think he's quite capable of *that*.'

'Perhaps not,' said Rowlands, wondering how much she knew of Harmsworth's nefarious goings-on.

'Care for a cigarette?' said his companion.

'Have one of mine,' he replied, taking out the case – quite a nice one, although it was only sterling silver – and offering it to her.

'Actually, I prefer these. They're Virginians,' she said. 'Got the taste for them when I was in New York, you know.' This allusion to what had happened since they'd last met momentarily silenced him. 'You don't really think poor old Cecil's a murderer, do you?' she said; then, perhaps sensing his alarm at this indiscreet line of questioning, 'It's all right, there's no one about. And even if there were, they're making such an infernal row in there that no one could possibly hear what we're saying.'

'There' was the summerhouse, from which the sounds of raucous laughter, and the raucous strains of 'Minnie the Moocher' — all too apposite, given the topic under discussion, thought Rowlands — grew ever louder. 'I don't know what to think,' said Rowlands. 'All I know is Harmsworth's got himself involved in something pretty nasty.'

'You mean the dope, I suppose?' she said. 'Oh, I know all about that! And before you ask, I don't indulge myself – at least, not any more. I find it all rather a bore if you want to know.'

They had by now reached the end of the garden. The sound of water lapping against a jetty, and the sleepy cry of a waterbird, told Rowlands they were very near the river. He felt the fronds of a weeping willow brush his face. 'Oh, look!' said Celia West in the same moment. 'There's the boat.'

His interest was instantly quickened. 'What kind of boat?'

'Quite a small one. A skiff. Olave keeps it for guests. Picnics and all that.'

'Of course.'

She must have seen something in his face, for she said, 'I don't suppose you know how to row?'

'I've rowed a bit in my time.'

'Have you? How absolutely marvellous! Wait here a moment, won't you?' As if, he thought, he'd be going anywhere. A few minutes elapsed during which the louche rhythms of the previous song gave way to the more mellifluous 'Dancing Under the Stars'. Breathing in the smell of the river, and with the feel of the night air against his face, he let the mood of it wash over him.

Then, she was back again, her sequinned frock making the faintest swishing sound as she strolled towards him.

302

Glasses clinked in her hand. 'I thought if we were taking to the river, we'd need this,' she said.

'"This"?'

'Champagne. I found some bottles of the stuff kicking around. Well, are you going to take me for a row, or not?' she said.

When she'd settled herself on the cushions in the prow of the boat, he cast off, and took up the oars, hoping that the current wouldn't be too strong at first so that he could get the hang of the thing. But the skiff handled well, and after a few experimental strokes, he took her out into mid-stream. 'You'll sing out if you see anything coming, won't you?' he said.

'Of course. Do you want me to keep time?'

'No, I can manage, thanks.' Then, for a few moments, there was nothing but the soft splash of the oars dipping into the water, the creaking of the rowlocks, and the gentle flurry of feathering. From across the water, the strains of music, with its murmured words of love and make-believe, were fainter now.

The air was pleasantly cool, out on the water. He drew a deep breath. It seemed to him at once fantastical that she was here with him, and at the same time the most natural thing in the world. 'You're very quiet, Mr Rowlands,' said his companion. 'I hope you're not regretting having left the party so soon?' The opposite was so much the case that he laughed.

'Not a bit.'

'Thought not. They're a funny lot, the air crowd. Very

much in one another's pockets if you know what I mean? It's all a bit incestuous. Although I'm very fond of Olave. She and I were at school together, in Switzerland. It sort of binds you together, an experience like that – the way being in the army does, I imagine.'

It didn't require an answer, and so he merely smiled and concentrated on his rowing. He'd missed this, he realised, feeling the skiff glide forward, responsive to the power of each stroke. It seemed effortless, and yet there was effort involved, of a satisfying kind.

'How's your sister?'

The question took him by surprise. If he'd been a less experienced rower, he might have caught a crab. As it was, he took his time before replying. 'She's well. At least,' he added guardedly, 'she was when I last saw her.'

'I'm glad. I've sometimes thought she paid a higher price for . . . what happened . . . than I did.' Her voice was calm and level, betraying none of the emotion she must have been feeling. 'In fact, one might have said that she did me a favour.' He did not reply. A moment later she said, 'I gather from what Olave said that she's back in England.' There was no point in denying it.

'Lady Celia,' he said urgently. 'I must ask you . . . implore you . . . to say nothing of this to anybody else. My sister's life may depend on it.'

'Oh, never fear. You can count on me for that,' she said. 'I say, there's a nice little spot just over there – the far bank, under those willow trees – where we can tie up for a bit. It seems a shame to waste this good champagne.'

Guided by her, he rowed them towards the bank, and tied the painter to a convenient tree root. Then for a while – he wasn't sure afterwards how long it had been – they talked of this and that, and fell silent, and talked some more. Much of what they said seemed inconsequential when he tried to recall it afterwards. Yet he knew it was not. She'd always had a way of saying exactly what she wanted to say, without ever putting things directly. And so he learnt that she was unhappy; that the American affair had hit her harder than she liked to admit; and that she'd come home, as she put it, 'to regroup – or do I mean retrench? Both, probably.'

Yes, she'd had her wings burnt, he thought, reflecting on this conversation later. At the time, all he'd been able to think about was that she was here, with him; the two of them gently rocked on the river's calm surface as the night breeze blew their words away like so much thistledown. 'And you,' she said, refilling their glasses (the bottle was almost empty by this time). 'How are things with you? It always seems to me that you've got everything worked out.'

He laughed at that. 'What makes you think so?'

'Why, because you're one of the few sane people I know. You've been through all kinds of hell – no need to shake your head, it's the truth – and yet you're not bitter in the slightest.'

'I'd rather not talk about myself if you don't mind,' he said. 'In fact, I'd rather not talk at all.'

'Oh,' she said. Then neither said anything for a while.

A little later, she said, 'This is impossible – you know that, don't you?'

'Oh, yes,' he said. 'I know that.'

Both were silent as he rowed them back – Rowlands because his heart was full, and Celia West . . . but what she was thinking, he could only guess. Even now, she remained an enigma to him. Once she said, 'Frederick . . .'

'Yes?'

'Oh, nothing.'

She fell silent once more. Then the only sound was of the oars, gliding through the water. Another few strokes and they'd have rounded the bend in the river. Already he could hear the strains of music from afar. Now they were in the home straight. 'I hope you won't think . . .' But whatever she'd been going to say was cut off by a different kind of sound, one whose shrill violence seemed to shatter the glassy tranquillity which surrounded them. It was a woman screaming.

'What on earth . . . ?'

Rowlands didn't waste time in speculation. A few more rapid strokes brought them to the bank. He held the boat steady while she jumped out and made fast the painter. Then he too got out, scrambling up the bank as fast as he was able. She took his hand. 'Come on,' she said, and the two of them began to run towards the house and the direction from which the scream had come. Nor were they the only ones: other guests were emerging from the summerhouse. 'What's going on?' Rowlands heard one man say.

'Damned if I know,' was the reply. 'Sounds as if someone's being murdered.'

Inside the house, all was confusion as people coming in from the garden bumped into those already milling around inside. In the crush, Rowlands lost hold of Celia West's hand, and found himself jostled hither and thither. A woman was sobbing uncontrollably. He heard a voice – Hank Harrington's – say, 'For Chrissakes! Somebody call an ambulance!' He pushed his way through the crowd, not caring too much whose feet he trod on, until he reached the American. The latter was standing in the narrow passage which separated the sitting room from the room beyond.

'What's happened?' said Rowlands. But before Harrington could answer, there came another voice, from within the room. 'My God! I think he's killed her . . .'

It was Celia West. She must have slipped ahead of him, Rowlands thought. With a murmur of apology, he shouldered Harrington aside and entered the room – a study, he guessed. 'Who is it that's been hurt?' Even as he asked the question, he was half-prepared for the answer.

'It's Olave.' Her voice came from somewhere just above floor level. She was kneeling, he realised. The girl must be lying on the floor. 'She . . . she's awfully white and . . . she's not moving. She's been hit on the head, I think. There's blood in her hair . . . I can't tell if . . . if . . .'

'Is she still breathing?'

'I . . . I don't know. Perhaps. I can't tell . . .'

'Do you know how to take a pulse?' Squatting down

307

beside her, he explained what it was she had to do, and the vital signs she ought to check for. It crossed his mind that she'd probably never had any first aid training, since she was too young to have been a VAD – a thought which could not but remind him, uncomfortably, of Edith.

'I think I can feel something,' she said after a minute had passed.

'Good,' he replied. She was near enough for him to feel that she was trembling. He resisted an impulse to put his arm around her. 'Now we just have to keep her warm until the ambulance arrives. You couldn't fetch a blanket, could you, Mr Harrington?'

'Coming up,' was the reply, and a few moments later, Harrington re-appeared with the said article. 'I'm told the ambulance is on its way,' he said as the three of them made the unconscious woman as comfortable as possible.

'Who found her?' said Rowlands as he got to his feet once more.

'Mrs Coulson. She's the one who was yelling her head off just now. Guess it must have given her a shock, walking in and finding Olave like that. Wish I knew who'd done it,' said the American fiercely. 'I'd be happy to knock his brains out for him, the bastard.'

'Do we have any idea who it was?' said Rowlands.

It seemed to him that Harrington hesitated a moment before replying. 'It's funny you should ask that,' he began. 'Because nobody seems to have seen anything.' Before he could expand on this, someone else put his head around the door of the study.

'I say, Harrington, oughtn't we to call the police?' It was 'Stinker' Coulson. 'For all we know, this burglar chappie might still be about.'

'Do we know for certain that it was a burglary?' interrupted Rowlands. 'I mean – has anything been stolen?'

'Couldn't tell you, old boy,' was the reply. 'All I know is, we ought to think of the women. Pamela's had the most awful fright, and . . .'

'Where's Harmsworth?' said Rowlands. There was a silence.

'He took off a while ago, didn't he, Coulson?' It struck Rowlands that Harrington sounded distinctly uneasy.

'Couldn't say,' was the reply. 'Hang on, though – I think I *did* hear his car, now you mention it. Drives a Bentley, doesn't he? Sporty little number.'

'When was this exactly?' said Rowlands. 'That you heard the car leave, I mean.'

'Quarter of an hour ago?' said Coulson. 'Certainly no more – wouldn't you say, Harrington?'

'I guess so,' said the American. 'But I don't see that it matters all that much. Peter's right. We should call the cops right away. Why, if that girl dies, we could be looking at a case of first degree murder.'

'Yes,' said Rowlands. 'Which is why I'm about to telephone Scotland Yard.'

'It appears I owe you an apology, Mr Rowlands,' said Chief Inspector Douglas. It was past one o'clock. Two hours had passed since Olave Malory had been attacked

– time in which the lady in question had been taken to hospital, and the police had been summoned. Now the remaining partygoers were having their statements taken in the next room by two of Douglas's subordinates, while the man himself sucked at his pipestem and ruminated on the evidence so far. 'You've said all along that Harmsworth was our man, and I'm sorry to say, I doubted you.'

'Mm,' said Rowlands, a shade distractedly. Something wasn't right, but he couldn't put his finger on it.

'Aye,' went on Douglas. 'It seems we've got a motive for these killings at last. Cocaine smuggling. Seems to me Captain Percival must've got wind of what Harmsworth was up to. Threatened to blow the gaff, no doubt, and so he had to be silenced.'

'No doubt,' echoed Rowlands. He tried to remember what it was that had struck him as odd about the events of that evening, but failed to do so. 'Have you found the weapon?' he asked.

'Not so far,' was the reply. Medical Officer said it was a blunt instrument of some kind. Same as the one that did for Farley,' he added meaningfully. 'To judge from where Miss Malory was lying, the assailant must have been hiding behind the door as she came in, hit her a blow on the back of the head, and scarpered through the French windows.'

'Do we know when this was?'

The Chief Inspector considered a moment. 'Well, the Coulson girl thinks it must have been around eleven-thirty that she stumbled across Miss Malory. Wanted to ask if she could use the telephone to call a taxi, she says. Must have come close to catching the fellow in the act. Thinks she heard someone running away, along the path that leads to the front gate.'

'Was it before or after Harmsworth's car was heard driving away?'

The Chief Inspector laughed softly. 'Now, wouldn't that be useful to know?' he said.

'But Coulson said . . .'

'I know what he said,' replied Douglas. 'He thought he heard Harmsworth's Bentley drive off about a quarter of an hour before Mrs P gave the alarm.'

'Then that means . . .'

'That the man she heard running along the path can't have been Harmsworth. I can work that out for myself,' said the policeman irritably. 'It doesn't alter the matter. Things still look very black indeed for Mr Cecil Harmsworth.'

'Yes, I see that,' said Rowlands. He was still trying to pin down what it was that had attracted his attention. Something someone had said, was it? Or perhaps some other sound. The trouble was, it had been pandemonium in that room, with everyone shouting together. It might have been anything, he thought.

'Consider the evidence against him,' Douglas was saying. He removed the unlit pipe from his mouth, the better to make his point. 'To begin with, he doesn't have an alibi for Farley's murder – in fact, he lied about the time he arrived at the aerodrome.'

'Yes, but . . .'

'He had a motive for killing Farley, who must have been blackmailing him about the cocaine shipments. And it was his plane that Percival was flying. He'd ample opportunity to sabotage the thing.' The Chief Inspector drew breath before continuing. 'As for motive, he was jealous of Percival – we'd already established that much – and had several other good reasons for wanting him out of the way. The fact that Percival must have tumbled to his dope smuggling racket being the best of 'em.'

'It does hang together, I suppose.'

'It's certainly enough to *hang him*,' said Douglas with grim humour. I mean to say,' he went on, 'he was lucky enough to get away with *one* murder; thinking he can get away with three – four, if this young woman dies – seems like pushing his luck.'

'So you think it was Harmsworth who killed Mrs Metcalfe?'

'I don't see who else it could have been,' replied the Chief Inspector. 'If we're agreed that Metcalfe didn't do it – and I must say, we haven't found a scrap of evidence that he did – then it must have been someone else. Harmsworth fits the bill. She was at the aerodrome that day and obviously overheard something she shouldn't have. Now we find him running away from the scene of a crime, having quarrelled with the victim.'

'What?'

'Oh, didn't I say?' There was a note of smug satisfaction in the Chief Inspector's voice. 'Aye, as it happens, we've a witness who says he overheard raised voices coming from this very room, not half an hour before Miss Malory was found.' Harrington, thought Rowlands, remembering how uneasy the American had seemed when Harmsworth's name had been mentioned.

'Did he actually hear what was said?'

'He says he didn't hear much. Went away as soon as he realised what was going on,' said Douglas. 'More's the pity,' he added grimly. 'One thing he did hear, though, pretty nearly clinches the affair, as far as I can see.'

'What was that?'

'He says he heard the girl – Miss Malory, that is – say something like, "I think you'd better leave". To which Harmsworth replied, "You'll regret this, Olave." There!' said the policeman. 'If that isn't a threat, I don't know what is.'

'He's in love with her,' said Rowlands.

'I don't see what that's got to do with it,' said Douglas. 'Yes, what is it, Withers?' he snapped, as his sergeant appeared in the door of the study.

'Just to say that the Yard have telephoned, sir, to inform us that the suspect was picked up ten minutes ago, as per your orders, at his flat in Bryanston Square.'

'Not a stone's throw from the Metcalfes' flat in Gloucester Place,' said Douglas pointedly. 'That'll do, Sergeant. You can bring the car round. I don't think there's much more we can do here. All right, ladies and gentlemen,' he went on as the two police officers, followed by Rowlands, emerged from the study and entered the sitting room where those that remained were closeted. 'You're free to go. I shan't need to talk to any of you again tonight. But please don't embark on any long journeys – by aeroplane or otherwise – without informing me or Sergeant Withers.'

'Dash it!' muttered a voice close to Rowlands' ear. 'I suppose that puts paid to my Biarritz trip.' It was hard to tell whether the speaker was joking or not. It occurred to Rowlands that he ought to be making tracks, too. It was a quarter to two; the trains from Richmond would have stopped running long ago. Well, it was a fine night, he thought – it wouldn't hurt him to walk. He accordingly took his leave of the Chief Inspector, who, perhaps thinking of what lay ahead – the interrogation of a suspect – replied with a preoccupied air.

'Ah, yes. Mr Rowlands. Quite so. Time you got yourself home. It's been a long night.' Although for him it would doubtless be a longer one.

Of Lady Celia there was no sign. Harrington, when questioned as to her whereabouts, was vague. 'Guess she must have taken off already. Her car's gone, anyhow.' Rowlands thanked him and took his leave. After all that had passed between them earlier, it didn't surprise him in the least that she wanted to avoid another meeting. But as he set out along the lane that led to the river, and the path that would take him to Kingston, a car pulled up alongside him, and a voice said, 'I waited for you.'

'Lady Celia.'

'Get in,' she said. 'I'll run you home.'

'There's no need,' he said; then, because it sounded

314

ungracious, 'It's such a nice night. I'll walk.'

'It's miles. And hardly the most auspicious circumstances.' She sounded utterly done in, he thought.

'You're right,' he said. 'I'd be glad of a lift.'

'You'll have to give me directions,' she said as he climbed into the front seat of the Hispano-Suiza beside her. 'I used to know this part of the world quite well, of course, but one forgets.' He knew she was referring to the time she'd lived not ten miles from here, at the great house in the countryside outside Esher which her family had owned for generations, and which had since been sold off, like many such since the war. Although it had not been the war which had brought about that particular catastrophe. He guessed the place must have evil memories for her now.

'Will she die, do you think?' she said, interrupting this melancholy train of thought with one still more so.

'I don't know,' he replied. She was silent a moment, then she said, 'I can't believe he would have done such a thing. Cecil, I mean. He's been in love with her for years.'

'Yes,' said Rowlands.

'I was forgetting how much you always seem to know about people,' she said. He smiled.

'It isn't my famous intuition this time,' he said. 'She told me so herself. Miss Malory, that is.' He hesitated a moment. 'I didn't get the impression that the feeling was reciprocated.'

Celia West laughed. 'You're right there! She found it rather a bore if you want to know. It was Alan she cared for . . .' She broke off. 'I shouldn't talk about her as if she

315

were dead. I say, light me a cigarette, will you? There are some De Reszkes in the glove compartment.'

He did so, using the trick he'd learnt long ago, in the early days of his blindness: holding the cigarette level with the matchbox as he struck the match so that the end ignited as the match caught fire. He slipped the cigarette between his lips and took a couple of drags before holding it out for her to take. 'Thanks.' He heard the sound of her indrawn breath as she drew deeply on the gasper. The sweet smell of Virginia tobacco filled the car, mingling with that of the intoxicating scent she wore. 'Have one yourself,' she said. He lit up, and for a while neither said anything.

When she spoke again, it was in a different tone of voice: softer; almost cajoling. 'About what happened earlier . . .' she began. He didn't let her finish.

'It's already forgotten.'

'I hope not entirely forgotten.'

He didn't respond to this sally.

'Of course, I know it's impossible,' she went on. 'We've already said as much. You're married and I'm . . .'

'From a different world,' he said. 'I know.'

'You sound rather angry.'

'Not angry,' he said. 'Resigned. We don't belong together, you and I. It was presumptuous of me to suppose otherwise.'

'Oh, I wish you'd drop that attitude,' she said. 'It's all rot, and you know it.'

'All I know is I shouldn't have let my feelings run away with me,' he said.

'It isn't the first time we've kissed.'

'No. But that was different.' On the occasion referred to, they'd been surrounded by the graves of tens of thousands of his comrades-in-arms, and their talk had been of the man both had loved, whose death was still fresh in memory.

'Was it?' she said. 'I think it was then I fell in love with you. You were angry with me that day too, as I recall.'

'You shouldn't say such things. It isn't fair. To me, or . . .'

'To your wife, you were going to say. No, it certainly isn't fair to her. But then love isn't fair,' said Celia West.

The rest of the journey passed in a silence broken only by Rowlands' brief directions as they reached Kingston. 'So this is where you live now,' said his companion as they drew up in front of the house in Grove Crescent. 'Rather a nice house.'

'It's certainly nicer than the one in Crofton Park.'

'Yes. Although I thought that had a certain charm,' she said. 'The garden especially.' He remembered that occasion, too. Another silence fell.

'Well,' he said at last. But she laid a finger on his lips. 'Don't say anything.' Slowly, she drew her finger across his mouth, as if she were trying to memorise its shape. 'Go,' she said softly. 'Before I change my mind.'

He got out of the car, and stood waiting on the pavement as she engaged the gears and drove off. He waited until the sound of the engine had died away into the distance before he went inside.

# Chapter Seventeen

He was awakened by the ringing of the telephone. He felt for his watch as, pulling on his dressing gown, he stumbled out of bed and down the stairs. A quarter to seven. Who could be calling at this hour? He was unable to suppress a clutch of alarm as he picked up the receiver. 'Hello? Hello? Fred, is that you?' Even though they'd had a telephone installed for nearly five years, his wife still tended to shout when she used the instrument.

'Yes, it's me. Whatever's the matter?'

'Matter? Nothing's the matter, except . . . Where were you, last night?' she said. 'I telephoned three times, but there was no answer.'

'I was out,' he said. As briefly as he could, he summarised the events of the previous evening.

'You don't mean to say there's been *another* murder?' said Edith when he'd got to the bit about Olave Malory's being attacked.

'Attempted murder,' he said. 'Of course I had to hang around until the police got there.'

'But how did you happen to be there in the first place?'

'She was having a party. Miss Malory, that is.'

'So you said. But you still haven't answered my question.'

'There's no particular mystery to it,' he said, aware that he sounded defensive. 'She was having a party. I was invited, that's all.'

'But you hardly know the woman.'

'That sort of thing doesn't matter to people like her. Did you have a reason for telephoning at this ungodly hour?' he said, hoping to distract her from what seemed a dangerous line of questioning. But she wasn't finished.

'I suppose she was there,' she said. 'That West woman.'

He felt a guilty flush creep up his neck and face. 'She was, as a matter of fact.'

'Yes, I saw in the paper that she was back in London. I suppose it was she who fetched you?'

At least he didn't have to lie about that. 'Miss Malory sent her car, if you really want to know. Edith, what *is* this?' Guilt sharpened his indignation. Perhaps it convinced her; perhaps not.

'Nothing. It's just that . . .'

A voice said, 'Three minutes. Would you like more time, call-ah?'

'No, thank you. We're catching the ten-fifteen from Truro. We'll be at Paddington at . . .' Then the pips went. No matter, Rowlands thought. He could easily find out what time the train got in. Sighing, he replaced the heavy receiver in its cradle. He thought, I suppose it's for the best, and went to run his bath, with a heavy heart.

With several hours to go before he was due at Paddington Station, he decided to go into the office. Not that there was much doing on a Saturday, but he could catch up with some filing, and generally get things in order for the following week. Besides which, it would give him a chance to think things out, undisturbed by ringing telephones or random droppers-in. Arriving, just over an hour later, at the grand Regency mansion which had served as St Dunstan's HQ since the second year of the war, he let himself into the office, whose smell – a composite of furniture polish, carbon paper and Churchman's cigarettes – was now as familiar to him as his own smell. Funny how rooms came to fit one, like a shell, or a second skin.

He threw his briefcase on the chair, and rifled through the latest batch of post. Mostly brown envelopes by the feel of 'em, and one other, of better quality. He fingered its smooth, square shape, the address inscribed with a firm cursive hand, before deciding to pocket it. He'd take it home for Edith to read to him. Not that he got many personal letters here. But every now and then, someone trying to trace a relative, or pass on information about a former inmate who had died, would write to 'The Secretary, St Dunstan's' – which was what he was, he supposed; the institution which had saved his life, in more senses than one, having also provided him with an income.

Setting aside the rest of the post for Miss Collins to deal with on Monday morning, Rowlands sat down at his desk, and reached, as he often did when a problem proved intractable, for the sea-washed pebble he'd picked up that day – *four years ago, was it?* – on the beach at Brighton. For a moment or two, he turned it around in his fingers, feeling the smooth, cool contours with something approaching delight. It was of her he was thinking, the woman he'd been with that day, and of their stolen kisses the night before. How sweet it had been to hold her in his arms at last. He knew he should feel sick and ashamed, not least for his betrayal of Edith. But he did not. 'After all, nothing will come of it,' he said aloud; knowing, as he said it, that the damage was already done.

Putting the stone aside, and with it, thoughts of the woman in question, he picked up the paperknife. This, too, had a pleasant weight to it; he fingered the blade with circumspection. He thought, I've been looking at this from entirely the wrong angle. In concerning himself with motive, he'd overlooked what was most obvious – which was opportunity. He began to go over the events of the previous evening, from the time, around half past eight, when he'd arrived at Olave Malory's riverside cottage, to the moment, nearly three hours later, when he'd heard Pamela Coulson scream.

There was something, he thought, if only he could put his finger on it. Was it something somebody had said? Snatches of conversation, inconsequential at the time, now came back to him. 'It's all a bit incestuous . . .' Yes, it was certainly that. Percival with his entourage of – mainly female – admirers, amongst them poor little Irene Metcalfe . . . and Olave Malory. Harmsworth the former fag, whose hero-worship had turned to bitter rivalry. 'Incestuous' was the word, thought Rowlands, weighing the knife in his hand.

The telephone rang – suddenly, shockingly – interrupting his reverie. He answered it. 'Hello?'

'He denies it, o' course,' said a voice, without preamble. Douglas. He sounded as if he hadn't had much sleep. 'But we'll break him yet. Just as soon as that girl wakes up.'

'She hasn't come round then?'

'Not as yet. We've just got to hope the operation will prove a success.' Then, when Rowlands interrogated him further, 'She'll be unconscious for a wee while yet. I'm told the doctors had quite a fight to keep her alive. It appears they had to remove a blood clot from her brain.' The Chief Inspector's tone was one of barely suppressed anger. 'I don't mind telling you that it'll give me great pleasure to see this fellow hang.'

'You're quite certain it's him? Harmsworth, I mean.'

'As certain as I am about anything,' was the reply.

'But is there any physical evidence that he was involved? Blood on his clothes or . . .'

'I know well enough what you mean,' said Douglas curtly. 'No, we've found nothing like that – so far, at least. But he had ample opportunity to change his clothes.'

'And the weapon?'

'I can see you've thought about this in great detail,' said the Chief Inspector drily. 'We'll make a policeman of you yet, Mr Rowlands. No, we've not found the weapon, either. But I can tell you where we will find it – if we ever find it – wrapped up inside a suit of clothes at the bottom of the river.'

Rowlands approached Paddington Station with plenty of time to spare – and not a little trepidation. He didn't for a moment think that Edith would take him to task in front of the children, but her offended silences could be bad enough. He decided that the line of least resistance was the one to take. But she greeted him with what seemed like a very good show of affection – if indeed it was a show, and not the genuine article – kissing him soundly on the cheek (they never kissed on the lips in public) and tucking her arm though his as they turned to make their way towards the ticket barrier, as if she were thoroughly pleased to see him.

The girls, inevitably, provided most of the commentary to this meeting, chattering incessantly and at the tops of their voices about all the things they'd done and all the places they'd been until reprimanded by their mother. 'You'd think this was the Parrot House at the Zoo.' Then, turning her attention to her husband, 'How are you, Fred? You look all right. A bit thinner, perhaps. Have you been eating properly?'

'It's only that I'm wearing fewer clothes,' he said. 'It's been so hot, this past few weeks. Did you have a good journey?'

'Yes, quite all right.'

'We had lunch on the train, Daddy,' said Anne, with an air of importance. 'The steward called us. We had . . .'

'Your father doesn't want to hear what you had for lunch,' said Edith firmly. 'Margaret, hold Joanie's hand, will you, while we're getting through this crowd? It is hot,' she said, fanning herself with her straw hat. 'Like an oven, after Cornwall. Porter, could you bring our luggage to the taxi rank, please? Have you got sixpence for him?' she whispered to her husband. He duly obliged. 'I must say,' said Edith as the five of them piled into the back of the taxicab. 'It's good to be back. Cornwall was lovely, but I've been looking forward to being in my own home.'

'Well, I'm glad you're back,' said Rowlands, conscious that this was not entirely true. At once he reproached himself. What sort of a man am I, he thought, as the taxi rattled its way through the afternoon traffic towards Waterloo. 'I gather you all enjoyed yourselves?' he remarked, in an interval between Anne's telling him about a day spent crab-fishing, and Joan's demanding an

324

ice cream, 'Which she'll have to do without,' said Edith. 'I'm afraid she's been rather spoilt by her Uncle Jack.'

'How is the dear old fellow?'

'Oh, he's all right,' said Edith. Something in her tone alerted him to the fact that there was more to the statement than met the eye.

'And Cecily?' But she wouldn't be drawn.

'We'll talk about it later,' she said. 'Cabbie, you can let us off here.'

It wasn't until they were back at Grove Avenue once more, that his wife was persuaded to expand on her cryptic remark. The girls had been sent to unpack their things, and were even now reacquainting themselves with their surroundings. 'I must say,' said Margaret. 'It'll be jolly nice to have a room to myself again.' He and Edith were having tea in the garden. It was another beautiful evening, with barely a breath of wind; the heady smell of night-scented stocks hung in the air. This time yesterday, he thought, he'd only just got in, and all that had since transpired had yet to transpire. Recalling those events, and certain things in particular, Rowlands felt a pang of guilt, sharp as dyspepsia. Perhaps construing his pained expression as a reproach, Edith said in a low voice, 'Look, I'm sorry for what I said earlier. On the telephone, I mean. It was quite uncalled for.'

'Oh, I wouldn't say that,' he said miserably.

'Well, I would. You were at that party on police business. Oh, don't tell me the Chief Inspector wasn't involved in some way, because I know better!'

'Edith . . .'

'I've been a silly jealous woman,' she said. 'I can't think what got into me.'

He could not have felt more of a worm. 'I don't deserve to have you,' he said.

'Oh, fiddlesticks!' Having got her confession off her chest, she was eager to tell him the rest. 'You haven't asked about your sister,' she said.

'I was waiting for you to tell me. From your tone of voice, I gather something's up.'

'I can see why you're such a good detective,' said his wife drily. 'Well, it really isn't my news to tell, but I suppose you'll hear soon enough. She and your friend Jack are engaged to be married.'

He let out a low whistle of astonishment. 'So that's what you meant when you said he was "all right"?'

'Yes.'

'How's Cecily talking it?'

'Very well. But then she always behaves beautifully. She's to live with them, of course.' Edith laughed. 'At first she offered to move out, but your sister wouldn't hear of it. In fact, she made it a condition of her marrying Jack. "This is your home," she said. "I've no intention of turning you out." You know how Dorothy goes on.' Rowlands did. 'They need her to help run the hotel, of course.'

'What about the boys?' he said, to cut short this less than charitable interpretation of his sister's motives. 'They've taken it quite well, all things considered,' was the reply. 'Victor's really too young to know much about it, and Billy . . .' Again, she laughed. 'Billy has his own view of the matter, as he does about everything. All I can say is, he and young Danny have had some spectacular fights since we first arrived there. Black eyes and bloody noses.'

'They're the age for fighting.'

'Perhaps,' she said, yawning. 'I must say, I'm rather glad we've only got girls.'

'So am I,' he said.

When congratulated on his good fortune, Ashenhurst had sounded pleased and slightly abashed. 'I was going to write – or get Ciss to write, rather – but then, as Edith was going to be seeing you in a day or two, I thought . . .'

'When did all this happen?'

'Exactly a week ago. We were walking back from church, Dorothy and I, and . . .' Church! That was a new one, thought Rowlands. To the best of his knowledge, his sister hadn't set foot in a church since deciding, at the age of fifteen, that 'God was all bunk', and that she'd rather read a good book than listen to a dull sermon any day of the week. '. . . decided to make it a quiet wedding,' Ashenhurst was saying. 'End of September, we thought. You'll be able to come, won't you, old man?'

'Just you try and keep me away,' said Rowlands.

'Splendid. Ciss is making all the arrangements. She's been a brick about the whole affair. Thrilled to bits, of course. She adores Dorothy. But I expect you'd like a word with the lady herself?'

'I would,' said Rowlands; then, when his sister came on the line, 'Well! This is good news.'

'We think so,' said Dorothy calmly. 'And of course it solves one particular problem. I won't be Mrs Lehmann for much longer.'

'No,' said Rowlands. 'There is that. Is Jack there with you?' he added, wondering a little at her frankness.

'He's taken the boys down to the beach. He says they need regular walking, like puppies. He's been marvellous with Billy,' she added, a real warmth in her voice now.

'It'll be good for the boys to have a home. What about Cecily?' he went on. 'I gather she'll be staying on at Cliff House?'

'Of course. It's where she's always lived,' said Dorothy. 'Except for a few weeks during the war before her husband got killed. She's been marvellous, too. I don't think,' she added, with a shade of her old sarcasm, 'she knows how to behave any other way. It's the way they were brought up, she and Jack.'

'Does he know?' said Rowlands abruptly.

'About my chequered past, I suppose you mean?' Her tone was acid. 'He knows I've been in prison.'

'Yes, but that was . . .' He broke off.

'For a minor offence, you were going to say. He doesn't know about the capital crime.'

'I'm sorry. I had to ask.'

'I know.' Her voice softened a little. 'You worry too much. It'll be all right, you'll see.'

'I hope so,' he said. 'One thing's certain, though. You

couldn't have wished for a better man than Jack Ashenhurst.'

'I know that, too,' she said.

'Not that he isn't lucky to have you.'

'I believe you mean that,' she said. 'You are a funny old thing, Fred. Sometimes you remind me awfully of Dad.'

'I'll take that as a compliment.' They both laughed; it seemed, after all, as if he and his sister might still be friends.

'Well,' said Dorothy. 'It's been lovely to chat. But this call must be costing you a fortune.'

'That's all right. It isn't often that a man gets the chance to congratulate his favourite sister on her engagement to his best friend.' He paused a moment. 'There was one other thing I wanted to ask you . . .'

'Oh?' she said. 'And what's that?'

'It's about that day – the day of the accident . . . when Captain Percival was killed. You remember.'

'Yes, I remember. And I'd really rather not have to be reminded of it again.'

'Please,' he said. 'I wouldn't ask if it wasn't important.'

'I suppose you're still after whoever it was that killed Alan?' she said. 'You and that copper friend of yours.'

'That's right,' he said. 'It's just that I can't help feeling that I might have missed something. I do miss quite a lot, you know,' he added humbly. His sister snorted.

'All right, I get the point. What is it exactly that you want to know?'

'That's just the trouble,' he said. 'I won't know

329

until . . . well, until I know. But it would be a tremendous help if you could tell me as much as you can remember of that day.'

'All right.' She paused for a moment, as if gathering her thoughts. 'Well, we arrived at the aerodrome, Alan and me. I'd spent the night with him in his flat in Cumberland Terrace, as I expect you'd guessed. That's something else Jack doesn't know about, by the by.'

'He won't hear it from me,' said Rowlands. 'Go on.'

'First we drove down to the hangar where Alan kept his plane . . . this must have been around a quarter to twelve, or thereabouts. He was furious when he found the place locked up. Said he'd have words to say to . . . what was the name of the bloke that was found murdered?'

'Farley.'

'That's the one. So, anyway, he was breathing fire all the way back to the Club House – Alan, I mean – saying he'd had his suspicions that Farley was a wrong 'un. Told me to sit tight in the car while he tracked the bloke down. When he didn't come back after ten minutes or so, I thought I'd investigate for myself. That was when I found you – and the Metcalfe woman, I think. She was creating an almighty fuss. It transpired she'd found a body. Farley's body, it turned out. So that explained what had happened to him. Then the police arrived, and . . .'

'You haven't mentioned Higgins. He was there, too.'

'Was he the bloke they arrested? Yes, he was there.'

'How was he dressed?'

'I don't remember. Overalls, I think. Navy, or brown, or some dark colour.'

'Anybody else you can recall?'

'Well, there was the barman. He'd just come on duty . . . and that girl – the one who knew such a lot about aeroplanes.'

'Can you remember what she was wearing?'

'A frock, I think. I didn't pay her much attention. Yes, that's right. A pale blue frock, with some kind of floral pattern. And white gloves. To tell you the truth, I hardly recognised her, she looked so smart. Then the police arrived – but you know most of this already, Fred.'

'I'm just trying to get a picture.'

'Well, then we all drove down to the hangar – you, me, Alan and the girl – and then you men went off with the police to view the body, and the rest of us just hung around until you got back.'

'What was she doing – the girl?'

'I don't recall. Hanging around too, I suppose. There was quite a crowd of people there by this time – pilots, mostly. I'm afraid I can't tell you their names. One was German, I think.'

'That's all right,' said Rowlands. 'I think the police have eliminated most of them from the list of suspects. Can you remember anything that was said?'

'Not a great deal,' she confessed. 'It *is* over six weeks ago. There was a lot of shouting and arguing about whether or not the race would go ahead. One of the angriest was that chap Harmsworth. He'd arrived with Olave Malory – Alan's old flame. Not that I realised that until later when she went for me in the bar.'

'What happened then?' he said, trying to keep her to the point. She thought about it.

'Alan was upset because the police had told him he couldn't fly the Moth,' she said. 'He'd been looking forward to the race as the Grand Finale to a year of triumphs.' Her voice failed her, momentarily. 'I wish to God he'd given it up. If I'd known then what I know now . . .'

'You couldn't have known,' said Rowlands gently.

'It was just that it meant so much to him to fly that day,' she said. 'And I encouraged him, God forgive me.'

'There's no sense in reproaching yourself.'

'No,' she said. She was silent a moment. 'Well, then we went back to the Club House,' she went on, her voice now steady. 'The police wanted to interview us all, and so . . .'

'Did anything happen before that?' he asked. 'Before the police interviews, I mean.'

'I can't think of anything in particular. People were standing about, I suppose. The place was rather full, by then. That silly little Metcalfe woman was fussing about something. Oh, and then that husband of hers arrived, to take her away.'

'Can you remember what was said?'

'Let me think. Yes . . . She said something about having seen the murderer, and he told her not to be so silly.'

'I don't suppose you can remember who else was

within earshot when she said it – that she'd seen the murderer, I mean?' She told him. 'Yes,' he said. 'That's rather what I thought.'

He found Lanark Road easily enough; deciding which direction to take was more problematic. He was hesitating on the pavement outside the Underground station, with others pushing past on either side of him when a voice said, 'Are you all right, sir? You look a bit lost.'

'Well, as a matter of fact . . .' Before Rowlands could finish, there came a roaring in his ears, and he felt his arm seized, none too gently.

'I say, watch out! You nearly stepped under the wheels of that lorry. I'll have *his* number, for a start,' said his saviour, now revealed as one the local constabulary. 'Speeding in a built-up area! You see if I don't. But you really ought to look where you're going,' he said severely.

'I'm sorry, I didn't see it coming,' said Rowlands, with a rueful grimace. As the truth of this struck the young policeman, he began stammering an apology. 'That's quite all right, officer,' said Rowlands; then, seizing his chance with alacrity, 'As a matter of fact, you're just the man to help me.'

Arriving some ten minutes later at his destination, Rowlands climbed the short flight of steps that led to the front door, and rang the bell. Number 125, Lanark Road, was one of a terrace of tall brick mansions, built some thirty years before; Constable Dawson had described it for him. 'They're big old places,' he'd said, escorting his charge along the road in question, this being part of his beat, he said, and therefore not out of his way. Inconveniently large, was his opinion. 'Quite a few of 'em have been turned into flats. No one's got the money these days to keep up a place that size. The one you want's still in private hands, I gather. Elderly lady. Keeps herself to herself, if you know what I mean. Relative, are you?'

'A friend,' said Rowlands. 'Well, I hope you find her in. And take care in future, won't you, sir?' admonished this cheerful custodian of the law. Rowlands agreed that he would. Now, hearing the echo of the bell jangle away into silence inside the house, he wondered if, after all, he would find the answer he was looking for – or if this journey would prove yet another wild goose chase. But then, just as he was raising his hand for another assault on the bell pull, the door opened, and a voice he recognised as that of the woman he had spoken to on the telephone said, 'Yes? What do you want?'

'The name's Rowlands. We spoke on the telephone. I'd like to speak to Miss Denham, please.'

'I'll tell her.' She turned and shuffled away into the depths of the house, leaving Rowlands to follow as best he could. He managed this without incident, apart from bumping into the hall-stand – a larger than usual object which was no doubt a relic of the Victorian Age – and soon found himself in what he supposed must be the sitting room. He guessed this to be a large room, although it was difficult to form an idea of it, so muffled was any sound by the furniture with which it was cluttered. He discovered this only when, in taking a tentative step into the room, he collided with the protruding edge of a sideboard, which was on the same massive scale as the hall-stand; then, in advancing further, with the back of a sofa, and, in skirting this, with a mahogany whatnot. He was still disentangling himself from these obstructions when a voice from across the room said sharply, 'You there, sirrah! What are you doing, hanging about by the door? Come here, into the light where I can see you.'

Surprised, he did so, moving cautiously to avoid walking into any more items of furniture. 'That's better,' she said, for it was a woman's voice, in spite of its gruffness. 'So you're the mysterious Mr Rowlands, are you? I suppose,' she said, 'you've come because of my letter?'

'I'm afraid I don't know anything about a letter,' he replied. 'It is Miss Denham, isn't it?'

'And who else would it be? You'll have to speak up, young man. I'm a little deaf, although there's nothing wrong with my eyes.'

'Then you have the advantage of me.'

'Blind, are you? I suppose that was why you were crashing into my furniture. You ought to carry a stick.'

'I've considered it,' he said meekly.

'Well, sit down,' she said. 'There's an armchair to your right. So, if you didn't get my letter, then why are you here?'

Rowland hesitated a moment, wondering how far he ought to take this forthright old woman into his confidence. 'It's about your niece . . .' he began. 'She isn't my niece, but my great-niece. Her mother died when she was born. She's lived with me since . . . well, since she was a child. What's the matter? Is she in some sort of trouble? Out with it, man!' she said, with some asperity when he did not reply at once. 'I can see from your face that something's wrong.'

She sat in silence until he had finished speaking; then she said, in a subdued tone which was in marked contrast to her earlier acerbity, 'I was afraid something like this might happen. It was why I wrote to you in the first instance. But I was forgetting. You didn't get my letter.'

'As a matter of fact, I believe I did,' said Rowlands. 'I just haven't read it. Perhaps,' he went on, 'you could tell me what it said?'

She did so. Now it was his turn to be silent. 'I've been worried for some time,' she said when she had told him what she had to tell. 'There've been so many odd things happening . . . things I couldn't explain, that were nothing in themselves, you know, but which taken together . . .' Her voice tailed off.

'You began to see a pattern,' said Rowlands.

'Yes. And then, when I found . . . what I found . . . under her bed . . . Well, I thought the time had come for me to speak out.'

'You did the right thing,' he said.

'For all the good it'll do,' she replied bitterly. 'If only I'd spoken out sooner! But I didn't know who to turn to, you see. There's her father, of course, but he's refused to have anything to do with her since it happened, and . . .'

'Since what happened?' interrupted Rowlands.

She told him. 'She was only a child,' she said as she came to the end of this. 'But still . . .'

Rowlands got to his feet. 'May I use your telephone?'

'Of course,' said Miss Denham. 'It's in the hall. I'll take you to it. Oh, don't look like that! I can't have you knocking into the furniture again.' She took his arm, and they crossed the room together, Rowlands adjusting his step to her slower pace. She was hardly any weight at all, he thought. Insubstantial as a doll, made of wood and wax – all her strength concentrated into her indomitable will.

They had not reached the door when he came to a halt, his attention arrested by something outside it – the creak of a footfall, perhaps. 'Who else is in the house?' he said in a low voice.

'Eh? I didn't catch that.' Then, when he'd repeated it, 'There's no one but myself and Truscott, my maid.' Miss Denham opened the door. 'Truscott!' she called. 'Where *has* the woman got to? Ah, there you are! Truscott, Mr Rowlands is going to make a telephone call. He will then be leaving. I'm going up for my rest. You may call me in half an hour. Goodbye, Mr Rowlands.' He felt her take his hand in her little claw. 'I won't pretend I've enjoyed our talk, but I'm grateful to you for coming.' She paused, and drew a wheezing breath as if there were something more she wanted to say. 'You've got children yourself, I believe? Oh, she told me,' she added when he expressed surprise that she knew as much. 'She was very taken with one of them.'

'That'll be Anne. They liked her too, my girls. We all did,' he said, to soften the horror of which they had been talking.

'Oh, she can be a very sweet child at times,' said the old woman. 'How many children have you?

'Three. All girls. As it happens, they're just back from three weeks in Cornwall – the quietest three weeks I can remember,' he said, with a laugh.

'Yes, the house does seems quiet without them, doesn't it?' agreed Miss Denham sadly.

He heard her slow and halting footsteps go upstairs, and waited until the sound had faded into silence before dialling the familiar number. It rang only once before somebody answered. 'Chief Inspector Douglas, please,' said Rowlands. 'It's urgent.' But the Chief Inspector wasn't in his office. Nor would the young sergeant – a new man, with whom Rowlands hadn't had dealings – cast any light on where he might be.

'I'm sorry, sir,' he said. 'But that's confidential information. If you'll just tell me what it was you wanted to say to the Chief Inspector, I'll make sure it gets passed on.'

'But it might be too late by then,' said Rowlands, exasperated.

'Sorry, sir,' replied the other, with wooden obstinacy. 'I've got my orders.' It was useless to argue, thought Rowlands. There was nothing for it but to go into the office and await developments. When questioned as to her niece's whereabouts, Miss Denham had been uncharacteristically vague.

'No, she's not here. I expect she's at her job. All young women have jobs these days, don't they? In my day,' she said wryly, 'we hoped to get married.' As to what the job entailed and where it was that Miss Wilkinson went to do it, the old lady was even vaguer. 'It's something in an office, I gather. I believe the office is in the West End. A firm of literary agents,' she added, with a faint shudder.

# Chapter Eighteen

Back in his own office, Rowlands found Miss Collins going through the second post. 'You can leave that for the moment,' he said. 'There's something I'd like you to do for me.' The list he got her to compile from the telephone directory was not extensive, but it still took Rowlands the best part of an hour to work through it, with his secretary reading out the numbers as he dialled. He had tried eight of a possible twelve firms before he got a result. 'Good afternoon. Is that Matheson and Reed? I wondered if a Miss Pauline Wilkinson works there?' Even then, it could only be counted as a partial success. Yes, there was a Miss Wilkinson, said the supercilious young woman who answered his call – and no, she hadn't been seen for several weeks. So that was that, thought Rowlands. He wondered where he should try next. The aerodrome, perhaps. As he sat deliberating, the telephone in front of him rang. He picked up the receiver he had so lately set down. 'Hello?'

'At last!' said the Chief Inspector, sounding disgruntled. 'Your line's been busy for the past hour.' Then, as Rowlands went to speak, 'I know, I know. You've a job to do. Well, I won't keep you from it for very long. I just thought you'd like to know that she's woken up, our young lady. Although she can't remember much about that night. In fact, nothing at all about what happened before she was attacked.'

'So she can't say what it was she and Harmsworth quarrelled about?'

'Not as yet. O' course, her memory might come back.'

'Or it might not. Can she remember anything about the attack itself?'

'It's funny you should ask that. She *does* remember one thing. It was something she *heard* . . .' The Chief Inspector allowed a pause to elapse as if to let this information sink in. 'This was after she'd been attacked, so she was semi-conscious. But she swears she wasn't mistaken. Well, aren't you going to ask me what it was?'

'It was the sound of a motorbike.'

There was a stunned silence at the other end of the line. 'How in the name of all that's wonderful did you guess that?' said Douglas.

'It wasn't a guess. I heard it myself,' said Rowlands. 'I just didn't realise that I'd heard it until now. More than that, I can tell you who was riding the motorbike. And who attacked Miss Malory, and murdered Mrs Metcalfe, and . . .'

'But we already know it was Harmsworth,' interrupted the other.

'Do we?' said Rowlands. 'Then how do you explain the motorbike that Miss Malory – and I – heard accelerating away just after the attack? According to Mr Coulson, Harmsworth had left at least fifteen minutes before then.'

'I think you're jumping to conclusions,' said Douglas. 'We don't know that this chap on the motorbike had anything to do with the attack.'

'Oh, but we do,' said Rowlands. He proceeded to give the Chief Inspector a précis of all that he'd learnt since that morning. The policeman listened without interruption, but when Rowlands had finished saying what he had to say, Douglas seemed distinctly unimpressed.

'But that's preposterous, man!' His Edinburgh accent grew stronger the more upset he became. 'You can't expect me to believe that that wee girl . . .'

'She's a strapping young woman.'

'Be that as it may, you surely can't be serious? Why, man, that would mean . . .'

'It would mean she killed Farley and all the others, yes. The method was the same for Farley's murder as it was for the attack on Olave Malory. The same disguise, and the same weapon. The one found under the girl's bed by her aunt, Miss Denham.'

'Hmm,' said Douglas, sounding far from convinced. 'You're telling me the weapon – that is, the alleged weapon – has now gone missing?'

'Yes. She's removed it, obviously. But Miss Denham says . . .'

'Miss Denham's an old lady, you tell me. Old people get things confused. She may think she saw what you said she saw, but she might have got it wrong.'

'I'm convinced she didn't,' said Rowlands. 'Besides, what about the motorbike?'

'What about it?'

'Miss Wilkinson rides a motorbike.'

'A very modern young woman,' said the Chief Inspector, with evident distaste. 'But that hardly signifies. Lots of people ride motorbikes. *Infairnal* machines,' he added.

'She had the expertise to sabotage Percival's plane,' said Rowlands. 'To say nothing of the opportunity.'

'Perhaps,' said the Scotsman guardedly. 'But what was her motive?'

'Disappointed love,' said Rowlands.

'Ah, we're back to love again, are we?' replied the policeman, with amused scepticism. 'It seems to me, Mr Rowlands, that you've got love on the brain, if you don't mind my saying so.'

'The murder of Irene Metcalfe,' said Rowlands, ignoring this barbed remark, 'was carried out by a youth in navy blue overalls.'

'Yes, and carried out with a knife,' retorted the Chief Inspector. 'What became of your alleged weapon, then?'

'The murderer seized the weapon that was closest to hand – a kitchen knife,' was the reply. 'That doesn't mean . . .'

'It disnae mean very much,' said Douglas wearily. 'But go on with your story. I can see you've thought it all out.'

'The motive for killing Mrs Metcalfe was, as we've suspected all along, because she knew or had guessed the identity of Farley's killer,' Rowlands went on doggedly. 'That still holds true. My sis . . . that is, my wife . . . has corroborated the fact that Miss Wilkinson was present when Mrs Metcalfe made her unfortunate remark about having seen the murderer.'

'There were a number of people present at that time, according to Inspector Hawkins' report,' said Douglas.

'Yes, but there's one other thing . . .' Rowlands described the moment, during the telephone conversation he'd been having with Irene Metcalfe later that day, when he'd had the uncanny feeling someone else was there. 'She was in the house at the time – Pauline Wilkinson, I mean. She must have overheard my arranging to visit Mrs Metcalfe the following day. So she knew she had to act quickly, to silence her.'

'You're making this puir young woman sound like a master criminal,' said Douglas. 'Planning and plotting to do away with one person after another, just because . . .'

'Just because they got in her way,' said Rowlands. 'I

think that is what happened. Farley's murder wasn't planned – he simply happened to turn up at an inconvenient moment when she was sabotaging the Gipsy Moth. Perhaps he threatened to expose her – we can only guess. What we do know is that there must have been a struggle, during which she overpowered him by the simple expedient of kicking his legs from under him. As a cripple with a tin leg, he'd have found it impossible to get up unaided. The spanner she'd been using to fix Percival's aeroplane finished the job.'

'Ah yes, that blessed spanner,' said Douglas. 'You're telling me it was the same one your Miss Denham found under her great-niece's bed?'

'That, or another like it,' said Rowlands. 'A spanner was found to be missing from the tool box in Hangar Three,' he reminded the other. 'What with that and the overalls . . .'

'The overalls were found in Higgins' locker.'

'Planted there,' said Rowlands. 'You've said yourself that there was no other real evidence against Higgins. Anyway, the overalls Miss Denham found wrapped around the spanner were a different set. Miss Wilkinson's own. There was blood on those, too. Irene Metcalfe's blood. Oh, I'm afraid to say she planned that murder very cleverly indeed.'

Douglas was silent a moment. 'If it's as you say – and I'm not saying it is, mind – then why carry on after she'd got rid of Mrs Metcalfe? Surely all the people she wanted dead were already dead? If, as you say, she was in love with Percival and out to punish him for not loving her back, then why go for Miss Malory?'

'Jealous rage,' said Rowlands. 'Olave Malory had been engaged to Captain Percival, remember. Cecil Harmsworth was also in love with her.'

'Och, we're back on love are we?' said the other drily. 'Ye'll be telling me next that our murderous young female had transferred her affections to Mr Harmsworth.'

'I'm not telling you anything,' was the reply. 'But you have to admit there's a pattern. We're dealing with someone for whom murder has become a way of dealing with those whom she perceives as standing in her way. From her stepsister onwards.'

'Ah, I was wondering when we'd come back to that!'

'It's a material fact,' said Rowlands. 'Even if she was only ten years old at the time.'

'Yes, I remember the case,' said Douglas grudgingly. 'It was never proven to have been a deliberate killing. The perambulator overturned and . . .'

'The child suffocated. No, they never proved that Pauline was responsible. Although she was the only one in the vicinity when it happened,' said Rowlands.

'You've got children of your own,' protested the other. 'You surely don't think think a child of that age could be capable of such a thing?'

'I don't know what to think,' said Rowlands grimly. 'All I know is, jealousy's a powerful motive. Jealousy and thwarted love. The child felt rejected when her father remarried. When another child came along – to supplant her, as she thought, in her father's affections – it was too much for her to bear. What she did next set up a pattern for everything that was to follow.'

The Chief Inspector sighed. 'Well, I suppose we can bring her in for questioning,' he said. 'Although I don't mind telling you, I'm getting awful tired of interrogating suspects and then letting them go for lack of evidence. Where can we find your Miss Wilkinson, do you suppose? I take it she's no longer at her aunt's address?'

'No,' said Rowlands. 'And I'm afraid that I haven't the least idea where she might be.' He summarised that afternoon's fruitless search. 'I was going to try the aerodrome next,' he added.

'Tell you what,' said Douglas. 'Why don't you do just that? You can let me know if your researches turn up anything, and I'll get on with interviewing Mr Harmsworth about his drug smuggling activities. Then we can put our heads together at some convenient time. How does that strike you for a plan?'

It struck Rowlands as a very poor plan, but he knew there was little point in saying so. And it was true that, with the bloodstained spanner and overalls now missing, the only evidence against Pauline Wilkinson was circumstantial. So why was it he was so convinced that she was the one who'd carried out these hideous acts? He couldn't say. Perhaps it was no more than intuition – the icy shiver up the spine which told you something was amiss. That, and the murderous rage with which the acts had been carried out. A child's rage, thought Rowlands, sick at heart. In spite of all the harm she'd done – not least of which was depriving another child of his mother – tracking her down wasn't something he relished.

Nor did it prove to be an easy task, for Miss Wilkinson (he couldn't bring himself to think of her by the jaunty soubriquet she preferred) seemed to have a talent for disappearing. She hadn't been seen at Croydon Airport for some weeks, George Potter said. 'Not since the day Captain Percival got back from Australia. That was a day, wasn't it?'

'It was,' said Rowlands.

'Who'd have thought it'd end the way it did?' said the Airport Manager mournfully. 'He was fine chap, was the Captain. One of the best.'

'He was indeed.'

'A terrible loss to aviation. Terrible,' said the other. But of Pauline Wilkinson's whereabouts he could give Rowlands no idea. Stag Lane proved no more informative; nor could Fairoaks help. Even the Air Park seemed uncertain whether the fugitive had ever been there.

'Pauline Wilkinson?' said the young woman at the reception desk doubtfully. 'No, I don't think . . .'

'She calls herself Wilkie,' said Rowlands. 'Tall girl with bobbed brown hair,' – this being the description with which his sister had furnished him. 'Often wears trousers. She likes helping out with the maintenance crews.'

'Oh, I know who you mean now!' said the receptionist. 'To tell you the truth, I've never paid much attention to her. Thought she was somebody's kid sister, you know.

We get a lot of enthusiasts,' she added. ''Fraid I haven't seen her around for a while.'

Replacing the receiver, Rowlands thought, people see what they expect to see. A young man, instead of a young girl. A harmless child, instead of a vengeful woman. It had been staring them in the face all the time – the truth of what she was – and yet none of them, himself least of all, had wanted to believe it. Now she had once more performed the vanishing trick by which she had eluded capture all these months. Although there'd been times when she'd come close to being found out, he thought, recalling what his sister had told him about that day at Hendon.

It had been during lunch; he and Dorothy had just sat down with Percival when the girl had appeared. 'I can't tell you how oddly she behaved when she first caught sight of us', Dorothy had said, towards the end of their telephone conversation. 'She looked . . . I don't know . . . furtive. Like a child caught stealing sweets. But it was what she did next that struck me as strange. There was a glass of red wine on the table and she tipped it all down her dress. It was quite deliberate. I don't think Alan saw – he had his back to her – but I did. Then she broke the glass, and made a terrible fuss as if the whole thing had been an accident. What happened afterwards put it out of my mind, of course.'

She'd just come from sabotaging Percival's plane, thought Rowlands. There must have been oil on her dress – she wouldn't have had time to change into overalls as she had with her first attempt. Confronted with the man she was about to kill, she'd had to think quickly. A ruined frock was a small price to pay to avoid being exposed as a murderess.

All along, she'd gone to great lengths to escape detection. There had been no need to kill poor little Irene Metcalfe – what, after all, had she seen? A youth in overalls, running away. Yet the risk was too great for her to be allowed to go on living. And so once again, the anonymous youth in his burglar's garb had made his appearance before changing himself back into the talkative young woman with a fondness for aeroplanes which had proved such an effective disguise.

Five o'clock came, and Rowlands sent Miss Collins home. There wasn't much more for him to do in the office, either, yet still he lingered. It was as if all the muddle and confusion of the past three months had fallen away, leaving the way ahead clear and stark. How blind he had been! He, who prided himself on not settling for the obvious, who thought he'd found the truth, but had in fact only stumbled across a different kind of lie. Thinking himself above prejudice, he'd allowed his dislike of Cecil Harmsworth to override any doubts he might have had about the man's guilt. Not that Harmsworth wasn't guilty, just not of murder.

Nor could he escape yet another reminder of his folly, in the person of Giles Stratham, encountered as he was crossing the forecourt in front of St John's Lodge on his way to Baker Street Underground Station. A crunch of gravel underfoot told him that someone was coming towards him. 'Evening,' he said, out of habit borne of more than common politeness: if you couldn't see the other person, hearing his voice was the next best thing. His greeting was returned, then, 'I say, Rowlands – is that you?'

'Hello, Stratham.'

'Haven't seen you around in a while.'

'I've been out and about.'

'Funny,' said the other, falling into step with Rowlands as they passed through the iron gates which opened onto the path that led towards the Inner Circle. 'I was thinking about the last time we met, only the other day. That conversation we had about Harmsworth.'

'What about it?' said Rowlands.

'Well, the fact is, it's been preying on my mind, rather.' Stratham paused a moment, then went on awkwardly, 'Talking about . . . all that business during the war. It made me think I'd been rather unfair to Harmsworth. He was young; we all were. He made a mistake. People do when they're young.'

'That's true.'

'So I wouldn't want anything I said to . . . well, to have repercussions,' said the former pilot.

'I wouldn't worry about that. I think you'll find the whole thing's been forgotten.'

'Glad to hear it,' said Stratham. 'I do think a man's reputation counts for a lot, don't you?'

'Yes,' said Rowlands. They had by now reached the

351

circular walk which surrounded Queen Mary's Gardens. A heady scent of full-blown roses came from a nearby arbour.

'It's been good to chat,' said Stratham. 'So long, old man.' The two shook hands, and Stratham walked off, his brisk steps those of man whose conscience has been relieved of its burden, Rowlands thought. His own conscience was not so light. Distracted as he had been by matters of a graver nature, he'd given little thought to what had happened the night of Olave Malory's party, in the hours leading up to its disastrous end. Now he faced it. His infidelity. For that, regardless of what had actually happened, was what it amounted to. A betrayal of trust. He thought, I must talk to Edith – then dismissed the idea. What would be the point of hurting her, just to make himself feel better?

The journey home seemed to take an age: the train dawdling along as if propelled, not by steam power, but by the wind-up mechanism of a child's toy on the verge of running down. Perhaps it was the weather, thought Rowlands. It couldn't have been much fun driving one of these things when it was this close and sticky, with the furnace chucking out a fearful heat. Reaching Kingston at last, he set out from the station at a pace he was soon obliged to modify once his shirt began sticking to his back. He could hardly wait to get out of his hot city suit and into his gardening togs. He'd see if Edith and the girls fancied a stroll by the river after supper.

Watson was washing his car again, whistling under his breath as he did so. 'Nice evening for it,' said Rowlands as he came level with the vehicle.

'What? Oh, rather,' was the reply before 'Sonny Boy' started up again.

He found Edith in the garden, with Joan. 'Daddy, I made biscuits!' cried the latter as soon as he came in view.

'That's nice.' He bent to kiss his wife. 'Where are the others?'

'Margaret's doing her homework. As for Anne . . .' Edith laughed. 'I wonder if you can guess?'

He smiled, and ruffled Joan's curls. 'I'm not very good at riddles.'

'Shall we tell him, Joanie?'

'Anne went in a motorbike,' said the child gleefully.

'What?'

'Oh, don't look so flabbergasted,' said Edith. 'I'm sure it's perfectly safe. She's in the sidecar, not actually on the motorbike, and I made them promise to be back before supper.'

'Made who promise?' he said, with a feeling of mounting horror.

'Didn't I say? I should have thought it was obvious. Who else do we know that owns a motorbike? Your young friend, Wilkie. Apparently, Anne's been pestering her for ages, and—'

'When did they leave?' said Rowlands.

'I'm not sure exactly. About twenty minutes ago, I think. Fred, what is this? You've gone as white as a sheet.'

'Listen to me,' he said. 'I want you to telephone Whitehall one-two-one-two and ask to speak to Chief Inspector Douglas. Tell them it's a matter of life and death.'

'But Fred . . .'

'When you speak to the Chief Inspector, tell him what you've said to me – that Pauline Wilkinson's got Anne. Say that I think she'll have headed for the Air Park, and that I'll meet him there. Have you got that?'

'Yes. But I don't understand . . .'

He took the letter – Miss Denham's letter – from his jacket pocket, and thrust it at her. 'Read this,' he said. 'But only after you've telephoned.'

'But . . .'

'Hendon Air Park,' he repeated. 'And for God's sake, hurry!' Without another word, he turned and ran back out through the side gate to where the Sunbeam stood. 'Mr Watson!' he cried. 'You must help me. I need to get to the Air Park . . . to Hendon Aerodrome . . . as quickly as possible. My daughter's life may be at stake.'

When he came to look back on that journey, Rowlands found he could recall very little of it. Just the muted roar of the engine and the sound of the wind rushing past (Watson drove with the windows rolled down). From time to time he'd shouted a direction, in answer to the driver's shouted enquiries. 'Yes . . . Teddington's your best way . . . then take the Whitton direction . . .' Other than that, the two men were silent, with Watson concentrating on his driving, Rowlands supposed, while he himself was caught in a kind of limbo, unable to think of anything but the unthinkable – that his child, his beloved Anne, might be killed, or might already be dead, and all through his stupidity.

A little over twenty-five minutes later, they were at the gates of the Air Park, Watson having broken the speed limit most of the way. 'Right or left?' he shouted.

'Right,' Rowlands shouted back. 'It's about a quarter of a mile along the perimeter road. We're looking for Hangar Three.'

'Right-ho.' They were there in under a minute. Rowlands jumped out of the car.

'Wait here,' he ordered, breaking into a run. He remembered the way from before: it was the path along which he had come that first time – the morning of Farley's murder. The path along which the murderer had run, almost, but not quite, colliding with Rowlands who'd been coming the other way. He found the alleyway that led between the hangars, and hurled himself along it, oblivious to the banged elbows and scraped shins he collected in so doing. His only thought was to find Anne. Outside Hangar Three, he paused for breath, his heart pounding. The metal front of the hangar had been raised, he found; it was what he had expected to find, but even so, the discovery made him grow cold all over.

What he heard as he stepped across the threshold, to where the great aircraft stood, did nothing to lessen this feeling of dread. And yet it was also oddly comforting. A voice, addressing another, meant that the 'other' was still there to be addressed. Unless . . . 'We've been having *such*

355

a lovely time, haven't we?' said the voice. 'We drove *ever* so fast along the road to get here, didn't we?'

Was there an answering murmur? He couldn't tell. He went closer. 'Ever so fast, and now we're ever so cosy . . .' The voice was coming from somewhere level with Rowlands' head. The aeroplane, he realised in that shocked instant. 'Ever so cosy, because we're all tucked up, aren't we? Nice and safe in Alan's plane. Don't come any closer!' said the voice, dropping its sing-song rhythm for a sharper tone.

Rowlands stopped dead. He drew a breath. 'Let her go,' he said. 'You've got me here, now. You don't need her any more.'

The peal of laughter which followed made his blood run cold. 'Oh, but I *do* need her, don't I, little Anne? We're having such fun. Tell him how much fun we're having.'

'Daddy,' said the child. Rowlands felt his heart turn over. She was alive. 'I'd like to go home now.'

'Oh, but you can't go yet,' said Pauline Wilkinson. 'I've heaps more things to show you. My knife, for instance.' She laughed again, evidently enjoying the impression she'd created. 'It's a wizard knife, isn't it, little Anne? It's got five blades, all lovely and sharp . . .' She giggled – a sound that sent a shiver up Rowlands' spine. 'It isn't as sharp as the one I found in that woman's kitchen,' she went on, in the same sing-song tone as before. 'That was jolly sharp, as that silly woman found! But my little knife's quite sharp enough,' she added. 'Don't you think so, little Anne?'

'Daddy . . .'

'Shut up,' said the girl, her voice suddenly cold. 'You talk too much, that's your trouble.'

'Listen, Pauline . . .'

'Don't call me that!'

'Wilkie, I mean. Let her go. You've got me now, to do whatever you want with.'

'I know,' said Wilkie. 'And you needn't think you're going to get away. You told on me to the police. I heard you. I heard what you said about me to Aunt Sophie, too.'

'So you were there,' said Rowlands.

'Of course I was there!' There was a triumphant note in the voice, now. 'I heard everything you said. She's deaf as a post, so she didn't hear me creep downstairs. I'm good at listening,' the girl went on, with a kind of pride. 'I've always been good at that.'

'You overheard my telephone conversation with Mrs Metcalfe, didn't you?'

'Yes,' she said. 'I guessed from what you said to her – about going to the police – that she'd recognised me that day.'

'She was here, hiding in the office, wasn't she?' he said. 'When Farley found you . . .'

'I suppose she must have been,' said Wilkie, offhandedly. 'I didn't mean to hurt him, you know – old Bill. I just wanted to keep him quiet. He must have banged his head when he fell over,' she added, seemingly forgetful of the fact that it was she who had pushed him, and she who had made sure of Farley's silence by bashing his brains out.

'I expect he did,' said Rowlands, to keep her talking, and also because the less said about the murder in front of his young daughter, the better, in his estimation. It would take Douglas around forty minutes to reach Hendon, he thought, always supposing he left Scotland Yard as soon as he received Edith's message . . . *if* he had received Edith's message. The disturbing thought that he might have to deal with this alone presented itself. 'You heard what Mrs Metcalfe said to the Inspector, too, didn't you?'

'What's it to you if I did?' said Wilkie, her tone changing swiftly from one of self-exculpation to one of furious resentment. 'Always poking your nose in where it's not wanted! I've had just about enough of you.'

'I expect you have,' he said, to placate her.

But she wasn't finished. 'Thinking yourself so clever, Mr Blind Man, when really you can't see a blessed thing.'

'Daddy doesn't need to be able to see,' said Anne. 'He can tell what's going on without that.'

'And who asked *you*?' snapped the girl. 'Don't you know it's very ill-bred to speak unless you're spoken to?' Then as Rowlands took a step towards the plane. 'Stay where you are! If you come any closer, I'll . . .' But they never got to hear whatever it was she was about to say, because just then there came the sound of footsteps on the concrete floor, and a voice that sounded familiar to Rowlands – a young man's voice – said, 'Hello! Anybody there?'

'Hello, Ginger,' said the girl. Of course, thought Rowlands. 'It's only me.' Wilkie's voice had the cheery note it had had the first time Rowlands heard it, all those months ago, on the telephone. 'Just giving a little friend a ride in the Moth. She begged and begged, didn't you, Anne? So Yours Truly gave in at last. We were just about to take her up for a spin, weren't we, my pet?'

'You can't do that,' said Rowlands.

Pauline Wilkinson let out another peal of girlish laughter. 'Listen to Daddy!' she cried. 'He's afraid something bad might happen to his baby girl. We've told him and told him that it's *perfickly* safe, haven't we, Anne?'

'Daddy . . .' Anne's voice was a terrified whisper.

'All right,' said Rowlands. 'Have it your own way.'

'That's the spirit! I say, give us a hand getting her out, will you, Ginger?' The youth must have looked uncertain, for a hard note entered Wilkie's voice. 'Go on. You wouldn't want me to tell Flight Lieutenant Crowther about those cigarettes I saw you pinching from his locker?'

'I never . . .' said Ginger weakly.

'Oh, but you did, you know,' was the reply. 'Stealing's very bad form, isn't it, Anne? You could be put away for that.'

'All right, all right,' muttered the boy. To Rowlands' dismay, there came the sound of the plane being dragged across the concrete. Before he could do anything to stop it, the machine was outside the hangar, its nose pointing towards the grass runway that lay beyond the apron.

'Stop!' he cried. 'You can't do this. You'll both be killed.'

'Silly Daddy!' laughed the girl. 'He's got the wind up, good and proper. I know *perfickly* well how to fly one of these things. Alan showed me, ages ago. It's easy-peasy once you get off the ground.' There came the sound of the engine being switched on. 'Come on,' she shouted to the hapless ground engineer. 'Give the prop a spin!' Ginger must have done so, for the engine's note changed, and a powerful gust of wind came from the moving propeller. 'Another one!' cried Wilkie. It was then that Rowlands made his move.

Knowing that at that moment her hands would be occupied with the controls, he flung himself at the plane. A desperate scramble up the wing and over the side and he was there. He grabbed wildly at where he guessed she must be sitting and got her by the head – a blunt shape in its leather helmet. At once she let out a scream – it was more of a bellow – and sank her teeth into his hand. The pain was intense, but he held on like grim death. She was flailing around in her seat now; he could feel how strong she was. 'Ginger!' he shouted, but the boy was already running to his aid. 'It's all right,' said Rowlands. 'I've got her. Just get my daughter out, will you?' Only when he felt Anne clamber across him to the safety of Ginger's waiting arms, did he relax his hold on his prisoner.

As soon as he did so, he felt her lunge towards him. 'Look out, sir! She's got a knife!' shouted Ginger; but Rowlands, perhaps half-instinctively, had already turned his face away so that the blade, instead of penetrating his eye, merely grazed his cheek. With a howl of rage, the girl leapt up out of her seat and over the side of the plane. 'She's getting away, sir!' Moments later, there came the low growl of a motorbike's engine revving up.

'Let her go,' said Rowlands. He had better things to think about just then. Trembling with the strain of the past few moments, he levered himself painfully out of his seat and climbed over the side of the plane. 'Are you all right, Anne?' He dropped to his knees beside her. He was still shaking. 'She didn't hurt you, did she?'

'No. But your face is all bleeding, Daddy.'

'It's nothing.' he took her in his arms and hugged her to him. 'You're safe. That's all that matters.' Then he said nothing for a while, thinking how close he'd come to losing everything.

A few moments later, a car – Douglas's Wolseley, thought Rowlands dully – came around the corner of the hangar and pulled up smartly in front of it. The Chief Inspector got out. 'Looks as if you've had a spot o' bother, Mr Rowlands,' he said. 'That's a nasty scratch. Our Miss Wilkie's doing, I take it?'

'Yes. You've just missed her,' said Rowlands flatly.

'Och, I don't think so,' was the reply. 'One of my officers is looking after her just now. We picked her up on the perimeter road a couple of minutes ago. Ran her motor bicycle into the ditch. She's a fierce one, I'll say that for her! She put up quite a struggle. It took two of my men to get the handcuffs on. As for her language!'

The Chief Inspector's Scotch Presbyterian upbringing revealed itself in his shocked tone. 'Not quite what you'd expect from a nicely brought-up young woman. No, I don't think Miss Wilkie will be going anywhere soon – unless it's to a cell in Holloway prison.'

# Chapter Nineteen

'What made you change your mind?' said Rowlands. Two days had passed since the events at Hendon Air Park in which he had played such a leading role, and the two men were in Douglas's office at Scotland Yard. It was still warm, but the sky had an overcast look, the Chief Inspector informed him.

'Looks as if we might be in for some rain at last.' The silence which followed Rowlands' question lasted so long that he wondered if perhaps the other hadn't heard him. But then Douglas laughed. 'Not much gets past you, does it, Mr Rowlands?'

'It just occurred to me that you'd had a change of

heart,' said Rowlands. 'When we spoke on the telephone on Monday afternoon, you didn't seem awfully convinced by my suggestion that Miss Wilkinson might have been responsible for the murders.'

'I wasn't,' said Douglas bluntly. He busied himself with filling his pipe. Only when it was lit, and drawing to his satisfaction, did he go on. 'To tell you the truth, I was pretty sure that Harmsworth was our man. But then after we'd spoken, I got a call from the hospital to say that Miss Malory had something to tell me.'

'She'd remembered what the quarrel with Harmsworth was about.'

'Exactly.' The Chief Inspector sounded faintly embarrassed. 'The fact is, he'd asked her to marry him, and she'd turned him down.'

'So it wasn't about his drug smuggling at all?'

'No. Although he'll still get a prison sentence for that. Six months, with time off for good behaviour,' said Douglas. 'What it is to have a Cabinet Minister for a father,' he added gloomily. 'So that washed him out as a suspect,' he went on. 'Seeing as we'd already got a witness who'd heard him drive off a quarter of an hour before the attack on Miss Malory took place. And with Metcalfe out of the running – his broker confirmed his story about the reason for his telephone call, by the way – that just left your Miss Wilkie. I was about to issue a search warrant for the girl's room when your wife telephoned.'

'And did you find anything – when you searched Miss Wilkinson's room, I mean?'

'We did. You were right about the overalls, it turns out.'

'Oh? But I thought she'd got rid of them.'

'She had. But one of our clever chappies – the Sherlock Holmes boys, I call 'em – found traces of blood on the rug by the girl's bed. Mrs Metcalfe's blood, we can assume. Then o' course there's the evidence of the aunt, Miss Denham.'

'Ah.'

'A very shrewd old lady,' said the Chief Inspector. 'No flies on her, I'd say.'

'No, indeed.'

'Tore me off a strip when I ventured to question whether her memory of events was all it should be. "Chief Inspector," said she. "I may have lost some of my faculties with advancing age, but my reason is not one of them." Sharp as a tack,' said Douglas ruefully.

'What will happen to her, do you think?' said Rowlands after a pause. They both knew it was not Miss Denham to whom he was referring.

'Not for me to say,' replied the policeman. 'If she's judged sane enough to stand trial, it'll prove an unedifying spectacle. Seeing as she's still a minor.'

'But if she's not considered sane?'

'There are places for those like her,' said the Chief Inspector. 'Fortunately, it's not up to me to decide where she's to go, or what's to happen to her afterwards. My job's over now, or as good as. Yours, too,' he reminded Rowlands.

'Has she said anything?' said the latter, ignoring this. 'Since she was arrested, I mean.'

'She's said plenty. Although it's not exactly what you'd call a confession,' said the other wryly. 'When I asked her about her relations with the late Captain Percival, she told me they were secret lovers. Seemed convinced that he intended to marry her once he'd broken off the engagement with Miss Malory.'

'But it was Miss Malory who broke off the engagement,' objected Rowlands.

'I don't doubt it,' said Douglas. 'I think it's all part of our Miss Wilkie's fairytale to pretend otherwise.'

'A pretty dark fairytale. What made her turn on Percival?'

'Apparently, she saw him arriving at his flat late one night with another lady.'

'When was this?' asked Rowlands, with a sinking heart.

'Och, the night before the accident, or faked accident, rather.' It was what Rowlands had guessed. He guessed who the lady in question was, too. In the hope of steering the conversation away from this dangerous ground, he said, 'Has she given any explanation of why she killed Irene Metcalfe?'

'Not a word. She denies ever having been to Gloucester Mansions. Although we know she must have been in the flat because of the scarf.'

'Oh?' said Rowlands. 'That wouldn't happen to be a white silk scarf, would it?'

'With gold initials. AVP – for Alan Vivian Percival,' said Douglas. 'She was wearing it when we picked her up at the aerodrome. She says Percival gave it to her as a token of his esteem. All lies, o' course.'

'It was the one Irene Metcalfe was returning to Percival that day.'

'The very same,' said Douglas. 'She must have taken it from the Metcalfes' flat after she'd killed the poor woman.'

'She boasted about the murder the day I was with her at Hendon.' Rowlands was unable to suppress a shudder at the memory.

'Aye, so you said. A pity she didn't mention the poor woman by name. The fact is,' Douglas went on, 'we know she's the one who did it, but we're going to have the devil's own job to prove it.'

'As you said, it may not come to trial.'

'Even so,' said the Chief Inspector, 'I'd like to think we could have secured a conviction.'

'Of course. But in this instance, it might be best for all concerned to leave well alone,' said Rowlands.

'Och, I'm a great believer in leaving things alone,' was the reply. A silence ensued, during which the voices of people passing in the street below could be heard distinctly, '. . . so I says to him, "If you don't like it, you know what you can do . . ."'

'I gather your sister's left London?' said Douglas, his tone seeming no more than one of casual enquiry. Rowlands' heart gave a thump. So he'd known all along, he thought. To have feigned incomprehension would have been futile.

'Yes,' he said.

'Getting married, too, I hear?' Rowlands bowed his head.

'Are you going to arrest her?' he said, in a low voice. There was another silence. It was hard to tell if this was a deliberate cruelty on the part of the Chief Inspector, or merely that he was taking his time replying. For the sighted, such conversational hiatuses, filled as they were with looks, smiles, frowns, were easier to read.

The policeman sighed. 'Now what,' he said, as if to himself, 'would be the good of that? Even if I thought I could get a conviction on the basis of the evidence, the question remains: what purpose would such a conviction serve? The two people most concerned – that is, the murder victim and the, ah, alleged perpetrator – are dead. To all intents and purposes, the case is closed.'

Douglas allowed another silence to elapse, during which he fiddled with his pipe. 'Drat the thing,' he muttered. 'It's never been right since the time I dropped it in the Farringdon Road, in the middle of the Connolly affair . . . Re-opening the case,' he went on, 'wouldn't be an easy matter. First I'd have to convince the powers that be that there was enough evidence to do so, then I'd have to get that evidence . . .'

'I can tell you now,' said Rowlands. 'I won't admit to anything I might have said.'

'Which would be time-consuming and expensive,'

said Douglas as if the other hadn't spoken, 'and might, in the end, fail to bring about the said conviction. It's four years ago,' he added glumly. 'Witnesses have died, or moved away. It'd be a tedious business, getting the facts together. After all, what have we got?' His voice assumed a sceptical tone. 'A suspicion in the mind of one person – that is, myself – and an accusation made by another. Yourself.'

'There were no witnesses to that conversation,' said Rowlands.

'There were not.' The Chief Inspector's intonation could not have been drier. 'It would be, as you have reminded me so succinctly, difficult to prove.'

Rowlands judged it expedient to say nothing. After a moment, Douglas went on, still in the same ruminative tone, 'Quite apart from the difficulties of re-opening such a case, to say nothing of securing a conviction, I find myself coming back to the central question: what would be the point? Perhaps you can tell me that, Mr Rowlands?'

'To uphold the law,' said Rowlands, the words bitter in his mouth.

'Aye. The law must be upheld. It's what we're here for,' said the other. 'Then there's the question of justice. Blind justice, as it's sometimes called.' He took the now extinct pipe from between his lips and knocked out the ashes in the saucer that stood on his desk. From outside, came the whirring sound of the mechanism as the great clock readied itself to strike. Four sonorous chimes followed, each reverberating like the stroke of doom.

When the last of these had died away, the Chief Inspector spoke again, in a softer tone, 'You can tell the lady that, as far as I'm concerned, it won't go any further.'

Rowlands found he could breathe again. 'Thank you,' he said. The other made a deprecatory sound.

'Och, as to that . . .' he began. But there was something more Rowlands had to know.

'When did you find out?' he said. 'That she was back in England, I mean.'

'I knew the day I came to see you,' was the reply. 'You don't suppose for a moment I really believed that one of my officers had got the name wrong, and written down "Miss" instead of "Mrs"?' He laughed. 'You were quick enough to agree with me, though, when I suggested it! But I'd already had my sergeant check up on the list of passengers arriving that month by steamboat from South America. There was a Mrs Lehmann on the SS *Cap Arcona*, arriving from Buenos Aires via Lisbon and Boulogne, on 15th May.'

'So you knew all along?'

'Well, let's say I had my suspicions,' said Douglas. 'You played along very well, I'll say that for you. Your sister should know what a champion she's got to defend her.'

'I don't think she sees it quite like that,' said Rowlands wryly.

Saturday 12th September was a perfect day for flying, with a visibility of twelve miles across Southampton Water. Or so Olave Malory said; he'd have to take her word for it, thought Rowlands, as their party – himself, Edith and the children, now joined by the Ashenhursts' three boys, and not forgetting Edith's mother – strolled along the clifftop. Here, a crowd of several thousand people had already gathered although the race would not start for at least another hour. In times of economic crisis, such as this, there was an appetite for distraction, thought Rowlands. At Westminster, three days before, the Prime Minister had exhorted members of the newly formed Coalition Government to 'face reality' with regard to the immediate crisis. This was no time, he said, for 'fiddling while Rome was burning.' On the cliffs overlooking the sea, the crowd was in the mood for doing just that, however.

They had watched as Captain Orlebar made a preliminary circuit of the course in his Atlas, followed by Flight Lieutenant Boothman and Flying Officer Snaith, and then by Flight Lieutenant Long in his Fairey Firefly seaplane. Listening to Anne's excited account of what was taking place at that moment – 'Daddy, I think that's an S6B going past now . . . the blue and silver one . . .' – he was relieved to find that she sounded just the same as always. Perhaps, after all, her ordeal had left her unscathed. In the month which had passed since, she'd seemed a little quieter, that was all. But her enthusiasm for aircraft and for those that flew them seem undiminished. 'Now they're towing the aeroplanes to the starting line, Daddy! It's so exciting! I wish you could see it.'

'I almost feel as if I can,' he said. 'She seems happier,'

he murmured to Edith as his daughter ran off to join her cousins.

'Yes. I think the week in Cornwall helped.' They'd gone down for Dorothy's wedding, the previous Saturday, returning the day before and bringing the boys with them, at Edith's suggestion. 'They ought to have a few days alone together,' she'd said, meaning the happy couple. He could only concur. And he was glad his sister was settled at last, if that was the word to describe her. Certainly she'd seemed contented enough in the new life in which she found herself. Well, so she should be, he thought. She couldn't have found a better man than Jack Ashenhurst. Whether their marriage would provide the safe haven she needed remained to be seen; but it was a start.

Getting a moment alone with her in order to tell her of the Chief Inspector's decision hadn't been easy on a day of festivities, but he'd seized the opportunity when it came. Her response had been typically sarcastic, 'I suppose you could say it's a reprieve rather than a full pardon,' she said. 'But beggars can't be choosers.'

'No.'

'It's certainly a relief,' she added.

'For me, too.'

'I can see that,' said Dorothy. 'Well, you can thank your policeman friend from us both. Tell him it's the nicest wedding present I could have had.'

'I'll do that,' said Rowlands, thinking that this was the nearest to an apology for all the harm she'd caused that he was ever likely to get from his sister.

'I hope you and your family are enjoying yourselves?' said Olave Malory, striding up to them at that moment.

'Oh yes,' said Edith. 'It's such a treat for the children.'

'Perfect day for it, you know,' said their hostess. She sounded wistful.

'You'll be flying with them this time next year, I'm sure,' said Rowlands.

'Do you think so?' It seemed to him that she brightened a little. 'I hope you're right. If only it weren't for these wretched headaches of mine.' A consequence, he supposed, of the injury she had sustained at the hands of Pauline Wilkinson.

Having brought the girl to mind, it was impossible to dismiss her, and he found his thoughts returning to the visit he'd paid a few days before to the place she was now incarcerated. 'And I don't see them letting her out for a very long time – if at all,' Chief Inspector Douglas had said, the last time the two of them had met in Douglas's office. 'Not after what she's done. Between you and me, she was lucky to get off with life. If she hadn't been a minor, and a female, at that . . .' He let his voice tail off, but Rowlands was able to fill in the blank for himself. At seventeen, Miss Wilkinson was still legally classed as a child. Had she been a few years older, she might have paid for her crimes at the end of a rope.

The hospital was a new one, opened only the year before. 'Oh, we're completely up to date here,' said the Medical Superintendent when Rowlands had remarked on this. 'Bathrooms on every floor, and the very latest equipment. I suppose you'd pictured some Victorian horror?' Rowlands had replied with a smile that he wasn't really in a position to 'picture' anything.

'Just a figure of speech,' said the other airily. 'I saw you were blind at once. Although your eyes aren't obviously damaged. What was it? Mustard gas?'

'Shrapnel.'

'Ah!' There was a note of satisfaction in the medical man's voice. 'Damaged the optic nerve, I shouldn't wonder. Have you any sight at all?'

'A little.'

'Hm. I thought as much. Your pupils still react to light, don't they? I trained under Captain Rivers at Craiglockhart, you know,' went on this genial physician. 'Some fascinating cases of hysterical blindness there.' Still talking, he drew Rowlands with him up a broad staircase, and along the first of a series of corridors that led to Pauline Wilkinson's room. 'We've over three hundred patients here – most of them in the locked wards. Only a few, like young Pauline, have their own rooms. But then she's rather a special case.' Which was one way of putting it, thought Rowlands. 'We're getting quite good results using hydro-therapeutic methods,' the doctor was saying. 'Cold water immersion seems the most efficacious . . . Ah, here we are! Open up, will you, Nurse?' – this to the silent orderly who had accompanied them on noiseless rubber-soled shoes. There came a jangling of keys, and the sound of a door opening. After the violence she had offered to him at their previous encounter, Rowlands had felt some apprehension about how Miss Wilkinson might react on seeing him again. But in fact she seemed entirely tractable, answering the doctor's enquiries as to how she was in a placid monotone, like that of a well-behaved child. 'You've a visitor, Pauline,' said the Superintendent when these preliminary exchanges were at an end. 'Say hello to Mr Rowlands.'

'Hello,' said the girl. She seemed not to remember that she and Rowlands had met before. A pause ensued.

'I've got something for you,' said Rowlands, having previously ascertained that this was in order. 'A present.'

'What do we say?' said the nurse, who had not spoken until now.

'What do we say?' the girl repeated. She sounded genuinely puzzled.

'We say thank you, don't we?' said the nurse encouragingly.

'We say thank you,' said her charge, in the same bright toneless voice with which she had earlier replied to the doctor's questions. Rowlands held out the package to her and she took it. There came the sound of paper being unwrapped. 'Oh,' said the girl flatly when she saw what it was.

'A nice book,' said the nurse.

'A nice book.'

'I thought you might like it,' said Rowlands. 'Since you're so interested in aeroplanes.'

'Yes.' Her voice conveyed no interest at all.

'We try to avoid too many reminders of the past,' put

in the doctor swiftly. 'I'll take that, shall I? The library here will be glad of it, I'm sure.'

'I'm sorry,' said Rowlands. 'I didn't think . . .'

'People never do,' said the doctor. 'As I said, she's an interesting case,' he went on as, some minutes later, the two of them walked back along the corridor towards the hospital's imposing entrance hall. 'She doesn't remember any of the things she's done – or at least, she doesn't admit to remembering.'

'Is she always like that?' said Rowlands. 'She seemed . . . I don't know . . . *different* from the last time I saw her. Rather subdued.'

'That'll be the paraldehyde,' said the Superintendent. 'A harmless sedative.' He laughed. 'We can't have her sticking a knife into one of the nurses, you know.'

'I see that.'

'Although I have great hopes of a new kind of treatment – quite experimental, you know. It involves injections of insulin. The Germans have achieved some impressive results with it. But I'm afraid it's all rather technical. I don't suppose it makes much sense to you.'

'No,' said Rowlands. 'It doesn't make much sense at all.'

The boom of the starting gun, from the *Medea*, anchored just off Southampton Water, recalled him to the here and now. A moment later, the deep roaring of a Rolls Royce engine told him that the Supermarine S6B monoplane had taken off.

'Oh!' cried Edith, her cry lost in the general exclamation arising from ten thousand throats. 'It's like . . . a bolt of lightning!'– her unusually poetic turn of phrase indicating how powerfully the sight had affected her.

'It reached three hundred and forty miles per hour in the trials,' shouted Miss Malory, on Rowlands' other side. 'Let's see if it can break Orlebar's record.' Seven times around the course went the great flying machine, each revolution accompanied by the *Oohs* and *Ahs* of the watching crowd. For Rowlands, on the periphery of this spectacle, the effect was that of a conjurer's trick at a children's party: a great deal of excitement and commotion generated by a clever illusion.

Of course he knew it was more than that. This was the future – wasn't that what everybody said? Perhaps he was just being contrary when he resisted the general enthusiasm. But he remembered a time, not so very long ago, when the 'future' had been hailed in much the same way. The old order was moribund, or so the advocates of the new thinking said. A New World, in which machines would do the work that men had once been forced to do, would supersede it. There would be machines for every conceivable purpose. Washing machines. Sewing machines. Machines to cook one's dinner and clean one's house. And the essence of all this mechanisation would be to increase the speed with which life could be lived. No more need man proceed at the slow pace of his ancestors; he could dash along at hitherto unthought of speeds in his motorcars and flying machines. Then the war had come, and suddenly, the machines that were to make life so much more efficient for human beings were transformed into the means of killing them in unprecedented numbers.

'Isn't it wonderful, Fred?' cried Edith, clutching his arm.

'Oh, yes,' he said. 'It's wonderful all right.'

The race was over. Flight Lieutenant Stainforth had received the trophy and the adulation of the crowd for his successful attempt on the world speed record, with an average speed of 386.1 miles per hour. Now the spectators, released from the extraordinary tension of those few moments, could look forward to the rest of the afternoon's entertainment – a programme of stunt flying and speed trials for the different classes of aeroplane. From all around came voices, excitedly commenting on what they had seen. Smells of fish and chips, lemonade, and burnt toffee came from the stalls selling refreshments. Nearby a band was playing 'Tea for Two'.

For Rowlands, who could take no more than a passing interest in the proceedings, there was enjoyment to be had from the very atmosphere of a crowd in holiday mood, as well as from the feel of the sea breeze on his face. For the first time in many weeks, he felt himself relax. The nightmare which had begun that day at Croydon Airport when events had been set in motion that would culminate in the deaths of three people, was over. He drew a deep breath of the salt-tasting air, and let it out: a sigh of relief, and regret for all that had passed. 'Why,' said Edith suddenly. 'That woman over there – in the pale yellow chiffon – it's Lady Celia! I didn't know she went in for flying.'

'I dare say she goes in for a lot of things,' he replied, hoping that the consternation he was feeling wasn't obvious from his expression.

'Oughtn't we to go and speak to her?' said his wife.

'Oh, I don't think so,' he said, keeping his voice casual. 'She'll be with her friends, I imagine.' In a crowd this size, it ought to have been easy enough to avoid a meeting, he thought, especially since he had a better excuse than most for not catching the other person's eye. But he had reckoned without the intervention of Olave Malory.

'I say, Celia!' she cried. 'Over here!' Then, to Rowlands, 'She's with Bryan Howard, of course, and all that crowd . . . Celia! Blast you. Over here!'

She must have seen them, then, because a moment later, she was with them. 'What are you shrieking about?' she said to Miss Malory. 'I could hear you halfway across the course. Hello, Mrs Rowlands. I hope you've been enjoying the races?'

'Very much,' said Edith.

'And the dear children, too, I see. How frightfully grown-up they look! Such ages since I saw them. But I was forgetting. You don't know Flight Lieutenant Howard. He was the one flying the S1595 – have I got that right?' she added, to her companion.

'Spot-on,' said a cheerful voice – the voice of a young man, Rowlands guessed. 'Bryan Howard, at your service.'

'Frederick Rowlands.' The two shook hands. 'I'm afraid I didn't see your attempt on the speed record,' said Rowlands. 'But I should congratulate you, just the same.'

'Thank you, sir.' So he was young, thought Rowlands. Either that, or he – Rowlands – was getting old.

'Bryan's going to take me across to Paris in his machine,' said Celia West, in the bright, artificial tone Rowlands had come to know in the years since they had first become acquainted. It meant she was trying rather too hard to convince herself that she was having fun. 'He says if we set out not too late, we can be at the Crillon in time for cocktails.'

'Oh, she's quite a fast little thing when she wants to be,' said the Flight Lieutenant modestly. A brief, faintly awkward silence ensued.

'I suppose we'd better go and put on our goggles – or whatever we have to do before taking off,' said Lady Celia. 'Lovely to see you, Mrs Rowlands, and the darling girls, too. Goodbye, Mr Rowlands.' She took his hand in her smooth gloved hand, and held it for a moment.

'Goodbye, Lady Celia,' he said. Then she was gone.

'Well, I can't offer cocktails at the Crillon,' said Olave Malory, 'but there is tea being served in that tent over there for anyone who's interested. Cakes, too. Coming, kiddies?' She led the way, with the children milling around her, Anne having transferred her affections, to Rowlands' considerable relief, from the late Captain Percival to his former fiancée. Evidently the unfortunate episode at Hendon Aerodrome hadn't killed her fascination with flying and fliers. He and Edith and Edith's mother followed at a slower pace.

'He seemed nice,' said his wife after a moment. It was

of course the Flight Lieutenant she meant. 'Rather handsome, I thought, with that fair hair. If perhaps a bit young.'

'Mm. I hope it hasn't been too long a day for you, Helen,' he said to his mother-in-law, by way of changing the subject.

'Oh, no! I'm not the least bit tired. Such a lovely afternoon,' said this obliging lady. 'So kind of dear Miss Malory to arrange it.'

'It's a pity,' said Edith, never one to be easily distracted, 'that she can't find someone to look after her – Lady Celia, I mean. Someone older, and more reliable. Don't you think so, Fred?'

'I don't think it's any of my business,' he said.

'Don't you? I thought you and she were such friends.' Was there an edge in her voice? He couldn't be sure.

'It isn't that kind of friendship,' he said.

# Acknowledgments

With thanks to Mike Sheppard, for letting me fly his aeroplane – a much more up-to-date version of the ones described here – and for taking me to see the Tiger Moth.

CHRISTINA KONING has worked as a journalist, reviewing fiction for *The Times*, and has taught Creative Writing at the University of Oxford and Birkbeck, University of London. From 2013 to 2015, she was Royal Literary Fund Fellow at Newnham College, Cambridge. She won the Encore Prize in 1999 and was long-listed for the Orange Prize in the same year.

*christinakoning.com*